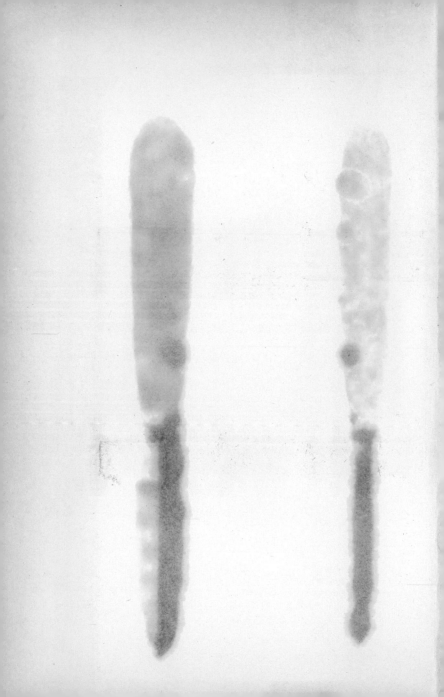

A STUDENT'S GUIDE
TO THE SELECTED POEMS OF
EZRA POUND

A STUDENT'S GUIDE
TO THE SELECTED POEMS OF
EZRA POUND

PETER BROOKER

FABER & FABER
LONDON AND BOSTON

First published in 1979
by Faber and Faber Limited
3 Queen Square London WC1
Printed in Great Britain by
Western Printing Services Ltd, Bristol
All rights reserved

For Liz, first

British Library Cataloguing in Publication Data

Brooker, Peter
A student's guide to the selected poems of Ezra Pound.
1. Pound, Ezra – Criticism and interpretation
I. Title
811'.5'2   PS3531.082Z/

ISBN 0–571–11011–8
ISBN 0–571–11012–6   Pbk

CONTENTS

5

800232

CONTENTS

6

7

CONTENTS

9

PREFACE

This Guide is not intended as a substitute for criticism, but as an assistance towards it: in Pound's case a necessary assistance, and not only in the obvious example of the *Cantos*. Pound's poetry is not uniformly difficult, and much of the early poetry is, in its immediate object and effect, in fact, far from obscure. But an important part of its meaning lies in the process and manner of its composition; in its being quarried from what are often now out-of-the-way sources, and in the extent and range of what becomes its increasingly cryptic allusion. It is these details which most of all require to be made explicit throughout the poetry, and this I have tried to do. Inevitably, however, one is directed in annotating these things by questions of relevance. The following notes are necessarily selective, and informed, as they must be, by a critical reading of the poetry, though I have attempted to make them instructive rather than interpretative. Certain readers will wish other items had been annotated, or feel that the information given is insufficient or prolix. I see no way of avoiding this, and only regret in advance any errors of fact which may have occurred, as well as any possible inconsistencies, and the cumbersomeness of indicating the great amount of cross-reference in Pound's poetry, though it seemed essential to record it. My hope is that the general function of the Guide is nevertheless served, and that the student will gain from it, not an abbreviated sense of 'what the poems are about', but some understanding of how they have been made.

It is with this in mind that I have avoided summary statements on the subject-matter of individual poems, not because these exist elsewhere, though they do, but because such state-ments pretend to a neutrality they cannot possess, and because they are far too pre-emptive. I have also chosen not to include a general introduction to Pound's poetry and career. Many such introductions also exist elsewhere, and yet another would I feel be redundant, and intervene too much between the student and the poems themselves. I have preferred rather to try to situate the poems in time and to suggest a focus for critical discussion in introductory notes attached to particular collections, or to important individual poems. In these head-notes I have been consciously dependent on Pound's own prose writings, in the belief that these still in many ways provide the most illuminating commentary on the poetry, and that it is an additional purpose of this Guide to direct the student to these.

The need for a book such as this has been suggested to me by the experience of teaching Pound, but I owe it in particular to Peter Widdowson of Thames Polytechnic for proposing that I might write it myself. To him too I am grateful for continued encouragement and advice, and for providing me with the time in which to do the book. To my colleagues at Thames Polytechnic I am grateful for their interest and their always helpful response to my enquiries. I am especially grateful also to Christopher Stray of University College, Swansea, for his careful reading of and advice on the notes to *Homage to Sextus Propertius*, and for his tolerating my obtuseness. I am bound also to acknowledge my debt to K. K. Ruthven's *A Guide to Ezra Pound's Personae (1926)* (1969), particularly for the notes on the *Lustra* poems, to J. H. Edwards and W. W. Vasse's *Annotated Index to the Cantos of Ezra Pound* (1957), without which this Guide would have been unthinkable, and to the journal *Paideuma*, for its elucidation of many items in the *Cantos*. To Donald Davie, and to George Dekker and Herbie Butterfield, I am grateful for a willingness to support the initial idea of such a Guide. To Donald Davie also, I owe a special debt for his having read the main portion of the book in typescript, for his salutary corrections and suggestions for improvement, and for his generous encouragement. I am pleased to acknowledge here too the continuing inspiration of his teaching and criticism. To Liz, first and last, for sharing the labour and pleasure of composing the Guide, and to the children for their interest and patience, my thanks are unending.

P.B.

September 1977

BIOGRAPHICAL TABLE

For details of the publication of Pound's works see the Select Bibliography.

1885   Ezra Weston Loomis Pound born 30 October in Hailey, Idaho. After eighteen months the family moved to Pennsylvania and later settled in Wyncote, Philadelphia.

1898   Three months tour of Europe with his great-aunt Frank.

1901–5 Studied at the University of Pennsylvania and at Hamilton College, Clinton, New York. Friendship with H.D. (Hilda Doolittle) and William Carlos Williams.

1902   Visited London and Venice with his father, Homer Pound.

1905   Ph.B., Hamilton College.

1906   M.A., University of Pennsylvania. Awarded a Harrison Fellowship in Romanics and travelled to Europe to work on Lope de Vega.

1907   Instructor in Romance Languages at Wabash College, Crawfordsville, Indiana. Resignation requested after four months when he put up a stranded chorus girl for the night.

1907–8 Travelled to Venice, where he published *A Lume Spento*. Settled in London, autumn 1908.

1909   Lectured at Regent Street Polytechnic on Romance Literature, and met W. B. Yeats, Ford Madox Hueffer (Ford), T. E. Hulme, and such figures as

Maurice Hewlett, Laurence Binyon, Victor Plarr and Selwyn Image.

1910–11　Met A. R. Orage, editor of the *New Age*, to which he made the first of many contributions.

1912　Appointed 'foreign correspondent' to *Poetry* (Chicago), edited by Harriet Monroe.

1913　Met Henri Gaudier-Brzeska.

1914　Married Dorothy Shakespear, 20 April. Met T. S. Eliot, September. Working on the Fenollosa papers. Edited *Des Imagistes: An Anthology* and contributed to Wyndham Lewis's *Blast* (1914–15).

1917　First versions of Cantos I–III published in *Poetry*. Met Major C. H. Douglas.

1920　June, met James Joyce briefly at Sirmione. Left London for Paris and there met Gertrude Stein, Ernest Hemingway, Brancusi, Jean Cocteau and George Antheil.

1922　Edited T. S. Eliot's *The Waste Land*.

1924–5　Visited Sicily and settled in Rapallo, Italy.

1925　Daughter, Mary, born to Olga Rudge, 9 July at Bressanone, Italian Tyrol.

1926　Son, Omar Shakespear Pound, born to Dorothy Pound, 10 September, Paris.

1939　Revisited U.S.A. in an attempt to avert the war. Received an honorary D.Litt. from Hamilton College.

1940–4　Broadcast over Rome Radio, with an interval in 1941 when the U.S.A. declared war on the Axis powers.

1943　Indicted *in absentia* for treason in Washington, D.C.

1945　Confined in the U.S. Army Detention Training Centre, near Pisa. Flown to Washington in November to stand trial for treason.

1946　Committed to St. Elizabeth's Hospital for the Criminally Insane, after being declared medically unfit to stand trial.

1949　*The Pisan Cantos* awarded the Bollingen Prize for Poetry.

1958   April, released from St. Elizabeth's after the efforts of Archibald MacLeish, Robert Frost, Ernest Hemingway, T. S. Eliot and others. Returned to Italy to live with his daughter at Schloss Brunnenberg, near Merano, and at Rapallo and Venice.

1965   Attended the memorial service for T. S. Eliot in London, and visited Yeats's widow in Dublin.

1969   Revisited U.S.A. briefly with Olga Rudge.

1972   Died in Venice, 1 November.

SELECT BIBLIOGRAPHY

Full bibliographical details of works by Pound are given in
Donald Gallup, *A Bibliography of Ezra Pound*, Rupert Hart-
Davis, London, 1963, 1966.

WORKS BY POUND

POETRY

A Lume Spento, A. Antonini, Venice, 1908; reprinted New
Directions, New York, and Faber & Faber, London, 1965

A Quinzaine for this Yule, Pollock & Co., London; Elkin
Mathews, London, 1908

Personae, Elkin Mathews, London, 1909

Exultations, Elkin Mathews, London, 1909

Provença, Small, Maynard & Co., Boston, 1910

Canzoni, Elkin Mathews, London, 1911

The Sonnets and Ballate of Guido Cavalcanti, Small, Maynard &
Co., Boston, and Swift & Co., London, 1912

Ripostes, Swift & Co., London, 1912; reprinted with *Canzoni*,
Elkin Mathews, London, 1913

Cathay, Elkin Mathews, London, 1915

Lustra, Elkin Mathews, London, 1916; unexpurgated edn.
including 'Three Cantos', Alfred A. Knopf, New York, 1917

The Fourth Canto, Ovid Press, London, 1919

Quia Pauper Amavi, Egoist Ltd., London, 1919, including
Homage to Sextus Propertius and 'Three Cantos'

Hugh Selwyn Mauberley, Ovid Press, London, 1920

Umbra, Elkin Mathews, London, 1920

Poems 1918–1921, Boni & Liveright, New York, 1921

A Draft of XVI Cantos, Three Mountains Press, Paris, 1925

17

Personae: The Collected Poems of Ezra Pound, Boni & Liveright, New York, 1926; reprinted as *Personae: Collected Shorter Poems of Ezra Pound*, New Directions, New York, 1949; Faber & Faber, London, 1952; enlarged edn., Faber & Faber, London, 1968

Selected Poems, ed. T. S. Eliot, Faber & Gwyer, London, 1928

A Draft of XXX Cantos, Hours Press, Paris, 1930; reprinted Farrar & Rinehart, New York, and Faber & Faber, London, 1933

Eleven New Cantos XXXI–XLI, Farrar & Rinehart, New York, 1934; Faber & Faber, London, 1935

Homage to Sextus Propertius, Faber & Faber, London, 1934

The Fifth Decad of Cantos [XLII–LI], Faber & Faber, London, and Farrar & Rinehart, New York, 1937

Cantos LII–LXXI, Faber & Faber, London, and New Directions, Norfolk, Conn., 1940

A Selection of Poems, Faber & Faber, London, 1940

The Pisan Cantos [LXXIV–LXXXIV], New Directions, New York, 1948; Faber & Faber, London, 1949

The Cantos [I–LXXI, LXXIV–LXXXIV], New Directions, New York, 1948; Faber & Faber, London, 1954

Selected Poems, New Directions, New York, 1949, 1957

The Translations of Ezra Pound, ed. Hugh Kenner, Faber & Faber, London, and New Directions, New York, 1953; enlarged edn., Faber & Faber, London, 1970

The Classic Anthology defined by Confucius, trans. by Ezra Pound, Harvard University Press, Cambridge, Mass., 1954; Faber & Faber, London, 1955

Section: Rock-Drill: 85–95 de los cantares, All' Insegna del Pesce d'Oro, Milano, 1955; New Directions, New York, 1956; Faber & Faber, London, 1957

Sophokles: Women of Trachis: A Version by Ezra Pound, Neville Spearman, London, 1956; New Directions, New York, 1957; Faber & Faber, London, 1969

Diptych Rome–London: Homage to Sextus Propertius & Hugh Selwyn Mauberley, New Directions, New York, 1958

Thrones: 96–109 de los cantares, All' Insegna del Pesce d'Oro,

Milano, 1959; New Directions, New York, 1959; Faber & Faber, London, 1960

Love Poems of Ancient Egypt, trans. Ezra Pound and Noel Stock, New Directions, Norfolk, Conn., 1962

The Cantos of Ezra Pound [I–LXXI, LXXIV–CIX], Faber & Faber, London, 1964; New Directions, New York, 1965

Selected Cantos, Faber & Faber, London, 1967

Late Cantos and Fragments, New Directions, New York, 1969; reprinted as *Drafts and Fragments of Cantos CX–CXVII*, Faber & Faber, London, 1970

The Cantos [I–LXXI, LXXIV–CXVII], New Directions, New York, and Faber & Faber, London, 1975

Selected Poems 1908–1959, Faber & Faber, London, 1975; reprinted with additions, Faber & Faber, London, 1977

Collected Early Poems, ed. Michael King, New Directions, New York, 1976; Faber & Faber, London, 1977

PROSE

The Spirit of Romance, Dent & Son, London, 1910; revised enlarged edn., Peter Owen, London, and New Directions, Norfolk, Conn., 1953, 1968

Gaudier-Brzeska, A Memoir, Bodley Head, London, and John Lane Co., New York, 1916; new edn., The Marvell Press, Hessle, Yorks., 1960; New Directions, New York, 1961, 1970

'Noh' or Accomplishment, by Ernest Fenollosa and Ezra Pound, Macmillan & Co., London, 1916; new edn. published as *The Classic Noh Theatre of Japan*, New Directions, New York, 1959

Pavannes and Divisions, Alfred A. Knopf, New York, 1918

Instigations, including *The Chinese Written Character as a Medium for Poetry*, Boni & Liveright, New York, 1920; Faber & Faber, London, 1967

The Natural Philosophy of Love, by Remy de Gourmont, trans. with a postscript by Ezra Pound, Boni & Liveright, New York, 1922; The Casanova Society, London, 1925

Antheil and The Treatise on Harmony, Three Mountains Press, Paris, 1924; Pascal Covici, Chicago, 1927

ABC of Economics, Faber & Faber, London, 1933; New Directions, Norfolk, Conn., 1940; Peter Russell, Tunbridge Wells, 1953

ABC of Reading, Routledge & Sons, London, 1934; Yale University Press, New Haven, Conn., 1934; Faber & Faber, London, 1951

Make It New, Faber & Faber, London, 1934; Yale University Press, New Haven, Conn., 1935

Jefferson and/or Mussolini, Stanley Nott, London, 1935; Liveright, New York, 1936, 1970

The Chinese Written Character as a Medium for Poetry, by Ernest Fenollosa and Ezra Pound, Stanley Nott, London, and City Lights, New York, 1936

Polite Essays, Faber & Faber, London, 1937; New Directions, Norfolk, Conn., 1940

Guide to Kulchur, Faber & Faber, London, 1938; as *Culture*, New Directions, Norfolk, Conn., 1938; new edn., New Directions, Norfolk, Conn., and Peter Owen, London, 1952

If This Be Treason, printed for Olga Rudge by Tip. Nuova, Siena, 1948

Patria Mia, Ralph Fletcher Seymour, Chicago, 1950; reprinted with *The Treatise on Harmony*, Peter Owen, London, 1962

The Letters of Ezra Pound, 1907–1941, ed. D. D. Paige, Harcourt, Brace & Co., New York, 1950; Faber & Faber, London, 1951; reprinted as *The Selected Letters of Ezra Pound 1907–1941*, New Directions, New York, 1971

Literary Essays of Ezra Pound, ed. T. S. Eliot, Faber & Faber, London, 1954, 1960; New Directions, Norfolk, Conn., 1954

Pavannes and Divagations, New Directions, Norfolk, Conn., 1958, 1974; Peter Owen, London, 1960. Reprints earlier prose and poetry.

Impact: Essays on Ignorance and the Decline of American Civilization, ed. Noel Stock, Henry Regnery, Chicago, 1960. Includes Pound's 'Money Pamphlets'

EP to LU: Nine Letters to Louis Untermeyer by Ezra Pound, ed. J. Albert Robbins, Indiana University Press, Bloomington, Ind., 1963

SELECT BIBLIOGRAPHY

Pound/Joyce: The Letters of Ezra Pound to James Joyce with Pound's Essays on Joyce, ed. Forrest Read, Faber & Faber, London, 1968; New Directions, New York, 1967, 1970

Confucius: The Great Digest, The Unwobbling Pivot, The Analects, New Directions, New York, 1969

Selected Prose 1909–1965, ed. William Cookson, Faber & Faber, London, 1973; New Directions, New York, 1975

Certain Radio Speeches of Ezra Pound, ed. William Levy, Cold Turkey Press, Rotterdam, 1975

ANTHOLOGIES

Des Imagistes: An Anthology, ed. Ezra Pound, Albert and Charles Boni, New York, and The Poetry Bookshop, London, 1914

Catholic Anthology 1914–1915, ed. Ezra Pound, Elkin Mathews, London, 1915

Active Anthology, ed. Ezra Pound, Faber & Faber, London, 1933

Confucius to Cummings: An Anthology of Poetry, ed. Ezra Pound and Marcella Spann, New Directions, New York, 1964

WORKS ON POUND

BIOGRAPHY

Hutchins, Patricia, *Ezra Pound's Kensington. An Exploration 1885–1913*, Faber & Faber, London, 1965

Norman, Charles, *Ezra Pound. A Biography*, 1960; rev. edn. Macdonald, London, 1969

Stock, Noel, *The Life of Ezra Pound*, Routledge & Kegan Paul, London, 1970; Penguin Books, Harmondsworth, 1974

EARLY POETRY

de Nagy, N. Christoph, *The Poetry of Ezra Pound. The Pre-Imagist Stage*, Francke Verlag, Bern, 1960

Espey, John J., *Ezra Pound's Mauberley: A Study in Composition*, University of California Press, Berkeley, and Faber & Faber, London, 1955

Jackson, Thomas H., *The Early Poetry of Ezra Pound*, Harvard

University Press, Cambridge, Mass., and OUP, London, 1969

McDougal, S. Y., *Ezra Pound and the Troubadour Tradition*, Princeton University Press, Princeton, N.J., 1973

Ruthven, K. K., *A Guide to Ezra Pound's Personae (1926)*, University of California Press, Berkeley, 1969

Schneidau, Herbert N., *Ezra Pound: The Image and the Real*, Louisiana State University Press, Baton Rouge, La., 1969

Sullivan, J. P., *Ezra Pound and Sextus Propertius: A Study in Creative Translation*, University of Texas Press, Austin, 1964; Faber & Faber, London, 1965

Yip, Wai-Lim, *Ezra Pound's Cathay*, Princeton University Press, Princeton, N.J., 1969

Witemeyer, Hugh, *The Poetry of Ezra Pound: Forms and Renewals 1908–1920*, University of California Press, Berkeley, 1969

THE CANTOS

Baumann, Walter, *The Rose in the Steel Dust: An Examination of the Cantos of Ezra Pound*, Francke Verlag, Bern, 1967

Bush, Ronald, *The Genesis of Ezra Pound's Cantos*, Princeton University Press, Princeton, N.J., 1976

Dekker, George, *Sailing After Knowledge. The Cantos of Ezra Pound. A Critical Appraisal*, Routledge & Kegan Paul, London, and Barnes & Noble, New York, 1963

Edwards, John Hamilton and Vasse, William W., *Annotated Index to the Cantos of Ezra Pound. Cantos I–LXXXIV*, University of California Press, Berkeley, 1957

Emery, Clark, *Ideas into Action. A Study of Pound's Cantos*, University of Miami Press, Miami, Fla., 1958

Leary, Lewis (ed.), *Motive and Method in the Cantos of Ezra Pound*, Columbia University Press, New York, 1954

Nassar, Eugene Paul, *The Cantos of Ezra Pound: The Lyric Mode*, Johns Hopkins University Press, Baltimore, Md., 1975

Pearlman, Daniel D., *The Barb of Time: On the Unity of Ezra Pound's Cantos*, OUP, New York, 1969

Stock, Noel, *Reading the Cantos: A Study of Meaning in Ezra Pound*, Routledge & Kegan Paul, London, 1967

SELECT BIBLIOGRAPHY

GENERAL

Brooke-Rose, Christine, *A ZBC of Ezra Pound*, Faber & Faber, London, and University of California Press, Berkeley, 1971

Chace, William M., *The Political Identities of Ezra Pound and T. S. Eliot*, Stanford University Press, Stanford, Calif., 1973

Davie, Donald, *Ezra Pound. Poet as Sculptor*, OUP, New York, 1964; Routledge & Kegan Paul, London, 1965

—*Pound*, Fontana, London, 1975

Davis, Earle, *Vision Fugitive: Ezra Pound and Economics*, University of Kansas Press, Lawrence, Kans., 1969

Dembo, Lawrence Sanford, *The Confucian Odes of Ezra Pound. A Critical Appraisal*, Faber & Faber, London, 1963; University of California Press, Berkeley, 1965

de Rachewiltz, Mary, *Discretions*, Faber & Faber, London, 1971; New Directions, New York, 1975

Fraser, G. S., *Ezra Pound*, Oliver & Boyd, Edinburgh, 1960; Grove Press, New York, 1961

Goodwin, K. L., *The Influence of Ezra Pound*, OUP, London, 1966

Hesse, Eva (ed.), *New Approaches to Ezra Pound*, Faber & Faber, London, and University of California Press, Berkeley, 1969

Heymann, C. David, *Ezra Pound: The Last Rower. A Political Profile*, Viking, New York, and Faber & Faber, London, 1976

Homberger, Eric, *Ezra Pound. The Critical Heritage*, Routledge & Kegan Paul, London and Boston, 1972

Kenner, Hugh, *The Poetry of Ezra Pound*, Faber & Faber, London, and New Directions, New York, 1951

—*The Pound Era*, University of California Press, Berkeley, 1971; Faber & Faber, London, 1972

Quinn, Sister M. Bernetta, *Ezra Pound. An Introduction to the Poetry*, Columbia University Press, New York, 1972

Rosenthal, M. L., *A Primer of Ezra Pound*, Macmillan, New York, 1960

Russell, Peter, *Ezra Pound: A Collection of Essays to be Presented to Ezra Pound on his 65th Birthday*, Peter Nevill, London,

1950; reprinted as *An Examination of Ezra Pound: A Collection of Essays*, New Directions, New York, 1950

Seelye, Catherine (ed.), *Charles Olson and Ezra Pound*, Grossman/Viking, New York, 1975

Stock, Noel, *Poet in Exile: Ezra Pound*, Manchester University Press, Manchester, and Barnes & Noble, New York, 1964

— (ed.), *Ezra Pound: Perspectives*, Henry Regnery, Chicago, 1965

Sullivan, J. P. (ed.), *Ezra Pound*, Penguin Books, Harmondsworth, 1970

Sutton, Walter (ed.), *Ezra Pound: A Collection of Critical Essays*, Prentice-Hall, Englewood Cliffs, N.J., 1963

Wilhelm, James J., *Dante and Pound: The Epic of Judgement*, University of Maine Press, Orono, Me., 1974

See also *Paideuma, A Journal devoted to Ezra Pound Scholarship*, University of Maine, Orono, Me., and *The Analyst*, ed. Robert Mayo, Northwestern University, Evanston, Ill.

EDITORIAL NOTE

Line references in the notes which follow are given where poems or Cantos, or sections of Cantos, are included in the *Selected Poems* (1975; reprinted with additions, 1977). Double page references to Cantos I–CIX are to the Faber 1964 and 1975 editions respectively. References to Cantos CX–CXVII are to the Faber editions of *Drafts and Fragments* (1970) and *The Cantos* (1975). Line-numbering of the Cantos follows throughout that of the Faber 1975 edition even where this differs substantially from the earlier Faber edition.

The following abbreviations are used for editions of Pound's works frequently cited:

POETRY

ALS	*A Lume Spento and Other Early Poems* (New Directions, 1965)
CEP	*Collected Early Poems* (Faber, 1977)
CSP	*Collected Shorter Poems* (Faber, 1968)
Tr	*The Translations of Ezra Pound* (Faber, 1970)

PROSE

ABC of R	*ABC of Reading* (Faber, 1951)
G-B	*Gaudier-Brzeska: A Memoir* (New Directions, 1970)
GK	*Guide to Kulchur* (Peter Owen, 1952)
J/M	*Jefferson and/or Mussolini* (Liveright, 1970)
LE	*Literary Essays of Ezra Pound* (Faber, 1960)
MIN	*Make It New* (Faber, 1934)
P and D	*Pavannes and Divagations* (New Directions, 1974)
PE	*Polite Essays* (Faber, 1937)

P/J	*Pound/Joyce: The Letters of Ezra Pound to James Joyce with Pound's Essays on Joyce* (New Directions, 1970)
PM	*Patria Mia* and *The Treatise on Harmony* (Peter Owen, 1962)
SL	*The Selected Letters of Ezra Pound 1907–1941* (New Directions, 1971)
SPr	*Selected Prose 1909–1965* (Faber, 1973)
SR	*The Spirit of Romance* (New Directions, 1968)

Although *Collected Early Poems* (1977) is occasionally cited, this volume appeared while the present Guide was in preparation and no extensive use could be made of it.

References to Sappho are in the first instance to *Greek Lyric Poetry*, trans. Willis Barnstone (Schocken, New York, 1975), cited as 'Barnstone'. Double line references to Ovid's *Metamorphoses* are respectively to the translation by F. J. Miller in the Loeb Classical Library (2 vols., 1951) and to the 1567 translation by Arthur Golding (reprinted as *Shakespeare's Ovid*, Centaur Press, London, 1961): the second because Pound found it 'the most beautiful book in the language'. In references to Dante I have sometimes offered the translation by Laurence Binyon (*Dante's Inferno*, 1933; *Dante's Purgatorio*, 1938; *Dante's Paradiso*, 1943), again because of Pound's personal interest in it. For the translation from Arnaut de Mareuil I am indebted to Dr. L. Paterson, Warwick University; other translations, unless otherwise indicated, are those offered in Edwards and Vasse's *Annotated Index to the Cantos* (1957), or my own.

Works on Pound which appear in the Select Bibliography (p. 17) are cited throughout the notes in short form, by author's surname or author and title only, e.g. 'Kenner, *Pound Era*, 342'.

P.B.

NOTES

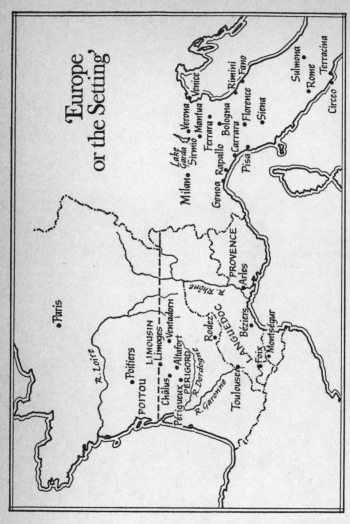

'Europe
or the Setting'

Langue d'oc, the tongue used by the Troubadours, was spoken south of the line running from the mouth of the Gironde to the Alps.

PERSONAE

(1908, 1909, 1910)

Personae was the title of Pound's third volume of poetry, including poems from his first volume *A Lume Spento* (1908). The title was used again for the collected poems of 1926, and for the selection from these of 1928. In itself this suggests the broad application of the term to Pound's early poetry. In Latin 'persona' signifies the putting on of a mask by the players in a drama, and Pound's earlier poetry is essentially a serial exercise in the adoption of the technique, voice, or character and situation of earlier poets: from the Provençal troubadours Bertran de Born, Arnaut de Mareuil and Peire Vidal, the early Italian poet Cino da Pistoia, and less directly Dante, to François Villon, Browning, Rossetti, the poets of the Nineties, and his contemporary W. B. Yeats. In one way Pound was evidently concerned in this to know and define, or re-define, the tradition of lyric poetry he saw as arising from Provençal (*LE*, 91), as one to which his own poetry might belong. He was concerned to bring this tradition and its exponents alive, primarily through the use of the dramatic lyric or dramatic monologue, derived from but not identical with Browning's use of that mode in his *Dramatis Personae*: he was consciously experimenting in 'melopoeia', in the forms of verse as speech, or song, so as to develop his own technique, and he was involved, crucially, in a personal 'search for oneself', for 'sincere self-expression':

> I began this search for the real in a book called *Personae*, casting off, as it were, complete masks of the self in each poem. I continued in long series of translations, which were but more elaborate masks.
>
> (*G-B*, 85)

Pound's translations are themselves an important dimension of his career, and as this suggests, inseparable from the purposes of his original poetry. But if the early translations, principally of Arnaut Daniel and Guido Cavalcanti, are masks, if they are prompted by Pound's taste and an identification with the poets themselves, they are primarily linguistic masks, and as such part of his exploration of 'melopoeia' and of viable poetic idioms. As Pound said of the problems of translating Cavalcanti,

> What obfuscated me was not the Italian but the crust of dead English, the sediment present in my own available vocabulary – which I, let us hope, got rid of a few years later. You can't go round this sort of thing. . . . Neither can anyone learn English, one can only learn a series of Englishes. Rossetti made his own language. I hadn't in 1910 made a language, I don't mean a language to use, but even a language to think in.
>
> (*LE*, 193–4)

Pound's aim in his translations, as in the varying strengths of his ventriloquism in the use of the dramatic monologue elsewhere, was to revivify and re-present the original integrity of his subjects, but also to shape a personal language. His success in either of these aims is a matter for discussion. In the first, as far as Provence at least and the general reader, or even modern poetry, are concerned, Pound was ready to acknowledge failure:

> I have proved that the Provençal rhyme schemes are not *impos*sible in English. They are probably *inadvis*able. . . . There is, however, a beauty in the troubadour work which I have tried to convey. I have failed almost without exception; I can't count six people whom I have succeeded in interesting in XIIth Century Provence.
>
> (*SL*, 179)

In the matter of a personal language, or perhaps more

accurately, the aggregation of consonant idioms, the test is of course the poetry itself, particularly those poems towards the end of the early period, *Homage to Sextus Propertius* and *Hugh Selwyn Mauberley*, and ultimately the *Cantos*, for which, one can see, Pound's early experiments were in many ways a preparation.

But the evolution of a language cannot be held separate from the broader search Pound describes 'for oneself' or for 'the real' – which does not necessarily, or at this stage, designate a single reality. The process to which Pound was committed was one that would lead to the certainty of what he described in an early and seminal essay as individual *virtù*:

> The soul of each man is compounded of all the elements of the cosmos of souls, but in each soul there is some one element which predominates, which is in some peculiar and intense way the quality or *virtù* of the individual.
>
> ('I Gather the Limbs of Osiris', *SPr*, 28)

'It is the artist's business', says Pound, 'to find his own *virtù*.' And once found, providing he has 'acquired some reasonable technique . . . the artist may proceed to the erection of his microcosmos' (ibid., 29). Again, as he had defined it in his introduction to his translations of Cavalcanti, '*La virtù* is the potency, the efficient property of a substance or person' (*Tr*, 18). It is this quality that Pound attempted to carry over from past literatures and to discover in himself. It follows also that the poets Pound chose to speak through were, in his eyes, examples of established *virtù*.

This estimate, one assumes, lies behind Pound's admiration of Yeats as 'the only poet worthy of serious study' ('Status Rerum', *Poetry*, January 1913, 123), behind too his admiration of Rossetti's and Swinburne's translations, his debt to Browning and praise of Villon, and behind his grouping the troubadour poets Bertran de Born, Arnaut de Mareuil and Peire Vidal with Villon as poets whose verse is 'real' because they 'lived it' (*SR*, 178). It is significant too that of these poets the earlier examples particularly are men of action, involved in

31

war, intrigue and even crime. One comes to recognize a composite personality type in which aggression and bitterness are weighed against directness, vigour and sincerity. Several of these figures also – Cino, Marvoil (Arnaut de Mareuil), Peire Vidal and Villon most clearly – are caught by Pound at points of crisis, during or on the point of exile, in situations where their values may have lost ground and the world to which they belong has receded. As such they anticipate the later personae of 'The Seafarer', Li Po in 'Exile's Letter', and Sextus Propertius and Hugh Selwyn Mauberley.

What one notices over this period is that the vigour and energy of the earlier examples – which in Bertran de Born for example, at one extreme, had in fact inspired, as it had been inspired by, active battle – is in Propertius re-oriented and in Mauberley totally lacking. In another way, one sees that this energy passes into the doctrine of the vortex and vorticism, in a transference that one can understand, perhaps, as part of Pound's response to the actuality of war in the years 1914–18. But it is true still that the personality type – the masculine values, the aggression, even a degree of physical brutality – persists in individuals like T. E. Hulme and Pound's Vorticist confrères Wyndham Lewis and Gaudier-Brzeska, as men and as artists.

Clearly Pound was attracted to this type, and to an analogous aesthetic, even if the extent to which he himself conformed entirely to it is uncertain. The flamboyance, bluster and intemperance that are widely attested to in Pound's early manner seem as much pose as reality. The recurrent theme of exile does no doubt correspond to his early situation: alienated, and eventually dismissed for bohemian conduct, from his first post at Wabash College, in Indiana, at a time when he was as the poem 'In Durance' tells us 'homesick after mine own kind', and when many of the early poems were also written. And perhaps a feeling of exile followed him to Venice and London. But what of course this reveals is that if Pound himself was 'living' his verse, he was doing so vicariously, and that the poetic masks he adopted functioned as much, or more, as a

form of protection as of direct expression. This would seem to
be the suggestion of an early poem, titled 'Masks':

> These tales of old disguisings, are they not
> Strange myths of souls that found themselves among
> Unwonted folk that spake an hostile tongue,
> Some soul from all the rest who'd not forgot
> The star-span acres of a former lot.

(ALS, 52)

The easy and uninterrupted passage from life to verse was
not a readily available reality to Pound. He was impressed by
it where he thought it existed (in Bertran de Born, in Villon),
but drawn equally towards indirection, disguise and evasion,
even anonymity. Consider, for example, the poem 'The
Flame':

> If thou hast seen my shade sans character,
> If thou hast seen that mirror of all moments,
> That glass to all things that o'ershadow it,
> Call not that mirror me, for I have slipped
> Your grasp, I have eluded.

(CSP, 65)

Or consider Pound's testimony that the poem 'Night Litany'
'seemed a thing so little my own that I could not bring myself
to sign it' ('How I Began', *T.P.'s Weekly*, 6 June 1913, 707).
Evidently one is dealing here, and Pound is dealing, with
another order of 'reality'. A clue to its character is given in
another early poem 'Histrion':

> Thus am I Dante for a space and am
> One François Villon, ballad-lord and thief.

(ALS, 108)

That Pound should name Dante and Villon here is significant,
since his discussion of Villon in *The Spirit of Romance* (pp.
166–78) is conducted with reference to Dante as an equivalent
but contrasting example. Where Villon, 'destitute of imagination', 'sings of things as they are' and 'dares to show himself',

where he 'speaks below the voice of his age's convention', and where he suffers as one man, like a character in Dante's *Inferno* too late for inclusion, Dante has 'boldness of imagination', he 'reaches out of his time', he 'lives in his mind', 'is many men, and suffers as many' and passes through hell 'to sing of things more difficult'. Dante and Villon are in all their differences, Pound wishes to say, 'admirably in agreement', and concludes, 'Dante's vision is real, because he saw it. Villon's verse is real, because he lived it.'

Rather than an agreement one feels more an arrangement here which is likely to yield under the pressure of its opposed terms; terms which in Pound's own practice were to incline him, one way towards uninterpreted experience and the claims of Imagism, and the other towards the involuntary 'madness' of vision and the mediated significance of myth. In the early years the particular example of myth perhaps was that exemplified in the metamorphoses of Apuleius' *Golden Ass* and in Ovid, and thence most obviously in poems such as 'The Tree' and 'La Fraisne'. The metamorphosis of man into tree appears also and interestingly, however, in Pound's presentation of Peire Vidal ('Behold me shrivelled as an old oak's trunk'), a poet presented otherwise with Villon and those who lived their verse, in a description ('that mad poseur Vidal') which already conflates realities. In Canto IV, Vidal is presented once more, in juxtaposition with Actaeon, as an example of metamorphosis.

Clearly for Pound there was a need to make these types of men and poetries compatible, even at the expense of some strain. And it is here that one arrives at a sense of his own *virtù*, as consisting in the search itself which he describes, but also in the impulse to balance, conjoin and compound vision with actuality, just as he attempted to infuse present with past literatures, and to synthesize 'a series of Englishes' into a personal idiom. One finds an analogy for this process in the figure of the radiant Lady, of Provençal and later poetry, including her manifestation in Pound's own verse. The Lady serves as an ideal, distilled like alchemist's gold from separable distinct virtues, and she is, or becomes, one is tempted to think, a metaphor for the making of poetry and an author's discovery of his *virtù*, 'compounded of all the elements of the cosmos of souls'. The conception of the Lady and of poetry share too the same imagery. Just as the Lady is suffused with light (in Pound's 'The House of Splendour' and 'Apparuit', for example), so 'Any author whose light remains visible in this place where the greater lamps are flashing back and forth upon each other is of no mean importance . . . he has attained his own *virtù*' ('Osiris', *SPr*, 30–1). One is reminded also by this of Pound's nostalgia for the 'radiant world', 'where one thought cuts through another with clean edge, a world of moving energies . . . magnetisms that take form, that are seen, or that border the visible' ('Cavalcanti', *LE*, 154). It is just such an interpenetrative world that Pound is in search of in 'the erection of his microcosmos', and, one might add, in the model of civilization that would sustain it. If both are in embryo in the early years, a course is nevertheless set and a design drawn by the pattern of authors Pound would want to maintain in orbit round himself, circulating in the terms of the poem 'Plotinus' like 'crescent images of *me*' (*ALS*, 56).

Cino (1908)

Written in Crawfordsville, Indiana, 1907, while Pound was teaching at Wabash College, where 'he felt a complete outsider' (Stock, *Life*, 47). Cino is the Italian poet, jurist and friend of Dante, Cino da Pistoia (1270–1337). Dante includes him with Arnaut Daniel, Bertran de Born and Gerard de Boneil, as a pre-eminent poet of love (*De Vulgari Eloquentia*, Bk. II, ch. 2), and Pound groups him with Cavalcanti and Dante as helping to bring 'the Italian canzone form to perfection' (*SR*, 109). Two early poems, rejected for *A Lume Spento*, were written under the name 'Cino': 'Roundel for Arms' and 'Roundel. After Joachim du Bellay' (*ALS*, 116, 117); cf. also 'Near Perigord', line 2.

On 21 October 1909 Pound wrote to William Carlos

PERSONAE

Williams: ' "Cino" – the thing is banal. He might be anyone. Besides he is catalogued in his epitaph.' (*SL*, 6.)

Subtitle: Pound's poem has its source in Cino's exile from Pistoia in 1303; 'the open road' perhaps alludes to Walt Whitman's 'Song of the Open Road', although Pound wrote in 1909 that he did not feel 'able to read Whitman' until he had settled in London ('What I feel about Walt Whitman', *SPr*, 115), and he is probably identifying more with Cino's wanderings in exile.

l. 1: Pound's poem begins as a dramatic monologue in the manner of Browning, but cf. Arthur Symons's translation of Paul Verlaine's 'Les Indolents', beginning, 'Bah! Spite of Fate' (*Silhouettes*, 1896).

ll. 1–2: the one textual allusion to Cino's poetry. Dante accused Cino of an inconsistency in love and Cino answered in Sonnet LXXVII that his banishment was to blame. As translated by Rossetti,

> One pleasure ever binds and looses me;
> That so, by one same Beauty lured, I still
> Delight in many women here and there.
>
> (*Poems and Translations*, 1968, 391)

Cf. also the line from Arthur Symons's 'Wanderer's Song', 'I have had enough of women and enough of love' (*Images of Good and Evil*, 1899). In his Preface to *The Poetical Works of Lionel Johnson* (1915), Pound said that Symons was amongst his early reading in America; 'One was drunk . . . with Dowson's "Cynara", and with one or two poems of Symons' "Wanderers" ' (*LE*, 367). Symons was also an influence on Pound's 'The Flame' (*CSP*, 64).

l. 14 wind-runeing: Pound's diction (cf. line 15 'us-toward', line 46 'way-fare', line 47 'wander-lied', line 50 'rast-way') often smacks of Anglo-Saxon. He wrote that the earlier poet Arnaut Daniel 'perhaps had heard . . . some song in rough Saxon letters' (*LE*, 109), and perhaps he supposed Cino would also be acquainted with Old English.

36

l. 22 Luth: (O.F.) 'lute'.

l. 25 Polnesi: Bolognese. Cino went to Bologna to study law in about 1290 and became a close friend of Dante there.

l. 30 Peste: (Ital.) 'plague'.

l. 36 Sinistro: (Ital.) 'left', or 'sinister'. In heraldry the 'bend sinister' was an indication of bastardy.

l. 40 grey eyes: this is an early appearance of a recurrent and important motif in Pound, summed up in *Homage to Sextus Propertius* VII (l. 12), 'Eyes are the guides of love'. Pound wrote from Crawfordsville to Mary Moore, whom he planned to marry, addressing her as 'Grey Eyes' (Stock, *Life*, 49). Cf. the descriptions of eyes 'as grey-blown mere' in 'Villonaud for this Yule' (l. 22) and 'like the grey o' the sea' in 'Ballad of the Goodly Fere' (l. 44).

l. 42: 'Pollo Phoibee: Phoebus Apollo, a designation of the sun.

l. 43 Zeus' aegis-day: Zeus was the principal god of the Greeks, in one of his functions god of sky and weather, and is commonly pictured holding a thunderbolt and aegis, or shield, sometimes interpreted as a thundercloud, which when shaken becomes a source of terror.

l. 45 boss: the convex projection at the centre of a shield; here, the sun.

l. 50 rast: path.

Na Audiart (1908)

Pound develops the reference to Lady Audiart in the fifth stanza of the poem 'Domna, puois de me no'us chal' (called 'The Borrowed Lady'), by the twelfth-century troubadour Bertran de Born (1140–1215). Cf. Pound's translation of this poem (*CSP*, 115), 'Near Perigord', 'Sestina: Altaforte', the translation 'Planh for the Young English King', and Pound's discussion and translations of Bertran in *The Spirit of Romance* (pp. 44–8). The Provençal text of Bertran's poem is given in H. J. Chaytor, *The Troubadours of Dante* (1901), pp. 25–7.

Na: (Prov.) 'Lady'.

Audiart: Aldigart of Malemort, a friend of Maria of Ventadorn, sister of the Lady Maent or Maëut (Matilda) to whom Bertran's poem is addressed.

The title and epigraph together make up line 1 of stanza 5 of Bertran's poem, translated by Pound as 'Of Audiart at Malemort,/ Though she with a full heart/ Wish me ill' (*CSP*, 116). The phrase is rendered four times here, at lines 1, 25, 32, 33, and repeated at the poem's close.

l. 3: based on Bertran's 'vuolh que'm do de sas faissos,/ que'lh estai gen liazos' ('I want her to give me her form/ for it is a gracious outfit for her', McDougal, 53), translated by Pound, 'I'd have her form that's laced/ So cunningly' (*CSP*, 116). 'Na Audiart' moves further from its source as the poem progresses.

l. 11 word kiss: though more sensual than Bertran's poem, 'Na Audiart' follows the convention of the lover's distant, vicarious contact with his lady, here and at lines 25 and 35.

l. 13 "Miels-de-Ben": Prov. Mielhs-de-be (Fr. Mieux que Bien), an appellation meaning 'Better than Good', for the Lady Guiscarda (Chaytor, 142). Pound translates in 'Dompna Pois',

> I of Miels-de-ben demand
> Her straight fresh body,
> She is so supple and young,
> Her robes can but do her wrong.

(CSP, 116)

l. 31 Aultaforte: Prov. Autafort (Fr. Hautefort), Bertran de Born's castle.

ll. 37–45: the source is probably Pierre de Ronsard's 'Quand vous serez bien vieille' (*Les Sonnets pour Hélène*, Bk. II, 42), the inspiration also of Yeats's earlier poem 'When You Are Old' (*Collected Poems*, 1967, 46) and of Symons's 'The Last Memory' (*Images of Good and Evil*). Pound had alluded to Ronsard in the poem 'Scriptor Ignotus' (*ALS*, 39), and quotes the phrase 'Quand vous serez bien vieille' in Canto LXXX (540/506). A translation of Ronsard's poem by Andrew Lang is included in *Confucius to Cummings* (p. 128).

l. 39 limning: embellishment as with gold or bright colour, generally in illuminated manuscripts; cf. the 'rose and gold' of line 26.

Villonaud for this Yule (1908, written 1907)

This poem and 'A Villonaud: Ballad of the Gibbet' have their source in the French poet François Villon (1431–63?). Villon, also called François de Montcorbier, was born in Paris where he lived a life 'between respectability, the demi-monde and crime' (de Nagy, 128). His first poem 'Le Lais' (called 'Le Petit Testament') was written in 1456 and the longer Testament (called 'Le Grand Testament') in 1461. He was probably a member of a national gang called Les Coquillards, and wrote also seven ballads in criminal slang. In 1463 he was under sentence of hanging, but instead was banished for ten years, from which point nothing is known of him.

Villon's importance for Pound appears first in ch. VIII of *The Spirit of Romance*. Villon, says Pound, was 'utterly mediaeval' though his poetry marked 'the end of mediaeval literature' (pp. 170–1); he carried on the Provençal tradition of 'unvarnished, intimate speech' though there were 'seeds or signs of a far more modern outbreak' in him than in Dante (p. 167). In particular Pound admires Villon's vitality and directness, 'Villon's art exists because of Villon', he 'has the stubborn persistency of one whose gaze cannot be deflected from the actual fact before him: what he sees, he writes' (p. 168). Where 'Dante lives in his mind', and where 'Dante's vision is real, because he saw it. Villon's verse is real, because he lived it' (p. 178).

It is this 'substance' in Villon which led Pound repeatedly to recommend him as indispensable to literary education (*LE*, 38), as a model of realism and good writing (ibid., 216, 276), and to link him with Tristan Corbière (ibid., 33, 45, 282). And it was Pound's enthusiasm in its turn, presumably, which led F. S. Flint to cite Villon directly as an influence on Imagism (*Poetry*, March 1913, reprinted *EP*, ed. Sullivan,

40–1). Villon had been popular in the late nineteenth century and Pound acknowledged particularly the earlier translations of Swinburne, as standing with Rossetti and with FitzGerald's *Rubáiyát* as the significant achievement of the Victorian period. But, as he wrote to Iris Barry, 'you should have a copy of Villon and not trust to Swinburne's translations (though they are very fine in themselves); they are too luxurious and not hard enough' (*SL*, 88), and again later, 'Swinburne's Villon is not Villon very exactly, but it is perhaps the best Swinburne we have' (*LE*, 36). Pound himself avoided direct translation and tried to present rather more of Villon the man than the artist.

> Technically speaking, translation of Villon is extremely difficult because he rhymes on the exact word, on a word meaning sausages, for example.

> The grand bogies for young men who want really to learn strophe writing are Catullus and Villon. I personally have been reduced to setting them to music as I cannot translate them.
>
> (*ABC of R*, 105)

Pound set himself to learn strophe writing and something of the constraints of rhyme in the ballad form in his two poems 'Villonaud for this Yule' and 'A Villonaud: Ballad of the Gibbet', but he intended also to carry over the substance of the original. As he wrote to W. C. Williams in 1908, 'The Villonauds are likewise what I conceive after a good deal of study to be an expression akin to, if not of, the spirit breathed in Villon's own poeting' (*SL*, 3). Pound's poems, as this suggests, are 'inspired' by Villon rather than attempts to translate an original poem or poems. As such they are a combination of homage, analysis and original poem, something of which Pound's term 'Villonaud' offers to convey.

Pound's attempt to set Villon to music (see above) resulted in a one-act opera based on Villon's life, called *Le Testament*. It was written in Paris in 1920–1, performed in part there in

June 1926, and broadcast in more complete form by the B.B.C. in October 1931 and June and August 1962.

Cf. also the reference to Villon in *Hugh Selwyn Mauberley*, 'E. P. Ode' (l. 18).

The source for 'Villonaud for this Yule' is two poems by Villon, 'Ballade des Dames du Temps Jadis' and 'Ballade de la Belle Heaumière' (*Oeuvres*, ed. André Mary, Paris, 1951, 31, 39). Translations of both poems, by Rossetti and Swinburne respectively, are included in the anthology *Confucius to Cummings* (pp. 117 and 111–13). Pound follows Villon in the use of the ballad form but restricts his rhyme scheme to two rhyme-words.

ll. 1, 3–4: derived from Villon's

> Sur le Noel, morte saison
> Que les loups se vivent de vent.
>
> ('Le Lais', ll. 10–11)

l. 2: the parentheses in each stanza refer to events surrounding the Nativity. Witemeyer suggests that the speaker in the poem finds no consolation in religion, and that the function of the parentheses 'is to convey Villon's "mockery", and they may be spoken almost bitterly' (p. 21). Pound had noted the element of mockery in Villon's voice in *The Spirit of Romance* (p. 168).

l. 3 everychone: Pound perhaps reaches for the authenticity of Villon through Chaucer, who 'wrote while England was still a part of Europe. There was one culture from Ferrara to Paris and it extended to England' (*ABC of R*, 101); cf. the use of 'gueredon' (l. 5), 'foison' (l. 13), 'feat' (l. 20).

l. 5 gueredon: (ME., O.F.) 'reward', 'requital'.

l. 7 skoal!: this is Pound's expansion of Villon, who never wrote a drinking song, although *Le Testament* ends with Villon drinking a glass of wine as if to scoff at the whole work.

l. 8: Pound adapts the refrain of Rossetti's translation of 'The Ballad of Dead Ladies', 'But where are the snows of yester-year?' (*Poems and Translations*, 101–2).

PERSONAE

l. 10 magians: the wise men who brought frankincense and
myrrh to Christ.

l. 13 foison: (ME., O.F.) 'plentiful', 'powerful'.

l. 18: the star of Bethlehem is thought to have occurred through
a conjunction of Jupiter (i.e. Zeus) and Mars.

ll. 19–21: the theme is that of the medieval 'ubi-sunt', as
detected by Pound elsewhere in the stanzas beginning 'Where
are the gracious gallants/ That I beheld in times gone by'
and 'I mourn the time of my youth,/ When I made merry
more than another' (*SR*, 171, 172).

l. 20 feat: (ME., O.F.) 'fitting', 'apt', 'neat'.

l. 22: cf. 'Ballad of the Goodly Fere', 'Oh we drank his
"Hale" in the good red wine' (l. 13) and 'Wi' his eyes like the
grey o' the sea' (l. 44).

ll. 25–8: cf. the closing lines of Villon's ballad, in Rossetti's
translation:

> Nay, never ask this week, fair lord,
>   Where they are gone, nor yet this year,
> Except with this for an overword,
>   But where are the snows of yester-year?
>
> (*Poems and Translations*, 102)

Pound's adaptation confirms the note of religious scepticism.

n. 1 Signum Nativitatis: (Lat.) 'sign of the nativity'.

The Tree (1908)

One of the 26 poems originally in the unpublished 'Hilda's
Book', given by Pound to H.D. (Hilda Doolittle). Pound
evidently associated H.D. with trees, as Hugh Kenner records:
'He had called her "Dryad" since Pennsylvania days, when a
crow's nest high in the Doolittles' maple tree had been one of
their adolescent trysting-places, and the little apple-orchard
in the Pounds' back garden at Wyncote another' (*Pound Era*,
174). According to Guy Davenport, 'Hilda's Book' was 'green
with trees, poem after poem' (Hesse, 146).

Cf. also the poem 'Aube of the West Dawn: Venetian June'

where Pound comments, 'I think from such perceptions as this arose the ancient myths of the demi-gods; as from such as that in "The Tree" . . . the myths of metamorphosis' (*ALS*, 94). In *The Spirit of Romance* Pound wrote, 'I believe that Greek myth arose when someone having passed through delightful psychic experience tried to communicate it to others and found it necessary to screen himself from persecution' (p. 92), a belief paralleled in the poem 'Masks':

> These tales of old disguisings, are they not
> Strange myths of souls that found themselves among
> Unwonted folk that spake an hostile tongue,
>
> (*ALS*, 52)

In a later essay on Arnold Dolmetsch (1918), the association between the making of myths and the making of poems becomes explicit:

> The first myths arose when a man walked sheer into 'nonsense', that is to say, when some very vivid and undeniable adventure befell him, and he told someone else who called him a liar. Thereupon, after bitter experience, perceiving that no one could understand what he meant when he said that he 'turned into a tree' he made a myth – a work of art that is – an impersonal or objective story woven out of his own emotion, as the nearest equation that he was capable of putting into words.
>
> (*LE*, 431)

l. 3: Daphne was turned at her own request into a bay tree (the Greek 'laurel') to escape the pursuit of Apollo (Ovid, *Metamorphoses* Bk. I, ll. 452–567/545–700). Cf. the poem 'A Girl' (*CSP*, 75), 'Dance Figure' (l. 10), *Hugh Selwyn Mauberley* XII (ll. 1–2), Canto II (ll. 124–5), Canto LXXVI (490/461), and also 'La Fraisne' (ll. 9–10) and 'Piere Vidal Old' (l. 52).
l. 4: i.e. Philemon and Baucis, a poor old couple who entertained the disguised Zeus and Hermes, and were as a reward protected by the gods and granted their request to die at the same time, when they were changed into trees whose boughs

intertwined. The story is told in Ovid, *Metamorphoses*, Bk. VIII (ll. 628–724/804–909); cf. also Canto XC (639/605). Pound was probably influenced by Yeats's line 'I have been a hazel-tree' in 'He Thinks of His Past Greatness When a Part of the Constellations of Heaven' (*Collected Poems*, 81). The hazel tree is the Gaelic tree of knowledge. Pound therefore, by allusion, joins Gaelic and Greek myth.

Sestina: Altaforte (1909)

First published in F. M. Ford's *English Review* (June 1909), Pound's first appearance in an English magazine; cf. 'Na Audiart', 'Planh for the Young English King' and 'Near Perigord'.

Pound's poem is based on a war song by the twelfth-century troubadour Bertran de Born, 'Be'm platz lo gais temps de pascor' (Chaytor, 28–9), usually called 'The Praise of War', of which Pound gives a fairly literal translation in *The Spirit of Romance* (pp. 47–8). Bertran's poem is composed of a series of vignettes of war each introduced by the phrase 'e platz mi' (it pleases me). Pound also structures his poem on variations of this sentiment, but in the form of a sestina. His own account of its composition is given in 'How I Began' (*T.P.'s Weekly*, 6 June 1913). Having found Bertran untranslatable, Pound realized he 'wanted the curious involution and recurrence of the Sestina. I knew more or less of the arrangement. I wrote the first strophe and then went to the British Museum to make sure of the right order of the permutations. . . . I did the rest of the poem at a sitting. Technically it is one of my best, though a poem on such a theme could never be very important' (p. 707).

The sestina rotates a set of six rhyme-words and was, said Pound, 'invented by Arnaut Daniel' (*SR*, 26). Pound therefore revivifies Bertran through his contemporary Arnaut as he attempts to do more fundamentally in 'Near Perigord' (cf. note on line 154). Though Pound stresses the poem's technique, Bertran de Born evidently signified more than this. Ford

Madox Ford recalled Pound braving the London traffic, 'waving his cane as if he had been Bertran de Born about to horsewhip Henry II of England' (quoted in Norman, 46), and Pound wrote to W. C. Williams in December 1913 that he liked the sculptor Gaudier-Brzeska because he was the 'only person with whom I can really be "Altaforte"' (*SL*, 27). Pound's public reading of his poem appears also to have been very much in character. He read it first on his introduction to T. E. Hulme and others of the 'Poets' Club' at the Tour Eiffel restaurant in Soho on 22 April 1909, and with such vigour, so it seems, that a screen was placed around the company's table (Stock, *Life*, 86). Pound tells also of how he read it to Gaudier-Brzeska.

> I was interested and was determined that he should be. . . .
> I therefore opened fire with 'Altaforte', 'Piere Vidal' and such poems as I had written when about his own age. And I think it was the 'Altaforte' that convinced him that I would do to be sculpted.
>
> (*G-B*, 45)

Gaudier, so it happened, was impressed for the wrong reasons, mistaking Pound's pronunciation of 'peace' for 'piss'. John Cournos who records Gaudier's response says, 'When I told this to Ezra, he was delighted' (*Autobiography*, 1935, 260).

Epigraph:
Loquitur: (Lat.) 'he speaks'.
En: (Prov.) 'Sir', 'Lord'.
Dante: Pound alludes to Dante's placing Bertran in the eighth circle of Hell as a 'Sower of Discord', for setting Prince Henry against his brother Richard and their father Henry II (*Inferno*, XXVIII, ll. 118–42). Cf. Pound's translation of this passage from Dante in *The Spirit of Romance* (p. 45) and in 'Near Perigord' (ll. 21–2, 163–8). Dante cites Bertran as an outstanding poet of war in *De Vulgari Eloquentia* (Bk. II, ch. 2).
Eccovi: (Ital.) 'Here you are.'
jongleur: the troubadour's singer.

Richard: Bertran's poem was a call to arms to the barons of Limousin against Richard, then Duke of Aquitaine.

l. 2 Papiols: some manuscripts of Bertran's poem contain an envoi in which he sends his jongleur Papiols to Richard Coeur de Lion to complain of too much peace. Bertran called Richard 'Oc-e-No' (de Nagy, 126). Pound glosses these lines, 'Papiol, be glad to go speedily, to "Yea and Nay", and tell him there's too much peace about' (*SR*, 48). By bringing Papiols forward into the Browningesque opening of the poem Pound launches his sestina as a dramatic monologue.

ll. 7–12: Bertran's poem refers to 'the sweet time of Easter'. Pound introduces here and in stanza IV the pathetic fallacy of a corresponding strife in nature.

l. 14 destriers: war horses, trained to rear up before an enemy.

l. 20: a metaphor anticipated in the lines from two earlier poems in *A Lume Spento*, ' "Red spears bore the warrior dawn of old" ' ('In Tempore Senectutis', p. 33) and 'Ye blood-red spears-men of the dawn's array' ('To the Dawn: Defiance', p. 67).

ll. 21–2: the sestina falters here, the rhyme pattern calling for a reversal of these lines.

ll. 37–9: Pound omits two of the rhyme-words ('opposing', 'rejoicing') which his envoi, as part of a sestina, should strictly include.

Ballad of the Goodly Fere (1909)

Pound wrote to his father in April 1909, 'I have this morning written a Ballad of Simon Zelotes, which is probably the strongest thing in English since "Reading Gaol" ' (quoted in Stock, *Life*, 83). Later, in the essay 'How I Began', he said that he had been provoked into writing the poem 'by a certain sort of irreverence which was new to me', that he had written the poem the next day in the British Museum reading room 'and later in the afternoon, being unable to study, I peddled the poem about Fleet Street, for I began to realise that for the first time in my life, I had written something that "everyone

could understand", and I wanted it to go to the people'
(*T.P.'s Weekly*, 6 June 1913, 707).

Only the *Evening Standard*, Pound recalls, even considered
the poem, but it was, in the event, well received. Edward
Marsh requested it for his first anthology of *Georgian Poetry* in
1912, although Pound declined 'as it doesn't illustrate any
modern tendency' (Norman, 82), and Yeats cited the poem in
March 1914 in an after-dinner address in Chicago as being 'of
permanent value' (Stock, *Life*, 191). Pound himself was
apparently more cynical. Malcolm Cowley records his saying,
'Having written one poem about Christ, I had only to write
similar ballads about James, Matthew, Mark and John and
my fortune was made' (Hutchins, 55). Eliot too had reservations about the poem and omitted it from the *Selected Poems*
(1928) 'because it has a much greater popularity than it
deserves' (p. 21).

Simon Zelotes: the apostle.
l. 2 gallows tree: cf. 'A Villonaud: Ballad of the Gibbet', line 1.
l. 3 lover . . . of brawny men: Pound owes something perhaps to
Walt Whitman's praise of 'manhood, balanced, florid, and
full' and his conception of 'the great Camerado, the lover true'
('Song of Myself', section 45).
l. 7: from the Gospel according to St. John:

> I have told you that I am he; if therefore ye seek me, let
> these go their way.
>
> (18:8)

ll. 11–12: from the Gospel according to St. Luke:

> Be ye come out, as against a thief, with swords and staves?
> When I was daily with you in the temple, ye stretched
> forth no hands against me.
>
> (22:52–3)

ll. 13–14: a reference to the Last Supper; cf. Matthew 26:27.
ll. 17–20: Christ drives the merchants from the temple; cf.
Matthew 21:12–13.
l. 44: cf. the reference to 'grey eyes' in 'Cino' (l. 40n.).

ll. 45–8: a reference to Christ's walking on the water; cf. Mark 6: 47–53.

l. 47 Genseret: Gennesaret.

ll. 53–4: derived from Luke 24: 42–3:

> And they gave him a piece of broiled fish, and of an honey-comb.
>
> And he took it, and did eat before them.

Planh for the Young English King (1909)

A translation of the second of two poems written by Bertran de Born on the death of Prince Henry (called 'the Young King' because he was crowned in 1170 before the death of his father, King Henry II, in 1189). Henry's younger brother Richard Coeur de Lion had supported Bertran's brother Constantin in his attempt to appropriate the Château d'Haute-fort (Pound's Altaforte). In revenge Bertran joined the league of Limousin barons against Richard, then Duke of Aquitaine, and contracted Prince Henry's support against Richard and King Henry II. Before the end of the campaign, Henry fell ill and died of fever, 11 June 1183, at Martel. The Provençal text is given in Chaytor (pp. 18–19).

Cf. 'Na Audiart', 'Sestina: Altaforte' and 'Near Perigord'.

Just as Bertran's 'Borrowed Lady' (cf. Pound's translation, *CSP*, 115) is an assemblage of an ideal lady, so Prince Henry is an exemplar of courtly virtues. Pound called the poem 'one of the noblest laments or "planh" in the Provençal' (*SR*, 45).

Planh: (Prov.) 'lament', 'elegy'.

ll. 1–5: Compare the translation of Ida Farnell in *The Lives of the Troubadours* (1896), a version known to Pound:

> If all the pain, and misery, and woe,
>   The tears, the losses with misfortune fraught,
> That in this dark life men can ever know,
>   Were heap'd together – all would seem as naught
> Against the death of the Young English King.
>
> (pp. 110–11)

l. 1: the Provençal, 'Si tuit li dol ëlh plor ëlh marrimen', is repeated in Canto LXXX (l. 754), and Canto LXXXIV (572/537).

l. 2 dolour: (cf. line 6, 'dolorous'). Pound matches the play in the first stanza of Bertran's poem on 'dol(h)', 'dolors', 'dolen' and 'doloros'; cf. also 'grief' (l. 1), 'grieving' (l. 3); 'every' (l. 2), 'ever' (l. 3).

l. 8 ire: gloominess, spite. Pound attempts to stay close to the sound of the Provençal 'ira'.

l. 9 bitterness: Pound drops the rhyme scheme of the original, ABABCDDE, but retains the repetition through the five stanzas of the final words of lines 1, 5 and 8.

l. 10 teen, liegemen: deliberate archaisms.

l. 12: Bertran's 'trop an argut en mort mortal guerrier' means 'They have found in Death a deadly warrior'. Pound apparently confuses 'en' meaning 'sir' with the preposition 'en', meaning 'in' (see McDougal, 23–4).

l. 18 Well mayst thou boast: adopted from Ida Farnell.

ll. 25–6: the sense of the Provençal ('If love flees from this weak world, full of sadness,/ I hold his joy to be untrue', McDougal, 24) is less pessimistic.

l. 35: the Provençal, 'e receup mort a nostre salvamen' ('And received death for our salvation', McDougal, 23) is more inert than Pound's version.

"Blandula, Tenulla, Vagula" (1911)

Pound's title is drawn from the dying words of the Emperor Hadrian:

> Animula vagula blandula
> hospes comesque corporis,
> quae nunc abibis in loca
> pallidula rigida nudula?
> (*Scriptores Historiae Augustae*, I, Loeb edn., 78)

('O blithe little soul, thou, flitting away,/ Guest and comrade of this my clay,/ Whither now goest thou, to what place/ Bare and ghastly and without grace?'). Pound quotes Fontenelle's French translation at the close of the last of his 'Twelve Dialogues of Fontenelle' in *Pavannes and Divagations* (p. 142), and includes his own adaptation of the first line of the Latin at the close of his obituary on Remy de Gourmont (*SPr*, 393). The Latin was adopted also by Walter Pater as the epigraph to ch. VIII of his *Marius the Epicurean*. Pound's 'tenulla' is perhaps a pun on 'tinnula' ('bell') and a sideways glance at Catullus' 'voce carmina tinnula' (*Odes* LXI, l. 13), quoted in Canto III (l. 25), and Canto XX (93/89). Alternatively, as Ronald E. Thomas suggests, Pound's 'tenulla' is drawn from the Latin 'tenellus' ('very tender', 'delicate'), especially as it occurs in the phrase 'ut flos tenellus' in the poem 'He compares his soul to a flower' by Marcus Antonius Flaminius (1498–1550), quoted (although 'tenellus' appears wrongly as 'tenellos') in *The Spirit of Romance* (p. 228) ('Catullus, Flaminius, and Pound in "Blandula, Tenella [*sic*], Vagula"', *Paideuma*, v, no. 3, 407–12). The phrase 'vagula, tenula' occurs much later in Canto CV (772/747).

l. 1: Pound's line recalls the rejection of a heavenly paradise by Aucassin in the story *Aucassin et Nicolette*. The story was discussed by Walter Pater in the opening chapter of *The Renaissance* and Pound praised the translation by Andrew Lang (*SR*, 84). Lang gives the opening of Aucassin's speech as, 'In Paradise what have I to win?' (*Aucassin and Nicolette*, 1896, 9). Aucassin rejects heaven for a hell accompanied by Nicolette. Pound rejects it for an earthly paradise.

l. 5 Sirmio: Latin name for Sirmione, a promontory on the southern shore of Lake Garda, where Catullus had a villa and which now contains a grotto to his name. Sirmio was among Pound's 'sacred places' (cf. Kenner, *Pound Era*, pp. 318–49). He first visited it in March 1910 and again, in the early years, in June 1911, April 1913, and May–June 1920 (when he met James Joyce there). His response in 1910, as he wrote to his parents, was that 'he knew paradise when he saw it' (Stock, *Life*, 107). Thomas argues that in its reference to

Sirmio Pound's poem asserts a poetic tradition which included Catullus, Flaminius and himself, and that Pound alludes to this effect to Catullus XXXI and Poem 1 of Flaminius' *Lusus Pastorales* (cited in *The Spirit of Romance*, p. 230). That this double association was in Pound's mind is suggested by a comment in a letter to his mother from Sirmione in March 1910, where he wrote of 'the same old Sirmio that Catullus raved over a few years back, or M. A. Flaminius more recently' (Stock, op. cit.). Cf. other references to Sirmio in 'The Flame', 'The Study in Aesthetics' (*CSP*, 64, 105), and in Cantos LXXIV (453/427), LXXVI (487/456) and LXXVIII (509/478).

ll. 6–15: Pound wrote in 1912 of his desire to 'lie on what is left of Catullus' parlour floor and speculate the azure beneath it and the hills off to Salo and Riva with their forgotten gods moving unhindered amongst them' (*LE*, 9).

l. 8 terrene: earthly.

l. 10: Pound consistently admired the blueness of Lake Garda; cf. the description 'sapphire Benacus' in 'The Flame', and Canto V, 'Topaz I manage, and three sorts of blue' (21/17). *cyanine*: a blue dye stuff.

l. 11 triune: three in one, a term suggested to Pound, says Thomas, by Flaminius' use of the Latin 'terna'. Pound translates the relevant lines, 'Thrice from the foam-filled bowl we pour/ Thee milk, and thrice of the honey's store' (*SR*, 230).

l. 12: cf. 'The Flame', 'Call not that mirror me, for I have slipped/ Your grasp, I have eluded', and 'Near Perigord', lines 191–2.

l. 15 Riva: a town to the north of Lake Garda.

Erat Hora (1911)

Title: (Lat.) 'It was an Hour'.
Similar fleeting and ecstatic moments occur in 'Horae Beatae Inscriptio' ('Inscription for an Hour of Happiness') (*CSP*, 65) and 'Shop Girl' (*CSP*, 123); cf. also 'The Needle', 'Here have we had our vantage, the good hour' (*CSP*, 81). The general

influence is perhaps Walter Pater's doctrine of attending to life's passing moments, 'simply for those moments' sake',

> who, in some such perfect moment, . . . has not felt the desire to perpetuate all that, just so, to suspend it in every particular circumstance, with the portrait of just that one spray of leaves lifted just so high against the sky, above the well, forever . . .

> > (from the original version of Pater's essay 'The School of Giorgione', quoted in Arthur Symons, *A Study of Walter Pater*, 1932, 29)

Pound himself wrote in 1912 of his belief that 'there are in the "normal course of things" certain times, a certain sort of moment more than another, when a man feels his immortality upon him' (*SR*, 94) and later that one of the ingredients of the *Cantos* was 'The "magic moment" or moment of metamorphosis, bust thru from quotidien into "divine or permanent world". Gods, etc.' (*SL*, 210).

The House of Splendour (1911)

'The House of Splendour' appeared first as poem no. VII in a series of twelve poems entitled 'Und Drang' (*Canzoni*, 1911; reprinted in *CEP*, 167–74).
l. 1 Evanoe: fictitious medievalism on Pound's part after the manner of William Morris in *The Defence of Guenevere*.
l. 2: cf. St. Paul's Second Letter to the Corinthians:

> we have a building of God, an house not made with hands, eternal in the heavens.

> > (5: 1)

Pound's source is also 'the golden house' to which Psyche is drawn in Walter Pater's translation of Apuleius' 'Cupid and Psyche':

> a dwelling-place, built not by human hands, but by some divine cunning. One recognized, even at the entering, the delightful hostelry of a God. Golden pillars sustained the roof,

arched most curiously in cedar wood and ivory. The walls
were hidden under wrought silver.

(quoted by Pound, SR, 17)

Pater's version of the tale appears in ch. v, 'The Golden Book',
of his *Marius the Epicurean*, and was a source also for Pound's
'Speech for Psyche in the Golden Book of Apuleius' (*CSP*, 53).
Cf. also ' "Blandula, Tenulla, Vagula" ' and 'Erat Hora' for
the influence of Pater.

ll. 6–8: cf. 'Apparuit', lines 13–16.

l. 10 sapphires: W. C. Williams records an incident when his
father objected to

> something Ezra had written: what in heaven's name Ezra
> meant by "jewels" in a verse that had come between them.
> These jewels – rubies, sapphires, amethysts and whatnot,
> Pound went on to explain with great determination and
> care, were the backs of books as they stood on a man's shelf.
> "But why in heaven's name don't you say so then?" was
> my father's triumphant and crushing rejoinder.

('Prologue to Kora in Hell', Selected Essays, 1969, 8)

Pound replied,

> remember we did talk about "Und Drang" but there the
> sapphires certainly are NOT anything but sapphires, per-
> fectly definite visual imagination. However, upshot (which
> you don't, certainly, imply) is that your old man was
> certainly dead right.

(SL, 159)

Sapphires (and other jewels) appear in 'The Flame', and in
'Horae Beatae Inscriptio', both also originally in 'Und
Drang'. Pound no doubt owes this reference to precious stones
to the poets of the Nineties.

La Fraisne (1908)

Originally intended as the title poem of *A Lume Spento* with
the dedication 'to such as love this same/ beauty that I love,

somewhat/ after mine own fashion'. (The title-page is reproduced in *A Lume Spento and other Early Poems*, 1965.)

In *A Lume Spento* and subsequently until 1920, 'La Fraisne'
appeared also with a long note in which Pound dilated on the
soul 'exhausted in fire' returning to the peace of 'its primal
nature':

> Then becometh it kin to the faun and the dryad, a
> woodland-dweller amid the rocks and streams
> > "*consociis faunis dryadisque inter saxa sylvarum*"
> > > > Janus of Basel.

Also has Mr. Yeats in his *Celtic Twilight* treated of such,
and I because in such a mood, feeling myself divided between myself corporal and a self aetherial, "a dweller by
streams and in wood-land," eternal because simple in
elements

> "*Aeternus quia simplex naturae.*"

The source of the poem, he suggests, is in the legend of the
fictitious troubadour Miraut de Garzelas who, ' "after the
pains he bore a-loving Riels of Calidorn and that to none
avail, ran mad in the forest" ' (*ALS*, 14).

This, as Pound suggests, resembles the story of Peire Vidal
(cf. 'Piere Vidal Old'). 'La Fraisne' is an example too of the
early influence of Yeats and of Pound's belief in the nature of
myth (cf. 'The Tree' and note). In *A Lume Spento*, and only
there, the poem appeared with a stage direction, 'Scene: The
Ash Wood of Malvern'. Patricia Hutchins suggests that 'If
this is a reference to an English region, presumably the poem
was drafted, or actually written, when Pound was in England
in 1906' (p. 64). Pound himself suggests he had looked,
without success, for someone who would publish the poem in
1907 (*SL*, 24).

Title: (Prov.) 'The Ash Tree'.
l. 3: Pound's variations on this line at lines 7, 11–12, 23, 24,
27–9, have as a common source Yeats's lines in 'In the Seven
Woods', 'I have . . . put away/ The unavailing outcries and

the old bitterness/ That empty the heart' (*Collected Poems*, 85).

l. 13 Mar-nan-otha: after the manner of Yeats's Celtic renderings, 'Pairc-na-lee' ('In the Seven Woods'), 'Clooth-na-Bare'
('Red Hanrahan's Song about Ireland'), for example.

l. 15 syne: (ME.) 'time since'.

l. 19: cf. the refrain, 'They will not hush, the leaves a-flutter
round me, the beech leaves old', in Yeats's 'The Madness of
King Goll' (*Collected Poems*, 17–20), a general influence on
Pound's poem.

l. 25 ellum: elm.

ll. 49–52: cf. the closing lines of 'Sandalphon', 'Even as I
marvel and wonder, and know not,/ Yet keep my watch in the
ash wood' (*ALS*, 102).

A Villonaud: Ballad of the Gibbet (1908)

Cf. 'Villonaud for this Yule' and accompanying note. Pound's
poem has some basis in Villon's 'L'Épitaphe de Villon', also
called 'Ballade des Pendus' (*Oeuvres*, 152), but in effect counters
this poem with the tenor of the so-called 'slang ballads'
written between *Le Testament* and Villon's disappearance, to
present the Villon who 'walked the gutters of Paris' described
by Pound in *The Spirit of Romance* (p. 167). Cf. also 'Histrion',
'Thus am I . . ./ One François Villon, ballad-lord and thief'
(*ALS*, 108).

Epigraph: the French phrase ('In this brothel we hold our
state') is from Villon's 'La Grosse Margot' (*Oeuvres*, 98),
where, says Pound, 'Villon casts out the dregs of his shame'
(*SR*, 176). The prose link is Pound's. Villon was condemned
to death by hanging in 1463 for his part in a brawl. After an
appeal the sentence was commuted to ten years' banishment.
It was probably at this time that he wrote 'L'Épitaphe'.
'*Frères . . . vivez*': the opening line of 'L'Épitaphe de Villon',
quoted by Pound with Swinburne's translation of the poem
beginning 'Men, brother men, that after us yet live' (ibid.,
178). Pound's scene-setting brings to Villon something of 'the

dramatic imagination' that Pound said was 'beyond him' (ibid., 173).

l. 1 gallows tree: cf. 'Ballad of the Goodly Fere', line 2.

l. 2 François . . . Margot . . . me: i.e. Villon, la grosse Margot and the sixth companion awaiting execution with Villon.

l. 5 Pierre: probably Pound's invention, as are 'Larron' (l. 6), 'Tybalde' (l. 7), 'Raoul de Vallerie' (l. 27), 'Maturin', 'Guillaume', 'Jacques d'Allmain' (l. 29) and 'Michault le Borgne' (l. 34).

l. 7 armouress: 'La Belle Heaumière' (*Oeuvres*, 39). Pound gives Swinburne's translation, 'The Complaint of the Fair Armouress', in *Confucius to Cummings*, pp. 111–13.

l. 8 poignard: dagger. Pound follows Villon's method of characterization by means of an associated object.

l. 9 Guise: the armourer to le duc de Guise and husband to 'la belle heaumière'.

l. 10: a pun; the 'Haulte Noblesse' ('the high nobility') are also those strung on the gibbet.

ll. 11–12: the armouress was abused 'right evilly' by her husband; cf. Swinburne's 'Fair Armouress', stanzas 3–4.

l. 12 drue: lover.

l. 15 Marienne Ydole: Marion l'Idole, a prostitute and one of the two criminals mentioned by Villon in *Le Testament* (CLI, CLV).

l. 16 brenn: burn.

l. 27 Jehan: Jean le Loup, the second of the criminals belonging to the Paris gangs named by Villon (*Le Testament*, CX).

ll. 30–32: Pound confuses Culdou with another character, Casin Cholet, to whom Villon bequeaths a coat so he can hide a fowl he has stolen ('Le Lais', stanza XXIV, *Oeuvres*, 9).

l. 30 Culdou: Michaut Cul d'Oue (*Le Testament*, CXXXV).

l. 32 St. Hubert: patron saint of hunters.

l. 40 faibleness: cf. French 'faiblesse' ('weakness').

ll. 41–3: cf. Villon's lines in 'L'Épitaphe', as translated by Swinburne:

> Prince Jesus, that of all art lord and head,
> Keep us, that hell be not our bitter bed;

We have nought to do in such a master's hall.
Be not ye therefore of our fellowhead,
But pray to God that he forgive us all.

(Confucius to Cummings, 114–15)

Pound's rendering undercuts Villon's piety.

Marvoil (1909)

Written early in 1908. Pound's 'Marvoil' is the Provençal troubadour Arnaut de Mareuil (1170–1200), born at Mareuil-sur-Belle in the Dordogne. Arnaut's family were servants and he was trained as a scribe, but preferred the wandering life of a troubadour. He left over twenty 'Canzos' or formal love songs, generally thought to be full of conventional panegyrics to his lady and clichéd expressions of his own hope and despair. Pound translates one song in *The Spirit of Romance*, and comments: 'For the simplicity of adequate speech Arnaut of Marvoil is to be numbered among the best of the courtly "makers" ' (p. 57). Pound's poem is a monologue presenting Marvoil's retrospective view of his career and exile. Here Marvoil can be frank about the identity of his lady and his contempt for Alphonso of Aragon, as he could not be in his poetry, Pound thereby removing Marvoil's mask to show him as one of those whose 'verse is real, because he lived it' (ibid., 178).

l. 1: Pound refers to the ' "lesser Arnaut" of Marvoil, possibly overshadowed in his own day by Daniel' (ibid., 57). The description derives from Petrarch's ' 'l men famoso Arnaldo' (*Trionfo d'Amore*, IV, l. 44). Pound credits Marvoil himself with an awareness of the comparison. His self-consciousness about his lowly station in relation to his lady appeared in a long didactic letter in which he gave special attention to clerks.

l. 4 Maître Jacques Polin: Marvoil's fictitious overseer while a clerk.

l. 6: Arnaut de Mareuil was at the court of Roger II, Viscount of Béziers.

l. 7 his lady: Alazais (Adelaide), daughter of Count Raymond V of Toulouse, and wife to Roger II.

l. 9: the Provençal biography, or *vida*, suggests that Alphonso II of Aragon, Alazais's suitor after Roger's death, became jealous of Arnaut and caused him to be expelled from the court. This is probably based more on Arnaut's verse than on fact, although Arnaut did leave Béziers in 1194.

l. 12 Mont-Ausier: Montausier, home of the Lady Tibors, Viscountess of Chalais (l. 18). In a note to the poem in *Personae* (1909) Pound said that though this lady was 'contemporary with the other persons' he had 'no strict warrant for dragging her name into this particular affair' (p. 59).

l. 20 Burlatz: Alazais was born in the castle of Burlatz and took the name Countess of Burlatz before her marriage. Since the lord of Béziers was only a viscount, she retained her inherited title.

l. 22 Quattro: Pound's 'Alfonso' was Alphonso II not IV. Ida Farnell, in a text known to Pound, includes a note which suggests some doubt: 'Diez considers this Alphonso to be Alphonso II of Aragon, while Millot declares him to be Alphonso IV of Castile' (*Lives of the Troubadours*, 1896, 75). This may be the source of Pound's confusion.

ll. 27–9: Pound echoes the lines from Arnaut de Mareuil:

> Bem' aucizetc, quan mi detz un baizar
> qu'anc pueys no fo mos cors meyns de dezir,
> mas be suy folhs, quar m'en auzi vanar
> be'm deuria hom a cavalh atraire.

(Canzone XX, de Nagy, 121)

('Truly you slew me when you gave me a kiss,/for never since that time was I any less full of desire./But I am mad, for you hear me boasting about it./I ought to be drawn by a horse!')

l. 31: in his poetry Arnaut in fact addressed a conciliatory envoi to Alphonso (Canzone XXI).

l. 34: Marvoil secretes his letter for posterity in a hole in the wall.

jongleur: singer.

l. 48: close to a characteristic simile in Arnaut de Mareuil: 'el cor m'a miral ab que 'us remir' (Canzone XXI, de Nagy, 121), ('In my heart there is a mirror for me in which I gaze on you').

Mihi pergamena deest: (Lat.) 'I do not have the parchment'. Pound uses the phrase 'Pergamena Deest' as the title of a chapter in *Guide to Kulchur* (pp. 342–4).

Piere Vidal Old (1909)

The Provençal troubadour Peire Vidal (1175–1215) 'was son of a furrier, and sang better than any man in the world' (*LE*, 95). Pound also translated Vidal's 'The Song of Breath' (*SR*, 49) and wrote a poem derived from Vidal, 'Canzon: To Be Sung Beneath a Window' (*Provença*, 1910; reprinted in *CEP*, 136).

His 'Piere Vidal Old' is not a translation but a 'persona' based on the incident Pound records in his epigraph from an early Provençal biography. This and other stories are probably apocryphal elaborations of references or fantasies in Vidal's poems, in this case of the lines,

> And although you call me a wolf,
> I do not hold myself in dishonour,
> Not even if the shepherds blame me
> Or if I am chased by them;
> And I prefer woods and thickets
> To palace and home.
> And with joy my path will be towards her
> Amid wind and ice and snow.
>
> (McDougal, 47)

Pound seems to accept the story either as fact or as the myth that a man makes when he walks 'sheer into "nonsense" ' (*LE*, 431). In *The Spirit of Romance*, he suggests that Vidal's verse is 'real' because, like Villon, Bertran de Born and Arnaut de Mareuil, 'he lived it' (p. 178), and in Canto IV he sets

Vidal with the myth of Actaeon pursued by the huntress Diana as an equivalent example of metamorphosis. Pound read 'Piere Vidal' with 'Sestina: Altaforte' to Gaudier-Brzeska (*G-B*, 45; cf. note to 'Sestina: Altaforte') and referred to Gaudier as 'like a well-made young wolf'. Gaudier himself presented Pound with a drawing of a wolf in admiration of Pound's poem (Stock, *Life*, 183), and either this or another similar drawing is included as Plate II in Pound's 'Memoir'.

Epigraph: Loba was mistress of Penautier in Toulousain, south of the Cabardes mountains (Prov. Cabaretz; Pound's 'Cabaret').

l. 1: Pound's poem sets Vidal's escapade in the past.

l. 23 guerdon: reward.

ll. 26–7: cf. the lines from Arnaut Daniel's 'Sols sui', praised by Dante as a model of excellent craftsmanship and by Pound for 'its vivid and accurate description of the emotion',

> for the Rhone, from the water that swelleth it, hath never such turmoil as doth that torrent which pools itself with love in my heart on seeing her.
>
> (*SR*, 27)

l. 29: cf. 'If she goes in a gleam of Cos, in a slither of dyed stuff' (*Homage to Sextus Propertius* v, l. 32).

ll. 34–42: Pound interpolates and enlarges on an alleged incident concerning Vidal and the Lady Azalais (Adelaide) of Marseilles, from whom he stole a kiss while she was sleeping. Vidal's songs, according to de Nagy, do 'occasionally display intensive erotic streaks' (p. 123).

l. 52: cf. 'The Tree', and 'La Fraisne', stanza 3.

ll. 66–7: Pound adopts the manner of Browning's 'Fra Lippo Lippi' as Vidal regains his old guise.

RIPOSTES

(October 1912)

If Pound came to London as he said to learn 'how Yeats did it'
(*SL*, 296), this influence was soon rivalled, if not overtaken, by
another, that of Ford Madox Ford. Writing a survey of the
London literary scene for *Poetry* in December 1912, Pound
found Yeats still 'the only poet worthy of serious study' and
'already a recognised classic', but set against him was Ford
(then known as Hueffer):

> I would rather talk poetry with Ford Madox Hueffer than
> with any man in London. Mr. Hueffer's beliefs about the
> art may be best explained by saying that they are in
> diametric opposition to those of Mr. Yeats.
>   Mr. Yeats has been subjective; believes in the glamour
> and associations which hang near words. 'Works of art
> beget works of art.' He has much in common with the
> French Symbolists. Mr. Hueffer believes in an exact
> rendering of things. He would strip words of all 'association'
> for the sake of getting a precise meaning. . . . He is objective.
>   ('Status Rerum', *Poetry*, January 1913, 125)

Pound had met Yeats in 1908 and Ford in 1909, through the
English Review of which Ford was then editor. In April of the
same year he met T. E. Hulme, F. S. Flint and members of the
'Poets' Club', whose theory and practice were to anticipate
Imagism. Hulme's thinking, his attack on sentimentality,
impressed Pound, and his prophecy of 'a period of dry hard
classical verse', made in a series of lectures Pound probably
heard him deliver at the end of 1911, confirmed Pound's own
early adumbrations of 'ultimate attainments in poesy' ('1. To

paint the thing as I see it. 2. Beauty. 3. Freedom from didacticism', *SL*, 6) and corresponded to Ford's own realization 'that poetry should be written at least as well as prose' and 'his insistence upon clarity and precision' (*LE*, 373, 377). But Ford again, as Pound recalled this period, was the stronger influence. 'The critical LIGHT during the years immediately pre-war in London shone not from Hulme but from Ford' ('This Hulme Business', Appendix I in Kenner, *Poetry of EP*, 307). Ford was gall to the English literary establishment, 'The old crusted lice and advocates of corpse language' (*SL*, 296), a champion and example of good writing and a personal influence on Pound.

The significant and famous episode concerns Ford's response to Pound's *Canzoni* (July 1911), told by Pound in his obituary of Ford in 1939. Pound met Ford in Giessen, Germany, and showed him *Canzoni*:

> And he felt the errors of contemporary style to the point of rolling (physically, and if you look at it as mere superficial snob, ridiculously) on the floor of his temporary quarters in Giessen when my third volume displayed me trapped, flypapered, gummed and strapped down in a jejune provincial effort to learn, *mehercule*, the stilted language that then passed for 'good English' in the arthritic milieu that held control of the respected British critical circles . . . .
>
> And that roll saved me at least two years, perhaps more. It sent me back to my own proper effort, namely, toward using the living tongue.
>
> (*SPr*, 431–2)

Ripostes was Pound's next volume and it has some of the merits of economy and hardness and good prose that one would expect after such a lesson. It is fair too perhaps to see Ford as at some point behind Pound's description of the poem 'The Return' as 'an objective reality', and as such, a second type of poem after *Personae*, made in the ' "search for oneself", . . . for "sincere self-expression" ' (*G-B*, 85). But one cannot ignore that Ford's roll, in Pound's opinion, sent him 'back' to his proper effort; that he had written to Williams of painting the thing as he saw it as early as 1908, and that he had praised Villon in *The Spirit of Romance* for singing of 'things as they are' (p. 171). Pound had his own *virtù* to pursue and his own routes to it. It is interesting, for example, that Ford should also cite Villon as an example to the modern poet. Ford's own object, he said in the Introduction to his *Collected Poems* (1916), was

> to register my own times in terms of my own time. . . . I would rather read a picture in verse of the emotions and environment of a Goodge Street Anarchist than recapture what songs the Sirens sang. That after all was what François Villon was doing for the life of his day and I should feel that our day was doing its duty by posterity much more surely if it were doing something of the sort.
>
> (p. 19)

Ford's modern poet, if he appeared, would 'voice the life of dust, toil, discouragement, excitement and enervation that I and many millions lead today' (p. 28). The thrust of this would seem to be a call for a poetry of shared contemporary reference. Ford's Villon is not Pound's Villon, who spoke 'below the voice of his age's convention, and thereby outlasts it' (*SR*, 170), nor is Ford's ideal of the modern poet Pound's. If any writer answered Ford's call in these years it was not Pound but D. H. Lawrence, a writer 'made by Ford', said Pound (*SPr*, 433), who 'learned the proper treatment of modern subjects before I did' (*SL*, 17) and who 'brought contemporary verse up to the level of contemporary prose' (*LE*, 388).

But the points of difference and contact between Ford (and Lawrence) and Pound focus, not unexpectedly, on the matter of the language of poetry. Though Pound acknowledges Ford's promotion of 'clarity and precision', Ford's own poems were 'gracious impressions, leisurely, low-toned' and in fact were too leisurely, it would seem, for Pound to quote from effectively (*LE*, 374). For his part, Ford, again in the Introduction to his *Collected Poems*, wrote that language was a secondary matter, that he preferred 'the language of my own day' and that Pound – and this is after the appearance of *Ripostes* – 'as often as not is so unacquainted with English idioms as to be nearly unintelligible' (p. 28). Plainly, Pound's 'living tongue' is not Ford's 'English idioms', at least at this point. The difference goes back to Pound's views in the essay 'I Gather the Limbs of Osiris', which first appeared in the *New Age* from 7 Dec. 1911 to 15 Feb. 1912, after his meeting with Ford at Giessen. He writes there of breaking up cliché, and of the need for poetry to stay 'close to the thing' if it is to be 'a vital part of contemporary life'. For this to come into effect,

> we must have a simplicity and directness of utterance, which is different from the simplicity and directness of daily speech, which is more 'curial', more dignified. . . . There are few fallacies more common than the opinion that poetry should mimic the daily speech. Works of art attract by a resembling unlikeness. Colloquial poetry is to the real art as the barber's wax dummy is to sculpture.
>
> (*SPr*, 41–2)

By 1915 and Pound's Preface to *The Poetical Works of Lionel Johnson*, there has been a change. Pound praises Johnson's 'precision' and 'hardness' but with an important reservation:

> Now Lionel Johnson cannot be shown to be in accord with our present doctrines and ambitions. His language is a bookish dialect, or rather it is not a dialect, it is a curial speech and our aim is natural speech, the language as spoken. We desire the words of poetry to follow the natural order.
>
> (*LE*, 362)

Ford's point is now taken. If Pound was not persuaded of it as immediately as he remembered in 1939, it would still be no easy matter to identify an exact, though later, point of change. In *Ripostes* there is an adjustment, but Pound's diction here is still perhaps 'curial'; it has the inversions, the formality, the 'old-fashioned kind of precision', the 'stately and meticulous speech' Pound finds in Lionel Johnson (*LE*, 361). 'The Sea-farer' too, as part of this collection, is part of Pound's acquaint-ing himself with 'English idiom', with what had been, and was still, or was no longer, possible within it. A further and major adjustment occurs also, evidently, during the series of events in 1912 that gave definition to Imagism: from Pound's meeting with H.D. and Richard Aldington in April, his promotion of their work and some of his own as 'Imagiste' in *Poetry* (of which he became 'foreign correspondent' in September), and his inclusion of T. E. Hulme's poems in *Ripostes* in October.

Certainly the authority of Imagism changed Pound's relationship with Yeats significantly. In the same month as the publication of *Ripostes* Pound received three poems from Yeats, for inclusion in *Poetry*, and without consent edited them (as he had edited his own and others' poems, and was to edit Eliot's *The Waste Land*; cf. Richard Ellmann, 'Ez and Old Billyum', in Hesse, 63–4). Yeats was suitably indignant, but soon accepted the reversal of roles and Pound's blue pencil. Pound, he wrote in 1913, 'helps me to get back to the definite and the concrete away from modern abstractions' (Ellmann, op. cit., 65). By 1913 too, Pound had learned his lesson so well that he was prepared to castigate a line in Ford's 'On a Marsh Road': 'Don't use such an expression as "dim lands of *peace*". It dulls the image. It mixes an abstraction with the concrete. It comes from the writer's not realising that the natural object is always the *adequate* symbol.' ('A Few Don'ts', *LE*, 5.) Pound can apply the doctrine so categorically at this stage, one feels, because he has made it his own, and in the process rejected its corollaries in Ford of a certain type of poet, and a certain relation of poetry to society. It is difficult to agree that Pound was prepared at any time to register his own times in their own terms rather than in his own, or to write of the experience that he 'and many millions' feel today. Pound's own view, very much from the beginning, is that an artist's first responsibility is to his art and not to his public (*SL*, 4); his concern is for the significant revealing fact, the 'luminous detail', for 'the particular case for what it's worth', since 'the truth is the individual' (*SPr*, 33). For him the poet as described in 1912 'is the advance guard of the psychologist on the watch for new emotions, new vibrations sensible to faculties as yet ill understood' (ibid., 331).

Other influences and associations too, besides Ford, or Yeats, had intervened in these years to confirm and broaden Pound's sense of poetry's function. One was Remy de Gourmont, cited by Pound, with like minds, in his review of Ford's *Collected Poems*:

> Shelley, Yeats, Swinburne, with their 'unacknowledged legislators', with 'Nothing affects these people except our conversation', with 'The rest live under us'; Rémy de Gourmont, when he says that most men think only husks and shells of the thoughts that have been already lived over by others, have shown their very just appreciation of the system of echoes, of the general vacuity of public opinion.
>
> (*LE*, 371–2)

Another influence was Allen Upward, whose *The Divine Mystery* and *The New Word* Pound reviewed enthusiastically in 1913 and 1914. Upward was 'intelligent', he had 'taken up the cause of the sensitive'; he argued 'That a nation is civilised in so far as it recognises the special faculties of the individual', and he propagandized 'for a syndicat of intelligence; of thinkers and authors and artists' (*SPr*, 374, 379, 381). Upward too, in *The Divine Mystery*, in a report quoted by Pound on the archetypal 'Genius of the Thunder', gave authority to the notion of the genius, the very special individual whose secret was sensitiveness, who 'was more quick than other men', who 'had learned to read his own symptoms as we read a barometer' (ibid., 373). Surely this in another guise is Pound's artist 'on the watch for new emotions, new vibrations'. With this belief secured one can see how Pound could 'advance by discrimination', how he could select from, synthesize and re-orientate Yeats and Ford within Imagism. If Yeats was 'subjective' and Ford 'objective', the Image could be both, but identical with neither:

The Image can be of two sorts. It can arise within the mind.
It is then 'subjective'. External causes play upon the mind,
perhaps; if so, they are drawn into the mind, fused, trans-
mitted, and emerge in an Image unlike themselves. Secondly, the Image can be objective. Emotion seizing up some
external scene or action carries it intact to the mind; and
that vortex purges it of all save the essential or dominant or
dramatic qualities, and it emerges like the external original.

('As for Imagisme', *SPr*, 344–5)

Ripostes: a fencing term, meaning counter-blows.
Earlier editions include the original dedication:

To
William Carlos Williams
'*Quos ego Persephonae maxima dona feram*'
Propertius

The American poet William Carlos Williams (1883–1963) was
the contemporary and friend of Pound. The Latin quotation,
used also as the epigraph to *Canzoni* (1911), is from Sextus
Propertius (*Elegies* II, 13B). Pound translates it in *Homage to
Sextus Propertius* as 'Which I take, my not unworthy gift, to
Persephone' (VI, l. 21). Persephone (Gk. Kore) is the queen
of Hades. Williams acknowledged a debt to Pound for the
form and title of his own *Kora in Hell: Improvisations*, 1920 ('*I
Wanted to Write a Poem*', 1958, reprinted 1967, 39, 41).

Portrait d'une Femme

Pound was perhaps inspired by Henry James's novel *The
Portrait of a Lady* (1881). (He first met James, appropriately, in
a London·drawing room in February 1912.) Cf. Pound's later
depiction of 'the stuffed-satin drawing-room', *Hugh Selwyn
Mauberley* XII (l. 3), and T. S. Eliot's poem 'Portrait of a Lady'
in *Prufrock and other Observations* (1917).

l. 1: Pound sent his poem in January 1912 to the *North American*

67

Review. It was rejected on the grounds that he had 'used the letter "r" three times in the first line, and that it was very difficult to pronounce, and that I might not remember that Tennyson had once condemned the use of four "s's" in a certain line of a different metre'. (Tennyson had objected to Pope's line 'What dire Offence from am'rous Causes springs' in *The Rape of the Lock*; Hallam, Lord Tennyson, *Tennyson*, 1897, II, 286.) Pound saw the incident as an example of the compliance of American editors with received formulae, 'and to formulae not based on any knowledge of the art or any care for it' (*PM*, 29, 30). Cf. the satirical attack on immovable editors in 'Phasellus Ille' (*CSP*, 75).

The Sargasso Sea between the Azores, the Canaries and the Cape Verde Islands in the North Atlantic collects masses of gulf-weed.

ll. 28–30: cf. the close of 'Near Perigord', 'And all the rest of her a shifting change,/A broken bundle of mirrors . . .!'

An Object

Pound's epigrammatic manner owes something perhaps to Catullus. The sense of a loss of identity in which people are known through or as themselves things occurs also in 'Portrait d'une Femme' and 'Phasellus Ille' (*CSP*, 75). It anticipates also the embattled dependence on 'selected perceptions' of *Hugh Selwyn Mauberley* (' "The Age Demanded" ', l. 40).

The Seafarer

'The Seafarer' first appeared in the *New Age* (30 Nov. 1911, 107) as the opening example in a series of twelve articles entitled 'I Gather the Limbs of Osiris', and then later in *Ripostes* (1912) and *Cathay* (1915). In the *New Age*, the poem was presented as an illustration of 'the New Method' in scholarship, and Pound appended the following 'Philological Note':

The text of this poem is rather confused. I have rejected half of line 76, read 'Angles' for angels in line 78, and stopped translating before the passage about the soul and the longer lines beginning 'Mickle is the fear of the Almighty', and ending in a dignified but platitudinous address to the Deity: 'World's elder, eminent creator, in all ages, amen.' There are many conjectures as to how the text came into its present form. It seems most likely that a fragment of the original poem, clear through about the first thirty lines, and thereafter increasingly illegible, fell into the hands of a monk with literary ambitions, who filled in the gaps with his own guesses and 'improvements'. The groundwork may have been a longer narrative poem, but the 'lyric', as I have accepted it, divides fairly well into 'The Trials of the Sea', its Lure and the Lament for Age.

Michael Alexander points out that Pound's conception of the poem is an example of an 'analytic' criticism which assumes the existence of an original text latterly revised and extended, and in Pound's view 'confused' by clerkly interference ('Ezra Pound's *Seafarer*', *Agenda*, XIII, no. 4–XIV, no. 1, 110–26). Not only does Pound on this reasoning omit the fourth, moralizing section of the extant poem, he also excludes the Christian reference in the text of the poem he does translate, most obviously in his rendering of Old English 'englum' as 'English' rather than 'angels' (l. 79), and in his ignoring the poem's references to God and the devil (ll. 43, 67, 76–7). As Alexander says, Pound as a result 'edited the poem into heathenism' (op. cit., 123), and although he might appear to ride roughshod in this way over questions of ambivalent morality in the poem that have concerned others (cf. *The Seafarer*, ed. I. L. Gordon, 1960, 4–12), Pound's position is even today far from unorthodox (Alexander, op. cit., 119). To this, however, one must add Pound's flagrant attempt on at least one occasion to 'modernize' the poem – in his reference to 'burghers' at lines 29 and 56, so that the Seafarer emerges as not only non-Christian, but anti-bourgeois – and also the whole manner of his translation.

In 1912 in answer to the query how much of the translation was his and how much the original, Pound was led to the brusque defence of 'The Seafarer' as 'as nearly literal, I think, as any translation can be' (*SPr*, 39). Though it has not been seen in this way, Pound's remark may well imply that *no* translation can be absolutely literal, but must contain some part, perhaps some large part, which is the translator's own. But if his defence is ambiguous, it is clear in his practice here and elsewhere that for Pound translation was not a business of literal fidelity but an art, and his sense of its boundaries the widest possible. In 1916, for example, Pound was to suggest that his search for 'sincere self-expression' in *Personae*, through 'a casting-off . . . of complete masks of the self in each poem' was continued in 'a long series of translations, which were but more elaborate masks' (*G-B*, 85). 'The Seafarer' is one such mask, and one can see Pound's concern in it to preserve and revive the integrity of the 'original' as intimately connected with his own practice and career as a poet.

There are two main respects in which Pound was attracted in this way to 'The Seafarer'. Firstly, as already suggested, it was a persona; as Pound himself said, 'a major persona', along with 'Exile's Letter' and *Homage to Sextus Propertius* (Note in *Umbra*, 138). 'Exile's Letter', as Donald Davie suggests, presents its author Li Po as 'a drunkard, an idler, disreputable, undependable, without self-respect' (*Poet as Sculptor*, 25). It is presumably Pound's and the Seafarer's lack of respect for Christianity, the Seafarer's extrapolated class enmity and his lauded 'malice' (l. 76), which as a persona bring him in line with Li Po and with the idleness and more subtle rebelliousness of Sextus Propertius. What they also have in common is something of the resilience and hold on life Pound identifies in 'The Wanderer' as illustrative of 'the English national chemical' expressed in the Anglo-Saxon poems. The 'doom-eager' man of 'The Wanderer' is, says Pound, 'the man ready for his deed, eager for it, eager for the glory of it, ready to pay the price' (*PM*, 45). Surely this is akin to the robust vitality Pound finds in the masks of Villon, Bertran de Born, Arnaut de Mareuil and Peire Vidal. 'For these men life is in the press,' says Pound (*SR*, 178); his composite persona is of a man and poet who 'sings of things as they are. He dares to show himself' (ibid., 171). More obviously, one can see that all are types of the exile, and that the Seafarer, in suffering the exile of a sea voyage, is spiritually kinsman to the figure of Odysseus. Pound is attracted therefore to a type and to a related theme which articulate his own case, and which found expression later in *Hugh Selwyn Mauberley* and the *Cantos*.

Pound's linking 'The Seafarer' in particular with 'Exile's Letter' suggests also, however, a second layer of personal interest. In the *ABC of Reading* (1934) Pound says,

> I once got a man to start translating the **Seafarer** into Chinese. It came out almost directly into Chinese verse, with solid ideograms in each half-line.
>
> Apart from the Seafarer I know no other European poems of the period that you can hang up with the 'Exile's Letter' of Li Po, displaying the West on a par with the Orient.
>
> (p. 51)

Both 'Exile's Letter' and 'The Seafarer' date from around the eighth century, and it is part of Pound's view of world poetry that he should want to recommend 'The Seafarer' as representing the English national chemical and as equivalent to Li Po (and also to Walt Whitman) (*PM*, 45). But this would seem to be as much a matter of the art of poetry, and of metrics, particularly, as of 'the temper of the nation' or of a literary canon. It is Pound's concern to 'break the pentameter' which interests him in the alliterative stress patterns of Anglo-Saxon, and which oversees his technique of translating by rhythm and sound rather than sense. It is easy to see how the consequent mimetic renderings of words like 'wrecan' (l. 1), 'monath' (l. 37), 'byrig' (l. 49) and 'englum' (l. 79), or of lines such as at 87–8, for example, have counted as blunders for those with perhaps more interest in Anglo-Saxon than in Pound's poetry (cf. Kenneth Sisam, for whom Pound's 'interpretation of the

71

Anglo-Saxon past is based on careless ignorance or mis-understanding', *T.L.S.*, 25 June 1954, 409).

The defence of Pound on this score is twofold: firstly, that his homophonic translation, as Alexander has most recently argued, recreates the reading experience of the Anglo-Saxon through a kind of 'phonetic simulacrum' (op. cit., 117); in which case one is dealing with a version or adaptation of the Anglo-Saxon rather than a strict translation. (This is supported by J. B. Bessinger, who in a discussion of Pound's recorded reading of the poem concludes, 'As the recording helps to demonstrate, it is a free imitation, phonic and rhythmic rather than thematic and verbal'; 'The Oral Text of Ezra Pound's "The Seafarer" ', *Quarterly Journal of Speech*, XLVII, 1961, 173–7). Secondly, one can see that Pound's translation is an example of his experimenting in 'melopoeia', in verse as speech, using a non-iambic measure. As such 'The Seafarer' is a moment in the effort Eliot identified in Pound 'towards the synthetic construction of a style of speech' (Introduction to *Selected Poems*, 1928, 12), an effort which bears especial fruit again in the *Cantos* and particularly Canto I, where Pound overlays and transmits Homer through the idiom learned here.

References to the Anglo-Saxon text are to *The Seafarer*, ed. I. L. Gordon (1960). References to Alexander's translation are to *The Earliest English Poems*, trans. Michael Alexander (1966), pp. 74–7.

l. 1 reckon: Pound translates by homophony. The Old English is 'wrecan' ('to utter', 'recite').

l. 5 care's hold: the OE. 'cearselda' means literally 'abodes of sorrow' (Gordon, 33). Alexander has 'care halls' (p. 74).

l. 6 sea-surge: cf. the line in *Hugh Selwyn Mauberley*,' Audition of the phantasmal sea-surge. (' "The Age Demanded" ', l. 45).

l. 8 tossed: OE 'cnossað' is present tense, meaning 'dashes' or 'drives'.

afflicted: Pound draws on the Latin 'affligo' ('to strike against', 'injure', 'weaken').

l. 15 wretched outcast: OE. is 'wræccan lastum', 'in the paths of exile' (Gordon, 63). Alexander has 'the wanderer's beat' (p. 74).

l. 16: a half-line in the OE. text; OE. 'bidroren' means 'bereaved of' rather than 'deprived of'.

l. 17 hail-scur: homophonic rendering of OE. 'haegl scurum' ('hail shower', or 'storm').

l. 21 Sea-fowls': OE. 'huilpan' is the curlew.

l. 22 mews': gulls.

l. 23 Storms . . . beaten: as in the OE. text, a 'swollen' half-line, with four beats.

fell on the stern: Pound mistranslates OE. 'stearn' ('tern'). The sense of the original, 'stearn oncwaeð', is that the cry of the tern answers the waves crashing on the rocks.

l. 25 pinion: the outer feathers of a bird's wing, or the whole wing.

ll. 25–6: Pound's break observes the uncertain state of the original text, where there is a probable omission (Gordon, 36). Otherwise a new verse paragraph begins in the original at Pound's line 27.

l. 29 burghers: OE. 'burgum' ('settlements' or 'dwellings'). Pound's anachronism is not without some strict authority. Gordon reports that 'From the Laws of Alfred . . . it appears that "burh" was used of the dwelling of any man above the rank of a peasant' (p. 37).

l. 34 Corn of the coldest: an ancient description of hail.

l. 35 high streams: OE. 'streamas' ('seas towering high', or 'deep seas'). The Seafarer is here thought to contemplate a new kind of voyage. Gordon says 'The use of "sylf" [I myself] implies that, though he has had experience of seafaring, he has not himself before made such a journey across the ocean' (p. 3).

l. 37 Moaneth: OE. 'monað' ('urges'). Pound's use of 'admonisheth' in line 51 shows that he understood the word but wished to render its sound.

l. 39 foreign fastness: Gordon points to a Christian reference in the OE. 'elþeodigra eard', which can mean both a 'foreign home' and also probably the heavenly home of those who are aliens in this life (p. 38).

l. 41 given his good: OE. 'gifena þæs god' means 'generous of gifts', and also more distantly here 'good in moral qualities' (Gordon, 38).

ll. 42–4: Pound obscures the sense by translating the OE. preposition 'tō' as 'to' rather than 'so'. Alexander translates these lines more clearly, 'so thoroughly equipped, so quick to do/ so strong in his youth, or with so staunch a lord' (p. 75).

l. 43 sorrow: OE. 'sorge' ('fear', 'anxiety').

l. 44: OE. 'to hwon hine Dryhten gedon wille' means literally '[as to] what the Lord will bring him to' (Gordon, 39). Pound ignores the play on the OE. 'dryhten' (earthly lord) in line 41, translating it as 'king', and here, OE. 'Dryhten' (heavenly lord).

l. 46 winsomeness to wife: the phrase 'is meant to mean "Nor winsomeness in women"; but it doesn't' (Alexander, *Agenda*, op. cit., 117).

l. 48 longing: Gordon suggests OE. 'longunge' refers to 'weariness of mind or distress' rather than 'a longing for the sea' (p. 39). The sense is therefore of the unabated distress of those who go to sea.

l. 49 berries: Pound's homophonic technique fails him here: OE. 'byrig' means 'town' or 'dwellings'.

l. 51 admonisheth: Pound retains the sense and echoes the sound of the OE. 'gemoniað'.

l. 54 Cuckoo: the cuckoo was traditionally a bird of lament; also referred to in line 63 as 'lone-flyer'.

l. 55 summerward: Pound's homophonic rendering of the OE. 'sumeres weard' (' "watchman" or "guardian" or perhaps "Lord" of summer', Gordon, 40).

l. 56 Burgher: Pound's extrapolation. The OE. refers to 'a man blessed with comforts'.

l. 59: The Seafarer's heart or spirit flies from its physical confines. Pound's 'breastlock' is faithful to the original kenning, 'hreþerlocan' ('enclosure of the heart', 'chest'). Gordon suggests the general sense at this point in the OE. is that 'the

74

Seafarer's spirit is impelled to traverse the ocean *because* the "joys of the Lord" mean more to him than "life on land" ' (p. 41).

l. 62 On earth's shelter: OE. 'eorþan sceatas'. Gordon suggests '(over) the expanse of the world' (p. 41).

ll. 65–7 seeing that . . . land: Gordon offers the literal translation of the OE. 'for the joys of the Lord are warmer (more living, more inspiring) to me than this dead, transitory life on land' (p. 42). This ends a verse paragraph in the original.

l. 66 My lord deems: OE. 'Dryhtnes dreamas', 'a conventional expression for the heavenly life' (Gordon, 42).

l. 70 tide go: OE. 'tide ge' ('tiddege': 'final hour', Gordon, 42–3).

turn it to twain: i.e. upset the balance. OE. 'tweo(n)' means 'doubt' or 'separation'.

ll. 73–81: Gordon offers the translation, 'Therefore for every man the praise of those who live after him and commemorate him is the best memorial, which he may earn, before he must depart, by good actions on earth against the wickedness of enemies (or fiends), opposing the devil with noble deeds, so that the children of men will praise him afterwards and his glory will live then among the angels for ever, [in the] blessedness of eternal life, bliss among the noblest' (p. 43). Kenneth Sisam comments on Pound's lines, 'So he eliminates the blend of Christian thought which is a main source of difficulty in the general interpretation of *Seafarer* and makes malice the source of everlasting renown among the English' (op. cit.).

l. 76 foes: OE. 'feonda' ('fiends' or 'enemies').

l. 77 Daring ado, . . .: OE. 'deorum dædum' ('brave deeds'). Pound's phrase, Alexander points out, is a 'corruption of Edmund Spenser's "derring-do", itself a false formation from Chaucer's "durrying don" ' (*Agenda*, op. cit., 116). Pound ignores the OE. 'deofle togeanes' ('oppose the devil').

l. 79 English: OE. 'englum' ('angels').

ll. 82–92 Days . . . earth's gait: of this section in the original Gordon comments, 'This eloquent lament for the golden age of the past is no doubt intended as a reminder of the mutability of earthly glory in contrast to the eternal glory described in the preceding lines' (p. 43). Compare this 'Lament for Age' with the elegaic passages in *Homage to Sextus Propertius* VI, and *Hugh Selwyn Mauberley* IV, V, X.

l. 83 earthen riches: OE. 'eorþan rices' ('earthly realm').

l. 84: cf. Canto LXXXI (552/517): 'Kings will I think disappear'.

ll. 89–90: Pound misconstrues parts of these lines. Alexander gives: 'it is a weaker kind who wields earth now,/sweats for its bread. Brave men are fewer' (p. 76).

l. 89 Waneth the watch: OE. 'wuniað þa wacran'. 'Wacran' means 'weak' and is used in the sense of 'morally infirm'. Pound mistakes it for a form of 'wacu' ('watch').

l. 90 Tomb hideth trouble: OE. 'brucað þurh bisgo' ('occupy it in toil and trouble', Gordon, 44). Pound confuses the preposition 'þurh' ('through', or 'by way of') with 'þruh', meaning 'coffin'.

The blade is layed low: OE. 'Blæd is gehnæged' ('glory is humbled'). Pound's concrete synecdoche replaces the abstract noun.

l. 95: Pound recalls this line in Canto LXXIV (ll. 267, 278).

ll. 96–8: the sense of the original is, 'Then when life escapes him, his fleshly form cannot taste what is sweet, nor feel pain, nor stir a hand, nor think with the mind' (Bessinger, op. cit., 176).

flesh-cover: OE. 'flæschoma' ('covering of flesh', 'body'). Pound's version would be more coherent if 'cover' were understood as a verb.

l. 101: Pound ends his translation at the original line 99 of a total 124 lines. Gordon gives the general sense of lines 97–102 as 'that wealth, whether expended on his grave by his brother, or hoarded in his lifetime, cannot help the sinful man at the Final Judgement' (p. 45). Pound's omission of the reference to sin and God's judgement is clearly consistent with his conception of the poem as indicated in his 'Philological Note'.

Δώρια

Title: Gk. Δώρεια (Doria). Dorian is the name given to the Dorian Greeks (from Dorus, son of Hellen), and has the association of strength and simplicity; cf. 'The Return' and 'The Coming of War: Actaeon', which also have this character. Charles Norman suggests that Δώρια is 'perhaps for Dorothy' (p. 80), i.e. for Dorothy Shakespear whom Pound married in 1914. One might also think, given the first line, that Pound has in mind Victor Plarr's *In the Dorian Mood* (1896). Plarr was a member of the Rhymers' Club and Pound knew him in his early years in London. In the article 'Status Rerum', Pound wrote that Plarr's 'volume, *In the Dorian Mood*, has been half-forgotten' (*Poetry*, January 1913, 127), and Plarr appears himself half-forgotten as M. Verog in *Hugh Selwyn Mauberley*. Δώρια was included in *Des Imagistes* (1914), the first anthology of Imagist poetry, edited by Pound.
l. 1: 'A god', wrote Pound, 'is an eternal state of mind' (*SPr*, 47).
ll. 6–7: defining the image by way of an analogy with analytic geometry in the essay 'Vorticism', Pound wrote,

> The statements of 'analytics' are 'lords' over fact. . . . And in like manner are great works of art lords over fact, over race-long recurrent moods, and over to-morrow. . . . By the 'image' I mean such an equation; not an equation of mathematics, not something about a, b and c, having something to do with form, but about *sea, cliffs, night*, having something to do with mood.
>
> (*G-B*, 91–2)

l. 10 Orcus: a synonym for the Roman Dis (Gk. Pluto or Hades), the god of the underworld. Pound probably alludes to the story of Persephone's being carried off to Hell while gathering flowers in the Vale of Enna.

Apparuit

The title is taken from the phrase spoken by Dante's animate spirit in the *Vita Nuova*, on his first seeing Beatrice, 'Apparuit iam beatitudo vestra', translated by Rossetti as 'Your beatitude hath now been made manifest unto you' (*Poems and Translations*, 1968, 326). Pound's attitude to Dante's Beatrice was somewhat ambivalent. In *The Spirit of Romance* he stated categorically: 'That the *Vita Nuova* is the idealization of a real woman can be doubted by no one who has, even in the least degree, that sort of intelligence whereby it was written, or who has known in any degree the passion whereof it treats' (p. 126). Similarly, his 'Donzella Beata' (*ALS*, 41) had supplied the 'real woman' lacking in Rossetti's 'The Blessed Damozel', a poem likewise indebted to Dante. At the same time, however, Pound saw Dante's 'glorification of Beatrice' as the 'consummation' of the cult of Amor and the increasing spiritualization of the Lady in Provençal and early Italian poetry (cf. ch. v, 'Psychology and Troubadours', in *The Spirit of Romance*). He explored this further in 'Canzoniere' (*Provença*, 1910), a series of derivations largely from early Italian poetry. The echoes in 'Apparuit' of poems in this series recalling Arnaut Daniel, Guido Guinicelli and Cavalcanti suggest again how far Pound views Dante and his own poem in terms of this literature.

'Apparuit' is in Sapphics (after the Greek poetess Sappho), a quantitative measure requiring stanzas with three lines of eleven syllables and a fourth of five syllables. It was probably this poem which Pound showed to Edward Marsh, secretary to Winston Churchill and editor of *Georgian Poetry*, in a restaurant in Soho in September 1912. Pound wished to discover any errors he had made in versification. Marsh's opinion was that 'He had; and when I pointed them out, he put the paper back in his pocket, blushing murkily, and muttering that it was only a first attempt.' When 'Apparuit' appeared without correction, 'it implanted in me', said Marsh, 'a lasting suspicion of his artistic seriousness.' (Quoted in Christopher Hassall, *A Biography of Edward Marsh*, 1959, 193.)

The use of Sapphics may have been suggested by the similarity Pound notes in *The Spirit of Romance* (p. 122) between a line in the eleventh sonnet of Dante's *Vita Nuova* ('Whence is he blest who first looketh on her') and the opening of a poem by Sappho translated by Catullus ('Godlike is the man who/ sits at her side, who watches and catches/ that laughter', *Odes* LI).

Cf. also Pound's free adaptation of lines from Sappho in the poem "Ιμέρρω".

l. 1 Golden . . . house: cf. the earlier 'The House of Splendour' (l. 2n.).

l. 3 Life . . . flickered: cf. Pound's translation of the line 'E quel remir contral lums de la lampa' in Arnaut Daniel's 'Doutz brais e critz': 'with the glamor of the lamplight about it' (*SR*, 34), and later, 'Where the lamp-light with light limb but half engages' (*Tr*, 175). William Carlos Williams recalled that during his stay with Pound in March 1910 there was a photograph of a woman on Pound's dresser with a candle always burning before it. Stock identifies the woman as Bride Scratton to whom Pound wrote on one occasion of a lamp burning before a shrine (*Life*, 105–6). But it is probably futile to attempt to discover the 'real woman', if any, that Pound's poem idealizes. The image, however, is a recurrent one.

l. 5: cf. the lines in 'Canzon: The Yearly Slain', 'Ah! red-leafed time hath driven out the rose/ And crimson dew is fallen on the leaf' (*Provença*, reprinted in *Selected Poems*, 1928, and *CEP*, 133).

the roses bend: an early translation of Cavalcanti's Sonnet VII, 'Sonnet: Chi è questa?', also in *Provença*, begins, 'Who is she coming, that the roses bend/ Their shameless heads to do her passing honour?' (*CEP*, 143). Cf. also the closing lines of 'Ballatetta' (*CSP*, 52).

l. 9: cf. the line in Pound's translation of the sonnet by Guido Guinicelli, 'The green stream's marge is like her, and the air' (*SR*, 106).

ll. 11–12: cf. 'Canzone: Of Angels' where the Lady 'presseth back the aether where it streameth' (*CEP*, 140), the line 'And left me cloaked as with a gauze of aether' in 'A Virginal'

(*CSP*, 83), and in 'Gentildonna', lines 2–3, 'Moving among the trees, and clinging/ in the air she severed'.

l. 13 shell of gold: this suggests Venus Aphrodite, born from the sea, and as depicted for example by Botticelli. It is perhaps this also which suggested to Edward Marsh that Pound's poem was a version of Sappho's 'Ode to Aphrodite'.

l. 15 oriel: probably 'aureole', or halo.

l. 20: cf. 'Erat Hora', line 4, 'Went swiftly from me'.

l. 23 slight thing: Beatrice was a girl of nine when first seen by Dante; cf. the image of the girl as a young maid and child in the poems 'N.Y.' and 'A Girl' respectively (*CSP*, 74, 75).

slight . . . cunning: cf. 'A Virginal', 'Slight are her arms . . . with her sleight hand she staunches' (*CSP*, 83).

The Return

Describing the ' "search for oneself", . . . for "sincere self-expression" ', Pound suggests that he first cast off 'masks of the self' in *Personae* and that secondly he 'made poems like "The Return", which is an objective reality and has a complicated sort of significance like Mr. Epstein's "Sun God" or Mr. Brzeska's "Boy with a Coney" ' (*G-B*, 85). For Pound Gaudier's statuette was an example of 'the combination of organic with inorganic forms', of what Lewis had called 'Brzeska's peculiar soft bluntness' (p. 26) and of a certain Chinese quality: ' "The Boy with a Coney" is "Chou" or suggests slightly the bronze animals of that period' (p. 29). More generally, Gaudier's and Epstein's sculpture represented for Pound the Vorticist use in sculpture of 'planes in relation'. 'The Return', then, is an equivalent exercise for the poet in free verse, where he '*expresses* his meaning *by* form' (p. 143): through 'the image' and also through 'movement' which belongs to 'the rhythm of music or verses' (p. 81).

'The Return' impressed W. B. Yeats, to whom it seemed as if Pound 'were translating at sight from an unknown Greek masterpiece' (*Oxford Book of Modern Verse 1892–1935*, 1936, xxvi), and who, as one of the first to admire its use of rhythm, felt it 'the most beautiful poem that has been written in the free form, one of the few in which I find real organic rhythm' (Stock, *Life*, 191).

'The Return' was included in *Des Imagistes* (1914).

ll. 1–4: cf. the lines 'High forms/ with the movement of gods,/ Perilous aspect' in 'The Coming of War: Actaeon'.

ll. 5–6: Pound's reading of 'The Return' was tested in 1920 by the French phonetician, Abbé Jean Pierre Rousselot, who, said Pound, 'had made a machine for measuring the duration of verbal components. . . . They return, One and by one, With fear, As half awakened each letter with a double registration of quavering' (*PE*, 129–30). It is significant perhaps that Pound was working at this time on his own musical composition *Villon*, that he had discovered the Vorticist composer George Antheil, and that he was concerned in *Antheil and The Treatise on Harmony* (1924) to stress the hitherto neglected element of time in music. 'The Return' Pound perhaps saw, or came to see, as evidence of the equal importance of sound and duration in poetry, of rhythm as a 'form cut into TIME' (*ABC of R*, 198).

l. 10 "*Wing'd-with-Awe*": an invented and deliberately mysterious attribution, suggesting perhaps Zeus or Jupiter, whose symbol is the eagle.

l. 12: perhaps Hermes or Mercury, principally the messenger of the gods and represented with wings on his sandals, but the reference is purposely vague.

LUSTRA

(Unabridged private edition September 1916;
abridged edition October 1916)

Though it appeared in 1916 *Lustra* properly occupies a place
between the volumes *Ripostes* (1912) and *Cathay* (1915), since,
as Pound explained to Kate Buss, 'the separate poems in *Lustra*
had mostly been written before the Chinese translations were
begun and had mostly been printed in periodicals either here
or in America' (*SL*, 101). In fact, the bulk of the *Lustra* poems
date from the period April 1913 to March 1915, and though
some of them (the translations 'After Ch'u Yuan', 'Liu
Ch'e', 'Fan Piece for her Imperial Lord', 'Ts'ai Chi'h',
'Ancient Wisdom, Rather Cosmic' and the poem 'In a Station
of the Metro') may be seen as prompting *Cathay*, they in
general show Pound as more concerned to apply the lesson
learnt at Giessen, when Ford Madox Ford rolled on the floor
at the archaisms of *Canzoni* (1911) (*SPr*, 431–2). Under this
reproof Pound accelerated through the years 1912–15 to bring
himself up to date, chiefly through the launching of Imagism,
the propaganda of *Blast* and his association with Vorticism,
the last providing him with a context in which the image,
already fallen foul of Amy Lowell and her attendant diluters,
could be redefined and repossessed.

The Imagist principles were announced in 1913 by F. S.
Flint on Pound's behalf:

1. Direct treatment of the 'thing' whether subjective or
objective.
2. To use absolutely no word that did not contribute to the
presentation.

3. As regarding rhythm: to compose in sequence of the musical phrase, not in sequence of a metronome.

(*EP*, ed. Sullivan, 41; cf. also *LE*, 3)

They combined with the anti-bourgeois missiles of *Blast* to give definition and edge to the *Lustra* poems, Pound finding through the precedents and models of Sappho, Ibycus, Martial, Catullus and Liu Ch'e an answer to the 'emotional slither' of current verse and to the assorted prudery, smugness and philistinism of the literary establishment and the metropolitan bourgeoisie. Judging by the nervous censorship the poems provoked in Harriet Monroe, the editor of *Poetry*, and in *Lustra*'s publisher, Elkin Mathews, Pound hit his target. (Cf. *SL*, 17–18, 37; *P/J*, 277–86; Homberger, 121–4.) Their response seems now absurdly out of proportion, if it did not then, and the poems' shock tactics probably no longer register, but both are relevant to Pound's immediate situation, and to his campaign in these years for standards of excellence and for a proper understanding and support of the arts which would foster, in his terms, a 'Renaissance' or 'Risorgimento' or 'Risvegliamento'. Pound addressed his campaign most explicitly towards America, in its earliest and most developed form in the work *Patria Mia* (1950; first published in the *New Age* 5 Sept.–14 Nov. 1912). Imagism was part of this new scale of values, and Pound's reworkings of Sappho, Ibycus and Catullus, as well as adding bite to his protest, were a necessary introduction of 'pure color' into the 'Renaissance palette' (*LE*, 214–15). But the most interesting voice adopted by Pound in the *Lustra* poems is that of Walt Whitman.

Whitman anticipated the first two Imagist criteria in his praise of 'simplicity' and 'definiteness' in the 1855 'Preface' to *Leaves of Grass* (*Complete Poems*, ed. F. Murphy, 1975, 749, 755), but it is rather in terms of the third principle, the matter of rhythm, and of a common message, that Pound acknowledges his own debt, in the essay 'What I feel about Walt Whitman' (1909): 'when I write of certain things I find myself using his rhythms. . . . "His message is my message. We will see that men hear it"' (*SPr*, 115–16). Whitman's expansive rhythms are plain to see and hear in poems such as 'Salutation the Second' and 'Commission', but it is also quite clear that Pound's 'message' is neither in those poems nor elsewhere Whitman's characteristic salute to 'the democratic average'. Pound's contempt for oppression carries over, one feels, to the oppressed themselves; to the failures and the frustrated, as well as to the complacent and ignorant. While Whitman can see no imperfection and absorbs all, indiscriminately, to himself, Pound appeals in, for example, 'Ité' and 'The Rest' from an embattled position, precisely to 'the lovers of perfection alone', the 'lovers of beauty' and those of 'the finer sense'. In *Patria Mia* Pound sees Whitman as representing the 'American keynote', the rude substance of American potential in need of the shape and polish of art (pp. 24, 31, 45–7), and that art, committed to the care of 'a class of artist-workers free from necessity' (p. 73), as in turn 'the acknowledged guide and lamp of civilisation' (*SL*, 48). Whitman's chant for democracy is perhaps constrained and befuddled by his own massive egoism, but it is a distant cry still from the meritocracy along European lines that Pound conceives of for America. And in so far as Pound concedes that Whitman was so close to the American temper as to be inseparable from it, that in short 'He *is* America' (*SPr*, 115), then his mixed feelings of repugnance and acceptance towards Whitman ('an exceeding great stench' and yet 'a forebear of whom I ought to be proud') are a measure of Pound's relation to his native country. Whitman, lacking art, is the 'reflex' of an America without a centre, the capital so important to the traffic of ideas necessary to a Risorgimento (*PM*, 42; *LE*, 214, 220–1). And though Pound in *Patria Mia* can set the pagan crowd and architecture of New York against 'the melancholy, the sullenness, the unhealth of the London mass' (pp. 13–14), it is clear that for him the lack of an American vortex, taking root in the capital, is what has driven American artists, including Henry James, Whistler and himself, to Europe (p. 43).

Pound was drawn to London, he later said, as to 'the capital of the U.S. so far as art and letters were concerned' (Rome Radio broadcast, 5 May 1942, quoted in Hutchins, 47). In 1912 or 1913, this was no longer true, or true to the same extent. The view that the 'Risorgimento', 'if it comes at all, will move from the centre outwards, and that "the center is in Europe"' had, Pound allowed, 'much to be said' for it (*PM*, 53). It had, in fact, all the more to be said for it because it was Pound's own case; a position only aggravated by his finding England in 1913 'dead as mutton' (*SL*, 24). If Pound thought his message Whitman's, then he had misconstrued both Whitman and the character of America (as his contemporaries W. C. Williams and D. H. Lawrence, on either side of the Atlantic, perhaps did not). But he had also, it seemed, misjudged England and London. Though he braved the hostility that surrounded *Lustra*, Pound recognized that his own values had in the process been tainted: 'I find I have been beguiled into leaving out the more violent poems to the general loss of the book, the dam'd bloody insidious way one is edged into these tacit hypocrisies *is* disgusting' (ibid., 81). This could only have confirmed his disenchantment with London, and though other factors intervene, particularly the effect of the war in these and later years, Pound's eventual departure from London for Paris, and his further removal from America, begin at this point to seem inevitable.

Earlier editions reprint the following:

> DEFINITION: LUSTRUM: an offering for the sins of the whole people, made by the censors at the expiration of their five years of office, etc. Elementary Latin Dictionary of Charlton T. Lewis.

Vail de Lencour
Cui dono lepidum novum libellum.

And the days are not full enough
And the nights are not full enough
And life slips by like a field mouse
Not shaking the grass.

'Vail de Lencour' was a name conferred by Pound upon Bridgit Patmore, a close friend in his early London years and a member of the '*English Review* Circle' gathered around F. M. Ford and Violet Hunt. Pound found her 'charming' (*SL*, 26) and Douglas Goldring tells how she was the first to be blessed by *Blast* (*South Lodge*, 1943, 68). Her memoir of Pound was published in the *Texas Quarterly* (Autumn 1964; included in *My Friends When Young*, 1968). The Latin quotation is from the opening of Catullus I, 'To whom should I present this little book' (*Poems of Catullus*, trans. Peter Whigham, 1966, 49).

Tenzone

Included with eleven other poems ('The Condolence', 'The Garret', 'The Garden', 'Ortus', 'Dance Figure', 'Salutation', 'Salutation the Second', 'Pax Saturni', 'Commission', 'A Pact', 'In a Station of the Metro') as 'Contemporania' in *Poetry* (April 1913). The series was saluted by Floyd Dell as having 'brought back into the world a grace which (probably) never existed, but which we discover by an imaginative process in Horatius and Catullus' (Homberger, 98, 99). 'Dell is very consoling,' said Pound. 'It's clever of him to detect the Latin tone' (*SL*, 19).

Title: (Ital.) the term for a debate or dialogue poem.

l. 3 centaur: in 'The Serious Artist' (1913) Pound had written, 'Poetry is a centaur. The thinking word-arranging, clarifying faculty must move and leap with the energizing, sentient, musical facilties. It is precisely the difficulty of this amphibious existence that keeps down the census record of good poets.' (*LE*, 52.)

The Garret

Pound thought this 'about the best' of 'Contemporania' (Chicago MSS, April 1913, quoted in Ruthven, 76).

ll. 6–7: Sappho writes of dawn 'In gold sandals' (Barnstone, 134).

l. 7 Pavlova: Anna Pavlova (1885–1931), the Russian ballerina who visited London with the Russian Ballet in 1910. In a later pseudonymous review for the *Athenaeum* (23 Apr. 1920) Pound referred to Pavlova as 'that image of whom no one was privileged to speak who could not compass blank verse . . . it was her own delicate and very personal comment of emotion upon the choreographic lines of Fokine which won her the myriad hearts' (p. 553). Cf. 'Les Millwin' and the references to Serafima Astafieva in Cantos LXXVII (495/466) and LXXIX (516/484, 522/489, l. 198n.).

l. 10 this hour: cf. 'Erat Hora'.

The Garden

Epigraph: from the opening of Albert Samain's *Au Jardin de l'Infante* (1893), 'Mon âme est une infante en robe de parade.' Later Pound felt that Samain, in comparison with Gautier, 'begins to go "soft", there is just a suggestion of muzziness . . Heredia and Samain have been hard decreasingly, giving gradually smoothness for hardness' (*LE*, 285, 288). Pound's poem was parodied by Richard Aldington:

> Like an armful of greasy engineer's-cotton
> Flung by a typhoon against a broken crate of ducks' eggs
> She stands by the rail of the Old Bailey dock.
> Her intoxication is exquisite and excessive,
> And delicate her delicate sterility.
> Her delicacy is so delicate that she would feel affronted
> If I remarked nonchalantly, 'Saay, stranger, ain't you
>   dandy'.

> (*Egoist*, 15 Jan. 1914)

Aldington also parodied the poems 'Further Instructions', 'April', 'In a Station of the Metro' and 'A Song of the Degrees'. Pound found them 'excellent' (*Poetry*, June 1915, 158); 'good art', he wrote, 'thrives in an atmosphere of parody. Parody is, I suppose, the best criticism – it sifts the durable from the apparent.' (*SL*, 13.)

l.1 : cf. the similar imagery of 'Liu Ch'e' and 'Shop Girl' (CSP, 123).

ll. 3–4, 8–9: cf. 'the bourgeoise who is dying of her ennuis' in 'Commission' and the portrait of the modern woman reduced to suburban morality in *Hugh Selwyn Mauberley* XI.

l. 4: an example of the 'mandarin-demotic' idiom employed by Pound (Fraser, 40).

ll. 5–7: cf. 'The Study in Aesthetics' (*CSP*, 105).

l. 7: Matthew 5: 5 reads, 'Blessed are the meek: for they shall inherit the earth'.

Salutation

Yeats's later 'The Fisherman' praises 'This wise and simple man . . . In scorn of this audience' (*Collected Poems*, 1967, 166–7). Pound's model is probably Walt Whitman's repeated paean to the common man in *Leaves of Grass*.

Salutation the Second

Elkin Mathews wrote to Pound that he 'must omit ll. 6 to end' of this poem (Homberger, 123) and it was in the event omitted as a whole from the trade edition of *Lustra* (October 1916); cf. also 'Salutation the Third' (*CSP*, 165).

ll. 1–4: cf. *Hugh Selwyn Mauberley*, 'E.P. Ode', lines 1–6.

l. 8 archaic: Pound confessed to Harriet Monroe that he 'wallowed in archaisms in my vealish years' (*SL*, 15). The versions of the poem before *Personae* (1926) contained the following three lines: 'Watch the reporters spit/ Watch the anger of the professors,/ Watch how the pretty ladies revile them'.

l. 9: added for the poem's appearance in *Personae* (1926).

l. 16: cf. 'Salutation' (l. 10); 'Further Instructions' (l. 15): 'Insolent little beasts, shameless, devoid of clothing' (*CSP*,103); and 'Dum Capitolium Scandet' (ll. 6, 8): 'O my unnameable children . . . Clear speakers, naked in the sun, untrammelled' (*CSP*, 105). The influence here is probably the open sensuality of Walt Whitman, his 'willingness to stand exposed' (*PM*, 45).

l. 25 "*The Spectator*": Pound included 'The "Spectator"' in his twenty-part 'Studies in Contemporary Mentality'. It was, he said, 'a sort of parochial joke . . . an unfailing butt', marked by a 'stupendous vacuity' whose keynote he found in the *Spectator*'s own 'It is not as if there were anything of more than usual interest to say.' (*New Age*, 6 Sept. 1917, 406–7.) Cf. line 30A.

l. 28: Pound refers to the 'Kordax', an ancient and licentious dance, common in Attic comedy, in the poem 'Our Respectful Homages to M. Laurent Tailhade' (*CSP*, 263). Charles Olson also reports that Pound told him of 'a dance of Astafieva, spermatopyros, done in her studio' (Seelye, 79).

l. 29 Cybele: an Asiatic goddess of nature.

l. 30A: earlier versions of the poem contain the line '(Tell it to Mr Strachey)', a reference to John Strachey (1860–1927), editor of the *Spectator* 1898–1925. Pound explained to his father that he used Strachey 'as the type of male prude' and was adopting 'the classic Latin manner in mentioning people by name' (*SL*, 21). Strachey was blasted in *Blast* (20 June 1914) and lampooned also in Eliot's 'Le Directeur' (*Collected Poems*, 1958, 46).

l. 33A: earlier versions have 'go! jangle their door-bells'.

ll. 34–5: cf. the earlier 'An Immortality' in *Ripostes*, 'Sing we for love and idleness,/ Naught else is worth the having' (*CSP*, 88) and 'Further Instructions', lines 1–7 (*CSP*, 103). Pound may be indebted to Whitman's posture: 'I loafe and invite my soul,/ I lean and loafe at my ease . . .' ('Song of Myself' 1).

The Spring

A version of a poem by the sixth-century Greek poet Ibycus (*Oxford Book of Greek Verse*, 164; *Penguin Book of Greek Verse*, ed. C. A. Trypanis, 1971, 68). Ibycus was a 'pure color' in Pound's 'Renaissance palette' (*LE*, 215, 216); he 'presented the "Image"' (*G-B*, 83).

Epigraph: (Gk.) 'In Spring the Cydonian quinces' (Trypanis), the opening line of Ibycus' poem, repeated in Canto XXXIX (203/195).

l. 1 Cydonian: of Cydonia, in Crete. Most translations render the association of Cydonia (Κυδωνία) with the quince (μῆλον Κυδώνιον).

l. 2 Maelids: fruit-tree nymphs. 'Maelids' is Pound's construction from the Greek 'μηλιδες' which John Quinn saw fit to correct to 'Meliads' in the American edition of *Lustra* (1917). Pound used the term also in Canto III (l. 11), and wrote to Quinn, ' "Maelids" is correct. They [,] the nymphs of the apple-trees [,] are my one bit of personal property in greek mythology' (Pearlman, 300).

l. 3 Thrace: ancient territory of the eastern Balkans.

ll. 11–13: Pound's addition to Ibycus (Kenner, *Pound Era*, 141).

Commission

Omitted from the trade edition of *Lustra* (October 1916). Elkin Mathews's note to Pound on this poem read, 'If included must be revised – delete last two lines on this page, and the lines "Go to the adolescent" to the end of p. 20' (Homberger, 123). Pound's sense of mission here and his use of syntactic parallelism is indebted to Walt Whitman.

l. 3: Pound praised Henry James as 'the hater of tyranny; book after early book against oppression, against all the sordid petty personal crushing oppression, the domination of modern life' (*LE*, 296).

ll. 9–10: cf. 'The Garden' (ll. 3–4, 8–9), and *Hugh Selwyn Mauberley* xi.

ll. 14–15: In *Patria Mia* Pound wrote, 'We in America are horrified at the French matriarchate, at the tyranny of family, but hardly so much, I think, as at the English "chattel" system' (p. 39).

ll. 16–17: in responding to Harriet Monroe, who objected to these lines, Pound wrote,

honi soit! Surely the second line might refer to the chastest

joys of paradise. Has our good nation read the Song of
Songs? No, really, I think this ought to stay. The tragedy as
I see it is the tragedy of finer desire drawn, merely by being
desire at all, into the grasp of the grosser animalities.
G – d! You can't emasculate literature utterly.

(SL, 17–18)

Richard Aldington satirized Pound's repeated use of 'delicate'
(also in 'Albatre', 'The Condolence', *CSP,* 91, and ''Ἰμέρρω')
in the parody 'Conviction'; cf. 'The Garden'.
l. 28: Pound praised Henry James for opposing 'the impinging
of family pressure, the impinging of one personality on
another' *(LE,* 296). Part also of his characterization of
'Mitteleuropa' in Canto XXXV is 'the intramural, the almost
intravaginal warmth of/ hebrew affections, in the family, and
nearly everything else . . .' (178/172–3).
ll. 29–30: Pound replied to Harriet Monroe's objection to
these lines,

> A poem is supposed to present the truth of passion, not the
> casuistical decision of a committee of philosophers. I expect
> some time to do a hymn in praise of 'race' or 'breed', but
> here I want to say exactly what I do say. We've had too
> much of this patriarchal sentimentality. Family affection is
> occasionally beautiful. Only people are much too much in
> the habit of taking it for granted that it is always so.

(SL, 18)

l. 35: Pound substituted this line for the following two earlier
lines, as the poem appeared in *Poetry* (April 1913): 'Speak for
the kinship of the mind and spirit./ Go, against all forms of
oppression'.

A Pact

Cf. also 'To Whistler, American' *(CSP,* 251).
l. 1 a pact: Pound had 'truce' in the first published version of
the poem, in *Poetry* (April 1913).

Walt Whitman: (1819–92), the American poet and author of *Leaves of Grass* (1855–1891/2). Pound expressed his relation to Whitman at greatest length in the essay, written in 1909, ' "What I feel about Walt Whitman" ':

> From this side of the Atlantic I am for the first time able to read Whitman. . . . I see him America's poet. . . . He *is* America. His crudity is an exceeding great stench, but it *is* America. . . . He is disgusting. He is an exceedingly nauseating pill, but he accomplishes his mission. . . . The vital part of my message, taken from the sap and fibre of America, is the same as his. . . . Personally I might be very glad to conceal my relationship to my spiritual father and brag about my more congenial ancestry – Dante, Shakespeare, Theocritus, Villon, but the descent is a bit difficult to establish.
>
> (*SPr*, 115–16)

Cf. also the remarks in *The Spirit of Romance* (pp. 155, 168–9), *Patria Mia* (pp. 24, 31, 45–7), *Selected Letters* (p. 21), *ABC of Reading* (p. 192) and Pound's 'commerce' with Whitman's 'Out of the Cradle Endlessly Rocking' in Canto LXXXII (561–2/526).

ll. 6–7: Whitman, wrote Pound, 'was not an artist, but a reflex, the first honest reflex, in an age of papier-mâché letters' (*PM*, 24) and to Harriet Monroe, 'but we can't stop with the "Yawp". We have no longer any excuse for not taking up the complete art' (*SL*, 11). Cf. also *Ta Hsio* (*The Great Digest*), II, 4, 'Hence the man in whom speaks the voice of his forebears cuts no log that he does not make fit to be roof-tree . . . *getting the grist of the phrase: Renew the people*' (*Confucius*, 39).

Dance Figure

Pound offered this poem as an example of the use of rhythm in free verse, 'with accent heavily marked as a drum-beat' (*LE*, 12), and with indeed 'little but its rhythm to recommend it' (*SL*, 11). Cf. also 'The Return'.

Epigraph: an allusion to the 'marriage in Cana of Galilee' (John 2: 1) where Christ performed the first miracle, changing water into wine.

l. 4: a Biblical construction, used by Swinburne in 'Aholibah': 'There was none like thee in the land' (Ruthven, 56).

l. 10: an echo of the story of Daphne, metamorphosed into a tree; cf. 'The Tree'.

l. 11: cf. lines 19–20, and the poem 'Ortus', 'I have loved a stream . . .' (*CSP*, 93).

ll. 12–13: Ruthven suggests Pound's most likely source was Swinburne's lines in 'At Eleusis',

> Also at night, unwinding cloth from cloth
> As who unhusks an almond to the white
> And pastures curiously the purer taste,
> I bared the gracious limbs and the soft feet.
>
> (Ruthven, 56)

In Greek mythology the nymph Phyllis is transformed into an almond tree. Cf. also Canto XXV (ll. 87–9), 'And Sulpicia/ green shoot now, and the wood/ white under new cortex.'

l. 18 Nathat–Ikanaie: derived perhaps from Ikhanaton (or Akhenaton), Egyptian pharaoh (1379–1362 B.C.), known for his worship of the sun disc, Aton.

"*Tree-at-the-river*": the name suggests the willow, sacred to Hecate, Circe, Hera and Proserpine, and also through a transference of the Greek word 'helice' to Helicon, sacred to poets; but it is obviously Pound's own concoction. Cf. the locution "Wing'd-with-Awe" in 'The Return' (l. 10).

April

One of sixteen poems, including the groups titled 'Lustra' and 'Xenia' which appeared in *Poetry* (November 1913).

Richard Aldington parodied 'April' in the poem 'Elevators':

> Let us soar up higher than the eighteenth floor
> And consider the delicate delectable monocles

Of the musical virgins of Parnassus:
Pale slaughter beneath purple skies.

(Egoist, 15 Jan. 1914)

Epigraph: (Lat.) 'the scattered limbs of the nymphs', adapted from the description of King Pentheus, torn limb from limb by the Dionysian maenads for opposing the new God (Ovid, *Metamorphoses*, Bk. III, l. 724/911).

l. 3 olive: sacred to Dionysus.

l. 5: in the poem's first appearance in *Poetry* this line was separated from the previous four. The effect is as of the summary images of 'Gentildonna' and 'Liu Ch'e', and like them owes something to the laconic juxtapositions of Chinese verse.

Gentildonna

Title: (Ital.) 'gentlewoman'.
ll. 2–3: cf. 'Apparuit' (ll. 11–12n.).

The Rest

Originally untitled, this formed the first of the group of 'Lustra' poems in *Poetry* (November 1913). Its address to kindred spirits was part of Pound's campaign for an American 'Risorgimento': he spoke, he said in the essay 'The Renaissance', to 'the fighting minority . . . a minority that has been until now gradually forced out of the country' (*LE*, 219); cf. also 'L'Homme Moyen Sensuel' (*CSP*, 255–63) and *Patria Mia*.

l. 7: 'The system of magazine publication', Pound wrote, 'is at bottom opposed to the aims of the serious artist in letters' (*PM*, 25).

l. 10 successes: in *Patria Mia*, Pound wrote, 'And, of course, the way to "succeed", as they call it, is to comply. To comply to formulae, and to formulae not based on any knowledge of the art or any care for it' (pp. 29–30).

ll. 18–19: cf. 'Epilogue', 'I bring you the spoils, my nation,/ I, who went out in exile,/ Am returned to thee with gifts' (*CSP*, 267). Pound may be remembering Walt Whitman's 'I have pressed through in my own right' in the poem 'So Long!', which he recommended to his father (*SL*, 21). D. H. Lawrence's second volume, similarly titled *Look! We Have Come Through!*, appeared in 1917.

Les Millwin

Originally the untitled second poem of the group 'Lustra' in *Poetry* (November 1913).

l. 1 Russian Ballet: Diaghilev's Ballets Russes. The ballet was a source of inspiration to the Nineties poets, for Arthur Symons concentrating 'in itself a good deal of the modern ideal in matters of artistic expression' (*Selected Writings*, ed. Roger Holdsworth, 1974, 82). Douglas Goldring reports that 'The Russian Ballet first electrified the town in 1913' (*South Lodge*, 1943, 72). Cf. 'The Garret' (l. 7n).

l. 6 "Slade": the Slade School of Fine Art, Gower Street, London.

l. 9 futuristic: the first Futurist Exhibition in London was held at the Sackville Gallery, 1 March 1912, and F. T. Marinetti visited London in 1912–13. He lectured twice at the Doré Gallery (the second lecture attended by Wyndham Lewis, T. E. Hulme and Gaudier-Brzeska), and read to a group, including Pound, at one of Yeats's evenings at 18 Woburn Buildings. Pound described Futurism as 'a kind of accelerated impressionism', distinct from both Imagism and Vorticism, and said he was himself 'wholly opposed' to Marinetti's aesthetic principles (*G-B*, 90).

l. 10 Exulted: reflecting on national variants in morality, Pound commented, 'The Russian dancers present their splendid luxurious paganism, and everyone with a pre-Raphaelite or Swinburnian education is in raptures. What "morality" will be like in two hundred years hence is beyond all prediction' (*PM*, 13).

Cleopatra: *Cléopâtre* was a one-act ballet performed by the Ballets Russes.

ll. 13–14: Hugh Kenner finds the centre of the poem 'in the ironic impersonality that reduces the writer to a recorder of social contours ... and locks into semi-comic relation scriptor, lector, Millwins, students and ballerinas alike' (*Poetry of EP*, 117–18).

A Song of the Degrees

Originally sections III–V in the series of seven poems ('The Street in Soho', 'The Cool Fingers of Science', 'A Song of the Degrees', 'Ité', 'Dum Capitolium Scandet') which appeared in *Poetry* (November 1913) under the title 'Xenia'. The Latin term 'Xenia', meaning 'a gift to friends', is derived from the collection of mottoes titled *Xenia* (*Epigrams*, Bk. XIII) by the Roman poet Martial (A.D. 40–104).

Title: Psalms 120–34 are subtitled 'A Song of Degrees'.
ll. 1–5: Parodied by Richard Aldington:

> Rest me with mushrooms,
> For I think the steak is evil.
>
> The wind moves over the wheat
> With a silver crashing,
> A thin war of delicate kettles.
>
> (*Egoist*, 15 Jan. 1914)

l. 1 Chinese colours: Donald Davie argues that this poem anticipates Pound's sense of 'the morality implicit in the painter's use of hue' in Cantos XLV and LI (*Poet as Sculptor*, 59, 157–8).
l. 2 glass: cf. 'The Flame' (ll. 40–3) (*CSP*, 65).
ll. 3–4: cf. 'The Alchemist' (l. 15), ''Mid the silver rustling of wheat' (*CSP*, 86).
l. 15 amber: an alloy, composed of gold and silver; ef. 'The Alchemist', lines 25–7.

two-faced: Ruthven (p. 225) suggests a pun on 'amber' and the Latin 'ambo' ('both', 'two together').

Ité

Title: (Lat.) 'go'.
l. 2 perfection: cf. 'Salvationists' 1, 'Come, my songs, let us speak of perfection –/ We shall get ourselves rather disliked' (*CSP*, 108). Pound questioned Harriet Monroe, 'Who in America believes in perfection and that nothing short of it is worth while?' (*SL*, 15).
l. 3 Sophoclean light: writing to Harriet Monroe in January 1915, Pound wished for 'a bit more Sophoclean severity' to counterbalance the current weakness of 'looseness, lack of rhythmical construction and intensity' (*SL*, 50). In 1916 Pound wrote that he was 'probably suspicious of Greek drama' and thought 'it would probably be easier to fake a play by Sophocles than a novel by Stendhal' (*SL*, 94). Much later, he was to translate Sophocles' *Trachiniae* as *Women of Trachis* (1956).

The Bath Tub

Originally poem VII of the ten-poem series titled 'Zenia' in the *Smart Set* (December 1913, 47–8). An earlier title, cancelled before publication, was 'Courtesy'. Pound wrote to Harriet Monroe:

> The 'Bath Tub' is intended to diagnose the sensations of two people who never having loved each other save in the Tennysonian manner have come upon a well-meaning satiety . . . No 'spiritual gravity' or 'quodlibet'. 2 bodies reduced to their chemical components . . .
>
> (Chicago MSS, 3 Dec. 1912, quoted in Ruthven, 44)

Liu Ch'e

'Liu Ch'e' appeared with the poems 'After Ch'u Yuan', 'Fan

Piece for her Imperial Lord' and 'Ts'ai Chi'h' in the first
Imagist anthology, *Des Imagistes* (March 1914). These poems,
together with 'Epitaphs' and 'Ancient Wisdom, Rather
Cosmic', also in *Lustra*, were probably derived from H. A.
Giles, *A History of Chinese Literature* (1901, reprinted 1967).
Giles's version of the present poem reads:

> The sound of rustling silk is stilled,
> With dust the marble courtyard filled,
> No footfalls echo on the floor,
> Fallen leaves in heaps block up the door . . .
> For she, my pride, my lovely one, is lost,
> And I am left, in hopeless anguish tossed.

(p. 100)

Arthur Waley made a later version of the poem in *170 Chinese
Poems* (1918, 49), reprinted in *Chinese Poems* (1976, 42).
Title: Liu Ch'e, or Wu-ti (157–87 B.C.), the author of the
poem, succeeded in 140 B.C. as sixth emperor of the Han
dynasty; cf. 'Old Idea of Choan by Rosoriu' (l. 28) in *Cathay*.
Pound felt that Liu Ch'e, like Ibycus, 'presented the "Image"'
(*G-B*, 83).
l. 6 wet leaf . . . clings: these ingredients recur in 'Gentildonna',
'Ts'ai Chi'h' (*CSP*, 119), 'Alba' and 'Coitus'.
threshold: recalled in Canto VII, 'My lintel, and Liu Ch'e's
lintel' (29/25).

Arides

Originally poem VIII of the series 'Zenia' (*Smart Set*, December
1913). Pound puns perhaps in the title on the Latin 'aridus'
('dry', 'arid').

Amities

Epigraph: from the line 'But think about old friends the most'
in Yeats's 'The Lover Pleads with his Friend for Old Friends'
(*Collected Poems*, 79), to which Pound's poem is a reply. The

earlier 'In Exitum Cuiusdam' (*CSP*, 71) opens with the phrase 'Time's bitter flood' from the same poem by Yeats.

l. 6 Te Voilà, mon Bourrienne: (Fr.) 'There you are, my Bourrienne'. Louis Antoine Fauvelet de Bourrienne (1769–1834) was private secretary to Napoleon and published his memoirs in 1829. Pound mentions him again in Canto XVIII (84/80) and repeats the French phrase in Canto XCIII (657/624).

l. 13 bos amic: (Prov.) 'good friend'. Richard Aldington suggested that this referred to Harold Monroe (1879–1932), editor of *Poetry and Drama* and owner of the Poetry Bookshop, Devonshire Street (J. Grant, *Harold Monroe and the Poetry Bookshop*, 1967, 44). Monroe published nine of the *Lustra* poems in *Poetry and Drama* (March and December 1914), and in April 1914 published the English edition of *Des Imagistes*, under the Poetry Bookshop imprint. Pound felt that Monroe's weakness was that he never had a 'programme' but allowed in his obituary notice that 'he certainly wrote poems that measured up to that [the Imagist] standard' (Stock, *Life*, 316, 384).

l. 16 moderate chop-house: Aldington thought this a reference to Bellotti's, in Pound's opinion the 'cheapest clean restaurant with a real cook' (*SL*, 97); cf. 'Black Slippers: Bellotti' (*CSP*, 121).

ll. 17–23: (Lat.) 'That chap was vulgar,/ Thank god he's buried,/ Let the worms feed on his face/ A-a-a-a-A-men/ Meanwhile, like Jove I/ Shall move in/ With his woman.' Pound adopts the rhythms of the *Dies Irae*.

l. 22 Gaudero: 'Gaudebo' in *Poetry* (August 1914).

Meditatio

Title: (Lat.) 'meditation'.
Elkin Mathews found this poem 'very nasty' and allowed it to appear only in the private unexpurgated edition of *Lustra* (September 1916) (Homberger, 123). 'The Seeing Eye' (*CSP* 114) was excluded by Mathews on the same grounds.

Ladies

To placate Harriet Monroe, Pound offered the present title
in place of the original 'Le Donne' ('tho' it don't mean the
same thing') and suggested the titles of the first and fourth
sections in place of the originals, 'Agathas Intacta' and
'Passante' (Chicago MSS, 8 July 1914, quoted in Ruthven,
157).

AGATHAS
l. 4: cf. 'The Tea Shop' where the girl is threatened with
middle age.

YOUNG LADY
l. 5 lar: (Lat.) the 'Lares Familiares' were gods of the hearth
in Roman religion.

LESBIA ILLA
Pound's source is Catullus LVIII:

> Caeli, Lesbia nostra, Lesbia illa,
> illa Lesbia, quam Catullus unam
> plus quam se atque suos amavit omnes
> nunc in quadriviis et angriportis
> glubit magnanimi Remi nepotes.

('Lesbia, our Lesbia, the same old Lesbia/ Caelius, she whom
Catullus loved once/ more than himself and more than all his
own,/ loiters at the crossroads/ and in the back-streets/ ready
to toss-off the "magnanimous" sons of Rome', trans. Whigham, op. cit., 118). Pound wrote to Harriet Monroe, 'Now
WHO could blush at "Lesbia Illa" ????????? WHO???' (*SL*,
37). Canto II originally included a more literal translation of
the Latin (*Poetry*, July 1917, 182).
l. 9 Memnon: legendary king of Ethiopia, son of Tithonus and
Eos ('the dawn'), who appears in Catullus LXVI.
ll. 12–13: cf. *Hugh Selwyn Mauberley* XI, on the decline of the
'Milésien' tradition to life 'in Ealing/ With the most bank-
clerkly of Englishmen?'.

l. 14 (Lat.) from Catullus III, 'Lugete, O Veneres Cupidinesque' ('Mourn, loves and cupids').

PASSING

An early, cancelled title was 'Cytherea in Furs', and the poem originally ended with the three lines, 'Neither upon you, unconscious,/ Nor upon that egoist who is longing to waste my time,/ Will I confer thought, or my hours' (Chicago MSS, quoted in Ruthven, 158).

l. 15 Aphrodite: the Greek goddess of love.

l. 18 patchouli: a perfume made from the patchouli plant.

Coda

Ruthven says this poem was originally planned as a tailpiece to 'Ladies', 'Phyllidula' and 'The Patterns' (p. 52).

The Coming of War: Actaeon

Norman considers this a 'war poem' (p. 158).

l. 1 Lethe: the river over which dead souls pass to Hades.

ll. 5–8: cf. 'Δώρια' (ll. 5–7), '. . the strong loneliness/ of sunless cliffs/ And of grey waters'.

ll. 11–12: cf. 'The Return' (ll. 1–4), '. . . the tentative/ Movements, and the slow feet,/ The trouble in the pace and the uncertain/ Wavering!'.

l. 14 Actaeon: the story of Actaeon, changed into a stag by the goddess Artemis (Diana) and torn to pieces by his own hounds because he had seen her bathing, is told in Ovid, *Metamorphoses*, Bk. III (ll. 143–252/168–304). Pound incorporates it into Canto IV (18–19/14–15) and mentions Actaeon in Canto LXXX (534/501). The story of a second Actaeon, a beautiful youth who drowned himself and caused a war between his father and would-be ravisher, is told in Plutarch.

l. 15 greaves: armour for the shins.

l. 19: identified as 'the dead warriors of Stonehenge' by Christine Brooke-Rose (p. 189).

In a Station of the Metro

Pound gave an account of the composition of this poem in
'How I Began' (*T.P.'s Weekly*, 6 June 1913, 707) and in the
essay 'Vorticism' (*Fortnightly Review*, 1 Sept. 1914, 465, 467,
reprinted in *Gaudier-Brzeska*, 1916). In the second of these
Pound writes,

> Three years ago in Paris I got out of a 'metro' train at La
> Concorde, and saw suddenly a beautiful face, and then
> another and another, and then a beautiful child's face, and
> then another beautiful woman, and I tried all day to find
> words for what this had meant to me, and I could not find
> any words that seemed to me worthy, or as lovely as that
> sudden emotion. And that evening, as I went home along
> Rue Raynouard, I was still trying and I found, suddenly,
> the expression. I do not mean that I found words, but there
> came an equation . . . not in speech, but in little splotches
> of colour. . . . That is to say, my experience in Paris should
> have gone into paint. If instead of colour I had perceived
> sound or planes in relation, I should have expressed it in
> music or in sculpture. Colour was, in that instance, the
> 'primary pigment': I mean that it was the first adequate
> equation that came into consciousness.
> . . . The 'one image poem' is a form of superposition, that
> is to say, it is one idea set on top of another. I found it
> useful in getting out of the impasse in which I had been left
> by my metro emotion. I wrote a thirty-line poem, and
> destroyed it because it was what we call work 'of second
> intensity'. Six months later I made a poem half that length;
> a year later I made the following *hokku*-like sentence:
> [quotes 'In a Station of the Metro'].
> . . . In a poem of this sort one is trying to record the precise
> instant when a thing outward and objective transforms itself,
> or darts into a thing inward and subjective.
>
> (*G-B*, 86–7, 88–9)

Pound's account recalls Arthur Symons's description of himself in *Spiritual Adventures* (1905) as devoutly practising the 'religion of eyes', 'I noted every face that passed me on the pavement; I looked into the omnibuses, the cabs, always with the same eager hope of seeing some beautiful or interesting person, some gracious movement, a delicate expression, which would be gone if I did not catch it as it went' (*Selected Writings*, 89). Cf. also Pound's 'Dans un Omnibus de Londres' (*CSP*, 179).

At Pound's insistence, the early printings of the poem (*Poetry*, April 1913; *New Freewoman*, 15 Aug. 1913) observed 'spaces between the rhythmic units' (*SL*, 17), as follows:

> The apparition   of these faces   in the crowd   :
> Petals   on a wet, black   bough   .

The poem was parodied in this arrangement by Richard Aldington:

> The apparition   of these poems   in a crowd:
> White faces   in a black   dead faint.
> > (*Egoist*, 15 Jan. 1914, 36)

It was, however, probably the appearance of 'In a Station of the Metro' in this form in the series 'Contemporania' in *Poetry* which persuaded Mrs. Mary Fenollosa to appoint Pound as the literary executor of her husband's papers (cf. headnote to *Cathay*).

Alba

Originally poem II of 'Zenia' (*Smart Set*, December 1913). 'Alba' is the term for a 'dawn-song'; cf. 'Alba *from* "Langue d'Oc" '.
l. 1 pale wet leaves: cf. 'Liu Ch'e', note on line 6.

Coitus

At Elkin Mathews's insistence the title was changed to 'Pervigilium' for the poem's appearance in the abridged edition of *Lustra* (October 1916). 'Pervigilium' alludes to the early anonymous Latin poem *Pervigilium Veneris* (Vigil of Venus), a celebration of the Spring festival of Venus Genetrix, discussed by Pound in *The Spirit of Romance* (pp. 18–21).

ll. 1–2: cf. in the *Pervigilium Veneris*, 'That glow which hides within the saffron sheath/ Shall dare at morn unbind the single fold' (*SR*, 19). Erotic flower symbolism occurs also in MAUBERLEY (1920) II.

l. 1 phaloi: Pound wrote to Mathews of William Clowes, the printer of *Lustra*, 'I judge he is not a hellenist, he seems to confuse the Greek PHALOS, plu. PHALOI (meaning the point of the helmet spike) with the latin Phallus, meaning John Thomas' (*P/J*, 286). Mathews replied, 'the Gk word Phallos means penis – *simply* and the Latin word Phallus is merely derived from it' (Homberger, 124).

l. 3: J. J. Wilhelm writes that the *Pervigilium Veneris* 'shows the inability of the aesthetic sense to function in a religious way, and . . . communicates the melancholy of a world view without a doctrine of salvation' (*Medieval Song*, 1972, 19).

l. 5 Giulio Romano: (1499–1546), Renaissance painter and architect whose most famous work, the Palazzo del Te in Mantua, contains erotic frescoes of the loves of the gods in the Sala di Psiche. Pound may be alluding to the streak of lasciviousness which runs generally through Romano's work.

ll. 7–8: probably derived from the *Pervigilium Veneris*, 'It is she who scatters damp of the gleaming dew, which the night wind leaves behind him' (*SR*, 19). Dione, the consort of Zeus and mother of Aphrodite, is the presiding deity of the *Pervigilium Veneris*.

l. 8 dew . . . leaf: cf. 'Liu Ch'e', note on line 6.

The Encounter

Originally poem IX of 'Zenia' (*Smart Set*, December 1913).

l. 1 new morality: Ruthven suggests (p. 63) that this may refer to the teachings of Sigmund Freud, whose *Three Contributions to a Theory of Sex* had appeared in 1910, and *The Interpretation of Dreams* in 1913. Pound's own ideas on sex would seem rather to derive from Propertius, 'the XIIth century love cult, and Dante's metaphysics a little to one side, and Gourmont's Latin Mystique' (*P and D*, 214).

ll. 4–5: cf. the fragile encounter in 'Shop Girl', 'For a moment she rested against me/ Like a swallow half blown to the wall' (*CSP*, 123).

'Ιμέρρω

Title: (Gk.) from the phrase 'Ατθιδος ἱμέρῳ'. ('for Atthis, longing') in a fragment by the seventh-century Greek poetess Sappho (Barnstone, 141; *Oxford Book of Greek Verse*, 145), incorporated also into Canto V (21–2/17–18). The Sapphic manuscript was published in the *Classical Review* (June 1909) and Pound was probably introduced to it by an earlier poem by Richard Aldington, 'To Atthis', included in *Des Imagistes* (1914). The poem 'Papyrus' (*CSP*, 122), also in *Lustra*, was similarly derived from a fragment by Sappho, published in Berlin in 1902 and in the *Classical Review* (July 1909). Hugh Kenner argues that these two poems form a suite with ' "Ione, Dead the Long Year" ' and 'Shop Girl' (*Pound Era*, 62–3).

l. 2: Aldington's poem 'To Atthis' ends 'I yearn to behold thy delicate soul/ To satiate my desire'.

delicate: Elkin Mathews commented that this poem was 'anything but *delicate*' and 'must be omitted' (Homberger, 124). It was as a result excluded from the trade edition of *Lustra* (October 1916).

"Ione, Dead the Long Year"

Title: Walter Savage Landor (1775–1864) used the name 'Iönè' for a young girl, Nancy Jones, in some early poems, and Pound's title was 'Dead Iönè' on the poem's first appearance (*Poetry and Drama*, December 1914, 353). Landor's collected works, Pound said, were 'the best substitute for a University education that can be offered to any man in a hurry' and his 'chiselled marmorean quatrain' the equal of Théophile Gautier's (*SPr*, 354–5). In May 1916 he reminded Elkin Mathews of 'the troubles over the printing of Landor's "Imaginary Conversations" and how foolish the opposers of them now seem' (*P/J* 285). The 'Imaginary Conversations' were probably an influence on Pound's 'Imaginary Letters' (*P and D*, 55–76).

' "Ione, Dead the Long Year" ' is recalled with the poem 'Liu Ch'e' in Canto VII (29/25).

l. 9: the theme of absence relates this poem to "*Ἰμέρρω*' and 'Papyrus' (*CSP*, 122).

The Tea Shop

Pound wrote to Harriet Monroe that this poem had that 'peculiar combination of sensuality and sentimentality to which we grossly apply the term "post-Victorian" ' (Chicago MSS, 3 Dec. 1912), and to A. C. Henderson that it was 'A poem still touched with Victorian Sentimentality' (Chicago MSS, April 1913; both quoted in Ruthven, 230–1).

l. 5: substituted for the earlier lines, cancelled before publication:

> And this teaches me
> Or at least draws my mind toward
> The thought here following,
> To wit:
>
> > Not only do the lights of love
> > Go dim with the years sliding by us,
> > But even these incidental girls,
> > To whom we have not spoken,
> > Lose their gay grace.

(Chicago MSS, Ruthven, 231)

middle-aged: cf. the poem 'Middle-Aged' (*CSP*, 252).
l. 9: substituted for the earlier lines, cancelled before publication,

They will have just that slight stiffness
        in moving
Which tells that the sap of youth
        is drying.

They will turn middle-aged

And in them we shall find a constant reminder

That she, whom we most desire,
Turns also her face toward the winter.

                    (Chicago MSS, Ruthven, 231)

The Lake Isle

A distant parody of W. B. Yeats's anthology piece, 'The Lake
Isle of Innisfree' (*Collected Poems*, 44). The printers of *Lustra*
declined to print this poem 'in any form whatever' (Homberger, 123) and it was excluded from both private and trade
editions in London, but published in the American edition
(September 1917).
ll. 1, 12 God: Elkin Mathews advised the substitution of
'Jupiter' (Homberger, 124).
l. 10 whores: Pound wrote to Mathews, 'I am not going to
quibble over a few words. I find I can change "whore" in
place to "volaille" ' (*P/J*, 285). The term 'volailles' appeared
in the version published in *Poetry* (September 1916).

Epitaphs

FU I
ll. 1–2: a version of the epitaph composed for himself by the
Chinese poet Fu I (A.D. 555–639), translated by H. A. Giles
as 'Fu I loved the green hills and the white clouds . . ./ Alas!
he died of drink' (op. cit., 135). Pound's original version of the
poem in *Blast I* (20 June 1914) followed Giles's translation
word for word, and included a footnote, 'Fu I was born in
A.D. 554 and died in 639. This is his epitaph very much as he
wrote it.'

LI PO

ll. 3–5: based on Giles's account of Li Po's death: 'After more wanderings and much adventure, he was drowned on a journey, from leaning one night too far over the edge of a boat in a drunken effort to embrace the reflection of the moon' (ibid., 153).

l. 3 Li Po: (A.D. 701–762), the author of twelve of the poems translated by Pound in *Cathay*. The poem 'Ancient Wisdom, Rather Cosmic' (*CSP*, 129), also in *Lustra*, is a version of Li Po's poem 'Ku-Feng 9'.

Villanelle: The Psychological Hour

Title: the 'villanelle' (from Ital. 'villanella', originally a pastoral song) is a strict form used in light verse, consisting of five tercets and a final quatrain, using two rhymes. The first and the third line of the first tercet are repeated as a refrain through the poem and form the final two lines of the quatrain. The form was adopted in the nineteenth century by W. E. Henley, Austin Dobson, Andrew Lang and Edmund Gosse. Pound's poem is obviously only loosely a villanelle.

It is possible that Pound draws in this poem on the experience of his first meetings with Henri Gaudier and Sophie Brzeska (whom Gaudier called his 'sister') in 1913. Pound had admired a clay figure by Gaudier at an art show at the Albert Hall and Gaudier had announced himself briefly there, only to disappear immediately. Pound relates that when he subsequently invited Gaudier to dinner, he did not arrive, and that when they did meet at Gaudier's studio in Putney, 'I knew that many things would bore or disgust him, particularly my rather middle-aged point of view' (*G-B*, 45).

l. 3 middle-ageing care: cf. 'The Tea Shop' (l. 5) and 'Middle Aged' (*CSP*, 252).

ll. 16–19: these lines were added after the poem's first appearance in *Poetry* (December 1915).

l. 27: borrowed from Yeats's poem 'The People' (*Collected Poems*, 169).

l. 30: Pound writes that Gaudier-Brzeska tried to persuade him he was not becoming middle-aged, 'but any man whose youth has been worth anything . . . knows he has seen the best of it when he finds thirty approaching; knows that he is entering a quieter realm, a place with a different psychology' (*G-B*, 45–6).

Alba
from "Langue d'Oc"

The series of poems titled 'Homage à la Langue d'Oc' appeared in the *Little Review* (May 1918), the *New Age* (27 June 1918) and with 'Mœurs Contemporains', 'Three Cantos' and *Homage to Sextus Propertius* in *Quia Pauper Amavi* (1919). The total sequence consists of six poems, three of which, including the present poem, are 'albas' or 'dawn-poems' (five of these poems are included in *Collected Shorter Poems*, pp. 189–95: the sixth, a version of Arnaut Daniel's 'Sols Sui', appears in *Translations*, p. 179). The term 'Langue d'Oc' refers to the dialects of southern France used by the twelfth- and thirteenth-century troubadours.

The present poem is a version of an anonymous Provençal poem ('Quan lo rossinhols escria') rendered in a prose translation by Pound in *The Spirit of Romance* as:

> When the nightingale cries to his mate, night and day, I am with my fair mistress amidst the flowers, until the watchman from the tower cries "Lover, arise, for I see the white light of the dawn, and the clear day".
>
> (pp. 40–1)

'Romance literature', said Pound, 'begins with a Provençal "Alba" supposedly of the Tenth Century' (*SR*, 11), and appropriately his own first published poem was called 'Belangel Alba' (*Hamilton Literary Magazine*, May 1905, reprinted as 'Alba Belingalis' in *Personae*, 1909). Cf. also 'That Pass Between the False Dawn and the True', 'To the Dawn: Defiance', 'Aube of the West Dawn, Venetian June' (*ALS*, 44, 67, 94) and the poem 'Alba' in *Lustra*.

Near Perigord

Before its appearance in *Lustra* (1916), 'Near Perigord' had
appeared in *Poetry* (December 1915) with Pound's notes and
with a translation of the poem it is concerned with, 'Dompna
pois de me no'us cal' (*CSP*, 115) by the warlike baron and
troubadour Bertran de Born (1140–1215). Pound glossed this
poem in his epigraph to 'Na Audiart' and again in *The Spirit
of Romance* (1910). It is to all appearances a love poem, in
which Bertran seeks consolation for being rejected by his Lady
Maent of Montaignac by constructing a 'borrowed' or ideal
Lady composed of the outstanding qualities of the pre-eminent
ladies of Provence ('of Anhes, her hair golden as Ysolt's; of
Cembelins, the expression of her eyes; of Aelis, her easy
speech; of the Viscountess of Chales, her throat and her two
hands; of Bels-Miralhs (Fair-Mirror), her gaiety', *SR*, 47).

The story of the relationship with Maent is now discredited.
As James J. Wilhelm, for example, says, 'There is no doubt
that any "amorous legends" about Bertran de Born are as
fictional as his own poem indicates' (*Seven Troubadours: The
Creators of Modern Verse*, 1970, 168). Pound, one can suppose,
accepted the story and was attracted to Bertran's poem on
another score: as a test case of the blend of fact and phantom
in the composition of the Lady, and of the poet's adoption of
a persona. Pound's translation of Bertran's poem was begun as
early as 1908, the same year in which 'Na Audiart', which
explores one of its aspects, appeared in *A Lume Spento*. In the
following year, two further poems, 'Sestina: Altaforte' and
'Planh for the Young English King', one an adaptation and
one a translation of Bertran de Born, appeared in *Exultations*.
If 'Na Audiart' and 'Sestina: Altaforte', most obviously, show
Bertran as respectively a writer of love poems and of war
songs, Pound asks in 'Near Perigord' to which category his
'Borrowed Lady' belongs. Was the poem an attempt to regain
the Lady Maent's favour, through flattery or by stirring her
jealousy, or was this a subterfuge, and the poem really a means
of infiltrating the neighbouring castles and of Bertran's
securing his position *vis-à-vis* local rival barons?

In one way, though it is not a direct answer to this question, Pound had attempted to understand Bertran by adopting him as a persona in the adaptations and translations mentioned, and more generally by his sustained study of Provençal. He had also, as part of this study, himself visited the sites associated with the troubadours, probably in the summer of 1908, and most significantly in the period May–August 1912 (he was to return to this area again with Dorothy Pound, and part of the time with T. S. Eliot, in 1919). It is fair to assume that two poems, 'Provincia Deserta' (*CSP*, 131) and 'Near Perigord', were inspired by his trip in 1912, and in a letter to his father of 3 June 1913, where Pound mentions 'doing a tale of Bertrans de Born' (*SL*, 21), we have what is perhaps the first reference to 'Near Perigord'.

The visit of 1912 would seem to be in Pound's mind also in the essay 'Troubadours – Their Sorts and Conditions' (October 1913), where he writes,

> Or, again, a man may walk the hill roads and river roads from Limoges and Charente to Dordogne and Narbonne and learn a little, or more than a little, of what the country meant to the wandering singers, he may learn, or think he learns, why so many canzos open with speech of the weather; or why such a man made war on such and such castles.
>
> (*LE*, 95)

One should note Pound's qualification here and also the place and value this knowledge is given in the essay. If a man wishes to acquire 'emotional, as well as intellectual, acquaintance with an age so out of fashion as the twelfth century', says Pound, 'he may try in several ways to attain it' (ibid., 94). Walking 'the hill roads and river roads' is one such way alongside others: reading the poems in manuscript, listening to the words with the music, and consulting the 'razos' or biographical notes on the troubadours. Each in its turn one might see as an instance of Pound's 'return to origins'; doubly so, since for Pound Provençal is at the root of modern lyric poetry, in the search for 'harmony, the fitting thing' (ibid., 92). These methods are examples collectively also of Pound's attempt, as always, to revivify the past in the present.

Again, if this does not answer Pound's question in 'Near Perigord', it enables us to ask a question ourselves of his method in that poem. It ends,

> And all the rest of her a shifting change,
> A broken bundle of mirrors . . . !

This is a description of the Lady Maent as she escapes definition in Bertran's poem, but it is a confirmation too of the broken image of Bertran himself, his head severed from his body, which we have received from Dante's *Inferno*, and which Pound reiterates through the poem. In seeking 'emotional acquaintance' with Bertran, in taking him as an exemplar of the problematic relation between the man and his persona, and of his own relation as a poet with the literary tradition, Pound turns on him the angled mirrors of fact (the geography of the region, fragments of recorded history), fiction (subjective re-creation) and of art (Bertran's own poem and the evidence of Dante).

This would seem to correspond to the several modes of access Pound indicates in 'Troubadours – Their Sorts and Conditions'. Pound revolves his subject, one is tempted to think, in the manner of Cubist or Vorticist art, but if this is so, it is in an attempt to find a single true reflection. 'Fact' and 'fiction' in 'Near Perigord' are not complementary but alternative ('End fact. Try fiction'), and it is 'art' which is seen to control experience and to endure. The Lady Maent, for example, has no existence, no form outside the tyranny of Bertran's poem, 'She who could never live save through one person'. The discord and contention represented in Bertran are similarly placed under a rule; in Dante's *Commedia*, 'an expression of the laws of eternal justice; "il contrapasso", the counterpass, as Bertran calls it' (*SR*, 127). Dante, whose intelligence in the *Commedia* journeys 'through the states of mind wherein dwell all sorts and conditions of men before death' (ibid.), stands as a model for an acquaintance with the inner life of men that is possible in art, for the data the arts give us 'of psychology, of man as to his interiors, as to the ratio of his thought to his emotions, etc., etc., etc.' ('The Serious Artist', *LE*, 48). The 'reality' of Bertran survives then in the certainty of Dante's vision:

> Surely I saw, and still before my eyes
> Goes on that headless trunk.

As Pound had said in *The Spirit of Romance*, 'Dante's vision is real, because he saw it' (p. 178). And one recalls the appearance of Dante in Canto XVI at the exit from hell, seeing it 'in his mirror'. His vision is not fractured, but whole.

What one must add to this, however, is that though Bertran is defined and categorized by Dante, his motives in the poem 'Dompna pois' remain enigmatic. 'Near Perigord' is therefore asking two questions. It interrogates Bertran's poem, but fails to detect the seam between its fact and fiction. To this extent, 'a broken bundle of mirrors' describes its own condition as well as the Lady Maent and Bertran's poem. Secondly and more fundamentally, Pound is weighing the relative claims to truth of art and other means of recovering and giving form to the past. As such the answer of 'Near Perigord' is quite clear and significant, but it ought to be taken too with the discussion Pound was conducting elsewhere on this same question.

By the date of 'Near Perigord's publication in *Poetry* (December 1915), Pound had drafted the first three Cantos and was at work on Canto V (Stock, *Life*, 237). These are concerned too with the purchase art and history can have on the past. The first version of Canto I (published in *Poetry*, June 1917, 113–21), which became, much revised, the opening of Canto II, begins for example with Pound's considering Robert Browning's *Sordello* as a model, since 'the modern world/ Needs such a rag-bag to stuff all its thought in'. It taxes Browning later on his inaccuracies ('half your dates are out'), but justifies the end since it is 'more real than any dead Sordello'. Amidst these questions of appropriate form and relative truths, the Canto moves through an associative flux of intermittent certainties and uncertainties:

> What have I of this life,
> Or even of Guido?
> Sweet lie! – Was I there truly?
> Did I know Or San Michele?
> Let's believe it . . . No, take it all for lies.
> I have but smelt this life, a whiff of it.

(Poetry, June 1917, 120)

The line 'Or even of Guido?' corresponds to Pound's confession of 'the depths of my ignorance, or my width of uncertainty' in his essay on Cavalcanti (*LE*, 160), a work he cited as evidence of his desire 'at all times . . . to know the demarcation between what I know and what I do not know' ('Date Line', *LE*, 85). In Canto V, Pound presents an analogous demarcation in the work of the sixteenth-century historian Benedetto Varchi, who confesses his inability to establish the motive of Lorenzino Medici, the murderer of his cousin Alessandro:

> "Whether for love of Florence," Varchi leaves it,
> Saying "I saw the man, came up with him at Venice,
> "I, one wanting the facts,
> "And no mean labour . . . Or for a privy spite?"
> Our Benedetto leaves it.

(Cantos, 23/19)

Varchi corroborates Pound's own attempt in 'Near Perigord' and in 'Cavalcanti' to distinguish 'the known and the unknown, in at least a few specimen areas' ('Date Line', *LE*, 86). Such an effort one might think informs too the editing, reshuffling and re-making of the early Cantos. In rejecting Sordello, in throwing off the model and voice of Browning for the persona of Odysseus, Pound gains the explorative assurance necessary for an epic which will 'include history'. 'Near Perigord', we can assume, sounds a preparatory note in this process.

Title: 'Perigord', i.e. Périgueux in the diocese of Perigord.
Epigraph: the opening lines of a 'sirvente' (a poem on political or moral subjects) by Bertran de Born. Pound translates, 'At Perigord near to the wall,/ Aye, within a mace throw of it' (*SR*, 45).
l. 1 '*You'd . . . dust*': a reply to Pound's 'Judge ye! Have I dug him up again?' in the epigraph to 'Sestina: Altaforte'.
l. 2 Cino: Pound's adopted persona is perhaps suggested by Cino da Pistoia (cf. 'Cino'), grouped by Dante with Bertran de Born and other poets in *De Vulgari Eloquentia*, Bk. II, ch. 2. Two very early unpublished poems, 'Roundel for Arms' and 'Roundel: After Joachim du Bellay', were also signed 'Cino' (*ALS*, 116, 117).
l. 3 Uc St. Circ: Uc de Saint Circ, a Provençal troubadour and biographer, possibly of Bertran de Born. Pound refers to him in *The Spirit of Romance* (p. 41).
l. 5 En: (Prov.) 'Lord' or 'Sir'.
canzone: Bertran's 'Dompna Soissenbuda' ('Borrowed Lady') which Pound proceeds to summarize; cf. his translation (*CSP*, 115) and 'Na Audiart'.
l. 6 Maent: the Lady Maent (or Maëut, i.e. Matilda) of Montaignac, to whom Bertran's poem is addressed. Bertran does not speak so directly of 'love' as Pound suggests.
l. 7 Montfort: the Lady Elis (or Alice) of Monfort, sister of Maent; cf. lines 110, 121.
Agnes: of Rochecouart; cf. lines 29, 70, 107, 122.
   Rejected by Maent, Bertran makes his 'borrowed' or ideal lady, begging 'from each pre-eminent lady of Provence, some gift, or some quality: of Anhes, her hair golden as Ysolt's . . . of Aelis, her easy speech' (*SR*, 47).
l. 8 Bel Miral: 'Fair Mirror', an unidentified lady of whom Bertran asks 'Tall stature and gaiety' (*CSP*, 116).
viscountess: the Viscountess of Chalais, Tibors of Montausier; also at lines 12, 71 and 122. Cf. 'Marvoil', line 12.
l. 9: it is rather Pound's view that the 'Borrowed Lady' is not worthy of Maent: 'Bertrans finds the song small consolation, as the patchwork mistress does not reach the lofty excellence of Maent' (*SR*, 47).

l. 11 Montaignac: site of Maent's castle, south-east of Périgueux; modern Montignac.

l. 12 another at Malemort: i.e. the Lady Audiart; cf. 'Na Audiart' and stanza 5 of Pound's translation, 'Dompna pois de me no'us cal' (*CSP*, 116).

l. 13 Brive: east of Périgueux.

l. 16 Tairiran: Maent's husband, Guillem Talairan or Tairilan (mod. Talleyrand).

l. 17 brother-in-law: Helias Talairan, Count of Perigord, Talairan's brother and therefore Maent's brother-in-law.

l. 20 Altafort: Bertran de Born's castle (Prov. Autafort, Fr. Hautefort, Ital. Altaforte).

ll. 21–7: Dante set Bertran with the 'Sowers of Discord' in the ninth ring of Hell for causing Prince Henry (the 'Young King' of Pound's 'Planh') to rebel against his brother Richard Coeur-de-Lion and their father King Henry II (*Inferno*, XXVIII, ll. 118–42). Cf. also lines 163–8, Pound's prose translation of the passage from Dante (*SR*, 45) and the epigraph to 'Sestina: Altaforte'.

l. 26: Bertran's grief over the death of Prince Henry is said to have moved King Henry to tears and effected a reconciliation between them; cf. lines 40–6. Pound suggests that Bertran was an opportunist, here as elsewhere.

l. 27 "counterpass": Dante's 'contrapasso' (*Inferno*, XXVIII, l. 142) spoken by Bertran and glossed by Pound as 'the laws of eternal justice' (*SR*, 127). The point is that Bertran's punishment, the severance of his head, is matched to his supposed crime.

l. 29 Poictiers: Poitiers, north of Périgueux, was the site of the famous court of Queen Eleanor, wife of Henry II, and of his defeat of Prince Henry in 1173.

Rochecouart: cf. line 7 note.

l. 32 Foix: in the foothills of the Pyrenees, at the junction of the rivers Arget and Ariège.

l. 35 four brothers: Bertran was confronted on all sides by brothers; his own, said to number three, particularly Constantine with whom he battled for possession of Hautefort, and locally the brothers Talairan: Guillem and Hélias, Olivier de Mauriac and possibly a fourth, called Ramnulf. Bertran was also constantly embroiled in the feuds amongst the Plantagenets, and the allusion is perhaps to Henry II's four sons, Prince Henry ('the Young King'), Richard of Aquitaine, later King Richard I of England, Geoffrey of Brittany and John ('Lackland'), later King John of England.

ll. 38–9: 'A vivid but distorted rendering of the Provençal' (McDougal, 61). Bertran's lines are 'Baro, metetz en guatge/ chastels e vilas e ciutatz'/ enanz qu' usquecs no'us guerreiatz' (H. J. Chaytor, *The Troubadours of Dante*, 1901, 29), from his poem, 'Be'm platz lo gais temps de pascor', translated by Pound in *The Spirit of Romance* as 'Barons! put in pawn castles, and towns and cities before anyone makes war on us' (p. 48). In 'Troubadours – Their Sorts and Conditions' Pound comments, 'De Born advises the barons to pawn their castles before making war, thus if they won they could redeem them, if they lost the loss fell on the holder of the mortgage' (*LE*, 94).

ll. 40–6: cf. line 26. The 'great scene' is the supposed scene of reconciliation between Bertran and King Henry after the death of Prince Henry at Martel, 1183. It is 'well recounted', said Pound, 'in Smith's *Troubadours at Home*. It is vouched for by many old manuscripts and seems as well authenticated as most Provençal history, though naturally there are found the usual perpetrators of "historic doubt" ' (*Poetry*, December 1915, 146).

l. 51 The Talleyrand: the Talairan family; cf. lines 16–19, 35.

ll. 54–68: Pound incorporates his own first-hand knowledge of the terrain: he had as he says in 'Provincia Deserta' 'walked over En Bertran's old layout' (*CSP*, 131, l. 39). In his note to 'Near Perigord', Pound wrote, 'as to the possibility of a political intrigue behind the apparent love poem we have no evidence save that offered by my own observation of the geography of Perigord and Limoges' (*Poetry*, December 1915, 145–6).

ll. 69–75: Pound adapts the envoi of the 'Dompna', which in his note he translates as 'Papiol, my lodestone, go, through all the courts, sing this canzon,/ how love fareth ill of late; is fallen from his high estate' (ibid., 145). Bertran was the composer of verses, Papiol his 'jongleur' or singer (cf. 'Sestina: Altaforte', l.2).

l. 70 Cembelins: from whom Bertran borrowed 'the expression of her eyes' (*SR*, 47).

l. 71 throat . . . two white hands: borrowed from the Viscountess of Chalais; cf. note on line 8.

l. 80: a general dilemma: 'For purpose of translation', wrote Pound, 'one has, as Rossetti remarks, to cut through various knots, and make arbitrary decisions' (*LE*, 160).

ll. 81–2: Pound wrote: 'No student of the period can doubt that the involved forms, and the veiled meanings in the "trobar clus", grew out of living conditions, and that these songs played a very real part in love intrigue and in the intrigue preceding warfare' (ibid., 94).

ll. 86–7 St. Leider: 'If you wish to make love to women in public, and out loud, you must resort to subterfuge; and Guillaume St Leider even went so far as to get the husband of his lady to do the seductive singing' (ibid., 94).

l. 89: Pound is perhaps attracted to the ironies of 'logopoeia' in the 'veiled meanings' of the troubadours.

l. 90: Pound gives this line as 'And sing not all they have in mind' in a song translated from 'the sardonic Count of Foix' (ibid., 101).

l. 93 heaumes: helmets or crests.

II

l. 100 'al' and 'ochaisos': Bertran's 'Borrowed Lady' begins, 'Domna, puois de me no'us chal/ e partit m'avertz de vos/ senes totas ochaisos' (Chaytor, 25), and this pattern of final sounds is repeated for the first three lines of each of its seven stanzas. The restraints for Provençal poets, said Pound, 'were the tune and rhyme-scheme' (*LE*, 115). He himself submitted to these restraints in his translations from Provençal, particularly of Arnaut Daniel's 'Autet et bas' and 'L' aura amara' (cf. *Tr*, 156–67).

l. 103: cf. the lines in 'Provincia Deserta', 'I have looked south from Hautefort,/ thinking of Montaignac, southward' (*CSP*, 133). Pound identifies with Bertran after the manner of Browning, or as Hugh Kenner suggests, Maurice Hewlett (Kenner, *Pound Era*, 359). Pound's beard was of course red, and Iris Barry remembered his 'greenish cat-eyes' ('The Ezra Pound Period', *Bookman*, October 1931, 165).

l. 104 "magnet": Prov. 'aziman'. Pound applies the term elsewhere to the figure of the Lady (*Tr*, 19).

l. 105 Aubeterre: east of Hautefort.

l. 117 Ventadour: Ventadorn, north-east of Hautefort, the home of the Lady Maria, Maent's sister.

l. 119 Arrimon Luc D'Esparo: an Arramon Luc d'Esparro appears in one of Bertran's poems, designed to stir up the lieges of the Count of Toulouse against the King of Aragon (cf. *SR*, 46).

ll. 123–5: in 1183, after the death of the 'Young King', Richard Coeur-de-Lion, in compact with the Count of Limoges, stormed and captured Hautefort because of the part Bertran had played in aiding his brother against him (cf. Bertran's lines translated by Pound in the poem from which he takes the title 'Near Perigord', 'and they destroy and burn my land, and make wreck of my trees, and scatter the corn through the straw', *SR*, 46). On 2 August 1919 Dorothy Pound wrote to her mother, during the Pounds' stay in Provence, 'Aug 2 at Montignac. We spent last night at Altaforte . . . we slept close to where Henry II's men probably camped, besieging B. de Born' (verso of postcard included in an exhibition catalogue, 'Ezra Pound. The London Years', prepared by Philip Grover, University of Sheffield, 1976). King Henry was not, it seems, present at the siege (Chaytor, 44).

l. 128 Arnaut: Arnaut Daniel, probably the most important Provençal poet for Pound (cf. *SR*, ch. II, and the essay 'Arnaut Daniel' in *LE*, 109–48). If, said Pound, Arnaut 'frequented one court more than another it was the court of King Richard Coeur de Lion, "Plantagenet"' (*SPr*, 26). Arnaut and Richard are pictured here in April 1199 at the siege of the castle of Châlus.

l. 133 leopards: a lion passant, called a leopard in early heraldry, was the device of Richard.

l. 137 de Born is dead: Bertran de Born died in fact in 1214 or 1215. He is said to have become a monk in 1196, in the Abbey of Dâlon, near Hautefort.

l. 140 trobar clus: a term designating the intricate verse forms and hermetic meanings of a type of Provençal poetry, exemplified by Arnaut Daniel.

l. 141 "best craftsman": Dante called Arnaut 'il miglior fabbro' ('the better craftsman') in the *Purgatorio* (XXVI, l. 117). Pound used the phrase as the title of his chapter on Arnaut in *The Spirit of Romance*, and Eliot later applied it to Pound in his dedication to him of *The Waste Land*.

friend: Arnaut addresses Bertran directly in the envoi of his 'Lancan son passat li giure', translated by Pound (*Tr*, 152–5).

l. 146 sister: Bertran wrote a poem in praise of Richard's sister Elena (real name, Matilda), wife of Duke Henry of Brunswick (F. Hueffer, *The Troubadours*, 1878, 210–11).

l. 149: after regaining his holdings, Bertran made peace with Richard and wrote two poems honouring him on his return to Aquitaine in 1194, after the crusades.

l. 152 you . . . métiers: Richard was both a man of action and a sometime poet, composing in both French and Provençal.

l. 154: if Arnaut could not explain Bertran the man, his own art was for Pound a gauge of Bertran's poetry: 'having analysed or even read an analysis of Arnaut, any other Provençal canzon is clearer to one. . . . We know in reading, let us say, de Born, what part is personal, what part is technical, how good it is in manner, how good in matter' (*SPr*, 43). Writing of Gaudier-Brzeska, 'the only person with whom I can really be "Altaforte"' (*SL*, 27), Pound reflected, 'yet what do we, any of us, know of our friends' (*G-B*, 44).

ll. 157–9: Richard was struck in the shoulder by an arrow while besieging Châlus and died of the wound, 6 April 1199. Pound adapted a 'Planh' on his death by Gaucelm Faidit in 'Five Troubadour Songs' (1920); cf. 'Provincia Deserta' (*CSP*, 131, l. 44), 'Here Coeur-de-Lion was slain'.

l. 161 "In sacred odour": a phrase applied to the death of a holy man; Daniel reputedly ended his days in a monastery.

Pound, affecting the style of the Provençal *vida*, writes, 'Nor
is it known if Benvenuto da Imola speaks for certain when he
says En Arnaut went in his age to a monastery' (*LE*, 109).
ll. 163–8: from Dante's *Inferno* (XXVIII, ll. 118–23, 139–42).
Cf. lines 21–7 and Pound's translation (*SR*, 45).

III

In the version in *Poetry* (December 1915) this section begins
with the lines since cancelled, 'I loved a woman. The stars
fell from heaven/ And always our two natures were in strife.'
The suggestion would seem to be that in this section we are
presented with Bertran's 'own speech' (cf. l. 79).
Epigraph: Pound translates 'and they were two in one and one
in two' (*SR*, 45).
ll. 170–6: cf. Pound's own knowledge of the terrain in 'Provincia Deserta', and the movement of a war song by Bertran,
translated by Pound (*SR*, 47).
l. 170 Auvezere: a river near Hautefort.
l. 171 day's eyes: daisies.
émail: (Fr.) 'enamel', used of enamel paintings.
ll. 191–2: cf. Pound's earlier 'Portrait d'une Femme' which
ends,

> In the slow float of different light and deep,
> No! there is nothing! In the whole and all,
> Nothing that's quite your own.
>   Yet this is you.

and also "Blandula, Tenulla, Vagula" (l. 12n.), 'Mirrors
unstill of the eternal change?'.
l. 192: this phrase was turned against Pound by John Gould
Fletcher who wrote in 1919 of Pound's last two volumes
(presumably *Lustra* and *Quia Pauper Amavi*) as 'almost value-
less. They are "a broken bundle of mirrors", the patchwork
and debris of a mind which has never quite been able to find
the living, vivid beauty it set out to seek' (Homberger, 171).

CATHAY

In the second half of 1913 Pound began to acquire the manuscripts, consisting of some sixteen notebooks, of the late Ernest Fenollosa. Fenollosa was an American of Spanish descent, educated at Harvard, who became Professor of Philosophy at the new University of Tokyo in 1878, and then Commissioner of Arts to the Imperial Japanese government. Fenollosa left notes on and prose versions of Japanese Noh plays, the material of an essay, *The Chinese Written Character as a Medium for Poetry*, and transcriptions into Japanese with English prose renderings of classical Chinese poetry. These papers came into Pound's possession through Mrs. Mary Fenollosa, who had already edited her husband's *Epochs of Chinese and Japanese Art* (1911) after his death in 1908 and who, so it seems, had decided to approach Pound on the evidence of his 'Contemporania' in *Poetry* (April 1913). Of the twelve poems in 'Contemporania' the most important in this respect was 'In a Station of the Metro', which Pound in March 1913 had referred to as a hokku, and where he had been careful originally to indicate spaces between the rhythmic units (*SL*, 17). Mrs. Fenollosa may have seen other of Pound's work, perhaps the essay 'A Few Don'ts by an Imagiste' which had appeared in *Poetry* the previous month; but if not, one can understand how 'In a Station of the Metro' would suggest affinities between Imagist practice and Chinese poetry. (Pound later made the connection explicitly, in an article, 'Imagisme and England', in *T.P.'s Weekly*, 20 Feb. 1915, 415.)

But whatever decided Mrs. Fenollosa on Pound as executor in 1913, the Fenollosa MSS clearly confirmed an emerging interest in Pound and his circle. Dorothy Pound had a developed taste in Chinese jade, and Pound reported in December 1913 that she was 'learning Chinese'; Allen Upward had published some 'Chinese stuff' in *Poetry* in 1913 which he had made 'up out of his head' (*SL*, 22), and John Gould Fletcher, an Imagist confrère, had included two poems, 'From the Chinese' and 'From the Japanese', in his *Visions of the Evening* (1913), though he 'knew nothing' of either language (Kenner, *Pound Era*, 196). Fletcher recalled (in 'The Orient and Contemporary Poetry', *The Asian Legacy and American Life*, ed. Arthur E. Christy, 1942, 149) the influence that Lafcadio Hearn and H. A. Giles's *History of Chinese Literature* (1901) and Judith Gautier's *Le Livre de Jade* (1867) had had upon himself; and Pound too had certainly drawn on Giles in making the poems 'After Ch'u Yuan', 'Liu Ch'e', 'Fan-Piece for Her Imperial Lord' and 'Ts'ai Chi'h' for the anthology *Des Imagistes* (1914), the manuscript of which Pound had sent to Alfred Kreymborg, co-editor of the *Glebe*, as early as the summer of 1913 (Gallup, 140). The scent was already there then when Pound received, via the Fenollosa notebooks, an opportunity to work from Chinese and Japanese literature at an unprecedentedly direct source.

Fenollosa's papers in the event provided for four works: *Cathay* (1915), *Certain Noble Plays of Japan* (1916), the four plays of which were reprinted in '*Noh*', or *Accomplishment* (1917), and *The Chinese Written Character as a Medium for Poetry* in *Instigations* (1920). Pound worked on the plays first at Colman's Hatch in Sussex with Yeats, for whom Noh drama was probably of more importance than it was for Pound himself. Pound clearly found at the heart of Noh drama a certain 'concentration', a 'unity of the Image' and an answer to the query as to whether there could ever be a long Imagiste poem, but just as clearly he had to overcome a fundamental lack of sympathy for its psychological, not to say spiritualist interest (cf. *Tr*, 236–7). The plays were perhaps too 'soft', too close to the 'mushy technique' Pound associated with Symbolism, to appeal strongly to him. (Cf. Davie, *Poet as Sculptor*, 47–53.) In 1917, for example, Pound wrote to John Quinn, 'China is fundamental, Japan is not. Japan is a special interest, like Provence, or 12th–13th Century Italy (apart from Dante). I don't mean to say there aren't interesting things in Fenollosa's Japanese stuff. . . . But China is solid' (*SL*, 102). The same letter is concerned with Pound's attempt to secure a publication for *The Chinese Written Character*, and it would be fair to assume that it was this essay which stimulated Pound's preference for China over Japan. (It was serialized after a good deal of difficulty and anxiety in the *Little Review*, September–December 1919, included then in *Instigations* (1920) and received its first separate edition only in 1936.)

In Pound's view, *The Chinese Written Character* was obviously seminal, it was 'a whole basis of aesthetic' (*SL*, 61). Fenollosa's central claim was that the Chinese ideogram retained its original pictorial representation of things and actions, 'based upon a vivid shorthand picture of the operations of nature' (*Chinese Written Character*, 1936, 8) which enacted 'the transference of force from agent to object' (p. 7). As such the lesson for English poetry was that an analogous energy lies, often submerged, in the active verb and therefore in the simple transitive sentence. Fenollosa read Chinese with the assistance of instructors, and it is clear that in so far as he (or they) persisted in seeing Chinese through the eyes of Japanese his magnificent insight is purblind. For while Japanese and Chinese share the same small set of 'radicals' or basic characters, so that it is possible for a Japanese to sight-read a Chinese text without being able to speak it, the two languages are quite distinct. In particular Fenollosa failed to allow that the radicals with pictorial origins have many possible applications which are realized in combinations with other characters having a purely phonetic function, and that these indicate their appropriate meaning in a given compound:

Chinese characters are made up of single diagrams or combinations of diagrams representing objects. . . . The 'radical' remains invariably an ideograph, but the other

component or one of the other components of the combination may be purely phonetic in its function. Thus the
diagram for horse 馬 *ma*, when combined with the mouth
diagram 口 repeated: 口 口, sheds its graphic significance
to serve as a mere indicator of the sound of the Chinese
character for *scold*: 罵 (also *Ma*).

(Hsieh Wen Tung, 'English Translations of
Chinese Poetry', *Criterion*, April 1938, 406)

(Cf. also the discussion in Kenner, *Pound Era*, 223–31.)

But if Fenollosa's inferences are somewhat discredited it
perhaps remains true, as Pound suggested, that 'the theory is
a very good one for poets to go by' (*SL*, 82), although it is not
altogether clear that Pound himself did go by it; 'he did not',
says Hsieh Wen Tung, 'apply his deductions in his translations
– fortunately' (op. cit., 407). Pound's self-confessed ignorance
of Chinese prompted, in 1915 perhaps, certain cautions.
Certainly later his reservations are exactly in line with expert
strictures on Fenollosa. Writing to Katue Kitasono in 1937, for
example, Pound said, 'When I did *Cathay*, I had no inkling of
the technique of sound, which I am now convinced *must* exist
or have existed in Chinese poetry' (*SL*, 293). And in 1940, to
Santayana, Pound wrote,

> Not the picturesque element I was trying to emphasize so
> much as the pt. re western man 'defining' by receding: red,
> color, vibration, mode of being, etc; Chinese by putting
> together concrete objects as in F's example:
>
> | red | cherry |
> | iron rust | flamingo |
>
> Am not sure the lexicographers back him up.

(ibid., 333)

Pound, one may suppose then, was attracted in Fenollosa and
in Chinese poetry to a way of seeing and thinking (of 'defining'),
that stays close to particulars and which therefore corroborated
and extended his Imagist programme.

Unlike Fenollosa (and unlike H. A. Giles and Arthur

Waley, whose *170 Chinese Poems* appeared in 1915), Pound had
no direct, personal knowledge of either Chinese or Japanese
and this was, paradoxically, his great advantage as a translator
in *Cathay*. (One cannot help but note that these poems – of
all Pound's translations the most removed in their source from
common access – were well received from the beginning.)
Pound's gift in *Cathay*, as elsewhere, was that he could enter
and recast an alien idiom. And if the Chinese of *Cathay*, like
other literatures, provided Pound with a mask, then it was
(as they were) as much a linguistic mask as any other. Like
earlier poems, *Cathay* was an exercise in invigorating the
English language and the English literary tradition and therefore, a way also of investigating poetic measure. Pound's citing
precedents and analogues for *Cathay*, his remark to Kate Buss
for example that 'all the verbal constructions of *Cathay* [were]
already tried in "Provincia Deserta" ' (ibid., 101), and his
discovering the convertibility of the Anglo-Saxon half-line
with the ideogram (*ABC of R*, 51), are remarks made at this
level of a sustained exploration of poetic language on different
fronts. *Cathay* then constitutes a moment in a concerted
apprenticeship which allowed here an emphasis and confirmation: of Imagism perhaps, but more precisely, in Pound's
preferred term, of 'phanopoeia'.

The anthology *Des Imagistes* had appeared under Pound's
editorship in February 1914, but by August he had dissociated
himself from the machinations of Amy Lowell and the diluted
productions of her forthcoming *Some Imagist Poets*. (Amy
Lowell with the aid of Florence Ayscough replied with a
jealous and blunted rebuff to Pound's *Cathay* in her *Fir Flower
Tablets*, 1921.) Pound insisted to Amy Lowell that 'Imagisme',
to have any meaning, must 'stand for hard light, clear edges',
for 'a certain clarity and intensity' (*SL*, 38, 39). And looking
back later, he was to write in the *ABC of Reading*,

 The defect of earlier imagist propaganda was not in mis-
 statement but in incomplete statement. The diluters took
 the handiest and easiest meaning, and thought only of the

STATIONARY image. If you can't think of imagism or phanopoeia as including the moving image, you will have to make a really needless division of fixed image and praxis or action.

I have taken to using the term phanopoeia to get away from irrelevant particular connotations tangled with a particular group of young people who were writing in 1912.

(p. 52)

Pound had extricated himself from the misfortunes of the Imagist movement through the designation 'phanopoeia': the 'casting of images upon the visual imagination', 'the greatest drive toward utter precision of word' in a mode which could 'be translated almost, or wholly, intact'. 'The Chinese', Pound added, '(more particularly Rihaku and Omakitsu) attained the known maximum of *phanopœia*' (*LE*, 25–7).

This rethinking and refinement was initiated in the period of *Cathay*, which is not then simply an exemplar of Imagism, but a defence and extension of Imagism as Pound understood it. The Fenollosa papers opened one extremely fruitful avenue for this realignment. Another was Vorticism, whose organ *Blast* appeared in June 1914 and July 1915. In September 1914, Pound published his article 'Vorticism' in the *Fortnightly Review* (1 Sept. 1914, 461–71, reprinted in *Gaudier-Brzeska*, 1916, 81–94), in which in attempting to ally poetry with the new painting and sculpture, he had presented the image as 'the poet's pigment', 'the primary form' upon which the poet as vorticist essentially relied: 'The image is not an idea. It is a radiant node or cluster; it is what I can, and must perforce, call a VORTEX, from which, and through which, and into which, ideas are constantly rushing' (*G-B*, 92). One can see here again a refutation of the 'stationary image' and an affinity, if nothing more, with Fenollosa's account of the noun and verb:

A true noun, an isolated thing, does not exist in nature. Things are only the terminal points, or rather the meeting points, of actions, cross-sections cut through actions, snapshots. Neither can a pure verb, an abstract motion, be possible in nature. The eye sees noun and verb as one: things in motion, motion in things, and so the Chinese conception tends to represent them.

(Chinese Written Character, 10)

It would be too much to claim the poems in *Cathay* as Vorticist, but their cleanness, the angled cuts Pound makes in the unit of the poetic line, and the vitality of his transpositions (often a matter of the choice of active verbs) surely situate them in the current of ideas that flowed through Fenollosa and Vorticism and helped constitute the tone of the period for which, as Eliot said, Pound 'invented' Chinese poetry (Introduction to *Selected Poems*, 1928, 14–15).

To recall the association with Vorticism is to return *Cathay* to its historical moment. The first number of *Blast* appeared eight days before the assassination of the Archduke Franz Ferdinand, and Pound's essay, 'Vorticism', one month into the First World War. Ford Madox Ford was perhaps the first to detect the contemporary reference in *Cathay* (Homberger, 168) and Hugh Kenner, principally, has since maintained that *Cathay* as a whole has war as 'its true theme' (*Pound Era*, 201–2). This is an enticing view, particularly as it concerns three poems: 'Song of the Bowmen of Shu', 'Lament of the Frontier Guard' and probably 'South-Folk in Cold Country', which Pound sent to Gaudier-Brzeska in the trenches at Aisne in December 1914. Gaudier felt that 'the poems depict our situation in a wonderful way' (*G-B*, 58 and cf. p. 68) and it does indeed appear that the involvement of men such as Gaudier and Hulme in the war moved Pound himself to respond to it. To *Cathay* one might add in this way the two items, 'Poem: Abbreviated from the Conversation of Mr. T. E. H[ulme]' subtitled 'Trenches, St. Eloi' (*Catholic Anthology*, November 1915), and a war poem, '1915: February', which Pound sent to Mencken's *Smart Set*, but which was never published.

But the fact that these two poems are forgotten or lost seems more significant than their composition, and Kenner's claim for *Cathay*, while it applies, if obliquely, to those poems sent to Gaudier, is really both extravagant and limited. Pound was concerned not so much with the war itself as with its consequences for 'civilisation'. As he wrote to Harriet Monroe, 'It's all very well to see the troops flocking from the four corners of Empire. It is a very fine sight. But, but, but, civilization, after the battle is over . . .' (*SL*, 46). In fact all Pound's activities in these years, from his visit in homage to the irascible opponent of Empire, Wilfrid Scawen Blunt, and his prospectus for a College of Arts in 1914, to his redefinition of Imagism and his part in Vorticism, register a resistance and an alternative to contemporary English art and culture. This stance, it is clear, implied some re-education for Pound as well as for others; in early 1915, for example, following a clue in Fenollosa, he had begun to read Confucius and was campaigning for an imminent 'renaissance' in *Poetry* and the *New Age*. In the series 'Affirmations', he wrote:

> China is no less stimulating than Greece . . . these new masses of unexplored arts and facts are pouring into the vortex of London. They cannot help bringing about changes as great as the Renaissance changes, even if we set ourselves blindly against it. As it is, there is life in the fusion. The complete man must have more interest in things which are in seed and dynamic than in things which are dead, dying, static.
>
> (*New Age*, 14 Jan. 1915, 277–8; reprinted in *G-B*, 116–17)

The hope and effort in such an awakening provide the measure, one feels, for Pound's 'invention' in *Cathay* and for its attachment to its times.

As originally published in April 1915, the sequence ended with 'South-Folk in Cold Country', and included 'The Seafarer' between 'Exile's Letter' and FOUR POEMS OF DEPARTURE. Pound closed with the note:

> I have not come to the end of Ernest Fenollosa's notes by a long way, nor is it entirely perplexity that causes me to

cease from translation. . . . But if I give [the poems] . . . with the necessary breaks for explanation, and a tedium of notes, it is quite certain that the personal hatred in which I am held by many, and the *invidia* which is directed against me because I have dared to declare my belief in certain young artists, will be brought to bear first on the flaws of such translation, and will then be merged into depreciation of the whole book of translations. Therefore I give only these unquestionable poems.

For its appearance in *Lustra* (1916), Pound omitted 'The Seafarer' and added the present last four poems. The existing 18 poems were selected from some 150 in Fenollosa's notebooks. Cf. Pound's discussion in the articles 'Chinese Poetry' and 'Chinese Poetry. II' in *To-Day*, April and May 1918.
Subtitle:
Rihaku: the Chinese poet Li Po (A.D. 701–762). Pound took the Japanese form from Fenollosa. Out of 27 poems by Li Po in the Fenollosa notebooks, Pound selected 12 for *Cathay* (see also his 'Epitaphs' in *Lustra*). Li Po was a poet of the T'ang dynasty. As Arthur Waley describes him he was an example of the concern of writers in this period with new form rather than new content.

Often where his translators would make us suppose he is expressing a fancy of his own, he is in reality skilfully utilising some poem by T'ao Ch'ien or Hsieh T'iao. It is for his versification that he is admired, and with justice. He represents a reaction against the formal prosody of his immediate predecessors.

(*170 Chinese Poems*, 1920, 16)

The resemblance one feels with Pound himself is confirmed in his own account of Li Po as 'a great "compiler"'; 'A compiler', he adds, 'does not merely gather together, his chief honour consists in weeding out, and even in revising. Thus, a part of Rihaku's work consists of old themes rewritten, of a sort of summary of the poetry which had been before him' ('Chinese Poetry', *To-Day*, April 1918, 55).

Ernest Fenollosa: (1853–1908); cf. headnote above. Some of the manuscript notes of the poems Pound translated have been reproduced in the following: Lawrence Chisholm, *Fenollosa: The Far East and American Culture*, 1963 (for the text of 'Song of the Bowmen of Shu', pp. 251–2); *Ezra Pound: Perspectives*, ed. Noel Stock, 1965 (for 'The Beautiful Toilet', p. 178); Wai-Lim Yip, *Ezra Pound's Cathay*, 1969 (Appendix I contains the texts for 'Song of the Bowmen of Shu', 'The Beautiful Toilet', 'Lament of the Frontier Guard' and 'South-Folk in Cold Country', pp. 169–79); M. Reck, *Ezra Pound: A Close Up*, 1968 (the last lines of 'Exile's Letter' and the full text of 'The River-Merchant's Wife', pp. 167–71); Hugh Kenner, *The Pound Era*, 1972 (texts of 'The Beautiful Toilet', the epigraph to 'Four Poems of Departure', 'South-Folk in Cold Country', sections of 'To-Em-Mei's "The Unmoving Cloud"', pp. 192–222).

Professors Mori and Ariga: Fenollosa worked under the instruction of Kainan Mori (1863–1911) between 1899 and 1901, with the further assistance of Nagao Ariga (1860–1921), a former philosophy student at the Imperial University, Tokyo. Mori was a distinguished Chinese scholar and 'Ranshi' poet (a Japanese writing poetry in the classical manner). Fenollosa had worked earlier in 1896 with the less distinguished Mr. Hirai and in 1898 with a Mr. Shida.

Many errors exist in the Japanese names given in the poems as they appear in *Collected Shorter Poems*, which have been corrected in the present *Selected Poems*. The incorrect forms are not given here.

The following commentaries on *Cathay* are referred to below in short form, by author's name and page number only:

Richard P. Benton, 'A Gloss on Pound's "Four Poems of Departure"', *Literature East and West*, September 1966, 292–301

Achilles Fang, 'Fenollosa and Pound', *Harvard Journal of Asian Studies*, xx (1957), 213–33

Pen-ti Lee and Donald Murray, 'The Quality of *Cathay*: Ezra Pound's Early Translations of Chinese Poems', *Literature East and West*, September 1966, 264–77

Wai-Lim Yip, *Ezra Pound's Cathay* (1969)

Song of the Bowmen of Shu

Writing to Kate Buss in 1917, Pound suggested she compare his poem with the version in William Jennings's *The Shi King* (1891) (*SL*, 101). The first two stanzas of Jennings's translation, 'Song of the Troops during the Expedition against the Hin-Yun', run as follows:

> They gather the fern, the royal fern,
>   Now at its first appearing.
> O when shall we turn, aye homeward turn?
>   One year its end is nearing.
> O still, because of the wild Hin-Yuns,
>   From house and home remain we;
> O still, because of the wild Hin-Yuns,
>   Nor rest nor leisure gain we.
>
> They gather the fern, the royal fern,
>   Now supple grown and flexile.
> O when shall we turn, aye homeward turn?
>   For grievous is this exile.
> Disconsolate hearts here ache and ache,
>   And thirst we bear, and hunger;
> And endless patrols forbid us make
>   The home inquiries longer.

Compare also Ode 167 in *The Classic Anthology defined by Confucius* (1954), pp. 86–7, for Pound's later version of this poem in ballad form.

l. 1: Gaudier-Brzeska responded from the trenches to this and two other poems Pound had sent him, 'The poems depict our situation in a wonderful way. We do not yet eat the young nor old fern-shoots but we cannot be over-victualled where we stand' (*G-B*, 58).

l. 3 Ken-in: Chinese Hsien-yün (the Huns).

ll. 9–13: Gaudier-Brzeska wrote to John Cournos in December 1914:

> When you have turned to a warrior you become hardened to many evils . . . like the Chinese bowmen in Ezra's poem we had rather eat fern shoots than go back now. . . . If you can write me all about the Kensington colony the neo-Greeks and the neo-Chinese. Does the Egoist still appear? What does it contain?
>
> (Kenner, *Pound Era*, 203)

ll. 11–15: Pound modifies the grandiose appearance of the General in the original and the soldiers' willingness to fight (Yip, 118).

ll. 13–14: Pound misses a line, 'Flowers of the Cherry', probably because of the confused state of Fenollosa's notes (Yip, 115).

l. 15: a good example of Pound's breaking the iambic pentameter.

tired: a departure from the text, prepared by Ariga, which has 'hitched'.

l. 17 By heaven: this has no equivalent in the Chinese line. Pound repeats 'tired' (cf. line 15) where Ariga has 'tied'.

Bunno: Pound originally ascribed the poem, wrongly, to Kutsugen. In the London edition of *Lustra* (1916) it was attributed to 'Bunno, Very Early', then in the American editions of both *Lustra* (1916) and *Personae* (1926) to 'Bunno, Reputedly 1100 B.C.' According to Lee and Murray (p. 275), 'Scholars have not determined the author of the poem.'

Bunno is Wen-Wang, i.e. King Wen of the Chou dynasty (Fang, 223). Ariga records that the poem refers to an incident at the close of the Yin dynasty (1401–1121 B.C.) when Bunno the commander-in-chief of the western princes was despatched against the Huns. He composed this poem in the person of a common soldier to show his sympathy and alleviate the condition of his men (cf. Yip, Appendix I, 169–70).

The Beautiful Toilet

Title: 'Ancient Poems no. 3' (Yip, 186); 'Seventeen Old Poems. 2' (Arthur Waley, *Chinese Poems*, 1976, 57). Pound takes his title from the fifth line of the Chinese, given by Fenollosa as

> beauty of (ditto) red powder toilet
> face

and then omits this line from the text of his poem. Pound suggested to Kate Buss that she compare his version with that by H. A. Giles (*History of Chinese Literature*, 1967 reprint, 97).

l. 1 Blue, blue: the first six lines of the Fenollosa transcript commence with a reduplication. Pound follows Fenollosa here and in line 4, but more subtly elsewhere. The word 'blue' is suggested by Fenollosa. Other translations (e.g. Giles and Waley) have the more obvious but perhaps more correct 'green'. 'Blue' appears for the same Chinese character, 'ch'ing', in the first line of 'Taking leave of a Friend' (cf. Kenner, *Pound Era*, 193–5, 216–17), at line 25 of 'The River Song' and at line 4 of 'The River-Merchant's Wife'.

ll. 5–6: Pound makes a definite break where the Chinese has none.

Mei Shêng: Giles had attributed the poem to Mei Shêng. In Fenollosa it appeared as anonymous.

The River Song

Title: 'Chanting on the river' (Yip, 149).

For Pound's earlier renderings of Japanese words, corrected here, see *Collected Shorter Poems*, pp. 138–40.

l. 1 satō-wood: Chinese 'sha-t'ang' ('spice-wood').

l. 6 Sennin: described by Pound as 'the Chinese spirits of nature or of the air' (*SL*, 180). Cf. 'Exile's Letter', line 26, and 'Sennin Poem by Kakuhaku'.

ll. 7–8 and . . . them: compare 'The Seafarer' (ll. 63–5), 'the crying lone-flyer,/ Whets for the whale-path the heart irresistibly,/ O'er tracks of ocean'.

l. 9 Kutsu: Chinese Ch'ü Yüan; cf. Pound's 'After Ch'u Yuan' (*CSP*, 118).

l. 11 King So: Chinese King Ch'u (Yip, 188).

l. 16 blue islands: a secluded fairyland (Yip, 151).

l. 18 Han: the Han River flows from north-east central China into the Yangtze at Hankow.

ll. 19–22: Pound's one infamous howler in *Cathay*, where he dissolves the title of a second poem by Li Po into the continuous text of a single poem. Kenner suggests that Pound's error can be traced to the Fenollosa MSS, Pound mistaking a blank left-hand page at this point in the notebook for absence of comment rather than the beginning of a new poem (Kenner, *Pound Era*, 204).

Yip translates the title as follows, 'Poem composed at the ✔ command of the Emperor/ in I-Chin Park on the Dragon-Pond as the willows are in their fresh green and the new/ orioles are singing in their thousand ways' (Appendix II, 188). It is just possible that Pound intended an irony here, such as he detects in Sextus Propertius, between Li Po living and writing in the first poem at his own pleasure, and in the second at the command of the Emperor. Certainly Pound's additions ('moped' and an exclamation mark in line 19 and 'aimlessly' in line 22) introduce a tedium and disrespect, delivered in the first person, which are not in the original.

l. 23 Ei-shū: Chinese Ying-chou (Yip, 188).

l. 25 half-blue: 'half-green' (Yip, 190); cf. note on 'The Beautiful Toilet', line 1.

l. 29 "Ken-kwan": onomatopoeic bird call; Chinese 'chien-kuan' (Fang, 224).

l. 32 Kō: the Chinese capital Hao, capital of the kings Wen and Wu of the Chou dynasty; cf. *Classic Anthology*, Part 3, Bk. I, esp. p. 160.

l. 33 Five clouds: 'auspicious breath', i.e. the imperial influences on man and nature (Yip, 190).

purple sky: 'dwelling of the celestial emperor' (ibid.).

ll. 36–40: T. S. Eliot compared these lines with lines 28–41 of 'Provincia Deserta' (*CSP*, 131). It shows, he says, 'The language was ready for the Chinese Poetry' ('Ezra Pound; His Metric and Poetry', 1917, in *To Criticise the Critics*, 1965, 180). Pound had written to Kate Buss, 'I think you will find all the verbal constructions of *Cathay* already tried in "Provincia Deserta"' (*SL*, 101).

l. 36 Hōrai: Chinese Penglai (Yip, 190), P'eng-lai (Fang, 224).
l. 37 Shi: Chinese Chih-shih (Yip, 190), ch'ih (Fang, 224).
l. 38 Jō-rin: the Shang-lin Park, famous for its court life.

The River-Merchant's Wife: A Letter

Title: 'The Song of Ch'ang-kan' (Yip, 192).
Arthur Waley responded to Pound's translation by a version of his own given to the China Society at the School of Oriental Studies, London, 21 Nov. 1918. The first ten lines of his 'Ch'ang-kan' ran as follows:

> Soon after I wore my hair covering my forehead
> I was plucking flowers and playing in front of the gate,
> When you came by, walking on bamboo-stilts
> Along the trellis, playing with green plums.
> We both lived in the village of Ch'ang-kan,
> Two children, without hate or suspicion.
> At fourteen I became your wife;
> I was shame-faced and never dared smile.
> I sank my head against the dark wall;
> Called to, a thousand times, I did not turn.
>
> (*The Poet Li Po A.D. 701–762*, 1919, 18)

George Steiner reports that 'on sinological grounds alone "The River-Merchant's Wife: A Letter" is closer to Li Po' (*After Babel*, 1975, 358). Pound said of the poem,

> Perhaps the most interesting form of modern poetry is to be found in Browning's 'Men and Women'. . . . From Ovid to Browning this sort of poem was very much neglected. It is interesting to find, in eighth-century China, a poem which

136

might have slipped into Browning's work without causing any surprise save by its simplicity and its naïve beauty.

('Chinese Poetry. II', *To-Day*, May 1918, 93–4)

The version Pound then gives in 'Chinese Poetry. II' differs slightly from the present poem.

ll. 1–3: compare the translation by Amy Lowell and Florence Ayscough, 'When the hair of your unworthy one first began to cover the forehead,/ She picked flowers and played in front of the door./ Then you, my love, came riding a bamboo horse' (*Fir Flower Tablets*, 1921, 28). Fenollosa offered, 'My hair was at first covering my brows (child's method of wearing hair).' Stock tells of how Pound considered using the word 'bangs' and that Dorothy Pound protested that the better word was 'fringe', before Pound decided on the present line (*Life*, 210).

l. 4 blue plums: Waley has 'green plums'; cf. note on 'The Beautiful Toilet', line 1.

l. 5 Chōkan: Chinese Ch'ang-kan (Fang, 224).

l. 7: in the later version Pound had, 'At fourteen I married you, My Lord' ('Chinese Poetry. II', op. cit., 94). Fenollosa had 'At fourteen I became your wife', as does Waley. Pound, says Steiner, 'communicates precisely the nuance of ceremonious innocence, of special address from child to adult which constitutes the charm of the original' (*After Babel*, 358).

l. 12: in the version given in *To-Day* Pound had, 'I desired my dust to be mingled with your dust' ('Chinese Poetry. II', op. cit., 94).

ll. 13–14: in the Chinese these lines 'allude respectively to (1) the story of Wei Sheng who drowned waiting for his girl who never showed up, (2) to the story of a woman turned to stone waiting for the return of her husband' (Yip, 142). Pound generalizes their reference.

l. 16 Ku-tō-en: Chinese Ch'ü-t'ang, which has an islet called Yen-yü-tui (Fang, 225). The original allusion here is to a warning in a popular song on the dangers of sailing by the Yen Yü rocks in the Chü-t'ang River (cf. Yip, 142).

l. 19: in the version given in *To-Day* Pound had 'You dragged your feet, by the gate, when you were departing' (Chinese Poetry. II', op. cit., 94).

l. 26 Kiang: (Chiang), generally the word for 'river' itself; cf. 'Separation on the River Kiang' (title and l. 5n.).

l. 29 Chō-fū-Sa: Chinese, Ch'ang-feng-sha (Fang, 225). Yip translates as 'Long Wind Sand' (p. 194). The reference is to a beach several hundred miles up river from Nanking.

Poem by the Bridge at Ten-Shin

Title: 'Ku Feng no. 18 (After the style of Ancient Poems)' (Yip, 196).

Ten-Shin: Chinese, T'ien-chin (Fang, 225).

l. 11 Sei-jō-yō: Chinese Hsi Shang-yang (Fang, 225). Yip translates as 'Shang-Yang Palace' (p. 196).

l. 14 far borders: the Chinese means 'the capital' (Lee and Murray, 269).

l. 28 yellow dogs: Li Po points a moral here, through a series of allusions, on the folly of Chinese ministers who outstayed their period of office or the reign of their emperors. These were annotated in the Fenollosa text by Professor Mori. Pound omits the stated moral ('Mission accomplished to stay on/ Means, in history, a greater downfall', Yip, 198) and was left in this line with Fenollosa's 'Yellow dogs useless lamented', a reference to a luckless minister Li Ssu who yearned on the point of execution to go rabbiting once more with his son and yellow dog (Kenner, *Pound Era*, 205). In Pound's line the dogs are made to howl a warning to those who indulge in court life.

l. 29 Ryokushu: Chinese Lu-chu or Lü-chu (Fang, 225). The allusion here is to a minister, Shih Ch'ung, who was disposed of because he would not surrender his mistress to the prince, Sun Hsin. The mistress, Lü Chu, was driven to suicide. Pound contrasts her with those who idle at court.

ll. 31–3 Han-rei: Chinese Fan Li (Fang, 225). The contrasting example in the Chinese of a minister who left the court incognito (*his* hair down) and in good time (Kenner, op. cit.).

The Jewel Stairs' Grievance

Title: 'Jade Steps' Grievance' (Yip, 200).
Yip suggests this is an example of a genre poem in Chinese and offers of the same type a poem by Hsieh Ti'ao, 'I let down the beaded blind in the hall at night/ Fireflies fly around and take rest/ Through the long night I sew gauze dresses/ How can there be an end to my thoughts of you?' (p. 66 and n.).

l. 3: a word-for-word annotation reads 'let down crystal blind' (Yip, 66). Pound supplies the personal pronoun.
NOTE: Pound introduces a similar note on the poem in his article 'Chinese Poetry', with the comment:

> I have never found any occidental who could 'make much' of that poem at one reading. Yet upon careful examination we find that everything is there, not merely by 'suggestion' but by a sort of mathematical process of reduction. Let us consider what circumstances would be needed to produce just the words of this poem. You can play Conan Doyle if you like.

(*To-Day*, April 1918, 55–6)

Lament of the Frontier Guard

Title: 'Ku Feng no. 14' (Yip, 202).
Fenollosa worked on this poem with Mr. Hirai. Pound sent his translation, with 'The Bowmen of Shu' and 'South-Folk in Cold Country' to Gaudier-Brzeska in 1914 (*G-B*, 58, 68).
l. 2: Yip comments that 'Fenollosa, or perhaps Hirai for that matter, did not even understand that the first two words are meant to be a compound, meaning the sound of leaves or grass blown by autumn wind, suggesting bleakness, dismalness, loneliness etc.' (p. 85). Pound restores the meaning of the original.
l. 7: a word-for-word version of the Chinese is 'border/ village/ no left-behind/ wall'. Fenollosa had given 'side   village not leave   fence' (Yip, 85).

ll. 11–13: these lines correspond to lines 10–12 of the Chinese, with Pound's translation of line 10 appearing as his line 13. Yip gives the word-for-word version:

10. Heaven's-pride (the Huns, the barbarians)/ malicious/ martial/ warlikeness.
11. awful(ly)/ anger (v.)/ our/ holy (majestic)/ emperor,
12. labor(v.)/ army/ employ/ war-drums.

(p. 87)

Fenollosa has no mention of 'barbarians' and his final gloss to line 12 ('to soothe the army it became a main matter of the Emperor to employ music') 'gives a meaning almost entirely opposite to the original' (ibid.). Pound intuitively corrects Fenollosa's omission and error.

ll. 23–4: Fenollosa's notes supply the information that the death of Governor Ri and the incident referred to in the last line '[. . . happened in Go, just before Rihaku. It was in the northwest of China]'.

l. 23 Riboku: ('Rihaku' in *CSP*, 143 and *Tr*, 195). Chinese Li Mu (Fang, 225), a famous general who died fighting the Huns, 223 B.C.

l. 24: Pound's 'fed to' clarifies Fenollosa's 'Frontiersmen feed the wolves and tigers'.

Exile's Letter

Title: 'Remembering our Excursion in the Past: A Letter sent to Commissary Yen of Ch'ao County' (Yip, 204).

Pound published this poem separately in advance of *Cathay* (April 1915), in *Poetry* (March 1915, 258–61), with a note that Li Po was 'usually considered the greatest poet in China'. This was Giles's opinion in his *History of Chinese Literature* (p. 151). Shortly after, Arthur Waley, publishing in 1919 a translation of the poem under the title 'Sent to the Commissary Yüan of Ch'iao City, in Memory of Former Excursions', found this a ridiculous judgement on Li Po (*The Poet Li Po A.D. 701–762*, 5). Later still he conceded that Pound's poem was a 'brilliant paraphrase' (*The Poetry and Career of Li Po 701–762 A.D.*, 1950, 12).

Pound himself clearly singled out 'Exile's Letter'. On the publication of *Cathay*, he sent a copy to John Quinn with the inscription, 'I rather like the "Exile's Letter". Yrs. E.P.' (quoted in Norman, 181), and in October he wrote to Harriet Monroe, 'The average of the year has been perhaps better than the two years before, but there has been no particularly notable work. Except "Prufrock" (and, si licet, "The Exile's Letter")' (*SL*, 64). In *Umbra* (1920) also, Pound cited 'Exile's Letter' with 'The Seafarer' and *Homage to Sextus Propertius* as one of his 'major personae' (p. 128). The connection with 'The Seafarer' here is significant. In *Cathay* 'Exile's Letter' had immediately preceded 'The Seafarer', Pound merely indicating their contemporaneity. Later, he elaborated his sense of their equivalence:

> I once got a man to start translating the **Seafarer** into Chinese. It came out almost directly into Chinese verse, with two solid ideograms in each half-line.
>
> Apart from the Seafarer I know no other European poems of the period that you can hang up with the 'Exile's Letter' of Li Po, displaying the West on a par with the Orient.
>
> (*ABC of R*, 51)

The following notes refer by author to the translations by Arthur Waley in *The Poetry and Career of Li Po* (1950), pp. 12–15; by Wai-Lim Yip in *Ezra Pound's Cathay* (1969), pp. 204–10; and to Achilles Fang's 'Fenollosa and Pound', op. cit., pp. 226–7.

l. 1 Tō So-kiu: a proper name for Chinese Tung Tsao-chiu (Yip).
Rakuyō: Chinese Lo-yang (Fang).
Gen: i.e. Commissary Yen (Yip); Chancellor Yüan (Fang).
l. 3 Ten-shin: Chinese T'ien-chin (Fang); cf. 'Poem by the Bridge at Ten-shin'.
l. 12 Wai: the Huai River (Yip).

l. 14 Raku-hoku: Chinese Lo (Yip).

l. 17 Sen-jō: Chinese 'hsien-ch'eng' (Fang), 'City of Immortals' (Yip).

l. 23 Kan: the river Han (Yip).

l. 24 "True man": the reference is to the Taoist hermit, Hu Tzu-Yang, for whose grave Li Po composed an inscription. Waley has 'Holy man'.

Shi-yō: Chinese Tzu-yang (Fang).

l. 25 mouth-organ: a deliberate anachronism. Waley has 'reed pipe', Yip 'jade flute'; cf. line 51.

l. 26 San-ka: Chinese Ts'ang-hsia (Fang). Yip suggests 'the Tower of Feasting Mist'.

Sennin: Chinese 'hsien-jen' (Fang), 'Spirits of the Air'; cf. 'The River Song' (l. 6 n.). This is Pound's addition to the line in the original.

l. 28 Kan-chū: Chinese Han-chung (Fang), 'Middle Han' (Yip), the region south of the river Han at line 23.

l. 34 So: Chinese Ch'u (Fang), a province north of Hankow.

l. 37 Hei Shu: Chinese Ping-chou (Fang), in central Shansi province.

l. 47 blue: 'green' (Waley), 'emerald' (Yip); cf. note on 'The Beautiful Toilet', line 1.

l. 50 blue: 'grey' (Waley), 'green' (Yip).

ll. 63–4: compare 'The Seafarer', 'Days little durable,/ And all arrogance of earthen riches,/ There come now no kings nor Caesars/ Nor gold-giving lords like those gone' (ll. 82–5).

l. 66 Yō Yū: Chinese Yang Hsiung (53 B.C.–A.D. 18), 'author of the rhymeprose on the Ch'ang-yang Palace' (Fang).

Chōyō song: Chinese Ch'ang-yang fu (Fang). The allusion here is to the practice of civil service promotion on the basis of literary competition. 'Yō Yū' (Yang Hsiung) had tried to secure promotion with his prose song 'Ch'ang Yang'.

l. 71 San palace: Chinese Ts'an-t'ai, 'Ts'an terrace' (Fang).

ll. 72–80: Waley closes the 'Exile's Letter':

And should you ask how many were my regrets at
    parting –

They fell upon me thick as the flowers that fall at
  Spring's end.
But I cannot tell you all – could not even if I went on
  thinking for ever,
So I call in the boy and make him kneel here and tie
  this up
And send it to you, a remembrance from a thousand
  miles away.

(p. 15)

ll. 72–6: compare 'The Seafarer', 'No man at all going the
earth's gait/ But age fares against him, his face paleth,/
Grey-haired he groaneth, knows gone companions,/ Lordly
men, are to earth o'ergiven' (ll. 92–5).

l. 76: cf. 'now in the heart indestructible' (Canto LXXVII,
494/465).

ll. 77–80: Fenollosa's gloss ran, 'So calling to me my son I
make him sit on the ground for a long time/ And write to my
dictation/ And sending them to you over a thousand miles we
think of each other at a distance' (Stock, *Life*, 211).

FOUR POEMS OF DEPARTURE

Epigraph:
Title: 'To See Yüan Erh off as Envoy to An-hsi' (Yip, 210).
Cf. Kenner for the Fenollosa notes and a discussion of the
'sonoric intricacies' of these six lines (*Pound Era*, 200–1).

l. 1: Lee and Murray suggest that the Chinese means 'Morning
rain wets the light dust at Wei' (p. 269), but that the Chinese
word Pound translates as 'light' can mean 'bright, light
morning'.

l. 6 Go: Pound misread Fenollosa's 'Yo', i.e. 'the Yang pass'
(Fang, 227) in Kansu on the extreme border with Mongolian
territory.

Rihaku or Omakitsu: the poem is by Omakitsu (Wang Wei,
A.D. 699–759). Pound described him as 'the real modern – even
Parisian – of VIII cent. China' (*SL*, 101).

Separation on the River Kiang

Title: 'To See Meng Hao-jan off to Yang-Chou' (Yip, 212). Meng Hao-jan was a poet, recluse and friend of Li Po (Benton, 294).
Kiang: river; cf. note on 'The River-Merchant's Wife: A Letter', line 26.
l. 1: Fenollosa gives:

ko	jin	sei	gi	Ko	Kaku	ro
old	acquaint-ance	west	leave	...	.....	..

An old acquaintance, starting further West, takes leave of KKR

(Kenner, *Pound Era*, 204)

Pound converts 'ko jin' into a proper name, fails to see (as Fenollosa did) that 'west leave' means to 'leave' not 'go to' the west, and gives a fictive Japanese place-name,' 'Ko-kaku-ro', where the Chinese (Huang-hao-lou, Fang, 227) refers to the Yellow Crane Tower overlooking the Yangtze at Wuchang, Hupeh.

Pound translates 'ko-jin' as 'friends' in the epigraph to FOUR POEMS OF DEPARTURE (l. 5), and as 'old acquaintances' in 'Taking leave of a friend' (l. 6).
l. 5 long Kiang: Chinese Ch'ang Chiang, the Yangtze (Yip).

Taking Leave of a Friend

l. 1 Blue: 'green' (Yip); cf. note on 'The Beautiful Toilet', line 1.
l. 6 old acquaintances: cf. note on 'Separation on the River Kiang', line 1.

Leave-taking Near Shoku

Title: 'To See a Friend off to Shu (Szechuan)', (Yip, 214).

Epigraph: *Sanso*: the Chinese Ts'an-ts'ung was the first king of Shu (Pound's 'Shoku'). Cf. *Jefferson and/or Mussolini*, 'So Shu, king of Soku, built roads' (p. 100), also 'Ancient Wisdom, Rather Cosmic' (*CSP*, 129) and Canto II, lines 5, 130, where however Pound's 'So-shu' is 'Chuang Tzu'.

l. 6 Shin: Chinese Ch'in (Fang, 228).

l. 9 Shoku: i.e. Shu Chuan, a province not a city.

l. 11 diviners: Pound's substitution for the name Yen Chün Ping, a fortune-teller.

The City of Choan

Title: 'Ascend the Phoenix Terrace in Chin-ling' (Yip, 214).

Choan: Chinese Ch'ang-an, a former capital, now the city of Hsian Fu in Shensi (Benton, 296).

l. 1 phœnix: phoenix were said to have alighted on a tower to the north of Chin-ling (Nanking) in the reign of Wên Ti. The tower or terrace of the original title was erected in their honour (Benton, 297).

l. 5 Go: Chinese Wu. The Wu dynasty lasted from A.D. 222 to 265.

l. 6 Shin: the Chin dynasty (A.D. 265–419).

l. 8 Three Mountains: south-west of Nanking.

l. 10: the Ch'in Huai River in the Shang-Yüan district of the modern province of Kiangsu divides into two streams at Chien-k'ang (Benton, 298).

ll. 12–13: the poem is a poem of departure in that the poet regrets his exile from the capital Ch'ang-an, after three years at the court of the Emperor, Hsüan Tsung (Benton, 299).

The poem is by Li Po.

South-Folk in Cold Country

Title: 'Ku-feng no. 6' (Yip, 216), by Li Po (Rihaku).

The Fenollosa transcripts of this poem, as given (supposedly with Mr. Hirai) by Yip (pp. 177–9) and (with Professor Mori) by Kenner (*Pound Era*, 220–1), differ radically.

Pound had finished his poem in November 1914 and sent it with 'Song of the Bowmen of Shu' and 'Lament of the Frontier Guard' to Gaudier-Brzeska, who acknowledged it on 7 April 1915 (*G-B*, 63). Pound cited 'South Folk' in the article 'Chinese Poetry' as an example of

> directness and realism such as we find only in early Saxon verse and in the Poema del Cid, and in Homer, or rather in what Homer would be if he wrote without epithet. . . . There you have no mellifluous circumlocution, no sentimentalizing of men who have never seen a battlefield and who wouldn't fight if they had to. You have war, campaigning as it has always been, tragedy, hardships, no illusions.
>
> (*To-Day*, April 1918, 56–7)

Cf. headnote, 'Song of the Bowmen of Shu', and 'Exile's Letter'. Pound's translation closed *Cathay* (1915). It is a striking example of variations in tone carried across a line unit, composed, until the poem's close, of the simple sentence (cf. Davie, *Poet as Sculptor*, 41–2).

l. 1 Dai . . . Etsu: Chinese 'Tai' (north) and 'Yüeh' (south). Pound said in 'Chinese Poetry', 'The writer expects his hearers to know that Dai and Etsu are in the south' (op. cit., 56). The distinction is clear in the Fenollosa notes given by Kenner; in the notes given by Yip, Fenollosa adds that 'Dai is a place famous for horses' and Etsu 'a place famous for certain kinds of birds' (p. 178).

l. 2 En: Chinese Yen (Fang, 228).

l. 6: an ideographic line presenting what Pound calls in *The Chinese Written Character* 'a vivid shorthand picture of the operations of nature' (p. 8). Fenollosa has

> surprised   desert   turmoil   sea   sun
>   sand-sea
> Sands surprised by wind cover in the turmoil the desert sea sun
>
> (Kenner, *Pound Era*, 220)

Pound wisely avoids Fenollosa's prose gloss. The desert referred to is the Gobi Desert.

ll. 9–11: compare the lines from 'The Wanderer', often recommended by Pound,

> Nor may the weary-in-mind withstand his fate,
> Nor is high heart his helping,
> For the doom-eager oft bindeth fast his thought in blood-
> bedabbled breast.

(PM, 45)

ll. 10–14: there are echoes here of the enigma and unrecompensed wastage of war recorded at the close of 'The Return' and in *Hugh Selwyn Mauberley* IV.

l. 12 Rishogu: i.e. Rishōgun (Shōgun is the Japanese title of a commander-in-chief). The name alludes to General Li Kuang (d. 125 B.C.), called 'the Winged General'. Fenollosa adds the note, '(. . . in Kan Dynasty was famous Ri Shogun who fought more than 74 battles with the northern barbarians who called him the Flying Shogun. So skilful, he was constantly sent out for some expedition, and was never recalled – so he died in old age in one of the border battles)' (Kenner, *Pound Era*, 221).

Pound refers to Li Kuang again in Canto LIV (289/278):

> And Li-kouang bluffed the tartars (the Hiong-nou)
> in face of a thousand, he and his scouts dismounted
> and unsaddled their horses, so the Hiong nou
> thought Li's army was with him.

Sennin Poem by Kakuhaku

Title: 'Poems of a Taoist Elite' (Yip, 218).
Sennin: the Chinese 'hsien-jen' ('Spirits of the air') does not occur in the original Chinese poem (Fang, 228). Pound commented, 'Sennin are the Chinese spirits of nature or of the air. I don't see that they are any worse than Celtic Sidhe' (*SL*, 180), and in 'Chinese Poetry. II', 'Chinese poetry is full of fairies and fairy lore. Their lore is "quite Celtic". . . . The desire to be taken away by the fairies, the idea of souls flying

with the sea-birds, and many other things recently made familiar to us by the Celtic school crop up in one's Chinese reading' (*To-Day*, May 1918, 93).

Cf. 'The River Song', line 6, 'Exile's Letter', line 26 and Canto IV (20/16).

Kakuhaku: the Chinese poet Kuo P'u.

l. 5: Fenollosa has: 'Darkly they cover the whole mountain'. Pound derives 'weave' from Fenollosa's annotation:

> to wear on the head   to put into
>   to cover   basket
>
> obscure, dim
>   (Kenner, *Pound Era*, 219)

l. 6: Fenollosa has 'In it there is a silent and solitary man'. Pound's 'shut speech' derives from Fenollosa's note:

> silent (lit. dark
>   sometimes used in
>   shutting the eyes)
>
>   (ibid.)

Pound's locution is virtually a transposed Anglo-Saxon 'kenning'. Commenting on 'the temper of the race' to be found in the Anglo-Saxon poems, Pound said it was 'hardly more than a race conviction that words scarcely become a man' (*PM*, 45).

l. 11 red-pine-tree god: Yip notes that 'Red Pine', 'Floating Hill' (Pound's line 13) and 'Vast cliff' (Pound's 'great water sennin', line 14) 'are the names of three famous Taoist elites. The names themselves show the emphasis in Taoist metaphysics on the desire to become consonant with nature' (Yip, 218).

l. 13 "Floating Hill": *Collected Shorter Poems* has Pound's note, 'Name of a sennin' (p. 150).

A Ballad of the Mulberry Road

Pound's 16 lines are a translation of the first 14 lines of a 53-line anonymous poem.

l. 2 Shin: Chinese Ch'in (Fang, 229), the name of a state.

ll. 3–4: Lee and Murray suggest 'For they have a pretty daughter/She named herself Rofu' (p.270). 'Rofu' or 'Rafu' (Chinese Lo-fu) is a proper name; it does not mean 'pretty girl' or 'Gauze Veil' (l. 4), which is Pound's invention.

l. 9 Katsura: Yip has 'Cassia bough for her basket-handle' (p. 220).

Old Idea of Choan by Rosoriu

Pound translates the first 16 of 64 lines in the original (Fang, 229).

Title: *Choan*: Chinese Ch'ang-an; cf. 'The City of Choan'.

Rosoriu: Chinese Lu Chao-lin.

l. 26 Riu: possibly Rosoriu, i.e. Lu Chao-lin. Yip has 'Liang' (p. 226).

l. 28 Butei of Kan: Yip has 'Emperor Han'. Possibly the Emperor Wu-ti (140–86 B.C.) is meant. Giles lists him as Liu-Chê (*A Chinese Biographical Dictionary*, 1898). He is the author of the poem Pound translates as 'Liu Ch'e' in *Lustra* (cf. Giles, *History of Chinese Literature*, 99–100).

To-Em-Mei's "The Unmoving Cloud"

Title: 'Still Clouds' (Yip, 228).

To-Em-Mei: the Japanese for T'ao Ch'ien (A.D. 365–427).

Cf. Kenner's admirable discussion of Pound's 'invention' in this poem (*Pound Era*, 207–16).

ll. 3–4: Fenollosa has

> eight surface   same   dark
> The earth in all directions is equally dark
>
> (ibid., 207)

W. Acker, in a complete version of the poem, has at this point, 'The Eight Directions are all alike in twilight' (*T'ao the Hermit*, 1952, 135).

'Eight' denotes the Chinese compass points.

ll. 10–16: Arthur Waley translates this stanza:

> The lingering clouds, rolling, rolling,
> And the settled rain, dripping, dripping,
> In the Eight Directions – the same dusk.
> The level lands – one great river.
> Wine I have, wine I have;
> Idly I drink at the eastern window.
> Longingly – I think of my friends,
> But neither boat nor carriage comes.
>
> (*Chinese Poems*, 1976, 107)

ll. 20–1: Fenollosa's prose gloss suggests an arbitrary pantheistic affirmation, 'Men often are saying/ The sun and moon have their turning/ Setting my mat where I can be at ease/ Let me take joy in this course of nature' (Kenner, op. cit., 211). Pound departs ingeniously from his source to retain the elegaic mood of the first two sections.

l. 21 soft seat: derived from the 'mat' which might be set for a possible visitor. Acker has, 'Would that I could sit face to face with you/ And settle the problems of our daily life' (op. cit., 135).

ll. 22–7: a fourth stanza, conflated by Pound with the third. T'ao Yuan Ming: the author is T'ao Ch'ien, called in early life T'ao Yüan-ming (Giles, *History of Chinese Literature*, 128).

HOMAGE TO
SEXTUS PROPERTIUS

(October 1919)

Pound's *Homage* is based on a series of poems from the extant four books of the Roman elegist Sextus Aurelius Propertius (born *c*. 50 B.C.). The poem was finished in 1917 and published in book form in *Quia Pauper Amavi* (October 1919) with 'Langue d'Oc', 'Mœurs Contemporains' and the original versions of the first three Cantos. Earlier, four sections of the poem were published in *Poetry* (March 1919). This first appearance, presenting 'a very mutilated piece' of the poem, said Pound, provoked the uncomprehending outrage of Professor W. G. Hale at Pound's 'three score errors' and perversion of the original ('Pegasus Impounded', *Poetry*, April 1919, reprinted in Homberger, 155–7). Hale's strictures were supported by *Poetry*'s editor Harriet Monroe, and virtually ended Pound's connection with that magazine. His reply to Hale, by way of a letter to A. R. Orage, that his job was 'to bring a dead man to life, to present a living figure' (*SL*, 149) and to Harriet Monroe later (*SL*, 229–30; cf. also 231), as well as the repeated insistence that he was not making a literal translation, did nothing to prevent a stream of unimaginative and self-congratulatory carping in the same vein from later scholars (Robert Nichols in Homberger, 165–7, also 170–1; Wilfred Rowland Childe, *New Age*, XXVI, 1920, 179; Martin Gilkes, *English*, II (1938), 74–83; Robert Graves in *The Crowning Privilege*, 1955, 212–14). Nevertheless, defenders of the poem and of Pound's practice as a translator have steadily gained voice, from the discussions by L. J. Richardson in the *Yale Poetry Review* (VI, 1947, 21–9) and Hugh Kenner in *The Poetry of Ezra Pound* (1951) to the elucidation by J. P. Sullivan in his *Ezra Pound and Sextus Propertius* (1964). The general issue is surely now settled. Pound's poem is not a 'literal' translation, but what Sullivan names as a 'creative translation' in a long tradition of 'adaptions', 'imitations' and poems inspired by other poems.

The issue might have been settled much earlier. Pound's brusque denial that the *Homage* was a 'translation' was perhaps an over-reaction which served only to enforce the battle lines between poetry and translation, and therefore to obscure his own achievement. But the terms in which we might properly read *Propertius* were understood as early as 1928 by T. S. Eliot. Although his care for his readers' difficulty persuaded him to exclude the poem from the *Selected Poems* (1928) as being 'not enough' and yet 'too much a translation', Eliot was in fact clear that

> it is not a translation, it is a paraphrase, or still more truly (for the instructed) a *persona*. It is also a criticism of Propertius, a criticism which in a most interesting way insists upon an element of humour, of irony and mockery in Propertius, which Mackail and other interpreters have missed.
>
> (p. 19)

The aspects of 'paraphrase', 'persona' and 'criticism' are interrelated and if 'paraphrase' seems too mean a term, like the others it has the authority of Pound's own scattered comments on the nature and function of translation. As his recommended reading to Iris Barry alone shows, Propertius evidently occupied a place in Pound's literary canon, as an essential ingredient in a 'Kompleat Kulture' before he had embarked on his *Homage* (*SL*, 87, 91). In the absence of an adequate translation, Pound's own was in a sense necessary. And what qualified Propertius for this place and attracted Pound was his irony, the 'germ' of which he detected in the 'Ride to Lanuvium' (Propertius IV, 8), and 'the juxtaposition of the words "tacta puella sono" and "Orphea delinisse feras" ' (Homberger, 163, also 170). This was the quality, as it existed elsewhere, in Jules Laforgue, which Pound identified as 'logopoeia':

> 'the dance of the intellect among words', that is to say, it employs words not only for their direct meaning, but it takes count in a special way of habits of usage, of the context we *expect* to find with the word, its usual concomitants, of its known acceptances, and of ironical play. It holds the aesthetic content which is peculiarly the domain of verbal manifestation, and cannot possibly be contained in plastic or in music. It is the latest come, and perhaps most tricky and undependable mode.
>
> (*LE*, 25, cf. also p. 33, and *ABC of R*, 37, 38)

'Logopoeia', Pound adds significantly,

> does not translate; though the attitude of mind it expresses may pass through a paraphrase. Or one might say, you can *not* translate it 'locally', but having determined the original author's state of mind, you may or may not be able to find a derivative or an equivalent.
>
> (*LE*, 25)

It is this condition presumably which accounts for Pound's recoiling at the word 'translation', for Eliot's use of the term 'paraphrase', and for Pound's claim that he 'certainly omitted no means of definition that I saw open to me, including shortenings, cross cuts, implications derivable from other writings of Propertius, as for example the "Ride to Lanuvium" from which I have taken a colour or tone but no direct or entire *expression*' (*SL*, 231).

Pound discovered then a state of mind, a tone and a use of language in Propertius, and sought to carry this over, for one thing, as a corrective to academic orthodoxy. Mackail, for example, '(accepted as "right" opinion on the Latin poets) . . . Doesn't see that S.P. is tying blue ribbon in the tails of Virgil and Horace, or that sometime after his first "book" S.P.

ceased to be the dupe of magniloquence and began to touch words somewhat as Laforgue did' (*SL*, 178).

Pound's argument was that Propertius' valued sentimentality and tenderness, such as it was, had been misread in terms of the taste and idiom of the Victorians, as though Propertius had 'been steeped to the brim in Rossetti, Pater and Co.' (Homberger, 163). One can easily see how in this way *Propertius* functions as 'criticism', as a swipe at the 'beaneries', and a discarding of the 'mask of erudition' (*SL*, 149). And one can see too the consequences of bringing this 'dead man to life', for in realigning Propertius with Laforgue Pound was making, as Eliot said of *Cathay*, a 'Windsor Translation', a translation, that is to say, of and for his own period, in the terms of a literary taste largely defined by Eliot and himself.

As the response to the poem shows only too well, there was also involved in this process a reappraisal of the very concept of translation. Logopoeia, Pound suggests, operates at the level of meaning, 'it holds the aesthetic content which is peculiarly the domain of verbal manifestation', and 'you can not translate it "locally" '. Pound's poetry in translation explores other modes than logopoeia, but what he says here is entirely consistent with his view of the translator's necessary priorities:

if a work be taken abroad in the original tongue, certain properties seem to become less apparent, or less important. Fancy styles, questions of local 'taste', lose importance. Even though I know the overwhelming importance of technique, technicalities in a foreign tongue cannot have for me the importance they have to a man writing in that tongue; almost the only technique perceptible to a foreigner is the presentation of content as free as possible from the clutteration of dead technicalities, fustian à la Louis XV; and from timidities of workmanship. This is perhaps the only technique that ever matters, the only *maestria*.

(*MIN*, 159–60)

As one would expect, the translators Pound recommends are

those such as Salel, Douglas and Golding who were 'absorbed in the subject-matter' of their originals at the expense of vocabulary and syntax (*LE*, 254, 273). Arthur Golding, for example, for whose translation of Ovid's *Metamorphoses* Pound has only the highest praise, 'was endeavouring to convey the sense of the original to his readers. He names the thing of his original author, by the name most germane, familiar, homely, to his hearers. He is intent on conveying a meaning, and not on bemusing them with a rumble. And I hold that the real poet is sufficiently absorbed in his content to care more for the content than the rumble' (*LE*, 239). Even Rossetti is seen as a poet of this calibre since 'when he says that the only thing worth bringing over is the beauty of the original . . . he meant by "beauty" something fairly near what we mean by the "emotional intensity" of his original' (*LE*, 268). And when Pound offers what came to constitute Canto I, his own translation of the 'Nekuia' (*Odyssey*, Bk. XI) as conveying no more or less than 'the meaning of the passage' (*LE*, 262), he is evidently placing himself in this tradition.

It is tempting to believe that the recognition of 'logopoeia' in Propertius similarly directed Pound to the 'meaning' or 'subject-matter' or 'emotional intensity' of his original; in short, as one might think, to the Propertian *virtù*, that which was essentially and uniquely his (cf. *SPr*, 28). 'Questions of local "taste" ' in such a venture get short shrift, at least in their own right, since what Pound had called earlier 'the technique of manner' or of 'surface' is decidedly subordinate to the 'Technique of Content' which is all that is perceptible to a foreigner (*SPr*, 34, *MIN*, 160). In which case, one can see, if Pound is to be believed, how Hale who 'never *understood* anything but syntax' (*SL*, 149), and readers under the influence of Mackail who are 'asked to read *one* word at a time, and one line at a time' (Homberger, 170), could hardly fail to disparage his poem.

But in fact this would be too neat. One cannot ignore Pound's obvious presence in the poem's structure and voice, or its implication. He was less absorbed in the subject-matter of his original than he might have been, as he realized. Writing in March 1921 in response to a much valued comment on the poem by Thomas Hardy, Pound confessed,

> I ought – precisely – to have written 'Propertius soliloquizes'
> – turning the reader's attention to the reality of Propertius –
> but no – what I do is borrow a term – aesthetic – a term of
> aesthetic *attitude* from a French musician, Debussy. . . . I
> ought to have concentrated on the subject – (I did so long
> as I forgot my existence for the sake of the lines) – and I
> tack on a title relating to the treatment.
>
> (Quoted in Davie, *Pound*, 49)

But Pound did not forget his own existence enough: 'treatment' competes with 'subject-matter', with the result that the *Homage* falls, awkwardly, between (in Pound's terms) the categories of 'interpretative translation' – a guide to 'where the treasure lies' in the original – and translation in new composition, a poem of its author's own making (*LE*, 200). What Pound identified in Propertius he also identified with, so that his poem, as Eliot pointed out, is a 'persona', and perhaps 'more truly' a persona than it is a 'paraphrase'. As such it is one in the series of masks which constitute the early poetry, and like those others, a search for ' "sincere self-expression" . . . for the real', for his own *virtù* (*G-B*, 85).

The degree to which Pound freed Propertius from Victorian taste is part then also of the personal search for a language which required him to slough off an obfuscating Victorian idiom, 'the crust of dead English, the sediment present in my own available vocabulary' (*LE*, 193). The ironic mode uncovered in Propertius, one which can traverse registers within a language and play across whole languages, was a testament to Pound's education in 'a series of Englishes', and is what in an important way this poem shares with *Hugh Selwyn Mauberley* and the *Cantos*. It was indeed 'the latest come and perhaps most tricky and undependable mode', and Pound's major poetry stands or falls by it.

What also, of immediate effect but of less permanence,

Pound saw in Propertius and enlarged and re-directed on his own behalf, was an alternative in 1917 to genuflecting patriotic verse, creating an emphasis that has meant for many a shift in the centre of gravity of his original from a pure and youthful passion to sophisticated bohemianism (cf. Sullivan, *EP and Sextus Propertius*, 57–8). Propertius, Pound wrote,

> presents certain emotions as vital to me in 1917, faced with the infinite and ineffable imbecility of the British Empire, as they were to Propertius some centuries earlier, when faced with the infinite and ineffable imbecility of the Roman Empire.

> (*SL*, 231)

As he had presented it earlier to Thomas Hardy, this 'doubling of me and Propertius, England today, and Rome under Augustus' (Davie, op. cit.), would seem to be Pound's own, and perhaps the only available explanation of the way 'treatment' pulls away from 'content' in the poem. To put it there he had not only to resuscitate but to re-make Propertius, omitting 'no means of definition that I saw open to me, including shortenings, cross cuts, implications derivable from other writings' (*SL*, 231). But we would be wrong to take *Propertius* as in truth a serious rebellion against British imperialism. It is a phase in the discovery of a mode free of both aestheticism and acquiescence in imperialism which would allow the poet an independent but still active and critical relevance. But it does not in the event supply this role and is in fact rife with a decadence not to be discarded until *Mauberley*, and then far from unambiguously. *Mauberley*, Pound said, was a 'popularisation' of *Propertius*, and the two poems do share an anti-imperialist stance and a disdain for current literary models. But *Mauberley* is more seriously troubled, more broadly disillusioned, and its diagnosis of the effects of Empire and the war more direct than *Propertius*. In its tone and sometimes condensed, accelerated structure (section VI, for example), *Propertius* anticipates *Mauberley* and also the *Cantos*, but in terms of the theme of the poet's station it relates only negatively to Pound's own career, since what Propertius is made to say is that Pound would not write to 'Imperial Order', not what kind of epic he was contemplating, and would write when historical figures and events were remembered as more than 'background'. Indeed, as *Cathay* in its oblique reference to the war had already shown, the alternatives for Pound, even in 1917, were not poetry in the shape of the love lyric, however wryly undercut, and 'the distentions of Empire'. The irreverence of *Propertius*, and its theme of poetry's immortality and the independence of the poet, were an interlude which events and Pound's own real concern made it impossible to sustain. Its real significance in 1917 lies in its combined distance and cogency; in short, in its irony.

The references to Propertius at the heads of sections in the notes which follow are to the translation by Lucian Mueller, used by Pound, *Catulli Tibulli Propertii Carmina recensuit Lucianus Mueller* (Leipzig: Teubner, 1892) and (in brackets) to the poems as they are presented in *The Poems of Propertius* (trans. Ronald Musker, 1972). The Teubner text is given by Sullivan (*EP and Sextus Propertius*, 114–71), and in Ruthven rearranged to correspond with Pound's poem. The line references given here similarly correspond to their order in Pound's translation. These differ in several respects from the table given in Sullivan (pp. 112–13), and very occasionally from Ruthven.

ORFEO: Orpheus. This appeared as the dedication to *Quia Pauper Amavi* (1919) ('because I was poor when I loved', from Ovid, *Ars Amatoria*, II, l. 165), in which the full version of Pound's *Homage* first appeared.

I

Propertius IV, 1 (III, 1 and 2), lines 1–11, 14–18, 20–3, 25–32, 35–64.
ll. 1–9: Hugh Kenner sees 'this extending of the curve of speech beyond the limits of the line' as 'nothing less than a new way of articulating extended passages of English verse' (*Poetry of EP*, 151, 156).

l. 1 Callimachus: (*c.* 305–240 B.C.), Greek elegiac poet, grammarian and cataloguer at the Alexandrian Library, chiefly known for his poem 'Dreams' and for epigrams and love lyrics. Callimachus engaged in a feud with Apollonius Rhodius over the merits of lyric and epic verse, and is credited with the phrase, '*μέγα βιβλίον μέγα κακόν*' ('the greater the book, the greater the evil'). Horace satirized Propertius' claim to be the Roman Callimachus (*Satires*, II, 2, ll. 90 ff.). Cf. also note on II, line 9.

Philetas: (*c.* 330–275 B.C.), Greek poet and grammarian from the island of Cos, in the Sporades. Like Callimachus he was a member of the Alexandrian school, famed as an elegist and a source of Latin love poetry.

ghosts: R. P. Blackmur cites this word, and others in this section: 'orgies', 'whistles', 'generalities', 'distentions', 'normal' and 'boom' as examples of 'conversational, colloquial ease' in Pound's adopted diction (*EP*, ed. Sullivan, 152–3).

l. 2: an admiration of literary forebears modernized in the line 'His true Penelope was Flaubert' in *Hugh Selwyn Mauberley* ('E.P. Ode', l. 13 and MAUBERLEY (1920) I, ll. 5–6).

l. 4 Grecian orgies: Latin 'orgia' ('mystcry'). Pound means perhaps to suggest that the original Bacchanalian mysteries have degenerated into sexual licence; cf. *Hugh Selwyn Mauberley* III, and *The Spirit of Romance*, where Pound writes 'we should consider carefully the history of the various cults or religions of orgy and of ecstasy, from the simpler Bacchanalia to the more complicated rites of Isis or Dionysus – sudden rise and equally sudden decline' (p. 95).

l. 10 Apollo: the Greek god of light and patron of the arts.

Martian generalities: commonplaces of war and battle.

l. 11: Latin 'Exactus termi pumice versus eat' ('let the verse glide, polished by the sharp pumicestone'). Blackmur suggests that Pound here 'transforms' the Latin as a result of the 'operation of a very definite taste' (*EP*, ed. Sullivan, 153).

l. 15: Latin 'Non datur ad Musas currere lata via' ('it isn't given to us to race to the Muses on a broad road'). An example for Blackmur of the value of Pound's version, 'the value, that is, in translation, of making a critical equivalent, rather than a duplicate of the original' (ibid.).

ll. 16–18: Latin 'Multi, Roma, tuas laudes annalibus addent/ Qui finem imperii Bactra futura canent' ('Oh Rome! Many will add your praises to their histories/ who will sing of the Empire's bounds extending to Bactra'). An early example in the poem of Pound's re-ordering the basic elements of the Latin into a new sense. Richardson comments, 'Pound performs deliberately . . . only the first and third of Pound's lines translate the Latin; the second is an invention from three isolated words: *Roma*, *laudes* and *Bactra*, two chosen because they are capitalized and the third fitted in and around them three ways' ('Ezra Pound's Homage to Propertius', *Yale Poetry Review*, VI, 1947, 22–3).

l. 16 Annalists: Roman historians.

l. 17 Trans-Caucasus: Bactra was the capital of Bactria (mod. Balkh), annexed by Rome in 20 B.C. Pound perhaps has in mind a parallel between the foundation of an independent kingdom at Bactria in 255 B.C., when it broke from Greek rule, and the separation of Transcaucasia from Russia in 1917.

l. 18 distentions: a Jamesian *mot juste* (cf. Kenner, *Pound Era*, 13–14).

l. 20 forked hill: Latin 'de monte sororum' ('from the mountain of the Sisters', i.e. the Muses of Parnassus). Robert Graves gibed amusingly at Pound's 'forked hill' ('Dr. Syntax and Mr. Pound', *The Crowning Privilege*, 1955, 212–14). Sullivan points out however that it is an 'accepted locution', occurring also in Pope's 'Epistle to Arbuthnot' (l. 231) (*EP and Sextus Propertius*, 12n.).

l. 27 deal-wood horse: the legendary wooden horse used as a stratagem by the Greeks to gain entry into Troy.

l. 28 Achilles . . . Simois: the legendary Greek hero Achilles was a principal figure in the siege of Troy. The Simois is a tributary of the Scamander, the river which rises against Achilles in Homer's *Iliad*, Bk. XXI (ll. 233–382).

l. 29 Hector . . . wheel-rims: Hector, son of Priam, king of Troy, was the Trojan commander. He was killed by Achilles, tied to a chariot by the heels and dragged through the dust (*Iliad*, Bk. XXII, ll. 395–405).

l. 30 Polydmantus: Polydamas, son of Panthoos, was a Trojan officer and advisor of caution to Hector.

Helenus and Deiphoibos: Helenus and Deiphobus, sons of Priam and Hecuba. After the death of Paris in the Trojan war, Helenus, who is said to have traitorously advised the Greeks on the building of the wooden horse, paid suit to Helen, but was rejected by her in favour of Deiphobus.

l. 31 Paris: son of Priam. Paris' abduction of Helen, wife of King Menelaus of Sparta, brother to Agamemnon, was the legendary cause of the Trojan war.

l. 32 Ilion . . . Troad: the Roman Ilium (Gk. Ilion, i.e. Troy) was the capital and stronghold of the district called Troad (Gk. Troias), the projection of Asia Minor into the Aegean.

l. 33 Oetian gods: Propertius has 'Oetia's god'. Pound defended his plural gods on the grounds that the singular would 'bitch the movement of the verse' (*EP*, ed. Sullivan, 97n.). Mt. Oeta in central Greece was the legendary site of Hercules' death as a mortal.

l. 38 vote: Pound puns in a resolutely secular direction on the Latin 'vota' ('votive offering' or 'prayer').

Phoebus in Lycia: Phoebus ('bright') was a name for Apollo (the god of light), whose cult in Greece probably originated in Lycia, an ancient coastal district of south-west Asia Minor.

Patara: the birthplace of Apollo and his twin sister Artemis was thought to be at Letoon, between the towns of Xanthus and Patara.

l. 40 devirginated young ladies: Latin 'Gaudeat in solito tacta puella sono' ('Let my girl be touched by the sound of a familiar music and rejoice in it'). Perhaps the most controversial line in the poem. Hale found Pound's rendering of 'tacta puella' 'peculiarly unpleasant', with no basis in the Latin (Homberger, 157), Robert Nichols found it an example of Pound's 'ignorance and bad taste' (ibid., 167, cf. also 170–1), and Martin Gilkes thought it 'beyond comment' ('The Discovery of Ezra Pound', *English*, II, 1938, 76). Pound replied in similar terms to

Hale and Nichols. Clearly he saw in Propertius' line an example of 'logopoeia'; 'if this sequence of phrases is wholly accidental, and if the division of "in" and "tacta" is "wholly" accidental, then Propertius was the greatest unconscious ironist of all time' (Homberger, 169–70; cf. also *SL*, 149–50, for the reply to Hale). A vindication of Pound's reading appears in Richardson: 'The *tacta* of Propertius is ambiguous; it includes both: touched at heart and the opposite of *intacta* (untouched, virgin); Pound's rendering . . . does violence to the context, but it is the meaning which will escape a casual reader' (op. cit., 23–4), and this has been endorsed by Kenner (*Poetry of EP*, 149n.), who sees in Pound's line 'a scepticism directed at Latin professors' (*Pound Era*, 285), and by Sullivan, who suggests the ambiguity was 'frequently found in classical Latin' (*EP and Sextus Propertius*, 96).

l. 42 Pound found confirmation of Propertius' irony in the juxtaposition of the Latin phrases 'Orphea delenisse feras' ('Orpheus tamed the wild beasts') and 'tacta puella sono' (Homberger, 163).

Orpheus: the legendary Greek poet and musician, born in Thrace, who enchanted men and beasts with the lyre presented to him by Apollo.

l. 43 Threician river: the lyre not the river is Thracian.

ll. 44–5: in legend Amphio enchanted the stones from Mt. Cithaeron to form the walls of Thebes, the capital of Boeotia and much celebrated in legend. Pound commented, 'I think it as likely that Mt. Cithaeron played the flute as that the walls of Thebes rose to magic of Amphion's solo on the barbitos' (Homberger, 164). Pound's 'Citharaon' (as well as the later error over mistaken Phaeacia, line 54), Richardson considers 'unpardonable catastrophes' (op. cit., 23).

l. 46 Polyphemus: the greatest of the Cyclops, blinded by Odysseus (*Odyssey*, Bk. IX, ll. 105–566).

Galatea: a sea nymph, loved by Polyphemus. Their story is told in Theocritus, *Idylls*, XI.

l. 47: the *New Age* reviewer felt this line was 'nonsense'; 'Even if Polyphemus had had any horses, they probably would not have been able to sing; and, anyhow, why should they drip? Galatea's horses naturally would, as they had just come out of the sea'. Pound replied, 'I don't think I actually turn P's horses into vocalists; but when some horses are able to fly, others might possibly sing' (Homberger, 161, 163).

Aetna: Mt. Etna, in Sicily, the supposed home of the Cyclops.

ll. 51–62: Hugh Kenner points out how modern and ancient dictions are overlaid in this passage and how 'the words lie flat like the forms on a Cubist surface' (*Pound Era*, 29).

l. 51 Taenarian: Taenarum (mod. Cape Matapan) was a promontory of Laconia, an ancient district of the south-east Peloponnesus, famous for its 'rosso antico' marble.

Laconia . . . Cerberus: Hale felt there is 'pure addition, and pure delay' in these 'Baedekeresque explanations' (Homberger, 156). Sullivan suggests that Pound's additions, after the manner of collage, are to be judged by the success of the resulting image (*EP and Sextus Propertius*, 101).

ll. 54–5 Phaeacia . . . Ionian: the Phaeacians were the people of Scheria, where Odysseus was cast ashore (cf. *Odyssey*, Bk. V, l. 35). Pound confuses it with the Ionian town of Phocaea, throwing the 'mask of erudition . . . on the dust heap' (*SL*, 149).

l. 56 Marcian vintage: Latin 'non operosa rigat Marcius antra liquor' ('the water of the Marcian aqueduct flows into no elaborate grottoes'). The Aqua Marcia fed the grottoes, pools and fountains of wealthy Romans. Propertius is regretting his lack of inspiration.

Hale commented, 'The Marcian aqueduct was Rome's best water supply, recently renovated by Agrippa. Mr. Pound seems to have taken *liquor* as spirituous. He must then have thought of age as appropriate, and so have interpreted *Marcius* as referring to the legendary King Ancus Marcius' (Homberger, 157). This is the one criticism of Hale's which Pound accepted: 'Do him the justice to say that the bloody Marcian aqueduct is very very familiar, and that it was a thing I might very well have remembered' (*SL*, 149).

l. 57 Numa Pompilius: Pound's addition to Propertius. Numa Pompilius was the second king of Rome.

l. 59: Pound's interpolation, obviously, which did not re-appear, after the first version in *Poetry* (March 1919), until *Personae* (1926).

l. 67 Jove in East Elis: the sacred precinct at Olympia in Elis (mod. Ilia), in the north-west Peloponnesus, contained a colossal statue of Zeus (i.e. Jove).

l. 68 Mausolus: the ruler of Caria, south-west Asia Minor, whose tomb (the Mausoleum) containing his statue and other sculptures was erected by his wife Artemisa at his death, 353 B.C. The Mausoleum was in ancient times one of the seven wonders of the world.

II

Propertius IV, 2 (III, 3).

This poem in Propertius is a 'recusatio', in which the poet excuses himself with self-flattering irony from writing an epic.

l. 1 Helicon: a mountain range in Boeotia, central Greece, and the celebrated home of the Muses.

l. 2 Bellerophon's horse: Bellerophon slew the Chimaera with the help of the winged horse Pegasus. The spring Hippocrene on the eastern slopes of Helicon is said to have been created by Pegasus' stamping hooves.

l. 3 Alba: Alba Longa, the oldest Latin city, destroyed and superseded in the Latin League by Rome under Tullus Hostilius, *c.* 600 B.C. According to literary tradition, Alba had twelve kings between Aeneas the founder of Lavinium and Romulus the founder of Rome.

l. 5: Latin 'tantum operis, nervis hiscere posse meis' ('such great labour to be able to tell of [your kings and kings' deeds, Alba] with my strength'). Pound draws out the latent meaning of 'hiscere' ('tell of' but literally 'to open the mouth', and 'yawning' when applied to caverns) and 'nervis' ('sinews' and therefore 'strength', but also 'the strings of a lyre'); 'tantum operis' refers back and forward syntactically in Propertius, hence Pound's repeated 'with such industry' and the note of boredom this carries.

l. 7: Latin 'unde pater sitiens Ennius ante bibit' ('from whence father Ennius in his thirst has drunk before [me]'). Pound's rendering of 'sitiens' ('thirsting') was attacked as inept by the Georgian poet Robert Nichols, and defended by Wyndham Lewis (cf. Homberger, 166–7, 168). Pound himself replied that all his revisions 'were made *away* from and not *toward* literal rendering' (ibid., 169).

Quintus Ennius (239–169 B.C.) was known as the father of Latin poetry on the basis chiefly of his *Annales*, an epic poem on the history of Rome.

l. 8 Curian brothers . . . Horatian javelin: the three Curian brothers from Alba Longa fought the three Horatian brothers from Rome in a very early attempt on Rome's part to rule Italy. They killed two of the Horace brothers, but were themselves killed by the third, who then set up their javelins at the corner of the basilica in the centre of Rome to celebrate the victory (cf. Livy, I, 24 ff.).

l. 9: i.e. in imitation of the Latin poet Horace (Quintus Horatius Flaccus). Horace was a member of the literary circle of Maecenas and there was perhaps some enmity between himself and Propertius (cf. note on I, l. 1), but this line is Pound's addition to the Latin text. His point is the denigratory comparison of Horace with his glorious namesake.

l. 10 Aemilia: probably Aemilius Paullus, the Roman consul victorious in 219 B.C., but killed in the Roman defeat by Hannibal on the Aufidus, below Cannae (216 B.C.).

memorial raft: used for conveying royal trophies.

l. 11 Fabius: Quintus Fabius Maximus, Roman consul, surnamed Cunctator ('the delayer'), for his having adopted eventually successful guerrilla tactics against Hannibal's forces. Ennius praised Fabius in the line 'one man by delaying restored our fortunes'.

Cannae: ancient city of Apulia and the site of the Roman defeat by Hannibal (l. 10 above).

l. 12 lares fleeing the "Roman seat": the Lares were the gods of the home and family and the guardians of Rome, thought to have aided in the expulsion of Hannibal, not to have themselves fled.

l. 14 Hannibal: the Carthaginian general who waged the Second Punic War against Rome (218–201 B.C.).

l. 15 Jove . . . geese: in legend, the geese sacred to Jove (i.e. Jupiter, the chief Latin god and patron of Rome), awakened the Romans to the invading Gauls by their cackling (Livy, V, 47).

l. 16 Phoebus . . . Castalian tree: the spring Castalia on Mt. Parnassus was sacred to Phoebus Apollo and regarded as a source of poetic inspiration.

l. 29 Silenus: in Greek mythology a satyr known for his prophetic song, drunkenness and lechery, generally shown on an ass or supported by other satyrs.

l. 30 Tegaean Pan: the Arcadian and Greek fertility god. Tegea was a town in Arcadia.

l. 31 Cytherean mother: Aphrodite, from her association with the Ionian island of Cythera, between the southern Peloponnesus and Crete. Aphrodite's chariot was pulled by doves.

l. 32 Punic faces: one of Pound's 'blunders' for W. G. Hale: 'Where Propertius speaks of the "purple beaks" (*punica rostra*) of the doves of Venus, Mr. Pound renders by the nonsensical phrase "their Punic faces" – as if one were to translate "crockery" by "China" ' (Homberger, 156). Pound replied in a letter to A. R. Orage that this was 'one of my best lines. Punic (*Punicus*) used for dark red, purple red by Ovid and Horace as well as Propertius. Audience familiar with Tyrrian for purple in English. To say nothing of augmented effect on imagination by using Punic (whether in translation or not) instead of 'red'' (*SL*, 149). For a similar, public, defence in the *New Age* cf. Homberger (p. 164).

In the Mueller text Pound used 'Punica' was already capitalized.

Gorgon's lake: a lake of blood flowing from Medusa's neck when killed by Perseus, from which sprang Chrysador and Pegasus.

l. 35 thyrsos: the thyrsus was the wand, bound with vines or ivy, carried by Dionysus and his followers in their orgiastic rites.

l. 39 Calliope: the Muse of epic poetry who speaks as if offended at Propertius' desertion.

l. 40 white swans: the swans who drew Venus' chariot as contrasted with the 'high horses' suitable to heroic verse.

l. 44 Aeonium: an error for Aonia, a part of Boeotia in central Greece, containing Mt. Helicon.

ll. 45–7: Germanic forces, called the Suevi, crossed the Rhine in 29 B.C. and were defeated by the Roman general Gaius Carinas.

l. 49: Latin 'nocturnaeque canes ebria signa fugae' ('You shall sing of the drunken signs of nocturnal fight'). W. G. Hale spoke for all outraged classical scholars in his response to this line:

> Mr. Pound mistakes the verb *canes*, 'thou shalt sing' for the noun *canes* (in the nominative plural masculine) and translates by 'dogs'. Looking around then for something to tack this to, he fixes upon *nocturnae* (genitive singular feminine) and gives us 'night dogs'! I allow myself an exclamation point. For sheer magnificence of blundering this is unsurpassable.
>
> (Homberger, 156)

Cf. also Gilkes (op. cit., 78–9). One would have thought that the answer in this case was that a pun on 'canes' was a stock pedagogic joke (cf. Richardson, op. cit., 24). Sullivan however feels that the kind of linguistic homophone which operates for 'tacta puella' (cf. I, l. 40) cannot support this line, which is justified rather by its 'success, the greater vividness of the image' (*EP and Sextus Propertius*, 99–100).

l. 54 stiffened: Hale feels that Pound's confusing 'rigat' ('moistens' or 'sprinkles') with the English 'rigid' produces 'a monstrous rendering' (Homberger, 156–7). Sullivan suggests it intensifies the poetic image and adds a note of personal feeling (op. cit., 100).

III

Propertius IV, 15 (III, 16).
l. 2 Tibur: a city to the north-east of Rome (mod. Tivoli).

l. 5 Anienan: the river Anio (mod. Aniene), the main tributary of the Tiber.

ll. 12–13: Pound converts Cynthia into a nagging hussy.

l. 15: Sullivan points out that this 'almost religious over-valuation of the lover's status' is one of the main themes of Latin love poetry (*EP and Sextus Propertius*, 56).

l. 16 Via Sciro: 'Sciron's Way'. Sciron was a notorious robber who terrorized the road between Athens and Megara. After compelling travellers to wash their feet, he kicked them off the Scironian rock.

l. 18 Scythian coast: for the Romans, Scythia denominated the greater part of Asia. Its people were barbarian nomads.

l. 27 Cypris: (Gk. Κύπρις) Aphrodite, commonly thought to have risen from the sea near Paphos in Cyprus where she was worshipped as a goddess of fertility.

l. 38: The ashes of well-to-do Roman families were deposited in family tombs in secluded gardens, or, like Cynthia's, along the highways outside the city.

IV Difference of Opinion with Lygdamus

Propertius IV, 5 (III, 6).

Both Gilkes (op. cit., 80–1) and Sullivan (*EP and Sextus Propertius*, 56–7) object to Pound's debunking sophistication in this section as being more in the manner of Ovid than of the passion of Propertius' original.

l. 1: Latin 'Dic mihi de nostra, quae sentis, vera puella'. Pound commented, 'What of Propertius' delicate use of "nostra", meaning "my" as well as "our", but in a stylist how delicately graduated against "mihi" by Propertius' (*SL*, 149). Propertius' irony registers the infidelity of his mistress Cynthia with Lygdamus, his slave.

ll. 3–4: Pound's addition to Propertius.

l. 10: Sullivan feels this is 'mere word-play and phrase-mongering' which has 'no connection at all with the poem'. Similarly with line 28 below (op. cit., 23, 57).

l. 19 gawds: trinkets.

orfevrerie: (Fr. 'orfèvrerie'), used of an ornament worked in gold.

ll. 22–3 and . . . dreams: Latin 'et tristes sua pensa ministrae carpebant' ('and the servants, desolate, were pulling their wool'). Pound construes the Latin 'pensa' ('the amount of wool to be spun daily') as 'dreams spun out'. This is perhaps also 'the parodied line from Yeats' Pound mentioned to Felix Schelling (*SL*, 178). The second line of the refrain in Yeats's 'The Withering of the Boughs' runs, 'The boughs have withered because I have told them my dreams' (*Collected Poems*, 1967, 87).

ll. 25–6: Gilkes offers, 'Did she press to her eyes the wool to dry her tears and repeat my chidings in sobbing voice' and comments on how the Latin is 'unimaginably changed into turgid tumescence' by Pound (op. cit., 81).

l. 28: cf. note on line 10.

l. 32 rhombus: instrument used in a lover's spell (cf. IX, l. 1).

l. 33 screech owls: supposed to be vampirish.

V

This poem, like II, is a 'recusatio', and its bombast (ll. 16–28) evidently ironic.

1

Propertius III, 1 (II, 10), with lacuna at line 20 in Mueller where Pound ends section 1.

l. 1 Helicon: cf. II, line 1.

l. 2 Emathian: Macedonian.

ll. 4–6: Pound's quotation marks point up his 'recusatio'.

ll. 7–9: Hugh Kenner discusses these lines as a 'homeomorphic' translation of the Latin (*Pound Era*, 168–70).

l. 9: Latin 'bella canam, quando scripta puella meast' ('let me sing of war, since I have written of my girl'). Pound adjusts the tense of 'canam' from present subjunctive to future indicative, and of 'scripta meast' from present perfect to future perfect, the implication being that the subject of his girl is not (and will never be) exhausted.

l. 11 gamut: generally, the musical scale, but an earlier meaning suggests the first or base note in a hexachord.

gambetto: (Ital.) 'gambit'.

l. 12 cantilation: chant, cf. 'Come My Cantilations' (*CSP*, 166).

l. 14 Pierides: the Muses, whose reputed home before Helicon was Pieria on the northern slopes of Mt. Olympus.

ll. 16–17 Euphrates . . . Crassus: Crassus crossed the Euphrates in the invasion of Parthia where he was defeated and killed at Carrhae (53 B.C.).

l. 19 Augustus: honorary title first conferred on Julius Caesar Octavianus in 27 B.C., and thence on succeeding emperors.

Virgin Arabia: Latin 'intactae' (cf. I, line 40). Augustus in fact abandoned plans for the invasion of Arabia to avenge Crassus' defeat.

2

Propertius II, 1 (II, 1), lines 1–26, 37–46.

l. 25 you: Maecenas (cf. line 39), friend and counsellor to Augustus and patron of the literary salon which included Virgil, Horace and Propertius.

l. 28: Latin 'Ingenium nobis ipsa puella facit'. Quoted elsewhere by Pound (*SR*, 96; *P and D*, 214; *LE*, 103, 151, 343), and an important node in his discussion of Provençal love poetry and the relation between sex and creativity, suggested by Remy de Gourmont.

l. 32 gleam of Cos: the island of Cos in the Dodecanese produced the sheerest and most expensive silk; cf. *Hugh Selwyn Mauberley* III, line 2.

l. 36 Iliads: Homer's epic poem, the *Iliad*, deals with the Trojan war.

l. 41 Titans: the twelve children of Heaven and Earth, who rebelled against Zeus and the Olympian gods. They were defeated and imprisoned in a nether world.

ll. 41–3 Ossa . . . Pelion: the allusion is to the attempt of the twin giants Otus and Ephiates to climb up to heaven by piling Mt. Ossa on Olympus, and Mt. Pelion on Ossa.

l. 44 Thebes: the chief city in Boeotia, central Greece, and famous especially as the location of the story of Oedipus.

l. 45 Pergamus: Pergamum in Mysia, Asia Minor, was the capital of the Attalid dynasty (241–133 B.C.) under whom it became a centre of literary studies to rival Alexandria.

l. 46 Xerxes: king of Persia (485–465 B.C.), who cut a canal through Mt. Athos in his campaign against the Greeks.

Remus: twin brother of Romulus, the legendary founder of Rome, and killed by him (753 B.C.) for ridiculing his walls on the Palatine.

l. 47 Carthaginian: the Carthaginians, led by Hannibal, were defeated by Rome in the Second Punic War (218–201 B.C.).

l. 48: Latin 'Cimbrorumque minas et benefacta Mari' ('the threats of the Cimbri and Marius's great services to his country'). Pound's line has been a source of irritation to classicists for whom the Latin refers to the timely defeat of the invading Cimbri by Caius Marius at Vercellae (101 B.C.). Pound with great licence takes the Cimbri to be inhabitants of Cumbria, reads 'minas' as 'mines' and Marius as Marus, although he retains a later reference to Marius (VI, ll. 4, 12). As in other simple misreadings (XII, l. 19) and departures from the Latin (XII, l. 31), Pound may mean to undermine the pomposity and indicate the (for him) residing tedium of this patriotic strain.

l. 49: Pound breaks off, omitting eleven lines of Propertius.

l. 51 Callimachus: cf. note on I, line 1.

l. 52 Theseus: legendary Greek hero who slew the Cretan Bull and Minotaur and was afterwards king of Athens.

l. 53 Achilles: cf. note on I, line 28.

l. 54 Ixion: the legendary king of Thessaly who in an attempt to seduce Hera, instead embraced a cloud and so fathered the Centaurs. Zeus bound him to a spinning wheel of fire for his presumption.

Menoetius: Menoitios was the father of Patroklos, Achilles' favourite companion in the *Iliad*, where he is killed by Hercules.

Argo: the name of the ship which carried Jason and the Argonauts in search of the Golden Fleece.

Jove's grave . . . Titans: Propertius refers to the strife between

Jove and Enceladus at Phlegra. Enceladus the Titan was slain by a missile hurled by Athene.

l. 55 Caesarial ore rotundos: bombast in the official, public style.

l. 56 the tune of the Phrygian fathers: the Asiatic style of the royal family of Troy. Augustus was the adopted son of Caius Julius Caesar and could claim Trojan descent through the Iulii family from Aeneas, and thence from the founders of Troy.

3

Propertius II, 1 (II, 1), lines 47–50.

l. 65: the conduct that offends Cynthia is presumably Helen's seduction by Paris, her marriage to Deiphobus after Paris' death, and her return to her husband, Menelaus, after the fall of Troy.

VI

Propertius III, 5 (II, 13B), line 1; IV, 4 (III, 5), lines 13–16; IV, 3 (III, 4), lines 1, 4–6; IV, 4 (III, 5), lines 13–16; III, 5 (II, 13B), lines 3–14, 19–20, 34–42.

l. 2 Acheron: the name of several rivers, especially that in Epirus, believed to flow to the underworld, and of one of the five rivers of Hades.

l. 4 Marius and Jugurtha: Caius Marius (157–86 B.C.), seven times consul, who captured and put to death Jugurtha, the tyrannous ruler of Numidia in 104 B.C. Marius himself died insane.

ll. 6–10: Ronald Bottrall cites these lines as an example of 'the extremest licence which Pound permits himself' ('XXX Cantos of Ezra Pound', *EP*, ed. Sullivan, 134).

l. 6: at his death Caesar was rumoured to be planning an expedition to India; cf. v, line 19.

l. 8: Latin 'sera, sed Ausoniis veniet provincia virgis' ('under Italy's rod this province shall yet fall'). Pound's policemen emerge from the Latin 'virgis', meaning 'rods' and by extension 'truncheons'.

l. 9 Parthians: after the disgrace of Crassus' defeat at Carrhae (cf. v, ll. 18–19), Augustus arranged peaceful terms with the Parthians.

l. 16 Atalic: Attalic. Attalus was ruler of Pergamum, and the reputed inventor of cloth-of-gold weaving (Pliny, *Natural History*, VIII, 196).

l. 21: the Latin, 'quos ego Persephonae maxima dona feram', appeared as the epigraph to both *Canzoni* (1911) and *Ripostes* (1912). In Greek legend, Persephone, the daughter of Zeus and Demeter and goddess of seed corn, was obliged to spend one half of the year in the underworld, as queen of the dead.

l. 25 Syrian onyx: the allusion is to a box of unguents placed on or perhaps thrown into a funeral pyre.

ll. 26–7: Sullivan prints these lines in capitals, following the 1934 edition of the poem. The inscription and the following comments from Nestor are much condensed from the Latin.

l. 33 Adonis: a vegetation god, gored by a boar while hunting in Idalium, Cyprus. The mourning of Aphrodite ('the Cytherean') at his death is the subject of Bion's 'Lament for Adonis'.

ll. 35–7: Aphrodite and Persephone were rivals for the love of Adonis. Zeus ruled through Calliope that he must spend four months of the year with each and have the remainder at his own disposal. Adonis, once he had descended to Persephone, could not answer Aphrodite's summons; no more could Propertius respond to Cynthia.

VII

Propertius III, 7 (II, 15), lines 1–16, 23–6, 29, 31, 32, 33–4, 49, 51–4, 50, 35–40.

One of the few sections which present the central love themes of Propertius with seriousness.

l. 12 a sentiment shared by Remy de Gourmont (cf. Pound's essay 'Remy de Gourmont', *SPr*, 389, and the note to MAUBERLEY (1920) II, lines 26–9).

l. 13 Paris: cf. note on I, line 31.

l. 14 Endymion: a shepherd loved by the moon goddess Diana

(Gk. Selene) who descended every night to embrace him while he slept.

l. 15: the cynicism is Pound's addition to Propertius.

VIII

Propertius III, 24 (II, 28), lines 1–19, 21–34.

ll. 1–9: this passage is threaded with an ironic use of Latinate diction: 'unfortunate', 'ornamental', 'debit', 'torridity', 'canicular', 'derelictions'.

l. 2 ornamental death: the Latin is 'formosa mortua' (beautiful dead woman').

l. 10 Venus: Venus (Aphrodite) contended with Athene and Hera for the golden apple inscribed 'for the fairest', and they were referred to Paris, who awarded the prize to Aphrodite and with her help abducted Helen.

l. 12 Juno's Pelasgian temples: Juno (Gk. Hera) was the female equivalent of Jupiter and the goddess of women. Since in legend Hera was brought up by Temenus, son of Pelasgus, in Arcadia, the Arcadians claimed their cult as the earliest. 'Pelasgian' generally denotes all pre-Grecian peoples in the Mediterranean.

l. 13 Pallas good eyes: Pallas Athene was the patron goddess of Athens and Greek cities in general. She was frequently referred to as 'glaukopis' ('grey-blue eyed'); cf. *Hugh Selwyn Mauberley*, 'Yeux Glauques'.

ll. 19–20: Io was turned into a heifer by Zeus and persecuted by the jealous Hera until she came to Egypt, where she gave birth to Epaphos and was worshipped by the Egyptians as Isis. As a goddess Isis would be expected to drink nectar, not water.

l. 21: Ino was the second wife of Athamus, king of Thebes. She was entrusted with Dionysus, the son of Zeus by her sister Semele, but, driven insane by Hera, she jumped into the sea and was transformed into the sea goddess, Leucothea.

ll. 22–3: Andromeda was offered to a sea serpent because her mother Cassiopeia had offended the Nereïds (sea maidens) by boasting of her beauty. Perseus, the slayer of Medusa, changed the monster into a rock and married Andromeda. Gilkes finds the 'modern snigger' in the word 'respectably' 'entirely alien to Propertius' intention' (op. cit., 82). Sullivan defends it as an example of 'logopoeia' (*EP and Sextus Propertius*, 73–4); cf. also XI, line 28.

ll. 24–6: in Greek myth Callisto was the mother by Zeus of Arcas, the legendary ancestor of the Arcadians. She was changed into a bear by Hera and almost killed by Arcas out hunting. Zeus intervened and changed them into the constellations Ursa Major (the Great Bear) and Arctophylax respectively.

l. 26: Latin 'haec nocturna suo sidere vela regit' ('Now she guides by her star's light the sails of the ships that journey through the night'). Pound puns on the Latin 'vela' ('sails', and by metonymy 'ships'); cf. also IX, line 6.

l. 31 Semele: Semele was consumed by Zeus' lightning in the conception of Dionysus.

l. 34 beauties of Maeonia: i.e. the beautiful women in Homer, whose reputed birthplace was in Maeonia, an ancient name for Lydia in Asia Minor.

ll. 38–9: Jove, identified with Zeus and Jupiter, was the principal Greek and Roman god. His affairs constantly aroused the jealousy and vengeance of Juno (Gk. Hera).

l. 42: Pound's addition to Propertius.

IX

1

Propertius III, 25 (II, 28B), lines 1–8, 10–12.

l. 1 rhombs: the noisy rhombus wheel of IV, line 32, is now still.

l. 3 moon: witches attempted to constrain the moon and redirect its power. Propertius refers elsewhere to this practice (I, 1, ll. 25–7).

l. 4 ominous owl hoot: the eagle owl's cry was a portent of death.

l. 6 Avernus: a lake in Campania, near Naples. Aeneas descended to the underworld through a near-by cavern, but the name is used also, as here, to refer to the underworld itself.

l. 7 Cerulean: azure, recalling Pound's descriptions of Lake Garda (cf. ' "Blandula, Tenulla, Vagula" ', and 'The Flame', *CSP*, 64). Kenner suggests Pound puns in 'tears for two' on the English idiom 'tea for two' (*Poetry of EP*, 148).

l. 10: Latin 'Per magnum est salva puella Iovem' ('By the might of Jove, my loved one's saved'). Pound's line, says Kenner, is 'merely suggested' by the Latin (ibid.). Zeus was the greatest of the Greek Olympian gods.

2

Propertius III, 26 (II, 28C), lines 1–3, 5–7, 9–12.

Cf. Pound's earlier version of these lines in 'Prayer for His Lady's Life' (*CSP*, 52). Replying to a review of the *Homage* in the *New Age*, Pound wrote 'And there is a perfectly literal and, by the same token, perfectly lying and "spiritually" mendacious translation of "Vobiscum est Iope" etc. in my earlier volume *Canzoni*, for whomsoever wants the humorless vein' (Homberger, 164). For the versification of this section see Sullivan, *EP and Sextus Propertius* (pp. 82–4).

l. 13 Persephone and Dis: Persephone was carried off by Pluto while picking flowers in the meadows of Enna, Sicily. She ruled as queen of the dead for half the year. 'Dis' is the Roman corruption of Gk. Pluto, also called Hades.

ll. 14–19: Gilkes comments, 'This is not Propertius speaking: it is perhaps the Ovid of the "Heroides", who had nothing to learn about what in our modern slang we call "debunking" ' (op. cit., 80).

l. 16 Iope: either Antiope, wife of Theseus, or the daughter of Aeolus, god of winds. The name was probably used by Propertius for metrical convenience.

Tyro: the lover of Poseidon, visited by him in the form of the river Enipeus.

Pasiphae: the daughter of the sun, wife to Minos and mother of the Minotaur.

Achaia: a name given to separate territories in the north and along the southern shore of Greece, or to Greece generally.

l. 17 Troad: the district of Troy.

Campania: a fertile and wealthy district, south of the Roman Latium. Propertius has 'numero Romana puella' and Pound in 'Prayer for His Lady's Life' rendered the phrase as 'all the maidens of Rome'.

l. 19 Avernus: cf. ix, line 6 above.

3

Propertius III, 26 (II, 28D), lines 13–16.

l. 24 Dian: Diana, the moon goddess, and also from her association with Hecate, patroness of witches.

l. 28: Pound comments that the humourless vein of his earlier version made it 'utterly impossible to translate the "Votivas noctes et mihi" at its termination' (Homberger, 164).

X

Propertius III, 27 (II, 29A, B), lines 1–7, 9–17, 20–6, 29–32, 35–8, 27, 42.

There is a detailed and sympathetic study of this poem in Richardson (op. cit., 24–9).

ll. 10–11: the Latin 'sed nudi fuerunt, quorum lascivior unus' should convey, says Gilkes, that the boys who waylay Propertius are not human but 'little cupids, divinely sent' and that they are ' "unrestrained" . . . sprightly or playful or forward, even wanton' but not 'lustful, lewd, licentious' (op. cit., 81–2). Pound clearly intends a pun on 'lascivior' and 'lascivious' at the expense perhaps of the artificial convention of the gang of Cupids.

l. 19 Sidonian night cap: a night cap from Sidon, Phoenicia, famous for its purple dye; cf. 'Punic faces', ii (l. 32n.).

ll. 27–43: the Mueller text that Pound used conjoins the sections presenting the gang of Cupids and the exchange between Propertius and Cynthia, which in the original elegy are distinct (II, 29A and B). Sullivan suggests this may have misled Pound 'into keeping the whole section rather light and jocular' in a way inappropriate to the force of Cynthia's passion (*EP and Sextus Propertius*, 57).

l. 29: Kenner points to the 'witty scepticism' here, by which this line refers either to the preceding or to the following sentence (*Pound Era*, 285).

l. 33: Pound injects a vorticist principle into the Latin. In the essay 'Vorticism' he wrote: 'It seems quite natural to me that an artist should have just as much pleasure in an arrangement of planes or in a pattern of figures, as in painting portraits of fine ladies. . . . There is undoubtedly a language of form and colour.' (*G-B*, 87, 92.)

ll. 39–40: Latin 'aspice, ut in toto nullus mihi corpore surgat/ spiritus admisso notus adulterio' ('look, no quick-drawn breath in my body which would confess my adultery to you'). Pound introduces a pun on 'incubus' (from 'spiritus', meaning 'breath' or 'kiss') and 'incumbent' (l. 37) which is not in the Latin. An incubus is a demon (a nightmare) who descended upon sleeping women.

XI

1

Propertius I, 15 (I, 15), lines 1–3.

2

Propertius III, 28 (II, 30A), lines 1–8; III, 30 (II, 32), lines 18–28, 31–4; III, 28 (II, 30B), lines 26–30; III, 30 (II, 32), lines 35–6; III, 28 (II, 30B), line 20; III, 30 (II, 32), lines 29–30; III, 18 (II, 24B), lines 11, 14.

Like VI this is a collage of the Latin. Sullivan suggests that Pound uses the 'logopoeia' of Propertius' II, 32, where it appears in an ironic and mocking series of mythological examples, as the basis of this section, but that he 'distorts it and by reinforcing this distortion with themes taken from other elegies, he produces a poem on the power of love, which is singularly free from irony' (*EP and Sextus Propertius*, 73; cf. also pp. 90–5 for a discussion of Pound's techniques of juxta-position and compression).

l. 5 Ranaus: a fictitious river, emended by Sullivan with Pound's approval to 'Tanais'.
l. 7 gilded Pegasean back: Bellerophon attempted to fly to heaven on Pegasus.
l. 8 feathery sandals of Perseus: Hermes lent Perseus wings for his feet as an aid in obtaining the Gorgon's head.
l. 10 Hermes: the Roman Mercury, who, as messenger of the gods, was looked on as the patron of roads and travellers.
ll. 20–2: spoken by Cynthia.
ll. 23–4: Propertius' defence of Cynthia's innocence.
l. 25 A foreign lover: Paris; cf. i, line 31.
ll. 27–8: Aphrodite (Cythera) was caught by her husband Hephaestus in an act of adultery with Ares (Mars), entangled by him in a net and exposed to the ridicule of the gods. On their release Aphrodite renewed her virginity in the sea.
l. 28 respectable heavens: 'logopoeia'; cf. viii, line 23.
l. 34 Semele . . . Io: cf. viii, lines 19, 31.
l. 35 bird: the eagle sacred to Jove who in legend carried off Ganymede, a son of Tros, and the most beautiful of mortals.
l. 36 Ida: Pound personifies Mt. Ida where Paris was brought up and fell in love with the nymph Oenone.
l. 38 Hyrcanian: Hyrcania was south of the Caspian Sea.
Eos: goddess of the dawn.
l. 40 Via Sacra: Rome's principal street, running past the Temple of Vesta, was the haunt of prostitutes (cf. Propertius ii, 23, ll. 15–16).

XII

Propertius II, 32 (II, 34A, B, C), lines 1, 3–8, 21, 12, 11, 13, 15–18, 33–4, 37–8, 41, 45–50, 61–78, 55–60, 79–80, 83–94.
l. 4: Pound's addition.
l. 6 Trojan: Paris; cf. i, line 31, xi, line 25.
Menelaus: the husband of Helen.

l. 7 Colchis, Jason: Colchis was the destination of Jason and the Argonauts. Jason returned with Medea (the king's daughter) but abandoned her for Glauce.

l. 8 Lynceus: one of the Argonauts, but here a fictitious name for a pompous and aspiring minor poet, rival for Cynthia's favours.

l. 18 Achelöus . . . Hercules: the river god, Achelous, twice fought Hercules for the hand of Deianira, the second time in the form of a bull.

l. 19 Adrastus: king of Argos and leader of the 'Seven against Thebes'. He escaped in defeat on his horse Arion who is said to have expressed grief at the grave of Archemorus.

Achenor: Propertius has 'Archemorus' ('Forerunner of Death'), a name given to Opheltes, son of the king of Nemea, by the 'Seven against Thebes', who saw his death as an ill-omen.

l. 20 Aeschylus: the founder of Greek tragedy, whose works include the drama *Seven against Thebes*.

l. 21 Antimachus: Greek writer and poet, author of the fifth-century epic poem *Thebaïs*.

l. 30: this comment is Pound's addition.

l. 31 Actian: Actium, the site of Octavian's defeat of Antony and Cleopatra (31 B.C.) which marked the end of the Roman Republic and the beginning of the Empire.

Virgil: P. Vergilius Maro, author of the *Eclogues, Georgics* and the *Aeneid* (30–19 B.C.), a national epic celebrating the origin and growth of Rome.

Phoebus: Phoebus Apollo whose temple was at Actium and who was supposed to have assisted Octavian against Antony.

Chief of Police: Pound puns on the Latin 'custodis' ('guard', 'sentinel').

l. 33 Ilian: i.e. Trojan, hence Roman.

l. 34 Aeneas: the hero of the *Aeneid*, who is described as founding a Trojan settlement in Latium which was the origin of Rome.

l. 35 Lavinian: i.e. Latium. Lavinia, the daughter of the king of Latium, was courted by Aeneas.

l. 38 larger Iliad: Virgil's *Aeneid*, for which Homer was a primary source. Pound says 'larger' not 'greater', finding perhaps a hint of irony in Propertius' description of the *Aeneid* as 'nesco iquid' ('something', 'I don't know what').

l. 39 to Imperial order: Virgil followed the prescriptions of Maecenas and Augustus for patriotic verse, while Propertius resisted them. This aside is Pound's addition.

l. 42 Thyrsis and Daphnis: characters in Bk. VII of Virgil's *Eclogues* (39 B.C.), where Thyrsis is defeated in a singing match presided over by Daphnis.

l. 43: Latin 'utque decem possint corrumpere mala puellas' ('and how ten apples can seduce girls'). Pound puns on 'mala' ('mālum' = 'apple', 'malum' = 'evil').

l. 46 Tityrus: a shepherd in Virgil's *Eclogues*, sometimes identified with Virgil himself.

l. 47 Corydon . . . Alexis: in Virgil, Corydon is a young shepherd enamoured of Alexis (*Eclogues*, II, VII).

l. 49 Hamadryads: tree nymphs.

l. 50 Ascraeus: Ascra in Boeotia was the home of Hesiod, the author of *Works and Days*, a realistic picture of rustic life. Hence the comparison with Wordsworth and the practical advice of line 52.

l. 51 Wordsworthian: amongst several ripostes to Hale's criticism of the *Homage*, Pound wrote to Felix Schelling in 1922, 'That fool in Chicago took the *Homage* for a translation, despite the mention of Wordsworth and the parodied line from Yeats' (*SL*, 178). Pound himself had something less than respect for Wordsworth, describing him as 'a silly old sheep' whose talent was 'buried in a desert of bleatings' (*LE*, 277).

l. 55 indeterminate character: Pound makes the ladies who are guests ('conviva puellas') in Propertius, more 'convivial'.

ll. 59–60: Kenner calls these lines 'a truly glorious botch', a 'superbly impressionistic distich' (*Poetry of EP*, 150); cf. also Richardson, op. cit., pp. 24–5, and Sullivan who feels that Pound's own dislike of Virgil ousts Propertius' original 'deferential compliment' (*EP and Sextus Propertius*, 101–104).

l. 59 tortoise: Pound puns on the Latin 'testudo' meaning either 'tortoise' or 'lyre'.

l. 60 your: i.e. Virgil's. Pound called Virgil a 'second-rater, a Tennysonianized version of Homer' (*SL*, 87).

ll. 61–5: Pound strays far from the Latin.

l. 65: the diction and modulated suspense of this line is in the manner, Kenner suggests, of Henry James (*Pound Era*, 14).

ll. 66–7 Varro . . . Leucadia: the Latin poet Publius Terentius Varro (b. 82 B.C.) wrote a free translation of the *Argonautica* of Apollonius Rhodius. His love poems to Leucadia are lost.

ll. 68–9 Catullus . . . Lesbia: Catullus (84–54 B.C.), a major Latin poet best known for his poems to Lesbia (Clodia).

ll. 70–1 Calvus . . . Quintilia: Calvus (82–47 B.C.), orator and poet, all of whose poems, including those to his wife or mistress Quintilia, are lost.

l. 72 Gallus . . . Lycoris: Cornelius Gallus (69–26 B.C.), friend to Virgil and first Prefect of Egypt, wrote four books of love poems, since lost, to the actress Cytheris (the Lycoris of the poems).

HUGH SELWYN MAUBERLEY

(June 1920)

In September 1920 the *Dial* followed the first London edition of *Mauberley* by reprinting the first six poems of the total sequence. This version may well account for the attribution to the poem of a Pre-Raphaelite emphasis it does not as a whole possess (cf. Yvor Winters, *Hound and Horn*, April–June 1933, 538, and *In Defence of Reason*, 1947, 68). The *Dial* text also significantly omitted the initials 'E.P.' from the title of the first poem, and this omission was repeated in the poem's first full appearance in America in *Poems 1918–21*. Not until the appearance of *Selected Poems* in 1949 were the initials 'E.P.' and the Ode's place as simply the first in a series firmly established (cf. Espey, *Ezra Pound's Mauberley: A Study in Composition*, 1955, ch. 1).

In these early publication details one might see the under-tow of what has become the essential critical debate on the poem: the relation of Pound to the fictitious Mauberley. Pound himself maintained that Mauberley was unequivocally a distinct persona. Writing to Felix Schelling, he said, '(Of course, I'm no more Mauberley than Eliot is Prufrock. Mais passons.) Mauberley is a mere surface. Again a study in form, an attempt to condense the James novel. Meliora speramus.' (*SL*, 180.) As such *Mauberley* is consistent with Pound's description of his poetry to W. C. Williams in 1908 as 'dramatic and in the character of the person named in the title' (*SL*, 3), and part too of the continuing 'search for the real' begun in *Personae* and conducted through the casting off of 'complete masks of the self in each poem' (*G-B*, 85). Pound's reference to Henry James also, in the letter to Schelling, helps uncover

183

his intention in *Mauberley*. One of his longest critical essays had been written on James two years before the publication of *Mauberley*. There he identified as James's particular subject the depiction of 'atmospheres, nuances, impressions of personal tone and quality', but entered also, à propos of James's *The Awkward Age* (1899), his own important proviso:

> These timbres and tonalities are his stronghold, he is ignorant of nearly everything else. It is all very well to say that modern life is largely made up of velleities, atmospheres, timbres, nuances, etc., but if people really spent as much time fussing, to the extent of the Jamesian fuss about such normal, trifling, age-old affairs, as slight inclinations to adultery, slight disinclinations to marry, to refrain from marrying, etc., etc., life would scarcely be worth the bother of keeping on with it. It is also contendable that one must depict such mush in order to abolish it.
>
> *(LE, 324)*

If Pound had one particular James story half in mind in composing *Mauberley*, it would seem to be, as Espey suggests, James's 'The Figure in the Carpet', a short story which appeared first in a collection titled *Embarrassments* (1896). As such it belongs to a period Pound labels as 'light literature'. 'Neither *Terminations*', he says, 'nor (1896) *Embarrassments* would have founded a reputation' *(LE, 323)*.

At approximately the same time as his essay on James, Pound had begun a series of 'Imaginary Letters' in the character of Walter Villerant (September 1917–November 1918 in the *Little Review*, reprinted in *Pavannes and Divagations*, 1958). Villerant, like James and Pound, is an American expatriate who, as Donald Davie points out, borrows from James in his first letter, and is 'in an unsubtle way a very Jamesian person, at least as "Jamesian" is commonly understood' *(Poet as Sculptor, 92)*. Villerant, Davie suggests, emerges 'not as a limited person whom Pound will surpass, but, much of the time, as an ideally civilised person whom Pound aspires to emulate' (ibid., 100). But in the face of this there is Pound's own reference, in a letter to Wyndham Lewis, from whom he took over the series, to Villerant's 'effete and over-civilised organism' (quoted in Gallup, 73). Villerant (and therefore perhaps Mauberley also) would seem from this exactly to represent the 'mere surface' that Pound found in the Henry James of the 1890s. Villerant and Mauberley are alike timorous and disdainful dandies, and even if we admit that they represent a tendency in Pound himself, we might also grant that he is free of their aestheticism, for immediately preceding (and, as it would seem, suggesting) his remark on Mauberley and James in the letter to Schelling, Pound writes, 'I am perhaps didactic. . . . It's all rubbish to pretend that art isn't didactic. A revelation is always didactic. Only the aesthetes since 1880 have pretended the contrary, and they aren't a very sturdy lot.' (*SL*, 180.)

The Henry James of the late 1890s would seem then to be one source for Pound's *Mauberley*. And if, as Pound says, he finds in James of that period only 'sweet dim faded lavender tone', a sentimentality which 'softens his edges', he finds something of a remedy in a second model, Théophile Gautier.

At a particular date in a particular room two authors, neither engaged in picking the other's pockets, decided that the dilutation of vers libre, Amygism, Lee Masterism, general floppiness had gone too far and that some counter-current must be set going. Parallel situation centuries ago in China. Remedy prescribed, *Émaux et Camées* (or The Bay State Hymn Book). Rhyme and regular strophes. Results: Poems in Mr. Eliot's second volume . . . , also 'H. S. Mauberley'.

(*Criterion*, July 1932, 590)

Gautier's *Émaux et Camées* (1852) was early on established in Pound's canon, and as Espey shows, the direct influence of Gautier on Pound's poetry appears before *Mauberley* in *Lustra* (op. cit., 27–8). But what Pound admired in Gautier's work is clearly what is lacking in James the sentimentalist. 'We may take it', says Pound, 'that Gautier achieved hardness in *Émaux et Camées*' ('The Hard and Soft in French Poetry', *LE*, 285). 'Hardness' as a virtue in poetry is clearly consistent with Imagist principles, with Pound's prophecy in 1917 of a new verse which will be 'harder and saner . . . austere, direct, free from emotional slither' (*LE*, 12), and is fundamental also to the analogy between the arts he suggests in the essay on Vorticism. There Pound presents a first type of poetry like music and 'another sort of poetry where painting or sculpture seems as it were "just coming over into speech." ' (*G-B*, 82). It is just this sculptural hardness, one might think, which distinguishes Pound from the James of the 1890s and from the Jamesian Walter Villerant. But this would hardly seem to distinguish Pound from Mauberley since it is in fact Mauberley himself who in his own defence invokes Gautier in the phrase 'the "sculpture" of rhyme'. And if the attribution here is uncertain, since the speaker at this point in the poem is uncertain, then what of 'Medallion', the last poem in the sequence and one generally agreed to be Mauberley's own? (But cf. notes on this poem.) Surely this poem has the virtue of 'hardness'? But then this is precisely the point. Mauberley's 'Medallion' has hardness and nothing else; he is like the Parnassian poet Heredia who, while following Gautier, 'fell short of his merit' and who is 'hard, but there or thereabouts he ends'. Gautier, by contrast, is not only 'hard'; he is 'intent on conveying a certain verity of feeling' and it is this, says Pound, which 'makes for poetry' (*LE*, 285).

Pound had detailed his own 'intentness on the quality of the emotion to be conveyed' in his account of the making of the poem 'In a Station of the Metro' (*G-B*, 86–7, 89). 'In a poem of this sort', he says, 'one is trying to record the precise instant when a thing outward and objective transforms itself, or darts into a thing inward and subjective' (p. 89) and his description echoes through the same essay's definitions of the image as 'that which presents an intellectual and emotional complex in an instant of time' (p. 86), and of the vortex as the 'radiant node or cluster; . . . from which, and through which, and into which, ideas are constantly rushing' (p. 92). Pound it

186

would seem had absorbed and extended Gautier's lesson, enriching his 'intentness' in the context of the 'intensive art' of Vorticism. At the same time, while recommending the model of Flaubert and admiring his 'impressionist' followers for their 'exact presentation', Pound felt 'They are often so intent on exact presentation that they neglect intensity, selection, and concentration' (*LE*, 399). The corrective in both cases would seem to have been the Vorticist who looked for the 'more intense', the 'more dynamic' forms of expression in the creation of the Vortex as 'the point of maximum energy'. It is this energy then, we can suppose, which distinguishes Pound the Vorticist poet from the inert Parnassian Mauberley, and if Mauberley, as Pound said, 'buries E.P. in the first poem' so as to remove 'all his troublesome energies' (T. Connolly, 'Further Notes on Mauberley', *Accent*, Winter 1956, 59), it is only to drift towards his own extinction, leaving 'Medallion' as his limited achievement and epitaph. Pound we remember, refusing to be buried, was already embarked on the 'long vorticist poem' of the *Cantos*.

Hugh Selwyn Mauberley is a suite of eighteen poems in two parts, the first running from the 'Ode' to 'Envoi (1919)', and the second, under the title MAUBERLEY (1920), from 'I' to 'Medallion'.

On the title-page of the poem in *Personae* (1926) Pound included the footnote (since deleted): 'The sequence is so distinctly a farewell to London that the reader who chooses to regard this as an exclusively American edition may as well omit it and turn at once to [the poem *Homage to Sextus Propertius*].' In *Selected Poems* (1949) the epigraph and the subtitle, 'Life and Contacts', are omitted. In a revised version of the poem in *Diptych Rome–London* (1958) they are re-introduced, but the subtitle is reversed to 'Contacts and Life', thus following, Pound wrote to his New Directions publisher James Laughlin, 'the actual order of the subject matter' (Ruthven, 127).

Epigraph: "Vocat æstus in umbram" (Lat.), 'The heat calls

187

us into the shade', from the fourth Eclogue of the Roman poet Marcus Aurelius Olympius Nemesianus, poet at the court of the emperor Caius in A.D. 283. Pound published the volume titled *Umbra* in the same month as *Mauberley*.

E.P. Ode pour l'Election de son Sepulchre

Title: adapted from Pierre Ronsard's 'De l'Élection de son sépulcre' ('On the choice of his burial place'), Pound adding a pun on the term 'Epode': in classical literature a lyric metre, or after-song of sombre character following a strophe and anti-strophe. Ronsard (1524–85) was a member of the Pléiade, a poetic group which aimed to enrich French poetry through the imitation of classical models: cf. lines 2–3 below, and the reference to the 'classics in paraphrase' (II, l. 8). Pound referred to Ronsard as 'still under-rated' (*SR*, 176) and to the Pléiade as a side line in 'lyricism and grace' to the main line of Villon, Heine and Gautier (*SL*, 88). He may have had in mind also the 'ardent Hellenists' (Richard Aldington and H.D.) who with himself formed the nucleus of the Imagist movement. Their poems were, he said, 'modern . . . even if the subject is classic' (*SL*, 11).

In a later comment on the critics of *Mauberley* Pound said, 'The worst muddle they make is in failing to see that Mauberley buries E.P. in the first poem; gets rid of all his troublesome energies' (Connolly, op. cit., 59). The 'Ode' follows the spirit and to an extent the letter of early reviews of Pound's work, cf. in particular Babette Deutsch, 'Ezra Pound, Vorticist' (*Reedy's Mirror*, 21 Dec. 1917) and Louis Untermeyer, 'Ezra Pound – Proseur' (*New Republic*, 17 Aug. 1918), reprinted in Homberger (pp. 131–7, 142–4).

l. 1: cf. the portrait of M. Verog (' "Siena mi fe' " ', l. 17), 'out of step with the decade', and (MAUBERLEY (1920) II, l. 1), 'For three years, diabolus in the scale'. Louis Untermeyer refers to Pound's *Pavannes and Divisions* as 'a queer, out of tune collection; queerer than ever this year, 1918' (Homberger, 144).

ll. 2–3 He strove . . . poetry: Pound had included Dante's phrase 'Ma qui la morta poesi risurga' ('Now that the grave re-awakens poetry') (*Purgatorio*, I, l. 7), as an epigraph to the section 'Canzoniere: Studies in Form' in *Provença* (1910). Babette Deutsch, referring to *Provença*, cites the poem 'Histrion' as 'eloquent of what he strove for in these reincarnations of dead singers' (Homberger, 132).

ll. 5–6: cf. the poem 'Salutation the Second', in *Lustra*, which begins, 'You were praised, my books,/ because I had just come from the country;/ I was twenty years behind the times/ so you found an audience ready'.

l. 6 half savage country: Pound was born in Hailey, Idaho, in 1885. But it was uninformed opinion which associated him with the American frontier. His family left for New York, and subsequently Philadelphia, before he was two years old. 'I left at the age of eighteen months', said Pound, 'and I don't remember the roughness' (*Writers at Work: The Paris Review Interviews*. Second Series, 1963, 45). Walter Villerant in the second of the 'Imaginary Letters' writes of having passed years in a 'barbarous country' (*P and D*, 58).

out of date: Pound wrote that Henry James's 'drawing of *mœurs contemporaines* was so circumstantial, so concerned with the setting, with detail, nuance, social aroma, that his transcripts were "out of date" almost before his books had gone into a second edition' (*LE*, 339). The phrase occurs also in Babette Deutsch who writes, 'It should be noted, though, that Pound does not in any sense believe, or lead those who know his work to believe, that he was born out of date' (Homberger, 132). Louis Untermeyer, as one of those who was not convinced, refers to *Pavannes and Divisions* as a 'collection of out of date manifestoes' and to Pound as 'an anachronism' (ibid., 143, 144).

l. 7 lilies from the acorn: the components of the image, Pound suggested, 'must be in harmony, they must form an organism, they must be an oak sprung from an acorn' (*LE*, 51). And in *Patria Mia* he wrote, 'As touching "art for art's sake": the oak does not grow for the purpose or with the intention of being built into ships and tables, yet a wise nation, will take care to preserve the forests. It is the oak's business to grow good oak' (p. 57).

l. 8 Capaneus: one of the seven warriors sent from Argos to attack Thebes. The best-known version of the myth is Aeschylus' *Seven Against Thebes*. Capaneus boasted that not even Zeus' thunderbolt would prevent him scaling the walls of Thebes, and was duly burnt to a cinder. In Dante Capaneus is presented as defiant even in hell. Virgil predicts for him the continued torment of 'thine own hot rage' (*Inferno*, XIV, ll. 43–72); cf. Pound's *The Spirit of Romance* (p. 132). Pound's early reviewers refer repeatedly to his own 'rebelliousness' or 'scorn' (cf. Homberger, 132, 136, 144).

l. 9 (Gk.) from the Sirens' song to Odysseus (*Odyssey*, Bk. XII, l. 189), recalled later by Pound in Canto LXXIX in reference to Henry James (521/488–9). With Homer's next line, ''Αργεῖοι Τρῶές τε θεῶν ἰότητι μόγησαν', it reads 'for indeed we know all that the Argives and Trojans have suffered at Troy by the will of the Gods'. 'Τροίη' rhymes for Pound presumably with 'lee-way' (l. 11).

Pound's identification with Odysseus had begun in earnest with the first three Cantos (published in *Poetry*, 1917), his translation of the first part of Bk. XI of the *Odyssey* being moved significantly, in the revision of these poems, from the third to the first Canto. The reference here to the Sirens' song contains also perhaps a covert allusion to the art of 'melopoeia', the charging of words with some musical property in which the Greeks 'attained the greatest skill'. 'In *melopœia*' we find, says Pound, 'a force tending often to lull, or to distract the reader from the exact sense of the language' (*LE*, 26).

l. 10: Odysseus plugs his crew's ears with beeswax, while he himself, bound to the mast, hears the Sirens' song (*Odyssey*, Bk. XII, ll. 173–200).

l. 12: Babette Deutsch refers to Pound's travels through Europe before he came to London (in 1906, and then in 1908) as 'his bathing all his sensibilities in a kind of golden other age. What lured and held him then was not so different, however, from the things that hold and lure him now' (Homberger, 131–2). Odysseus had stayed on Circe's island of Aeaea for one year (*Odyssey*, Bk. X).

l. 13: repeated in MAUBERLEY (1920) I, lines 5–6.

Penelope: Odysseus' faithful wife, to whom he eventually returned.

Flaubert: Gustave Flaubert (1821–80), the French novelist. Flaubert, for Pound, was the 'archetype' in a tradition of prose writing – including Stendhal, Turgenev, the brothers Goncourt, Maupassant and Henry James – of 'An attempt to set down things as they are, to find the word that corresponds to the thing' (*ABC of R*, 74). In England the tradition 'becomes operative' in Ford Hueffer (Madox Ford), in whom Pound finds 'a sense of the *mot juste*. The belief that poetry should be at least as well written as prose' (*G-B*, 115). James Joyce also, Pound wrote, 'went back to Papa Flaubert' (*P/J*, 248) and in his discussion of Joyce's *Ulysses*, 'The *mot juste* is of public utility. I can't help it. I am not offering this fact as a sop to aesthetes who want all authors to be fundamentally useless. We are governed by words, the laws are graven words, and literature is the sole means of keeping these words living and accurate' (ibid., 200, *LE*, 409). The doctrine of the *mot juste*, particularly through Ford's influence, led Pound himself directly to the first two tenets of the Imagist programme, 'direct treatment of the "thing" ', and 'to use absolutely no word that does not contribute to the presentation' (*LE*, 3). If a reference to 'melopoeia' is contained in lines 9–10 above, the reference here is to 'phanopoeia', 'the greatest drive toward utter precision of word' (*LE*, 26).

l.14 obstinate isles: Hugh Kenner suggests 'both the British Isles and recalcitrant aesthetic objectives' (*Poetry of EP*, 170).

l. 15 Circe: the goddess of Aeaea who is introduced and often subsequently referred to in the *Odyssey* by mention of her 'lovely hair' (cf. Bk. X, l. 136). Odysseus obtains an antidote from Hermes to the drug by which Circe has converted his crew to swine, and delays on Aeaea for a year. The *Cantos* begin at the point of his departure from Circe.

l. 17 "the march of events": 'As far as the "living art" goes', wrote Pound, 'I should like to break up *cliché*, to disintegrate these magnetised groups that stand between the reader of poetry and the drive of it' (*SPr*, 41), and again to Harriet Monroe, 'There must be no clichés, set phrases, stereotyped journalese. The only escape from such is by precision, a result of concentrated attention to what is writing' (*SL*, 49). Cf. note on line 13.

ll. 18–19 He passed . . . eage: Pound adapts the opening line of *Le Testament* by François Villon (1431–63?), 'En l'an trentiesme de mon eage' (*Oeuvres*, ed. André Mary, Paris, 1951, 17). Cf. also his 'Or perhaps I *will* die at thirty?' in the poem 'Salutation the Third' (*CSP*, 165). Earlier editions of *Mauberley* contain 'trientiesme'. The present 'trentuniesme' appeared first in *Diptych Rome–London* (1958) and would suggest in terms of Pound's own career the year of the publication of *Lustra* (1916). Babette Deutsch closes her review 'Ezra Pound, Vorticist' on the obituary note, 'Pound may be remembered for many things. . . . He is now thirty-two years old, and by his own count, a man of middle age' (Homberger, 136). Pound may also have detected a parallel between his own imminent departure from London and Villon's banishment from the Paris region to obscurity at the age of thirty-two. Certainly his admiration for Villon is everywhere apparent. In *The Spirit of Romance* Pound places him in the Provençal tradition of 'unvarnished, intimate speech' (p. 167). Villon, he says, 'has the stubborn persistency of one whose gaze cannot be deflected from the actual fact before him: what he sees, he writes' (p. 168). Villon emerges therefore as a model of precision and intensity comparable to Flaubert (*LE*, 26) and as an influence on Imagism (R. S. Flint, 'Imagisme' in *EP*, ed. Sullivan, 40). Cf. also the poems 'Villonaud for this Yule' and 'A Villonaud: Ballad of the Gibbet' in *Personae*.

II

l. 1 The age demanded: repeated line 9, and in the title of the later poem ' "The Age Demanded" '. Cf. 'Imaginary Letters 1 : Walter Villerant to Mrs. Bland Burn',

> Art that sells on production is bad art, essentially. It is art that is made to demand. It suits the public. The taste of the public is bad. The taste of the public is always bad because it is not an individual expression but merely a mania for assent, a mania to be 'in on it'.
>
> *(P and D*, 55–6)

and from Pound 'in propria persona':

> As for 'expressing the age', surely there are five thousand sculptors all busy expressing the inanities, the pettinesses, the sillinesses . . . of the age. Of course the age is 'not so bad as all that'. But the man who tries to express his age, instead of expressing himself, is doomed to destruction.
>
> *(G-B*, 102)

l. 2 accelerated grimace: Pound referred to Futurism as 'a kind of accelerated impressionism'. He was 'wholly opposed', he said, to its aesthetic principles, and as a Vorticist had not its 'curious tic of destroying past glories' (*G-B*, 90).

l. 3 the modern stage: Pound was drama critic for the *Outlook* in October 1919 under the name of M. D. Atkins, and for the *Athenaeum*, under the initials T.J.V., from March to July 1920. He was abruptly fired from both.

l. 4 Attic grace: a pure classical style associated with Attica, a region forming the south-east promontory of central Greece. The Attic dialect was a special form of the southern Ionic dialect and was superseded under the Athenian Empire and Macedon by a single common Greek dialect, though Lucian is an example of its later revival.

ll. 7–8 Better mendacities . . . paraphrase: a reviewer (Adrian Collins?) of Pound's *Quia Pauper Amavi* (1919) referred to Pound's 'paraphrases from the Provençal and from Propertius' (Homberger, 160). Pound replied, defending Propertius, 'there is a perfectly literal and, by the same token, perfectly lying and "spiritually" mendacious translation of "Vobiscum est Iope etc." in my earlier volume *Canzoni*' (ibid., 164). Pound had discovered in Propertius an example of 'logopoeia', a mode he said which 'does not translate; though the attitude of mind it expresses may pass through a paraphrase' (*LE*, 25).

l. 9 a mould in plaster: Gaudier-Brzeska had planned to use plaster for his hieratic head of Pound. Pound found it 'a most detestable medium' and bought instead a half-ton block of marble (Norman, 135).

ll. 10–11 Made . . . kinema: Pound's lines echo a similar sentiment in Henry James, 'As we all know, this is an age of prose, of machinery, of wholesale production, of coarse and hasty processes' ('A Little Tour in France', quoted in A. Holder, *Three Voyagers in Search of Europe*, 1966, 223).

l. 11 prose kinema: 'The logical end of impressionist art', wrote Pound, 'is the cinematograph. . . . Or, to put it another way, the cinematograph does away with the need for a lot of impressionist art' (*G-B*, 89).

l. 12 "sculpture" of rhyme: Pound's phrase recalls Théophile Gautier's 'Vers, marbre, onyx, émail' in the poem 'L'Art' (*Émaux et Camées*).

III

Pound's (or Mauberley's) portrayal of cultural decline, aside from the debt to Théophile Gautier, owes something perhaps to Henry James whom Pound presents as 'concerned with mental temperatures, circumvolvulous social pressures, the clash of contending conventions' (*LE*, 339).

l. 1: Pound is indebted to Gautier's 'La Rose-Thé' and 'À une Robe rose' (Espey, 35–6). Cf. the reference to 'Pierian roses' (XII, l. 28) and 'As roses might in magic amber laid' ('Envoi', l. 13).

tea-rose: a hybrid rose especially popular in England between 1830 and 1900.

l. 2 mousseline of Cos: transparent muslin from the Greek island of Cos in the Sporades; cf. 'If she goes in a gleam of Cos, in a slither of dyed stuff' (*Homage to Sextus Propertius* v, l. 32). Remy de Gourmont lists a 'robe de mousseline' in his 'Litanies de la Rose' (quoted by Pound in 'French Poets', *MIN*, 189).

l. 3 pianola: in the essay 'Arnold Dolmetsch' Pound describes a process of decline from the ancient music of the clavichord and virginal to the piano and so 'we have come to the pianola. And one or two people are going in for sheer pianola' (*LE*, 433).

l. 4 Sappho: Greek poetess of the seventh century B.C. Fragments of three poems by Sappho came to light in Berlin in 1896. Pound was made aware of them by Richard Aldington's poem 'To Atthis' which he published in the first Imagist anthology, *Des Imagistes* (1914). Of five related poems in *Lustra* ('Papyrus', 'Love', "Ἰμέρρω", 'Shop Girl' and 'To Formianus'), 'Papyrus' is derived from the Sapphic manuscript and "Ἰμέρρω" from a detail of Aldington's poem. Pound refers to Atthis also in Canto V (22/17–18), first published in 1921.

barbitos: an early form of lyre or lute. Pound traced all lyric poetry to the traditions of Greece and Provence, 'when the arts of verse and music were most closely knit together', and praises 'the cadences of those earlier makers who had composed to and for the Cÿthera and the Barbitos' (*LE*, 91).

l. 5: Pound is probably indebted to Gautier's 'Bûchers et Tombeaux', 'Mais l'Olympe cède au Calvaire/ Jupiter au Nazaréen' (Espey, 36).

Christ: Pound distinguished between Christ and the Christian religion. In 'Provincialism the Enemy' (1917) he wrote, 'I think the world can well dispense with the Christian religion. . . . But I think also that "Christ" . . . is a most profound philosophic genius', even if 'a provincial genius' (*SPr*, 163), and to Harriet Monroe, 'Christ can very well stand as an heroic figure. . . . Also he is not wholly to blame for the religion that's been foisted on to him' (*SL*, 183).

Dionysus: a Greek god of fertility, especially the god of wine, worshipped in the orgiastic Dionysian rites.

l. 6: may refer to either Christ or Dionysus. In *The Spirit of Romance* Pound talks of Christianity as an enrichment of paganism (p. 98) and as a form of ecstatic religion which was 'not in inception dogma or propaganda of something called the *one truth* or the *universal truth*' (p. 95). Cf. MAUBERLEY (1920) II, line 2, and ' "The Age Demanded" ', line 34.

l. 7 macerations: a wasting of the flesh resulting from the Christian rites of abstention and fasting.

l. 8 in Shakespeare's *The Tempest* Caliban is 'a savage and deformed slave' to Ariel's 'airy sprite'.

ll. 9–13: cf. the lines from Gautier's 'Ars Victrix', given by Pound in the translation by H. Austin Dobson in *Confucius to Cummings*: 'All passes. Art alone/ Enduring stays to us;/ The bust outlasts the throne;/ The coin, Tiberius./ Even the gods must go . . . (p. 221).

l. 10 Heracleitus: the Greek philosopher Heraclitus (540–480 B.C.) of Ephesus, popularly credited with the view that all things are in a constant state of flux. In *Guide to Kulchur* Pound said 'It is quite foolish to suppose that Heraclitus . . . merely said "Everything flows", or that any one abstract statement wd. have made him his reputation' (p. 31). Cf. MAUBERLEY (1920) II, line 3, 'All passes . . .' In Canto LXXVII Pound remembers the philosopher Henry Slonimsky, author of *Heraklit and Parmenides* (1912) (*Cantos*, 498/469). Cf. also Canto XCVIII, line 38.

l. 14 Samothrace: the Greek island, home of the winged Victory and renowned for Dionysian worship. Samothrace was visited by St. Paul and was as such the first Greek island to feel the influence of Christianity. Pound is therefore perhaps distinguishing between the Christian ideal and its degeneration in the Christian religion; cf. note on line 5. Writing to Harriet Monroe he said that Paul 'neither wrote good Greek nor represented the teaching of the original Christian' (*SL*, 54). (Lawrence W. Mazzeno, 'A Note on "Hugh Selwyn Mauberley" ', *Paideuma*, IV, no. 1, 89–91.)

ll. 15–16: St. Luke in Acts of the Apostles 17 refers to Paul's speech in Athens, delivered at the Agora, the city marketplace, and Pound may have this particular reference in mind (Mazzeno, op. cit., 90). But cf. also in the eighth 'Imaginary Letter' by Walter Villerant, 'Vomit, carefully labelled

"Beauty", is still in the literary market, and much sought-after in the provinces' (*P and D*, 74) and Canto LXXIV, 'the useful operations of commerce/ stone after stone of beauty cast down' (476/448).

l. 15 τὸ καλόν:(Gk.) 'the beautiful'; cf. ' "Quasi KALOUN." S.T. says Beauty is most that, a "calling to the soul" ', in the poem 'In Durance (1907)' (*CSP*, 34) and cf. also the discussion by John Espey, 'The Inheritance of Tò Kalón' (Hesse, 319–30).

l. 19 the press: in *Instigations* (1920), Pound comments that 'the root of the difference' between journalism and literature is that 'in journalism the reader finds what he is looking for, whereas in literature he must find at least *a part of* what the author intended. . . . In journalism or "bad art", there is no such strain on the public' (p. 246). In Canto XIV 'the press gang' is set in hell, alongside 'the betrayers of language' and 'those who had lied for hire' (*Cantos*, 65/61). Pound conducted an analysis of British journals in twenty instalments under the title 'Studies in Contemporary Mentality' in the *New Age* (August 1917–January 1918).

wafer: the symbol of Christ's body eaten in the Eucharist.

l. 20 Franchise: 'We most of us believe, more or less,' said Pound, 'in democracy' ('Studies in Contemporary Mentality' XI, *New Age*, 1 Nov. 1917, 11), and in 'The Revolt of Intelligence' V, objecting to a plan for appointed as against elected representatives at the League of Nations, he called for 'an International Chamber . . . a larger body elected by direct vote of the people' (*New Age*, 8 Jan. 1920, 153).

circumcision: referring to the incident where Zipporah circumcises her son (Exodus 4: 25–6), Pound comments, 'that twentieth century man should be influenced by this antique abracadabra is a degredation, an ignominy past all bounds of the comic' ('The Revolt of Intelligence' VI, *New Age*, 15 Jan. 1920, 176).

l. 21: reminiscent of the opening of the Declaration of Independence, 'we hold these truths to be self-evident, that all men are created equal'.

l. 22 Pisistratus: a beneficent Athenian tyrant (605–527 B.C.) who encouraged the Dionysian rites, particularly in their dramatic aspect, and is said to have helped lay the foundations of Greek drama. Pound refers elsewhere to Pisistratus as having compounded the 'sacred book' of his age, alluding presumably to the tradition that Pisistratus first collected or recensed the Homeric poems (*SPr*, 364).

l. 23 eunuch: Pound exposes the corrupt political influence of eunuchs in Canto LV (303–7/291–5).

l. 25 Apollo: the Greek god of music and poetry.

l. 26: (Gk.) 'what man, what hero, what God', adapted from Pindar's 'τίνα θεόν, τίν᾽ ἥρωα, τίνα δ᾽ ἄνδρα κελαδήσομεν' ('What god, what hero, what man shall we loudly praise?', *Olympian Ode* II, l. 2). Pound cites this line elsewhere as an example of Pindar's 'big rhetorical drum' (*SL*, 91).

l. 28 tin wreath: i.e. in place of the traditional laurel. Pound puns on the Greek 'τίν᾽' of line 26, suggesting the arts have become mechanical, anticipating also poem IV, and the effects on artists of the war.

IV

A retrospect on the First World War. Pound it would seem was unaffected by the war until T. E. Hulme had enlisted and Gaudier-Brzeska began to send him first-hand accounts of the front (Stock, *Life*, 216–17). On 18 February 1915 he sent H. L. Mencken a war poem, '1915: February', for the *Smart Set*, but it was never published (*SL*, 51). A second war poem, 'Poem: Abbreviated from the Conversation of Mr. T. E. H[ulme]', subtitled 'Trenches, St. Eloi', appeared in the *Catholic Anthology* (November 1915) and in *Umbra* (1920). Otherwise Pound's contemporary response to the war appeared more obliquely in *Cathay* (April 1915). Gaudier-Brzeska wrote to Mrs. Shakespear that he kept this book in his pocket and used the poems 'to put courage in my fellows' (*G-B*, 68); cf. also Canto XVI (74–8/70–4).

l. 3 pro domo: (Lat.) 'for the home'.

ll. 4–10 Some quick . . . slaughter: Pound wrote that 'The metre in *Mauberley* is Gautier and Bion's "Adonis"; or at least those are the two grafts I was trying to flavour it with. Syncopation from the Greek; and a general distaste for the slushiness and swishiness of the post-Swinburnian British line' (*SL*, 181). Espey finds these lines particularly influenced by the rhythms of Bion's *Lament for Adonis* (op. cit., 44).

ll. 11–12 pro patria . . . "decor": excised from the line in Horace, 'Dulce et decorum est pro patria mori' ('It is sweet and fitting to die for one's country'), *Odes* III, ii, 13. The phrase supplies the title of the well-known poem by Wilfred Owen, in which it is indicted as 'the old lie' (*Collected Poems*, ed. Day-Lewis, 1963, 55). The notice of Gaudier-Brzeska's death at the front appeared in *Blast*, July 1915, under the heading 'Mort Pour La Patrie' (cf. *G-B*, 17).

The association of war with hell was common in First World War poetry. It impressed itself on Pound perhaps through Gaudier's description of the trenches at Aisne as 'a sight worthy of Dante, there was at the bottom a foot deep of liquid mud in which we had to stand two days and two nights' (*G-B*, 59). Pound had drafted the 'hell Cantos' (XIV and XV) in 1919 and in Canto XIV (ll. 68–9) hell is 'the slough of unamiable liars,/ bog of stupidities'.

l. 17 lies . . . infamy: cf. Canto XXIV, 'These are the sins of Georgia/ These are the lies/ These are the infamies' (175/171). In one of several attacks on passports in the *Nation*, 1927, Pound recalled an 'executive infamy', a 'new zealous bossiness' after the war which obstructed his leaving and returning to England from France in 1919 (quoted in Stock, *Life*, 281, 344).

l. 18 usury: *Mauberley* was the first of Pound's poems to contain the word 'usury'; its use coincided with his meeting and reading the economic theory of Major C. H. Douglas, whose *Economic Democracy* Pound reviewed in April 1920 for both the *Athenaeum* and the *Little Review* (*SPr*, 177–82). Cf. also the references in Cantos XIV, XV (67, 68/63, 64), Canto XLV, especially line 17, 'with usura the line grows thick', and Canto LI.

ll. 20–7: Pound's lines retrace the increasing realism and disillusionment of war poetry from Rupert Brooke to Wilfred Owen and Siegfried Sassoon. Pound's own concern was neither for the glory, nor particularly the horrors of the war, but rather for 'civilization'. In a letter to Harriet Monroe, November 1914, he had written, 'This war is possibly a conflict between two forces almost equally detestable. . . . It's all very well to see the troops flocking from the four corners of Empire. It is a very fine sight. But, but, but, civilization, after the battle is over and everybody begins to call each other thieves and liars *inside* the Empire' (*SL*, 46).

V

l. 2 best: Pound was thinking perhaps of T. E. Hulme, who was killed in France in 1917, perhaps of Rupert Brooke, killed in the Dardanelles in 1915 and whom he considered 'the best of all that Georgian group' (*SL*, 59). More probably he was remembering Gaudier-Brzeska (Henri Gaudier) who died on 5 June 1915 at Neuville St. Vaast. Pound described him to Joyce as 'the best of the younger sculptors and one of the best sculptors in all europe' (*P/J* 36). Pound's *Gaudier–Brzeska: A Memoir* was published in April 1916. Cf. also Canto XVI (75/71).

l. 5 Charm: possibly a further reference to Rupert Brooke and Pound's attempt to make amends for an allusion to him in 'Our Contemporaries' (*Blast*, July 1915) which many found offensive. In a letter to Milton Bronner Pound wrote that 'Brzeska's death is, so far, the worst calamity of the war. There *was* a loss to art with a vengeance. In Brooke's case I think it was more the loss of a charming young man' (Stock, *Life*, 228).

l. 6 Quick eyes: Wyndham Lewis recalling Gaudier's departure for the front in *Blasting and Bombardiering* (1967) remembers his 'excited eyes' (p. 161), and Pound in *Gaudier-Brzeska* refers to his eyes as ' "almost alarmingly intelligent" ' (p. 39).

ll. 7–8: in general, an attack on establishment attitudes to art.

In 'The Curse', January 1920, Pound wrote that 'the utter condemnation of today's British civilisation . . . might be found in the fact that uncountable excellent things are housed in a horror like the "Victoria and Albert"' (Stock, *Life*, 286). He shared also Gaudier's disdain for Greek sculpture, which as Kenner points out 'constituted in wartime much of the official inventory of culture' (*Pound Era*, 259).

l. 7 two gross of broken statues: in *Gaudier-Brzeska* Pound writes, 'one does not believe in having even columns made by the gross; one has the tradition that columns should be hand-cut and signed' (p. 96), where he is thinking of the signed column at San Zeno, in Verona, referred to in Canto XLV (l. 33) as free of the taint of usura. Cf. also *Patria Mia*, pp. 18–19.

broken statues: Gaudier worked of necessity mostly from discarded chunks of marble and the sense here is perhaps as much that he would have continued to produce, or produced more, great art if he had a plentiful supply, as that he was sacrificed uselessly for an already worthless official sculpture: 'his own genius', said Pound, 'was worth more than dead buildings' (*G-B*, 54).

l. 8 battered books: Canto XVI refers to T. E. Hulme's having 'a lot of books' from the London Library which were buried in a dug-out, much to the Library's annoyance (75/71).

Yeux Glauques

This and the following six poems present a gallery of symptomatic writers, representing the character of literary culture in the latter half of the nineteenth and the early twentieth centuries. Their inherent limitations and the philistinism of the age are precedents for Mauberley's own 'case'.

Title: derived most probably from Gautier's expression 'L'œil glauque' in his *Mademoiselle de Maupin* (Espey, 33).
Glauque: (Fr.) 'glaucous', dull bluish-green or grey. In 'French Poets' Pound wrote, 'The period was "glauque" and "nacre", it had its pet and too-petted adjectives, the handles for parody'

(*MIN*, 232), and, writing to W. H. D. Rouse, offered the gloss, '*Glaux*, owl, totem or symbolic bird . . . glare-eyed, owl-eyed Athena' (*SL*, 273). The goddess Pallas Athene was referred to by Homer as 'glaukopis' ('grey-blue eyed'); cf. *Odyssey*, Bk. I, l. 44, and also Canto XX (ll. 172–4n.).

l. 1 Gladstone: William Ewart Gladstone, Chancellor of the Exchequer 1859–66 and four times Liberal Prime Minister in the period 1868–94. Pound suggests that to be 'really conversant' with Gladstone's activities would secure a knowledge of his period (*SPr*, 43), and that though Russell and Gladstone were 'comics' by later standards, they were in their own time 'serious matters' (*GK*, 262).

l. 2 John Ruskin: (1819–1900), the art historian and social critic, author of *Modern Painters* (1843–60) and *The Stones of Venice* (1851–3). Ruskin defended Pre-Raphaelitism in *The Times* in 1851, and later befriended and championed Rossetti.

l. 3 "Kings' Treasuries": Ruskin's 'Of Kings' Treasuries' forms the first section of *Sesame and Lilies* (1865). Its argument, 'that valuable books should, in a civilised country, be within the reach of every one, printed in an excellent form, for a just price', would have appealed to Pound.

Swinburne: Algernon Charles Swinburne (1837–1909). On Tennyson's death in 1892, Gladstone made 'a very careful examination' of Swinburne's case for the Office of Poet Laureate; 'I fear', he wrote to Lord Acton, 'he is *absolutely* impossible' (Alan Bell, 'Gladstone Looks for a Poet Laureate', *T.L.S.*, 21 July 1972, 847). In his review of Edmund Gosse's *Life of Algernon Charles Swinburne* (1917), Pound praised particularly Swinburne's 'magnificent adaptations from Villon' as standing 'with Rossetti's and the *Rubaiyat* among the Victorian translations' (*LE*, 292, 293); cf. Pound's homage to Swinburne in the poem 'Salve O Pontifex' (*ALS*, 63).

l. 4 Rossetti: Dante Gabriel Rossetti (1828–82). A leader of the Pre-Raphaelite movement in painting and poetry, and an influence on Pound's early poetry and enthusiasm for pre-Renaissance poetry (cf. *SR*, ch. VI). In his translation of Guido Cavalcanti Pound acknowledged 'In the matter of these

HUGH SELWYN MAUBERLEY

translations and of my knowledge of Tuscan poetry, Rossetti is my father and my mother' (*Tr*, 20). Pound's special interest in Provençal, however, had no precedent in Pre-Raphaelitism, and cf. also his parody of Rossetti's 'The Blessed Damozel' in the poem 'Donzella Beata' (*ALS*, 41). It is interesting that Robert Browning, arguably the strongest influence on Pound among the Victorian poets, makes no appearance in this poem.

l. 5 Fœtid Buchanan: the poet and reviewer Robert Buchanan (1841–1901), who attacked Rossetti's *Poems* (1870), especially the poem 'Jenny', in his article 'The Fleshly School of Poetry' (*Contemporary Review*, 1871). Buchanan wrote under the pseudonym of 'Caliban'; cf. iii, line 8 (Ruthven, 131). Cf. also the reference to 'pickled foetuses' (' "Siena Mi Fe' " ', l. 1) and the use of 'foetus', 'foetor', 'foetid' in Cantos XIV and XV (66–8/62–4).

l. 6 faun's head: cf. iii, line 17, and line 18 below. An allusion probably to Rimbaud's 'Tête de faune', a poem praised by Pound in the *New Age* (16 Oct. 1913, 726) (Ruthven, 134).

hers: the reference is to Elizabeth Siddall, a seamstress discovered by Walter Deverell in 1849 or 1850. She modelled for Holman Hunt's *Sylvia*, Millais's *Ophelia* and many of Rossetti's drawings and paintings, including his *Beata Beatrix*. After ten years in which they were more or less engaged she and Rossetti married in 1860; their child was stillborn (cf. line 15).

l. 9 Burne-Jones: Sir Edward Burne-Jones (1833–98), painter and member of the Pre-Raphaelite Brotherhood; cf. Canto LXXX (l. 613 n.).

cartoons: drawings for paintings or tapestries.

l. 10 eyes: cf. title and 'Medallion', line 16, 'The eyes turn topaz'. William Rossetti described Elizabeth Siddall's eyes as 'greenish-blue', Burne-Jones as 'golden-brown, agate colour' (Friar and Brinnin, *Modern Poetry*, 1957, 529). The detail of Elizabeth Siddall's eyes places her among many incarnations of Pallas Athene and Aphrodite in Pound's work.

l. 12 Cophetua: Elizabeth Siddall modelled for Burne-Jones's *Cophetua and the Beggar-Maid* (1884), a painting now in the Tate Gallery.

ll. 13–14 Thin . . . gaze: cf. line 17, 'The thin, clear gaze', MAUBERLEY (1920) II, line 26, 'inconscient, full gaze', and ' " The Age Demanded" ', line 10.

l. 15 The English Rubaiyat: Edward FitzGerald's translation of the *Rubáiyát* of Omar Khayyám (1859). It was ignored until in 1860, as Pound records in Canto LXXX (l. 594), 'Rossetti found it remaindered/ at about two pence'. Pound valued the *Rubáiyát* with Rossetti's and Swinburne's translations (cf. note on line 3). It was, he said, 'the only good poem of the time that has gone to the people' (*LE*, 34).

still-born: cf. 'pickled foetuses' (' "Siena mi Fe' " ', l. 1).

l. 20 poor Jenny's case: the phrase 'poor Jenny' recurs through Rossetti's poem 'Jenny' which has as epigraph Shakespeare's ' "Vengeance of Jenny's case! Fie on her! Never name her, child" – (*Mrs. Quickly*)' (*Poems and Translations*, 1968, 62).

ll. 23–4 maquero's/ Adulteries: an allusion perhaps to Rossetti's infidelities with Fanny Cornforth and possibly Janey Morris; cf. line 8, 'Painters and adulterers'. A 'maquero' is a pimp.

"Siena Mi Fe'; Disfecemi Maremma"

A portrait of the combined religiosity and dissipation of the Nineties. 'The "nineties" ', said Pound, 'have chiefly gone out because of their muzziness. . . . They riot with half decayed fruit' (*LE*, 363).

Title: (Ital.) 'Siena made me: Maremma undid me' from Dante's *Purgatoria* (V, l. 134), a source echoed also in T. S. Eliot's 'Highbury bore me. Richmond and Kew/ undid me' (*The Waste Land*, ll. 293–4). Dante refers to the story of 'La Pia dei' Tolomei', imprisoned by her husband, the Guelph lord Paganello dei Pannocchieschi, in the marshland of the Maremma, where she died of malaria or from poison. Lines 133–6 of Dante's Canto V, with the present line translated as 'Siena, me Maremma, made, unmade' were placed upon the frame of Rossetti's picture of *La Pia*, for which Jane Morris had modelled. Dante places 'La Pia' in Purgatory as an example of sudden and unprepared death, and Pound's title therefore looks back to the conditions of the First World War in poem IV, to Rossetti's betrayal of Elizabeth Siddall and to her suicide in 'Yeux Glauques', and also forward to the sudden and unprepared deaths of Dowson and Lionel Johnson.

l. 1 pickled fœtuses: cf. 'Yeux Glauques', 'foetid' (l. 5n.) and 'still-born' (l. 15n.).

l. 4 Monsieur Verog: Victor Gustav Plarr (1863–1929), a member of the Rhymers' Club, author of *In the Dorian Mood* (1896) and a biography of Ernest Dowson. Plarr was born near Strasburg but came to England after the Franco-Prussian War of 1870, becoming Librarian for the Royal College of Surgeons, for whom he prepared *A Catalogue of Manuscripts in the Library of the Royal College of Surgeons of England*. Pound 'devoted' his Sundays to Plarr in 1909 (Stock, *Life*, 85), and later, reviewing his *Ernest Dowson* (1914) in *Poetry* (April 1915), referred to him as 'a survivor of the Senatorial families of Strasburg', and in his Preface to *The Poetical Works of Lionel Johnson* (October 1915) as 'delightful, a kind of half-French, half-Celtic Dobson with nature and the past and dying traditions and wild races for his Theme' (*LE*, 367). The name 'Verog' may have been suggested to Pound by the name 'Virag' given by Joyce to Leopold Bloom's father in *Ulysses*, which Pound was reading in sections between 1918 and 1920 for its serial publication in the *Little Review* and the *Egoist*. Cf. also note on line 16, the section 'Plarr's narration' in Canto XVI (74/70) and Canto LXXIV, note on line 274.

l. 5 Galliffet: Gaston Alexander Gallifet, a French general in the Franco-Prussian War who led a cavalry charge at Sedan, recalled via Plarr in Canto XVI (74/70).

l. 6 Dowson: Ernest Dowson (1867–1900). Pound thought Dowson in 1911 'a very fine craftsman' who 'epitomised a decade' (letter to Floyd Dell, quoted Ruthven, 136) and agreed with the moderation of Plarr's biography: Dowson was 'a delicate temperament that ran a little amuck towards the end, an irregular man with nothing a sane man would call vices' (Stock, *Life*, 224). He also lists 'Cynara' as a very early influence upon himself in America (*LE*, 367); cf. also 'In Tempore Senectutis, An anti-stave for Dowson' (*ALS*, 80).

Rhymers' Club: the circle of poets including Ernest Dowson, Lionel Johnson, Yeats, Arthur Symons, Plarr and Image, formed in 1891 in the Fleet Street pub The Cheshire Cheese. Pound wrote to Floyd Dell that ' "The Rhymers" did valuable work in knocking bombast, & rhetoric & Victorian syrup out of our verse' (Ruthven, 136). Yeats gives an account of this period in his 'The Tragic Generation' in *Autobiographies* (1965).

l. 7 Johnson: Lionel Johnson (1867–1902). Pound edited Johnson's *Poetical Works* (1915); cf. his Preface to this edition (*LE*, 361–70). The myth of Johnson's death may have its origin in a meeting Yeats records, 'when he [Johnson] rose from his chair, took a step towards me in his eagerness, and fell on the floor; and I saw that he was drunk' (*Autobiographies*, 309); cf. also the line in Johnson's 'Mystic and Cavalier', 'Go from me. I am one of those who fall', recalled in both Yeats's 'In Memory of Major Robert Gregory' and Pound's 'A Virginal' (*CSP*, 83). Johnson's 'falling' parallels also Elpenor's fall to his death, when intoxicated, from the roof of Circe's house (*Odyssey*, Bk. X, ll. 552–60). Cf. also Canto I (ll. 51–3), and in Canto V of Dante's *Purgatorio*, which provides Pound's title, the fate of Jacopo del Cassero and Buonconte da Montefeltro who both fall literally at their deaths (ll. 82–4, 101–2).

ll. 9–12 But . . . warmed: Yeats records in his *Autobiographies* that Johnson 'at the autopsy after his death was discovered never to have grown, except in the brain, after his fifteenth year' (pp. 310–11), and that in life he became more ascetic as he drank more wine (p. 223).

l. 12 Newman: John Henry Newman (1801–90), Cardinal and leader of the Oxford Movement. Johnson and Dowson were both converts to the Roman Catholic Church. Yeats discovered that Johnson's supposed meeting with Newman (and with Gladstone) and his quotations from him were in fact Johnson's own invention (*Autobiographies*, 223).

l. 13: Yeats characterizes Dowson's life as a solid round of drink and cheap harlots (*Essays and Introductions*, 1961, 492).

l. 14 Headlam: the Reverend Stewart D. Headlam (1847–1924), who resigned his curacy in 1878 after a lecture at a working-men's club on the theatre and dancing.

Image: Selwyn Image (1849–1930), artist and poet, a member of the Rhymers' Club and Slade Professor of Fine Arts at Oxford, who had shared 20 Charlotte Street, Fitzroy Square, with Johnson and Herbert Hone. His *Poems and Carols* appeared in 1894. With Headlam he founded the Church and Stage Guild, and was co-editor of the *Hobby Horse*, a periodical connecting the Nineties poets with the Pre-Raphaelites. Pound met Image early in 1909 through the Poets' Club and num-bered him with Olivia and Dorothy Shakespear as 'about the most worth while out of the lot I have come across' (Stock, *Life*, 78).

l. 15 Bacchus: the Thracian name for Dionysus, the Greek god of wine.

Terpsichore: the Greek Muse of the dance.

the Church: the Catholic Church. Yeats remembers hearing Johnson say, 'I believe in nothing but the Holy Roman Catholic Church' after having just left him amid the debris of a night's drinking in Dublin (*Autobiographies*, 223).

l. 16 "The Dorian Mood": Victor Plarr's *In the Dorian Mood* (1896). Writing in the article 'Status Rerum' for *Poetry* (January, 1913), Pound described how Plarr's volume 'has been half-forgotten, but not his verses "Epitaphium Citharis-triae"' (p. 127). Pound had copied Plarr's poem in his own hand on to the rear flyleaf of his copy of *The Poems of Ernest Dowson* (1909) (Exhibition Catalogue, 'Ezra Pound: The London Years', Sheffield University 1976, item 17). Cf. also Pound's poem 'Δώρια' ('Doria') in *Ripostes*.

l. 17 out of step: cf. 'E.P. Ode', lines 1, 6.

l. 20 reveries: cf. the mention of Mauberley's 'porcelain revery', ' "The Age Demanded" ', line 18.

Brennbaum

Title: (Ger.) 'burnt tree', suggesting 'burning bush'.

ll. 1–4 The . . . grace: the portrait suggests Max Beerbohm

(1872–1956), caricaturist, essayist and parodist of limited achievement. In Beerbohm's own words, 'my gifts are small' (quoted *Twentieth Century Authors*, cd. Kunitz and Haycraft, 1942, 102).

l. 5 The heavy . . . years: the Hebraic exodus and forty-year-long quest for Canaan. Moses made water flow from the rock of Mt. Horeb and received the Ten Commandments on Mt. Sinai (Exodus 3: 2, 19: 20). Beerbohm was not Jewish as this would suggest, but of mixed Dutch, Lithuanian and German blood. He is recorded, however, as saying that he 'would be delighted to know that the Beerbohms had that very agreeable and encouraging thing, Jewish blood' (David Cecil, *Max*, 1966, 4).

l. 8 "The Impeccable": Beerbohm was known popularly as 'the incomparable Max'. Pound refers elsewhere in passing to 'the impeccable Beerbohm' (*LE*, 340).

Mr. Nixon

Pound said Mr. Nixon was 'a fictitious name for a real person' (Friar and Brinnin, op. cit., 529), and probably intends Arnold Bennett (1867–1931), prolific journalist, editor and novelist.

l. 1 steam yacht: Bennett had bought his first yacht, the *Velsa*, in 1912, a very successful year in which he made £16,000. Pound had probably met Bennett at one of the dinner parties given by Ford Madox Ford for contributors to the *Little Review*, and certainly dined with him in mid-March 1911 (Stock, *Life*, 122).

ll. 3–11: Pound had referred to 'the click of Mr. Bennett's cash-register finish' in a review of Wyndham Lewis's *Tarr* (*Little Review*, 11 Mar. 1918). For its later appearance Pound included the footnote, 'E.P. rather modified his view of part of Bennett's writing when he finally got round to reading *An Old Wives' Tale* many years later' (*LE*, 429). Pound appeared to modify his opinion in other ways too. Writing to Harriet Monroe in September 1912, to accept the post of 'foreign correspondent' for *Poetry*, he said, 'If I were in the trade for the cash to be gotten from it, I should have quit some time ago' (Norman, 87). Yet in 1946 he said of Bennett, 'I might have made money if my snobbishness, which was at its height, hadn't made me sneer at this commoner', and in 1959, 'I mean we were [in 1911] so aesthetic that Arnold Bennett got on my nerves, and I lost great opportunities' (Seelye, 78, 142).

l. 13 Dr. Dundas: perhaps Sir Robertson Nicoll, who as editor of the 'despicable paper *The Bookman*' is associated with Bennett in Pound's review of Wyndham Lewis's *Tarr* (*LE*, 429).

l. 21: 'Blougram' is 'a reference', Pound said, 'to Browning's bishop, allegoric' (Friar and Brinnin, op. cit., 529). Browning's poem is 'Bishop Blougram's Apology'; like Nixon, Blougram sacrifices all integrity for creaturely comforts: 'How we may lead a comfortable life/ How suit our luggage to the cabin's size'. Blougram's image of man 'each in his average cabin of a life' reinforces the parallel with Mr. Nixon.

a friend: i.e. Gigadibs, 'the literary man' of Browning's poem. At its close Gigadibs buys 'not cabin furniture/ But settler's implements (enough for three)/ And started for Australia'. His choice finds an echo in the pastoral retreat depicted in poem x.

X

Pound may have drawn on the comparable scene depicted in Gautier's 'Fumée':

> Là-bas, sous les arbres s'abrite
> Une chaumière au dos bossu;
> Le toit penche, le mur s'effrite,
> Le seuil de la porte est moussu.

(quoted Ruthven, 139)

l. 2 The stylist: perhaps James Joyce whom Pound had referred to directly in 1917 as 'the stylist' (P/J, 115). Joyce, Pound said, had 'lived for ten years in obscurity and poverty, that he might perfect his writing and be uninfluenced by commercial demands and standards' (ibid., 39). As Hugh Kenner has suggested, Pound may also have in mind Ford Madox Ford's decision to move in May 1919 to the village of Hurston in West Sussex (*Poetry of EP*, 174–5).

l. 6 placid and uneducated mistress: Ford lived in Sussex with Stella Bowen, a young Australian painter.

l. 8 the soil meets his distress: Hurston provided Ford with 'chickens and ducks for eggs and meat, a garden full of tomatoes, beans and sweet corn' (F. McShane, *The Life and Work of Ford Madox Ford*, 1965, 138).

l. 11 succulent cooking: in September 1919 Ford moved from Hurston to a larger house in nearby Bedham and there planted potatoes and raised pigs.

XI

l. 1: adapted from Remy de Gourmont's 'Des femmes . . . ces conservatrices des traditions milésiennes' from the story 'Stratagèmes' in *Histoires magiques* (1894). Pound quotes the phrase in his essay on de Gourmont (*LE*, 345) and glosses it again as 'Woman, the conservator, the inheritor of past gestures' in the 'Postscript' to his translation of de Gourmont's *The Natural Philosophy of Love* (*P and D*, 213). In a letter to John Quinn in 1918 Pound applied the phrase to Maud Gonne:

> The other point M.G. omits from her case is that she went to Ireland without permit and in disguise, in the first place, during war time.
>
> "Conservatrice des traditions Milesienne," as de Gourmont calls them. There are people who have no sense of the value of "civilization" or public order
>
> (*SL*, 140)

Milésien: the 'Milesian Tales' were a series of erotic romances of the first century B.C., none of which are extant. The term 'Milesian' also designates a member of the Irish race (after King Milesius whose sons are reputed to have conquered ancient Ireland).

l. 3 Ealing: cf. the disquisition on suburbia in the fourth of the 'Imaginary Letters' from Walter Villerant to the newly remarried 'Ex Mrs. Burn' (*P and D*, 64–5).

l. 6 instinct: 'Instinct', Pound writes, 'conserves only the "useful" gestures' (*P and D*, 211).

XII

ll. 1–2: a translation of Gautier's lines from 'Le Château du souvenir' in *Émaux et Camées* : 'Daphné, les hanches dans l'écorce,/ Étend toujours ses doigts touffus'. In Greek mythology Daphne was transformed into a bay tree when pursued by Apollo. The tree thenceforth became sacred to Apollo and the laurel the symbol of the poet's crown; cf. 'The Tree' and 'A Girl'.

ll. 3–4 In . . . commands: Pound, Eliot and Yeats were collected together on 2 April 1916 for the first performance of Yeats's 'At the Hawk's Well' in the drawing-room of Lady Cunard in Cavendish Square (Norman, 182–3).

ll. 5–8: Pound's lines recall the tone and idiom of Eliot's 'The Love Song of J. Alfred Prufrock' and 'Portrait of a Lady' (*Collected Poems*, 1958, 11, 16). Eliot himself had been introduced to the circle gathered by Lady Ottoline Morrell at Garsington Manor by Bertrand Russell in 1915.

ll. 13–16: In *Patria Mia*, Pound wrote:

> It has been well said of the 'lady in society' that art criticism is one of her functions. She babbles of it as of 'the play', or of hockey, or of 'town topics'. She believes in catholicity of taste, in admiring no one thing more than anything else. But she is not ubiquitous. Even in London one may escape from her paths and by-ways.

(p. 43)

l. 17 Lady Jane: Lady Jane appears as a literary hostess in Henry James's story 'The Figure in the Carpet', in *Embarrassments* (1896).

*　　*　　*

ll. 21–2: a translation of Jules Laforgue's 'Menez l'âme que les lettres ont bien nourrie' from 'Complainte des Pianos' (Espey, 65). In 'Irony, Laforgue, and Some Satire' Pound wrote of how Laforgue's 'verbalism', his use of 'an international tongue common to the excessively cultivated', would dumbfound 'the man in the street', and since the scholar plays safe, avoiding contemporary literature, 'The journalist is left as our jury' (*LE*, 280–4).

l. 24 Dr. Johnson: Samuel Johnson (1709–84). Forced by poverty to leave Oxford, Johnson came to London in 1737 to make a living as a hack journalist and Parliamentary reporter. He could not be said to have 'flourished' until 1762, when he received a state pension.

l. 28 Pierian roses: an allusion to the line from Sappho, 'for you have no claim to the Pierian roses', addressed to a young girl excluded from the world of letters (Barnstone, 199; *Oxford Book of Greek Verse*, 143). Pieria in Greece is a reputed home of the Muses.

Envoi (1919)

Pound's 'envoi' recalls the English moment in the tradition of poetry as song. In 1918 he had written to Margaret Anderson, 'I desire also to resurrect the art of the lyric, I mean words to be sung. . . . And with a few exceptions (a few in Browning) there is scarcely anything since the time of Waller and Campion. AND a mere imitation of them won't do' (*SL*, 128). The present poem is modelled on Edmund Waller's 'Go, Lovely Rose!', included in the anthology *Confucius to Cummings* (p. 175). Cf. also Canto LXXXI (ll. 97–115n.).

l. 2 her: Charles Norman reports that when he asked Pound in 1959, 'Who sang you once that song of Lawes?' Pound replied, 'Your question is the kind of damn fool enquiry into what is nobody's damn business' (p. 224). Nonplussed, critics have suggested most recently that Pound is referring here to the singing of Raymonde Collignon, who in April 1918, at the

Aeolian Hall, London, sang the Provençal songs Pound had contributed to Morse Rummel's *Hesternae Rosae* (1913). As music critic of the *New Age*, writing under the name of William Atheling, Pound reviewed this and two subsequent concerts, the last on 15 April 1920, the year of *Mauberley's* publication. (Cf. Jo Brantley Berryman, ' "Medallion": Pound's Poem', *Paideuma*, II, no. 3, 391–8, and Donald Davie, *Pound*, 52). Both Berryman and Davie suggest that Miss Collignon's singing is the subject also of the later 'Medallion'.

Lawes: Henry Lawes (1596–1662), English composer and musician. Lawes set to music Waller's 'Go, Lovely Rose!', Milton's *Comus* and, Pound recalls, 'a number of Greek and Latin poems' (*ABC of R*, 156); cf. also note on line 23, and Canto LXXXI, line 101.

l. 13 roses: cf. earlier references to 'tea-rose' and 'Pierian roses' (III, l. 1 and XII, l. 28).

amber: cf. 'From metal, or intractable amber' in 'Medallion' (l. 12).

l. 17 her: 'England or the English poetic tradition, perhaps the English "muse", certainly the English language' (Davie, *Pound*, 54). Pound had said on the title-page of the first American edition of *Mauberley* that the sequence was 'distinctly a farewell to London' and would seem to refer here to the English ignorance of and indifference to its lyric tradition as good reason for his departure. In *Antheil and The Treatise on Harmony* (1924), commenting on the unavailability of Lawes's 'Ayres and Dialogues', and of Arnold Dolmetsch's arrangements of this music, Pound said, 'Only in a nation utterly contemptuous of its past treasures and inspired by a rancorous hatred of good music could this state of affairs be conceivable' (quoted Davie, op. cit.).

l. 20 some other mouth: Pound himself perhaps, as an American poet who values the English tradition.

l. 23 Waller's: Edmund Waller (1606–87), the poet. Pound compared Waller unfavourably with Henry Lawes; 'Lawes' position in English music is proportionally much more important than Waller's position among English poets' (quoted Davie, op. cit.), and in the *ABC of Reading* described Waller as 'a tiresome fellow' whose 'natural talent is fathoms below My Lord Rochester's. BUT when he writes for music he is "lifted"; he was very possibly HOISTED either by the composer or by the general musical perceptivity of the time' (pp. 154-5). Cf. Canto LXXXI, line 113.

MAUBERLEY (1920)

Epigraph: (Lat.) 'his empty mouth bites the air', adapted from Ovid's *Metamorphoses* (Bk. VII, l. 786/1021), Pound substituting 'vacuos' for Ovid's 'vanos' ('vainly'). The phrase refers to Cephalus' dog Laelaps who snaps at the empty air in a vain attempt to grapple with the monster sent to terrorize Thebes. Cephalus turns aside to adjust his javelin and looks back to see both the monster and dog turned to stone (cf. II, lines 34-7). The Latin phrase is repeated in the essay 'Mediaevalism', 'The God is inside the stone, *vacuos exercet aera morsus*. . . . The shape occurs' (*LE*, 152; cf. also Canto XXV, ll. 90-5n.).

I

l. 1 eau-forte: (Fr.) 'etching'.
l. 2 Jacquemart: Jules Jacquemart (1837-80), Parisian water-colourist and etcher. An etching by Jacquemart of Théophile Gautier in three-quarter face was included as the frontispiece to his *Émaux et Camées* (1881).
l. 4 Messalina: Valeria Messalina, the unfaithful wife of the Roman emperor Claudius, murdered at the age of twenty-four. Her head appeared on coins struck early in Claudius' reign. Pound communicated to Friar and Brinnin that 'he had in mind a particular portrait, but that he cannot now remember which' (op. cit., 530). His source may have been the engravings which appeared in J. J. Bernoulli's *Römische Ikonographie* (1886).
ll. 5-6: repeated from 'E.P. Ode', line 13.

ll. 12–16 In profile . . . To forge Achaia: recalled in Canto LXXIV (ll. 660, 756).

l. 14 Pier Francesca: Piero della Francesca (1420–92), Italian painter of the Umbrian school, renowned for his geometrical composition and as a colourist; cf. the description of the Burne–Jones cartoons as 'Thin like brook-water', 'Yeux Glauques', line 13, and Canto XLV, note on line 30.

l. 15 Pisanello: Antonio (or Vittore) Pisano (1397?–1455), Veronese painter and medallist. Salomon Reinach in his *Apollo* (1904) refers to him as 'an engraver of admirable medals, a draughtsman of genius' (p. 192). Pound included the reproduction of a letter seal by Pisanello as the frontispiece to his *Guide to Kulchur* (1938), 'to indicate', he said, 'the thoroughness of Rimini's civilization in 1460'. Pound refers to Pisanello again directly in Cantos XXVI (131/126) and LXXIV (464/437).

l. 16 Achaia: a name originally for two territories to the north and south of ancient Greece, but taken later to represent the whole. One of Pisano's earliest medals was of the Greek emperor of the East John VII Palaeologus.

II

Epigraph: (Fr.) 'What do they know of love, and what can they understand? If they don't understand poetry, if they have no feeling for music, what can they understand of this passion, in comparison with which the rose is gross and the perfume of violets a clap of thunder?' The flower symbolism and the association of 'amour and aesthetics' here suggest a possible model in Remy de Gourmont (cf. *LE*, 339–58).

Caid Ali: a Persian pseudonym in allusion perhaps to the *Rubáiyát* of Omar Khayyám.

l. 1 Cf. 'E.P. Ode', line 1.

diabolus in the scale: the devil in music is the augmented fourth, creating discord. Pound said of Yeats, 'he has nothing against them (*les Imagistes*), at least so far as I know – except what he calls "their devil's metres" ' (*LE*, 378).

l. 2 ambrosia: the food of the gods, cf. 'Phallic and ambrosial' (*Mauberley* III, l. 6), and 'amid ambrosial circumstances' (' "The Age Demanded" ', l. 34).

l. 3 All passes: cf. 'All things are a flowing' (poem III above, l. 9). *ANANGKE*: (Gk.) 'Necessity' or 'Fate'. Pound wrote in 1935 that Henry James 'perceived the *Anagke* of the modern world to be money' (*SPr*, 242).

l. 4 Arcadia: in ancient Greece, the central district of the Peloponnesus. In its pastoral isolation it came to represent an image of paradise in Greek and Roman poetry and in the Renaissance.

l. 5 phantasmagoria: Hugh Kenner has suggested the probable source is Henry James's *The Ambassadors* (1903), in which Strether remarks at one point, 'Of course I moved among miracles. It was all phantasmagoric' (Kenner, *Poetry of EP*, 176). Pound used the term elsewhere in association with 'imagism, or poetry wherein the feelings of painting and sculpture are predominant (certain men move in phantasmagoria; the images of their gods, whole countrysides, stretches of hill land and forest, travel with them)' (*SPr*, 394). Cf. also Ian Bell, 'The Phantasmagoria of Hugh Selwyn Mauberley', *Paideuma*, V, no. 3, 361–85.

l. 7 NUKTOS' AGALMA: (Gk.) 'jewel of the night', a phrase used by Bion in apostrophe to the evening star (Barnstone, 502; *The Greek Bucolic Poets*, Loeb edn., IX, 410).

* * *

l. 8 precipitate: Pound perhaps draws on the meaning of the term for the chemical action by which solids are deposited from solution in a liquid. Here, as in his use of the terms 'seismograph', 'diastasis' and 'anaesthesis', also in this poem, Pound, like Jules Laforgue, dips 'his wings in the dye of scientific terminology' (*LE*, 283).

l. 13 time for arrangements: cf. J. Alfred Prufrock's 'And indeed there will be time . . . In a minute there is time/ For decisions and revisions which a minute will reverse' (T. S. Eliot, *Collected Poems*, 12).

l. 17 TO AGATHON: (Gk.) 'the good'.

l. 18 sieve: in a discussion of correlated forms of intellectual and sexual failure in his 'Postscript' to Remy de Gourmont's *The Natural Philosophy of Love*, Pound writes, 'You have the man who wears himself out and weakens his brain, echo of the orang, obviously not the talented sieve; you have the contrasted case in the type of man who really can not work until he has relieved the pressure on his spermatic canals' (*P and D*, 213).

l. 19 seismograph: an instrument for the automatic recording of earthquakes. Pound had used the word in making a distinction between the passive and the creative (vorticist) artist: 'The good artist is perhaps a good seismograph, but the difference between man and a machine is that man can in some degree "start his machinery going". He can, within limits, not only record but create' (*SPr*, 346). Elsewhere, in his essay on Henry James, Pound suggests our chief interest in a writer is in his 'degree of sensitization' and that 'on this count we may throw out the whole Wells–Bennett period, for what interest can we take in instruments which must by nature miss two-thirds of the vibrations in any conceivable situation?' (*LE*, 331).

ll. 20–1: Mauberley's urge is that of the impressionist who would 'try to imitate in words what someone has done in paint'. Such poets, says Pound, are 'a rosy, floribund bore' (*LE*, 400).

ll. 22–3 cheek-bone/ By verbal manifestation: repeated in Canto LXXIV in connection with Sandro Botticelli's *La Nascita di Venere* (The Birth of Venus), 'cheek bone, by verbal manifestation,/ her eyes as in "La Nascita" ' (474/446). 'Verbal manifestation' is an expression used by Pound elsewhere to suggest the medium of language (cf. *LE*, 25).

l. 27 irides: the plural form for 'iris', referring to both the flower and the membrane of the eye. Pound possibly alludes also to Iris, the messenger of the gods, whose sign to men was the rainbow. The phrase 'rose iridine' occurs in de Gourmont's 'Litanies de la Rose' (*MIN*, 190). Pound quotes also de Gourmont's 'J'ai plus aimé les yeux que toutes les autres manifestations corporelles de la beauté' (*SPr*, 389).

l. 28 botticellian sprays: an allusion to Botticelli's *The Birth of Venus*.

l. 29 diastasis: separation, dilation. Pound records a visitation from Aphrodite in Canto LXXXI (ll. 123–4) 'Saw but the eyes and stance between the eyes,/ colour, diastasis'.

l. 30 anæsthesis: loss of feeling or sensation.

l. 31 affect: passion, desire, but also perhaps with the sense of 'pretense' or 'affectation'. Pound used the word in both his translations of Cavalcanti's 'Donna mi priegha' (*LE*, 155; Canto XXXVI, l. 3n.).

l. 32 (Orchid): a pun, as on 'Irides' (l. 27). 'Orchid' (from Gk. ὄρχεις) is both the flower and the testicles. For Mauberley the moment of sexual invitation has passed unnoticed and he can only appreciate his insensibility after the event. (Cf. Espey, 51.)

*   *   *

ll. 34–7: cf. the epigraph to MAUBERLEY (1920).

"The Age Demanded"

l. 3 red-beaked steeds: the doves and swans who pull Aphrodite's chariot and who would be unfit for a harness.

l. 4 the Cytheræan: Aphrodite, who is said to have landed on the island of Cythera after her birth from the sea.

ll. 13–15: He made . . . individual: Pound had stated his own sense of the application of art to the state in 'The Serious Artist' in 1913: 'Men still try to promote the ideal state. No perfect state will be founded on the theory, or on the working hypothesis that all men are alike. No science save the arts will give us the requisite data for learning in what ways men differ' (*LE*, 47). More directly, in 'How to Read', he wrote:

Has literature a function in the state, in the aggregation of humans, in the republic. . . . It has . . . the individual cannot think and communicate his thought, the governor and legislator cannot act effectively or frame his laws, without words, and the solidity and validity of these words is in the care of the damned and despised *litterati*.

(*LE*, 21)

Cf. also the *ABC of Reading* (p. 32).
l. 21 neo-Nietzschean clatter: 'Nietzsche', wrote Pound, 'made a temporary commotion' (*LE*, 32). Pound's portrait in this and immediately surrounding stanzas recalls his discussions of Remy de Gourmont. In 1915 he wrote, 'Nietzsche has done no harm in France because France has understood that thought can exist apart from action . . . so Diomedes in De Gourmont's story is able to think things which translation into action would spoil', and of de Gourmont generally he added that he

had written throughout his life in absolute single-blessedness; it was to express his thought, his delicate, subtle, quiet and absolutely untrammelled revery, with no regard whatsoever for existing belief, with no after-thought or beside-thought either to conform or to avoid conforming.

(*SPr*, 391)

Later Pound wrote of de Gourmont as 'intensely aware of the differences of emotional timbre' and of his holding 'ideas, intuitions, perceptions in a certain personal exquisite manner' (*LE*, 340, 343). Yet for Pound de Gourmont retained his vigour and relevance, his essays were 'the best portrait available, the best record that is, of the civilized mind from 1885–1915' (ibid., 344) and his sonnets 'are among the few successful endeavours to write poetry *of our own time*' (*SPr*, 388).
l. 33 Minoan: a term introduced by Sir Arthur Evans to denote the period of Bronze Age culture established at Knossos in Crete, the first centre of high civilization in the Aegean. Cf. the reference to King Minos in 'Medallion' (l. 11).
ll. 38–9: Pound wrote of de Gourmont, 'In Diomède we find an Epicurean receptivity, a certain aloofness, an observation of contacts and auditions' (*LE*, 343).
l. 39 apathein: (Gk.) 'impassivity', 'indifference' as of the gods to men.

ll. 44–5 imaginary . . . sea-surge: a rendering of Homer's

παρὰ θῖνα πολυφλοίσβοιο θαλάσσης

(*Iliad*, Bk. I, l. 34), which Pound cited in his 'Translators of Greek' as an example of 'untranslated and untranslatable' onomatopoeia (*LE*, 250). Writing to W. H. D. Rouse, Pound described the present lines as a 'cross cut' to Homer, and the 'Best I have been able to do', but as 'totally different, and a different movement of the water, and inferior' (*SL*, 274–5). De Gourmont's 'Litanies de la Rose', said Pound, was a poem that 'must come to life in audition, or in the finer audition which one may have in imagining sound' (*MIN*, 188). Pound had used the term 'sea-surge' earlier in 'The Seafarer' (l. 6), and in Canto VII he refers to Homer's 'Ear, ear for the sea-surge' (28/24).

l. 47 conservation . . . tradition": cf. note on poem XI above, line 1. *"better tradition"*: Pound had written to H. L. Mencken in September 1916, '"Better" is such a bloody ambiguous word' (*SL*, 97). His quotation marks here register a similar inadequacy and his own irony. As Donald Davie has said, for Pound '*All* the traditions are precious' (*Pound*, 84). Cf. ' "his betters" ' (l. 58 below).

ll. 48–9: Pound held firmly to the Imagist principles of economy, direct statement and precise definition. Mauberley's art would seem to represent neither Imagist nor Vorticist principles but Impressionism. In the essay 'Arnold Dolmetsch', Pound had written, 'Impressionism has reduced us to such a dough-like state of receptivity that we have ceased to like concentration' (*LE*, 433).

ll. 58–61: Pound notes that de Gourmont had been denied membership of the French Academy (*SPr*, 392), and is perhaps thinking also of his own exclusion from the pages of the *Quarterly Review* in 1914, subsequent to his involvement in *Blast* (cf. *LE*, 357–8).

IV

The presence of 'the palms, the coral, the sand, the quiet water, the flamingoes' in this section lead Espey to suggest it has its source in Flaubert's African travels and his novel *Salammbô* (p. 39), Jo Brantley Berryman, who feels that Mauberley is 'a portrait drawn from historical example' argues that his passivity and impressionist sensibility correspond to the critic Huntley Carter, author of the articles 'Poetry versus Imagism' (*Little Review*, September 1915) and 'Towards a Human Aesthetic' (*Egoist*, May 1914). In the second of these, Carter talks of the recovery of his '(Art) Soul' in two years spent in the Pacific islands, removed from the corruptions of civilization (Berryman, 'Ezra Pound versus Hugh Selwyn Mauberley. A Distinction', Ph.D. dissertation, University of Southern California, 1973, 117–30). Pound may allude also to the lotus-eaters sunk in lassitude and forgetfulness (*Odyssey*, Bk. IX, ll. 82–104, and cf. Canto XX, line 150 ff.), and perhaps to Plotinus' *Enneads*, where prior to a reference to Odysseus Plotinus considers the individual who would withdraw into himself in pursuit of beauty, 'is there not a myth telling in symbol of such a dupe, how he sank into the depths of the current and was swept away to nothingness?' (trans. S. MacKenna, 1969, Bk. I, Sixth Tractate, 8, p. 63).

l. 1 Moluccas: the spice-producing Moluccan Islands in the Malay Archipelago.

l. 5 Simoon: the hot, dry, sand-wind which sweeps across the African and Asian deserts during spring and summer.

l. 12 juridical: *le mot juste* from Pound. The flamingoes have the formal, authoritative demeanour of the law.

ll. 14–17: a further reference to impressionism. Pound described the poet John Gould Fletcher as 'sputter, bright flash, sputter. Impressionist temperament, made intense at half-seconds' (*SL*, 49).

ll. 20–5: Pound alludes perhaps to the fate of Odysseus' companion, Elpenor, who falls to his death from the roof of Circe's palace after a bout of drinking (*Odyssey*, Bk. X, ll. 552–60). In Canto I (ll. 54–7), Elpenor's soul bids Odysseus,

> remember me, unwept, unburied,
> "Heap up mine arms, be tomb by sea-bord, and inscribed:
> "*A man of no fortune, and with a name to come.*
> "And set my oar up, that I swung mid fellows."

l. 25 hedonist: in *Blast* I (June 1914), Pound defined hedonism as 'the vacant place of the Vortex, without force, deprived of past and future'.

Medallion

'Medallion' is often thought of as a companion poem to 'Envoi'. Their relation can perhaps be explained by Pound's distinction between two types of verse, the lyric and the imagist; the first type is 'a sort of poetry where music, sheer melody, seems as if it were just bursting into speech', the second 'where painting or sculpture seems as if it were "just coming over into speech"' (*G-B*, 82). If 'Envoi' therefore is an example of Pound's attempt to 'revive the lyric', 'Medallion' would seem to be an attempt at the 'Image', an example of 'the "sculpture" of rhyme', which takes its cue from Théophile Gautier's account in 'Les Progrès de la poésie française depuis 1830' of his own *Émaux et Camées*, 'Chaque pièce devait être un médaillon . . . quelque chose qui rappelât les empreintes de médailles antiques qu'on voit chez les peintres et les sculpteurs' (quoted in Espey, 30–1). Whether the poem is then to be regarded as Pound's own or as Mauberley's is a question of its success in these terms. Certainly the possibility of failure is suggested at many points earlier in the poem, particularly in the implied comparison with Piero della Francesca and the medallist Pisanello (MAUBERLEY (1920) I, ll. 14–15). Just as, in Pound's view, the Parnassian poets though following Gautier 'fell short of his merit' (*LE*, 285), so by as early as 1915 he had felt that those associated with Imagism had fallen below the 'critical standard' he had been at pains to set (cf. *SL*, 48–50), and been led himself to re-situate 'the doctrine of the Image' within Vorticism. (But cf. J. B. Berryman, ' "Medallion": Pound's Poem', op. cit.)

l. 1 Luini: Bernardino Luini (*c.* 1470–1532), Lombard painter, known for his religious frescoes and for his secular paintings dealing with the stories of Europa, Cephalus and Procnis. Salomon Reinach (l. 8 below) suggests that Luini's 'characteristic trait is a certain honeyed softness that delights the multitude' (*Apollo*, 191).

ll. 1–4 porcelain . . . soprano: Berryman argues that the reference here as for 'Envoi' is the singing of Raymonde Collignon. In Pound's third and final review of her singing (*New Age*, 15 Apr. 1920), he wrote, 'As long as this diseuse was on the stage she was non-human; she was, if you like, a china image: there are Ming porcelains which are respectable; the term "china" is not in this connection ridiculous' (op. cit., 397–8).

ll. 2–4 The grand piano . . . Protest: Pound alludes perhaps to Jules Laforgue's 'Complaintes des Pianos', included in his 'French Poets' (*MIN*, 168). The protest here is on behalf of the 'old music', the grand piano seeming to occupy a position midway between 'the gracious, exquisite music' of the clavichord and the 'sheer pianolo' described by Pound in the essay 'Arnold Dolmetsch' (*LE*, 433).

ll. 5–6: Pound perhaps owes something to the opening of Robert Browning's poem 'A Face' which refers to 'that little head of hers/ Painted upon a background of pale gold'. The same poem includes the expressions 'pure profile', 'honey-coloured' and 'Breaking its outline'. It was included by Pound in the anthology *Confucius to Cummings* (p. 252).

l. 5 sleek head: cf. Canto LXXIX, 'Sleek head that saved me out of one chaos' (516/484). James Joyce apparently expressed his sole praise of Pound's work by way of the comment, 'The sleek head of verse, Mr. Pound, emerges in your work' (Seelye, 104).

l. 6 gold-yellow: this term and the word 'topaz' (l. 16 below) recur in Canto V (21/17). Hyphenated adjectives of this type (cf. also 'honey-red', 'face-oval') were common in the poetry of Dante Gabriel Rossetti.

l. 7 Anadyomene: in Greek 'rising out of the sea', i.e. Aphrodite, 'born of the sea foam'. The allusion is to the head of Aphrodite by Praxiteles reproduced in Reinach's *Apollo* (fig. 83, p. 59). Pound quotes in his 'French Poets' from Arthur Rimbaud's 'Vénus Anadyomène' as an example of Rimbaud's presenting 'a thick suave colour, firm, even' (*MIN*, 182).

l. 8 Reinach: Salomon Reinach (1858–1932), French archaeologist and art historian, author of *Apollo* (1904). Pound suggests the limitations of Reinach in his description of Gaudier-Brzeska as a man 'who knows not merely the sculpture out of Reinach's Apollo but who can talk and think in the terms of world-sculpture' (*G-B*, 105).

l. 9 face-oval: Reinach suggests the 'head of Aphrodite', 'hitherto round, has become oval' (*Apollo*, 58).

l. 11 Minos: king of Crete, whose palaces were at Knossos. Minoan civilization reached a high level of achievement in design and metal work; cf. 'Minoan undulation' (' "The Age Demanded" ', l. 33).

l. 12: cf. Pound's earlier 'The Alchemist', 'Midonz, with the gold of the sun, the leaf of the poplar, by the light of the amber . . . Give light to the metal' (*CSP*, 86).

metal: writing under the pseudonym of B. H. Dias, Pound described Wyndham Lewis's 'consummate ability to define his masses by line and to express the texture of soft substance without sacrifice of an almost metallic rigidity of boundary' (*New Age*, 29 Jan. 1920, 205). As Walter Villerant also, he said of Joyce, 'The metal finish alarms people' (*P and D*, 73).

l. 14 suave: Reinach describes Praxiteles' head of Aphrodite as 'exquisitely suave in expression' (*Apollo*, 58).

l. 16 eyes: a common designation for Aphrodite in Pound's poetry (cf. 'Yeux Glauques', title and note on line 10).

topaz: a yellow or pale blue or pale green stone, lustrous and transparent. Daniel Pearlman suggests, 'Topaz belongs in the range of yellow and golden colors classically associated with

Aphrodite' (p. 61). In *The Spirit of Romance* Pound translates Dante's *Paradiso*, XXX, lines 76–8, 'The river and the topaz-gems which enter and go forth are shadowy prefaces of their truth' (p. 151).

THE CANTOS

The *Cantos* occupied Pound, it would appear, from as early as 1904 or 1905 when he had 'various schemes' for the poem (*Writers at Work: The Paris Review Interviews*. Second Series, 1963, 36) until his death in 1972, and for the student of his poetry, indeed for the student of modern poetry at large, they are as Basil Bunting has suggested, like the Alps: 'You will have to go a long way round if you want to avoid them' ('On the Fly-leaf of Pound's Cantos', *Collected Poems*, 1968, 122). The *Cantos* make undeniably and unprecedentedly monumental demands on their readers. What is more, one cannot assume they have yet been crossed, though camps and markers have been pitched at different heights by lone inspired individuals and more recently by bands of intrepid and diligent scholars, whose honest labours, though more modest, are seemingly without end. One thing, however, ought to be clear: the *Cantos* will not flatten out into an ornamental garden. Detailed and piecemeal explication of at least parts of the poem is inescapable and indispensable, and this, it is important to realize, cannot then be put to the back of one's mind as though preliminary to a full experience of the poetry. The demands the poem makes and the reader's willingness or reluctance to meet them are part of our experience of the *Cantos*, and part therefore of its meaning as a modern epic, and all that this implies in Pound's case of an uncompromising and estranged relationship between the epic poet, his readers, and the society whose tale he means to tell.

The *Cantos* are arguably the most significant poem of this century, because of their intrinsic merit, the sheer scale of

Pound's ambition, and their influence on later, mostly American, poets, but also because of their difficulty, the sense of failure that surrounds them and because Pound *in toto* as man and poet presents us with a paradigm of the relation of poetic form to ideology and of modern poetry's relation to history. We cannot have Pound the poet, that is to say, and at the same time ignore or excuse or dismiss Pound the supporter of Social Credit, the disciple of Confucius, the anti-Semite and fascist. As the American poet Charles Olson has said, speaking as one of those influenced by Pound and troubled by this question,

> Shall we talk a 100 Cantos and not answer the anti-Semite who wrote them? Shall we learn from his line and not answer his lie? . . . For Pound is no dried whore of fascism. He is as brilliant a maker of language as we have had in our time. The point is not that this mitigates, or in any way relates to the punishment the U.S. shall deal to him as an American citizen. What is called for is a consideration, based on his career, of how such a man came to the position he reached when he allowed himself to become the voice of Fascism. For Pound is not isolated in this, among artists of his time. He is only, as so often, the more extreme. Yeats, Lewis, Lawrence have also been labelled fascist.
>
> (Seelye, 17, 19)

Olson's remarks were made some thirty years ago, but they have yet to be answered. Criticism has alerted itself, it is true, to Pound's economic thinking and to his politics, but the most recent studies in these areas (Earle Davis, *Vision Fugitive; Ezra Pound and Economics*, 1969; William Chace, *The Political Identities of Ezra Pound and T. S. Eliot*, 1973; David Heymann, *Ezra Pound. The Last Rower*, 1976), aside from other weaknesses, signally fail to consider them at any depth as of a piece with Pound's poetry. Even the very real advance in Pound studies represented by Hugh Kenner's *The Pound Era* (1972) fails, in the midst of so much that it does do, to consider Pound's fascism or the broader paradox, which Olson and others have

pointed to, of to say the least a 'disposition' on the part of
writers such as Yeats, Eliot, Wyndham Lewis and Lawrence
towards reactionary ideologies. Otherwise the general state of
critical opinion on the *Cantos* is in fact much as it is presented
in Daniel Pearlman's Introduction to his *The Barb of Time*
(1969), with critics divided on what Pearlman takes to be 'the
crux of *Cantos* criticism, the question as to whether this
physically enormous, sprawling poem has *major form* – an
over-all design in which the parts are significantly related to
the whole' (p. 3). Criticism which shares this assumption is
limited to internal aesthetic and thematic questions in the
Cantos, and is locked moreover – its differences notwithstanding
– in an organicist aesthetic which values formal unity to a
degree probably inappropriate to a poem which, like the Alps
or the ocean, has mass and boundaries but hardly coherence.

It is true that organicist criteria have the authority of
Pound's own pronouncements on the *Cantos*' over-all design
(as a 'fugue', an 'Odyssey', a 'Divine Comedy', a 'vortex',
composed according to 'the ideogrammatic method' or made
out of 'interlocking rhythms of recurrence'), and also of his
late confessions of failure ('I cannot make it cohere', Canto
CXVI, 26/796, or 'a mess', 'It's a botch', *EP*, ed. Sullivan,
354, 375). Pound himself evidently subscribed to these criteria,
but is more interesting than most of his commentators because
he also explicitly and in practice contradicted them. Against,
for example, Pound's remarks on the scheme of the *Cantos* as
'Rather like, or unlike subject and response and counter subject
in fugue' (*SL*, 210) or the elaborate parallel he suggested to
Yeats with the three-tiered Renaissance fresco by Cosimo
Tura ('A Packet for Ezra Pound' in *A Vision*, 1956, 4–5), one
can (and must) set his reminder of 'the number of very
important chunks of world-literature in which form, major
form, is remarkable mainly for absence' (*LE*, 394). And
against Pound's most categorical avowal of an analogy with
Dante's *Divine Comedy*, that he had schooled himself 'to write
an epic poem which begins "In the Dark Forest" crosses the
Purgatory of human error, and ends in the light, and "fra i

maestri di color che sanno"' (*SPr*, 137), one is bound to set the caution of 'By no means an orderly Dantescan rising/ but as the winds veer' (Canto LXXIV, 471/ 443) and his proviso 'I was not following the three divisions of the *Divine Comedy* exactly. One can't follow the Dantesquan cosmos in an age of experiment' (*Writers at Work*, 52).

At the outset we know also that the *Cantos* were neither conceived or begun according to a settled plan. The first sixteen especially evolved in the period 1915–25, most intensely in the years 1923 and 1924, out of false starts and substantial revisions made in the actual process of composition (cf. Myles Slatin, 'A History of Pound's Cantos, I–XVI, 1915–1925', *American Literature*, xxxv, 1963, 183–95). As Pound wrote to Felix Schelling in July 1922,

> Perhaps as the poem goes on I shall be able to make various things clearer. . . . the first 11 Cantos are preparation of the palette. I *have* to get down all the colours or elements I want for the poem. Some perhaps too enigmatically and abbreviatedly. I hope, heaven help me, to bring them into some sort of design and architecture later.
>
> (*SL*, 180)

As this suggests Pound was evidently constructing the *Cantos* in the dark, moved more by a compulsion than a preconceived design, and could at most promise, and himself hope for, a final order and clarity. Pound had referred to the *Cantos* at their beginning as 'endless' (Slatin, op. cit., 185), had written to Hubert Creekmore in 1939, 'As to the *form* of *The Cantos*: All I can say or pray is: *wait* till it's there. I mean wait till I get 'em written and then if it don't show, I will start exegesis' (*SL*, 323), and in the late *Paris Review* interview felt still he had to discover a 'principle of order', 'I must clarify obscurities; I must make clearer definite ideas or dissociations' (*Writers at Work*, 51). If we are to understand from this that the *Cantos*' final design and architecture were postponed even until their completion, we can assume they do not appear since the poem is ended only arbitrarily by the event of Pound's death. Just as the first thirty Cantos were published and still stand as a 'Draft', and just as their last instalment is titled 'Drafts and Fragments', so we may conceive of the whole as provisional, open, exploratory and unfinished.

But in fact this would be no more an adequate description of the whole than claims for the *Cantos*' firm, accomplished design. One is reminded of Pound's comparison of the *Cantos* with a performance of Bartók's Fifth Quartet heard at Rapallo as having alike 'the defects inherent in a record of struggle' (*GK*, 135), and reminded too of his defence of Sigismondo Malatesta's Tempio at Rimini, 'If you consider the Malatesta and Sigismundo in particular, a failure, he was at all events a failure worth all the successes of his age. . . . If the Tempio is a jumble and junk shop, it nevertheless registers a concept. There is no other single man's effort equally registered' (note to frontispiece, *GK*). It is just this success in failure, a combination of chaos and partially achieved form, which one encounters in the *Cantos*. And Pound again provides the best gloss to it:

> Art very possibly *ought* to be the supreme achievement, the 'accomplished'; but there is the other satisfactory effect, that of a man hurling himself at an indomitable chaos, and yanking and hauling as much of it as possible into some sort of order (or beauty), aware of it both as chaos and as potential.
>
> (*LE*, 396)

Pound's 'struggle' is essentially, as a poet, between the rival aesthetics he indicates here, and as this comes to imply, between rival conceptions of history; his *conscious* effort is, as criticism has largely presented it, to shape water into stone, to convert flux into permanence and to pull the disarray of the *Cantos*' materials into order. And this effort is repaid in the moments of transcendence and stillness from which 'integrative' critics are prone to extrapolate the character of the entire work. The *Cantos* in this way are for Hugh Kenner 'a timeless frieze' ('New Subtlety of Eyes' in Russell, 91) and for Daniel Pearlman a conflict of time systems in which Pound's own 'ahistorical cyclical time-consciousness' is triumphant over the linear and mechanical clock-time of history (esp. pp. 21–7). Both Kenner and Pearlman understandably make much in this reckoning of the 'dimension of stillness' in Canto XLIX, for Kenner 'one of the pivots of the poem: the emotional still point of the *Cantos*' (*Poetry of EP*, 326), and for Pearlman a paean to 'Confucian order' which he relates, rightly, to the definition of the essential or ideal form of love, in Pound's second translation of Cavalcanti's 'Donna mi priegha', as that which 'moveth not, drawing all to his stillness' (Canto XXXVI, l. 59; cf. Pearlman, 207–10). For Pound, says Pearlman, Cavalcanti's Canzone represents 'a touchstone of aesthetic and intellectual order' (p. 154) and the idea of 'stillness' he sees as 'the metaphoric and conceptual center of the only sustained vision Pound has yet offered us of a paradise' (p. 158). Here, in Canto XXXVI, in revitalizing a significant moment, a 'luminous detail' in the literary tradition, Pound sets art in defiance of time and presents its truth as one with the Confucian scheme of order of Canto XLIX as a rebuff to an Einsteinian theory or relativity which would define 'time' itself and not 'stillness' as the 'fourth dimension', and so undermine the moral and artistic absolutes on which these Cantos depend. If this is so, it is at the same time surely significant that the concept of individual and social order is so cryptically closed to a system of ideas which would threaten its serenity, and significant too that Pound's translation in Canto XXXVI is among the most inaccessible sections of the poem, that its definition of Love is an abstruse and privileged one, and that the poet (Pound as much as Cavalcanti) can at its close so arrogantly jettison those who do not share or understand it.

The connections over these Cantos between ideals of social and artistic order are already plain; what Pound called the 'scholastic definition in form' in Cavalcanti's poem ('Cavalcanti', *LE*, 161), which stands opposed to 'the general indefinite wobble' of 'Mitteleuropa' in Canto XXXV, as both Pearlman (p. 155) and Clark Emery (p. 126) have pointed out, stands also as co-extensive with the Confucian axis or 'unwobbling pivot', 'the calm principle' in Nature and in man's ethical and social organization. Nor is it difficult to see how the authoritarianism of Confucian doctrine, in its emphasis upon the state and upon the enlightened Prince in whom this principle is maintained, would support, if not direct Pound to, a view of history in terms of the words and deeds of single 'factive' personalities rather than of collective action. Nor is it difficult to see how its principles would attach themselves to the Adams brothers ('our 中 chung[1] [the axis, the pivot], Canto LXXXIV, 575/540), and inform also his view of Mussolini as a man of genius filled with 'the will towards *order*' (*J/M*, 128, and cf. pp. 112–13). The notion of art as transcendent, the value placed upon the thing itself, upon the isolated epiphany which was implicit in the Imagist programme, if indeed not before, and which comes to inform Pound's terrestrial paradise, is entirely consistent, one can see, with his neo-Platonism and Confucianism, just as these are consistent with his view of fascism. At their most determined these criteria will turn art into the immobility of metal or stone just as they will revere the established code of law (the Stone Classics, the Magna Charta, the U.S. Constitution), and at their fiercest grind down complex ethical, social and political questions to the dogma and *idées fixes* of Pound's faith in Social Credit and the excesses of his anti-Semitism.

The axis, the pivot, develops one might think an unfortunate or at times deplorable wobble, but we will not, I suggest, rescue Pound or, what is more important, understand the dynamic of the *Cantos* or Pound's historical situation and our own divided response, if we adhere to these same terms, but fall short of their logic. As a poet Pound is aware of both chaos and potential order, of change and permanence, and what the *Cantos* accustom us to, even in spite of Pound's express predilection for order over chaos, is the intermediary realm which is neither, but both. It is in this sense that the *Cantos* are truly exploratory and testing, requiring of us as of Pound something akin to Keats's idea of negative capability, 'when man is capable of being in uncertainties, Mysteries, doubts, without any irritable reaching after fact and reason' (*Letters of John Keats*, ed. R. Gittings, 1970, 43). It is in this spirit, I believe, that Pound writes of at all times desiring 'to know the demarcation between what I know and what I do not know' (*LE*, 85), admitting in his study of Cavalcanti to 'the depths of my ignorance, or my width of uncertainty' (ibid., 160). And it is in this spirit certainly that he talks in 1963 of realizing 'the consciousness of doubt' and 'the uncertainty of knowing nothing' (*Delta*, Montreal, 22 Oct. 1963, 3–4). In Pound's poetry this corresponds most, one feels, to the mode he identifies as 'logopoeia':

> 'the dance of the intellect among words', that is to say, it employs words not only for their direct meaning, but it takes count in a special way of habits of usage, of the context we *expect* to find with the word, its usual concomitants, of its known acceptances, and of ironical play. It holds the aesthetic content which is peculiarly the domain of verbal manifestation, and cannot possibly be contained in plastic or in music. It is the latest come, and perhaps most tricky and undependable mode.
>
> (*LE*, 25)

'Logopoeia' is usually confined to irony but I suggest it extends to the vocabulary and syntax, the ellipses, the suspensions, the lapsed and accretional reference, and the literal foreignness, of the *Cantos*. It is here as Pound checks and replenishes and surpasses habits of usage and known associations that his relation to his readers is at its most potentially enriching, and most at risk. The Cavalcanti translation of 1928 was, Pound suggested, a means to establishing a viable English (*LE*, 193–4), and Canto XXXVI is presumably a stage in this process, but Pound's translation of Cavalcanti here is remarkable precisely to the degree that its broken and curiously unfamiliar locutions and syntax render it virtually unintelligible as English. Terms such as 'affect', 'diafan', 'intention', 'emanation', even '*virtú*' and 'quality', rise from the page as detached from their surroundings but barely register even an independent meaning. What they do convey is their own aura, a sense of possible depth or of emptiness above which they have surfaced. And this is costly precisely because it has none of the play of 'logopoeia', because Pound here eschews common habits of usage, most evidently in his preference for the term 'affect' over the more literal 'accident', because the latter was subject to extraneous associations (*LE*, 159). The suppression of contingency in this way is the linguistic equivalent of the timeless 'dimension of stillness' the Canto otherwise seeks to define. In such an instance, Pound in his attitude towards language is, in the terms of Jean Paulhan introduced by Donald Davie long ago, a 'terrorist' who seeks to master and confine and atomize discourse (*Articulate Energy*, 1955, 140). When his poetry is at its most transcendent Pound's language, one suspects, is at its most constrained. The alternative to the 'terrorist' is the 'rhetorician' who can allow language to run freely, confident of its direction and fluent in tongues not necessarily his own. And Pound at moments is this too.

The corollary of negative capability, one remembers, is a preparedness to go out of one's ego in a non-possessive empathy with others as in the famous examples of Keats's empathy with a sparrow (*Letters*, 38) and his sense of a loss of identity on entering a crowded room (ibid., 158). Pound has said himself how 'The Thrones in the *Cantos* are an attempt to move out from egoism and to establish some definition of an order possible or at any rate conceivable on earth' (*Writers at Work*, 52), and the qualifications which hedge this projected order are significant. But Pound had in fact already moved out of egoism in the earlier *Pisan Cantos*; in one way, in the humility and respect of his attitude towards Nature, Pound's wasp corresponding as Donald Davie has pointed out to Keats's sparrow (*Poet as Sculptor*, 176), and in another way in the series of tessellated voices and rhythms (of, for example, Aubrey Beardsley, Arthur Symons, Chu Hsi, Browning, William Stevenson, Bertran de Born, FitzGerald's *Rubáiyát*, Tennyson or of Richard Lovelace, Ben Jonson, Chaucer and the Authorized

Version of the Bible) as they advance and recede through Cantos LXXX and LXXXI. Pound occupies but does not appropriate these voices, releasing them as freely back into themselves as into his own discourse. The *Cantos*, he had said in 1920, 'come out of the middle of me and are not a mask' (Pearlman, 301), but his poetry, at a point such as this, speaks more than anywhere through remembered authors with the effect of dissolving and simultaneously extending personal identity and 'self-expression' into a more impersonal and faceted idiom. If Pound does not inhabit a recognizable English in Canto XXXVI, he here inhabits several so that we witness 'the synthetic construction of speech' which Eliot saw Pound as moving towards. But at the same time we witness the synthetic construction of an idea of English culture, known through its literature, and in the form Pound had known at first hand in pre-war Edwardian London, then recalled through personal reminiscence. The two are connected as has often been shown through the associative method of these Cantos, by which in Canto LXXX thoughts of England suggest the Magna Charta, the Talbots, Christmas in Salisbury with Maurice Hewlett, the Blunts, Swinburne, Mary Stuart, the Wars of the Roses and the war with France, and Kensington (see the notes to this Canto).

But Pound does not, I believe, thread the Canto on these details as if they were recoverable, or in a pretence to coherence. We are in the double realm of chaos and potential order. His questions to England are for example speculative, if not cynical, and a hope such as that 'the bank may be the nation's' or that 'money be free again' is roundly answered as soon as raised by Pound's pessimism. His general purpose here is suggested by a comment in the chapter 'Tradition' in *Guide to Kulchur*. 'I am not in these slight memories, merely "pickin' daisies". A man does not know his own ADDRESS (in time) until he knows where his time and milieu stand in relation to other times and conditions' (p. 83). Pound is at the close of Canto LXXX (and elsewhere) as he says later in the same chapter, 'attempting to discover "where in a manner of speaking etc.

we have got to"' (p. 84). Where Pound had got to, as one is reminded in this passage, is the D.T.C. at Pisa, and the enormous gulf between this reality and a remembered English past is nowhere fudged. The predominant tone of the passage is one of loss, of 'Tudor indeed is gone' and of surviving remnants (the Serpentine, the gulls, the sunken garden) in the midst of a significantly shared sense of uncertainty and dispossession, 'and God knows what else is left of our London/ my London, your London'. In seeking his 'address' Pound discovers, as indeed he had before in less drastic circumstances, that he has none. Just as he employs several Englishes, and indeed of course in the *Cantos* as a whole several languages, to the extent that he is in George Steiner's expression, 'linguistically unhoused', so Pound is also culturally exiled, connected positively with none of the aspects of English or American or Italian or Chinese culture he admired and would have wished into being. It is Pound's ability to write out of this alienation, out of a sense of culture now 'sunken', which allows us to think of him as an example of negative capability. This is evident finally in the climactic moment of visitation in Canto LXXXI by Aphrodite, the symbol of all Pound's effort to extract permanence from flux. In the event, the experience is not one of vision but of partial fulfilment, 'careless or unaware it had not the/ whole tent's room/ nor was place for the full εἰδώς' (knowing). The strength of this moment is not in its transcendence but in its demarcation of the known from the unknown, its awareness of the disparity between consummate form and a falling short of it. Pound is true moreover, in this way, to his sense of an authentic history, 'when the historians left blanks in their writings,/ "I mean for things they didn't know' (Canto XIII, ll. 69–72). And the *Cantos* we can accept as a poem 'including history' by very virtue of their fragmentation, their ellipses and blanks, their record of loss, their unfulfilled paradise and their uncompleted journey home. What we have still to understand is not Pound's inclusion of history, or the perhaps stronger motive to escape it, but the forces of actual history which wrenched both poem and poet in two.

Canto I

Canto I originally formed the latter part of what was Canto III, first published in *Poetry* (August 1917, 248–54), and subsequently, in a condensed form, in the private American edition of *Lustra* (1917) and in *Quia Pauper Amavi* (1919). The present Canto I did not exist as such until *A Draft of XVI Cantos* in 1925. (Cf. John L. Forster, 'Pound's Revisions of Cantos I–III', *Modern Philology*, LXIII, 1966, 236–45.) Its opening 67 lines are a translation in the rhythm and diction of Pound's 'Seafarer' from a Renaissance Latin translation by Andreas Divus of the Nekuia passage ('The Book of the Dead') in Homer's *Odyssey* (Bk. XI). Pound described how he came upon Divus's translation along the Paris quais in '1906, 1908, or 1910' in his 'Translators of Greek' (*LE*, 259–67), and gives there also Divus's Latin and his own translation as it was for ur-Canto III. The effect of this re-setting of Homer's Greek via Renaissance Latin into Pound's Anglo-Saxon manner gives a sense of the continual renewal of the *Odyssey* and anticipates the interleaved strata of languages and motifs in the Cantos to come. Pound wrote later, 'The Nekuia shouts aloud that it is *older* than the rest, all that island, Cretan, etc., hinter-time' (*SL*, 274) and this is perhaps one indication of why he should have chosen this passage to begin the *Cantos*. It suggests too why he should think Anglo-Saxon appropriate, since he found in the early English poems an equivalent root of the English sensibility, 'trace of what I should call the English national chemical' (*PM*, 45). Pound had also suggested earlier a similarity in 'directness and realism' between certain Chinese poems, early Saxon verse, the *Poema del Cid* and Homer 'or rather what Homer would be if he wrote without epithet' (*To-Day*, April 1915), and in 'Early Translators of Homer' had written that 'Homer *is* a little *rustre*, a little, or perhaps a good deal, mediaeval' (*LE*, 254). Forrest Read argues that the choice of Homer and Odysseus was the result largely of the influence on Pound of James Joyce's *Ulysses* ('Pound, Joyce and Flaubert: The Odysseans' in Hesse, 125–45).

Pound's Canto I virtually begins where Joyce leaves off, at the point where Odysseus, after a year spent on Circe's island Aeaea, leaves as she directs him to seek Tiresias in Hades. From Tiresias he gains the prophecy of how he will return home to Ithaca.

l. 7 Circe: the goddess and sorceress of Aeaea who, after delaying Odysseus for one year (cf. *Odyssey*, Bk. X, ll. 135–574), provides his ship with a favourable wind on his departure.
l. 12 Kimmerian: the Cimmerians were an ancient people whose land, shrouded in perpetual mists and clouds, and standing at the limits of the world, gave Odysseus access to Hades.
l. 17 place: Hades.
l. 19 rites: blood sacrifice to raise the dead.
Perimedes, Eurylochus: companions of Odysseus. Eurylochus was Odysseus' second in command.
l. 21 pitkin: i.e. small pit. Odysseus is following instructions given him by Circe.
l. 25 Ithaca: island home of Odysseus, off the west coast of Greece.
l. 27 Tiresias: prophet of Thebes. Odysseus obtains from him the prophecy of his return to Ithaca; cf. lines 65–7.
l. 29 Erebus: the place of utter darkness from which dead souls rise.
l. 23 dreory: the earlier text (*LE*, 263) has 'dreary'; 'dreory' is OE. 'dreorig' ('bloody'). It occurs in the lines from 'The Wanderer',

> forðon domgeorne   dreorigne oft
> in hyra breostcofan   bindað fæste,

which Pound translates, 'For the doom-eager oft bindeth fast his thought in blood-bedabbled breast' (*PM*, 45).
l. 38 Pluto: a name in Greek for Hades, lord of the dead.
Proserpine: the Roman equivalent of Greek Persephone, the queen of the dead.
l. 42 Elpenor: Odysseus' companion, who waking from a drunken stupor at the sound of Odysseus' departure, had

fallen to his death from the roof of Circe's palace; cf. lines 50–3. Cf. *Hugh Selwyn Mauberley*, ' "Siena Mi Fe' " ' (l. 7n.). Elpenor is referred to again in Canto XX (l. 170) and Canto LXXX (549/514).

l. 50 ingle: hearth or chimney.

l. 53 Avernus: a small lake in Campania, Italy, close to the cave by which Aeneas descended to hell (*Aeneid*, Bk. VI).

l. 56: Elpenor's epitaph is repeated in the plural in Canto LXXX (548/514), and cf. also MAUBERLEY (1920) IV (ll. 22–5).

l. 58 Anticlea: Odysseus' mother, who had died in his absence from Ithaca. He beats her off because Circe had instructed that no one should drink the blood until he had questioned Tiresias.

ll. 65–7: Tiresias' prophecy introduces the major epic theme of the 'nostos' or return home. Cf. also Canto LXXIV, where Pound remembers Yeats, Ford, Joyce and others as 'these the companions' (l. 268).

l. 68 Divus: cf. note above. Divus is addressed as though he is himself a departed soul.

l. 69 In officina Wecheli: (Lat.) 'at the workshop of Divus'. Pound gives the imprint of Divus's volume, 'Parisiis, In officina Christiani Wecheli, MDXXXVIII' in *Literary Essays* (p. 259).

l. 70 Sirens: sea creatures who entice men to their doom with their singing. Odysseus encounters them in the *Odyssey*, Bk. XII (ll. 165–200). Cf. *Hugh Selwyn Mauberley*, 'E.P. Ode' (ll. 9–10).

l. 71: in the *Odyssey*, Odysseus first rejoins Circe and then sails to meet the Sirens.

ll. 72–5: a rendering of the second Homeric Hymn to Aphrodite, dealing with the courtship of Venus and Anchises. Pound quotes here from the Latin translation by Georgius Dartona Cretensis, included in the volume by Andreas Divus, and given by Pound in 'Early Translators of Homer' (*LE*, 266).

l. 72 Venerandam: (Lat.) 'compelling admiration', the first word of the second Homeric Hymn.

l. 74 Cypri munimenta sortita est: (Lat.) 'the citadels of Cyprus were her appointed realm'.

oricalchi: (Lat.) 'orichalci' ('copper'), in reference to Aphrodite's earrings.

l. 76: from the Latin 'habens auream virgam Argicida' from Homeric Hymn V, also to Aphrodite.

golden bough: a golden bough enables Aeneas to cross the Styx and enter Hades (*Aeneid*, Bk. VI). Aeneas was the son of Venus and Anchises, and is referred to many times in subsequent Cantos. As the defender of Troy and founder of Rome he is introduced here as the mirror-image of Odysseus, who helped in Troy's destruction. The significance of the golden bough in classical mythology is discussed in Sir James Frazer's *The Golden Bough* (1890).

Argicida: (Lat.) either 'slayer of Greeks', and therefore Aphrodite who supported the Trojans against the Greeks in the Trojan war, or more probably here 'slayer of Argus', and therefore Hermes, the messenger of the gods and the conductor of souls to hell. Hermes is the subject of the fourth Homeric Hymn (cf. Canto XXIV, 119/114). In the *Odyssey* Hermes 'of the golden staff' gives Odysseus the magic herb 'moly' to resist Circe's drugs (*Odyssey*, Bk. X, ll. 277–306); cf. Canto XLVII, line 43.

So that: a phrase in Browning's *Sordello* (Bk. I, l. 567), reference to which follows in Canto II. The words 'so that' also open Canto XVII.

Canto II

First published as the 'Eighth Canto' in the *Dial* (May 1922). *ll. 1–4*: all that remains from the 1917 version of the first Cantos of a long colloquy between Pound and Robert Browning on the appropriate form of the modern epic. The original Canto I began:

Hang it all, there can be but one *Sordello*!
But say I want to, say I take your whole bag of tricks,

Let in your quirks and tweeks, and say the thing's an
   art-form,
Your *Sordello*, and that the modern world
Needs such a rag-bag to stuff all its thought in;

                (*Poetry*, June 1917, 113)

l. 1 Robert Browning: the Victorian poet (1812–89) and a major influence on Pound's early poetry, particularly in the use of the dramatic monologue. Pound here adopts Browning's manner.

l. 2 "*Sordello*": the title of Browning's poem published in 1840, based on the Italian troubadour Sordello (?1180–?1255). Pound admitted to finding Browning's poem 'obscure' (*LE*, 381), but admired its 'limpidity of narration' and thought its 'continued narrative having such clarity of outline without clog and *verbal* impediment', comparable to Dante's *Divine Comedy* (*ABC of R*, 191).

l. 3: the historical Sordello, and the Sordello that Pound would make.

l. 4: (Ital.) 'The Sordellos are from the region of Mantua'; a reference to the Sordello of the *Vita e Poesie de Sordello di Gioto* (1896) by Cesare de Lollis, a text Pound had consulted in the Ambrosian Library, Milan (*LE*, 97). The present phrase, repeated in Cantos VI (26/22) and XXXVI (185/180), is a conflation of two phrases, 'Sordels fo de Mantoana' and 'Lo Sordels si fo de Sirier de Mantoana' from de Lollis' *Vita* (pp. 147, 148) (Bradford Morrow, 'De Lollis' *Sordello* and Sordello: Canto 36', *Paideuma*, IV, no. 1, 98).

l. 5 So-shu: Sō-shu is the Japanese equivalent of the Chinese name Chuang Tzu, a Taoist philosopher. He is presented in Pound's 'Ancient Wisdom, Rather Cosmic' as 'having dreamed that he was a bird, a bee, and a butterfly' (*CSP*, 129).

churned in the sea: Pound's 'Ancient Wisdom, Rather Cosmic' is a translation of a poem by Li Po (A.D. 701–762) who 'died drunk', trying to embrace the reflection of the moon in the water (cf. 'Epitaphs', *CSP*, 129). Pound seems here to confuse Chuang Tzu with Li Po. Cf. also lines 130–1.

l. 7 Sleek head: cf. MAUBERLEY (1920), 'Medallion' (l. 5n.).

Lir: the Celtic god of Ocean, Mamannan mac Lir. Branwen is the daughter of the sea-god Llŷr (Irish Lir) in the Welsh epic *The Mabinogion*.

l. 8 Picasso: Pablo Picasso (1881–1973), the painter and famous instigator of Cubism. Pound at one time contemplated a book on Wyndham Lewis, Brancusi, Picasso and Picabia (*SL*, 166).

l. 11: an adaption of Aeschylus' description of Helen of Troy in the *Agamemnon* (ll. 689–90) as 'elandros' ('man-destroying'), 'elenaus' ('ship-destroying') and 'eleptolis' ('city-destroying'). Cf. Canto VII (28, 29/24, 25), and the application to usury in Canto XLVI (245/235).

Eleanor: Eleanor of Aquitaine (1122–1204), wife of King Louis VII of France, and subsequently of Henry II of England. She is held to have been the source of strife between the king and his sons, Guillem, Henry, Richard and John, and a cause of the Hundred Years War. Cf. also Canto VI (25–6/21–2).

l. 13: 'Of Homer', Pound wrote, 'two qualities remain untranslated: the magnificent onomatopœia, as of the rush of the waves on the sea-beach and their recession in:

$$\pi\alpha\rho\grave{\alpha}\ \theta\hat{\imath}\nu\alpha\ \pi o\lambda\upsilon\phi\lambda o\acute{\imath}\sigma\beta o\iota o\ \theta\alpha\lambda\acute{\alpha}\sigma\sigma\eta\varsigma$$

untranslated and untranslatable; and, secondly, the authentic cadence of speech . . . This quality of actual speaking is *not* untranslatable' (*LE*, 250). For Pound's own closest approximation to the quality of onomatopoeia, cf. MAUBERLEY (1920), ' "The Age Demanded" ' (ll. 44–5n.).

murmur: perhaps Pound's equivalent for the Greek ῾Ηκα meaning, says Pound, 'low, quiet, with a secondary meaning of "little by little" ' (*LE*, 252).

ll. 14–22: Pound's attempt at the 'quality of actual speaking' is from Homer's *Iliad*, Bk. III (ll. 139–60) where the old men of Troy speak of Helen. Cf. Canto XX (95/91) where Pound draws momentarily on the same source, and his discussion of early translations of this passage (*LE*, 250–4).

l. 19 Schoeney's daughters: the daughter of Schoeneus was Atalanta. Pound gives the relevant passage from Ovid in the for him unsurpassed translation of Arthur Golding (*Metamor-*

phoses. The Eight Booke, ll. 427–35), in his 'Notes on Elizabethan Classicists' (*LE*, 236). Golding has 'one/Of Schoenyes daughters'.

ll. 23–8: Tyro, the daughter of Salmoneus, was loved by Poseidon, the sea god, in the form of the river Enipeus (*Odyssey*, Bk. XI, ll. 235–9). Poseidon caused a great wave to envelop and conceal them. Cf. lines 132–9.

l. 34 Scios: the island of Chios off the coast of Asia Minor.

l. 35 Naxos: an island in the Aegean Sea and a centre of Dionysian worship.

l. 36 Naviform: in the shape of a ship.

ll. 40–118: the story of the kidnapping of the young Dionysus and of the resistance to the new god is told in Ovid (*Metamorphoses*, Bk. III, ll. 547–691/759–873) and in the Homeric Hymn to Dionysus.

l. 42 young boy: Dionysus (the Roman Bacchus), a vegetation god, but chiefly the god of wine, and associated therefore with artistic inspiration and ecstacy. The plants and animals of this passage (the vine, ivy, grape, leopards, lynxes and panthers) are sacred to Dionysus.

l. 46 I: Acoetes; cf. note on line 62.

l. 47 ex-convict: the pirate Lycabas (the 'Lycabs' of line 104).

l. 59 King Pentheus: Pentheus, king of Thebes, opposed the Dionysian rites and attempted to arrest Dionysus. He was instead presented with Acoetes. As Tiresias had predicted, Pentheus was torn to pieces by his own mother and aunts (*Metamorphoses*, Bk. III, ll. 692–733/874–921).

l. 62 Acœtes: the pilot of the ship taking Dionysus to Naxos. He alone of the crew believed in the god and was spared. Here he relates his conversion before Pentheus.

l. 95 Lyæus: a name meaning 'deliverer from care', applied to Dionysus as the god of wine.

l. 100 Olibanum: frankincense.

l. 113 Medon: a member of the pirate crew.

l. 115 Tiresias: the Theban prophet who foretold the coming of Dionysus and the death of Pentheus (*Metamorphoses*, Bk. III, ll. 516–27/649–64).

Cadmus: founder of Thebes, the grandfather of Pentheus, and also of Dionysus, who was born of Zeus and Semele, Cadmus' daughter. Cadmus too warns Pentheus (ibid., Bk. III, ll. 564–5/715–16).

l. 124 Ileuthyeria: a sea nymph, transformed into coral. The name is probably of Pound's own making.

Dafne: Daphne who was transformed into a laurel tree to escape the pursuit of Apollo. Cf. Pound's earlier 'The Tree'.

l. 127: repeated Canto XXIX (146/141). 'Tritons' are mermen in Greek mythology.

l. 144 Hesperus: the evening star.

l. 151: a cryptic identification of Apollo (Bush, 102). Cf. Canto XXI, 'Phoibos, turris eburnea' ('Phoebus [Apollo], tower of ivory') (103/99).

l. 153 And we have heard: cf. Acoetes' repeated 'I have seen what I have seen' (ll. 107, 112).

fauns: a 'symbol of masculine fertility' (Quinn in Leary, 87).

Proteus: in Homer, 'the old man of the sea', with the ability to change shape. He would disclose knowledge of future events if caught and held still (cf. *Odyssey*, Bk. IV, ll. 365–570).

l. 155 frogs: a 'symbol of metamorphosis' (Quinn, op. cit.).

Canto III

The present Canto includes material that had appeared in a very different form in the 1917 version of the early Cantos. It is also the first mention in the poem of Venice, which Pound returned to many times but visited first in 1898, 1902 and 1908, after his dismissal from Wabash College. It is to this third visit that the Canto refers: 'Venice is', said Pound, 'after all, an excellent place to come to from Crawfordsville, Indiana' (*P and D*, 5). Cf. for further reference to Venice, 'Night Litany' (*CSP*, 40), Canto XVII, Canto XXVI (126/121), Canto LXXXIV (489/460).

ll. 1–3: cf. the first version of Canto I:

> Your "palace step"?
> My stone seat was the Dogana's curb,
> And there were not "those girls", there was one flare, one
> face.
> 'Twas all I ever saw, but it was real. . . .
>
> (*Poetry*, June 1917, 116–17)

l. 1: Pound no doubt remembers Browning's lines in *Sordello*, 'I muse this on a ruined palace-step/ At Venice' (Bk. III, ll. 676–7), a reference to Browning's visit to Venice in 1838, at a time when he revised the conception of *Sordello*. Cf. the opening of Canto XXVI (126/121).

Dogana's steps: the steps of the custom-house in Venice, the Dogana di Mare.

l. 3 "those girls": Browning makes reference to 'those girls' at line 699 of *Sordello*, Bk. III, in a description of peasant girls journeying by gondola to market.

l. 4 Buccentoro: the Bucintoro was originally the ship used by the Doge of Venice for the ceremony of marriage between Venice and the Adriatic; more recently it has been adopted as the name of a Venetian rowing club.

"Stretti": (Ital.) 'embraced one another', the title of a popular song, repeated in Canto XXVII (135/130). Perhaps Pound is thinking of the meeting between Dante and Sordello (*Purgatorio*, VI, ll. 72–5), paraphrased by Pound, 'and the shade, so self-contained, leapt towards him from the place where it first was, saying, "O Mantuan, I am Sordello, of thy land", and they embraced each other' (*SR*, 58).

l. 5 Morosini: the Palazzo Morosini, Venice.

l. 6 And peacocks in Koré's house: a phrase from Gabriele d'Annunzio's *Notturno*, mentioned by Pound in his 'Paris Letter' (November 1922) in the *Dial* (pp. 552–3). Pound translates the relevant line ('La casa di Core e abitata dai pavoni bianchi') as 'In Koré's house there are now only white peacocks' (*Analyst*, III, 10–11).

Koré: (Gk.) 'daughter', i.e. Persephone, daughter of Demeter.

ll. 9–11: cf. in the ur-Canto I: ''Tis the first light – not half-light – Panisks/ And oak-girls and the Maenads/ have all the wood' (*Poetry*, June 1917, 118).

l. 10 Panisks: gods of the forest; the term is a diminutive of Pan, and Pound may have found it in Cicero's *De Natura Deorum*.

dryas: tree nymphs.

l. 11 mælid: a fruit tree nymph; cf. 'The Spring', note on line 2.

l. 13 the lake: cf. the descriptions of Lake Garda in ' "Blandula, Tenulla, Vagula" ' and in 'The Flame' (*CSP*, 64).

l. 17 Poggio: Gian Francesco Poggio Bracciolini (1380–1459), Papal Secretary and humanist, who revived Latin texts by Plautus, Valerius Flaccus and Lucretius. Kenner records that Poggio 'observed A.D. 1451 bathers in a German pool. . . . Its ultimate source is Catullus 54: 18 – *nutricium tenus exstantes e gurgite cano*. Poggio's phrase has not been located' (*Pound Era*, 143).

ll. 20–37: a paraphrase of the twelfth-century Spanish epic, the *Poema del Cid*, I, iii–x. Pound praises the poem for its 'swift narration, its vigor, the humanness of its characters' (cf. his discussion in *The Spirit of Romance*, pp. 66–73).

l. 20 Cid: Rodrigo Diaz de Bivar (or Vivar), the Cid, Spanish soldier of fortune and hero of the *Poema del Cid*.

Burgos: the birthplace of Pedro I; cf. note on line 38.

l. 23: (Sp.): 'a nine-year-old girl', the only person in Burgos who dared to tell Ruy Diaz of Alfonso's threat to confiscate the possessions and cut out the eyes of anyone who assisted him (*Poema del Cid*, I, iv). Pound visited Spain in 1906, and wrote of his visit in an article 'Burgos, a Dream City of Old Castile'. He was guided around the area by a small boy and then, Noel Stock writes, 'came upon a pair of very big black eyes and a very small girl tugging at the gate latch, and he "knew of a surety" that this was the little girl who had delivered the King's command to the Cid' (*Life*, 41).

l. 25 voce tinnula: (Lat.) 'with a ringing voice', repeated in Canto XXVIII (143/137). The source is Catullus LXI (l. 13).

l. 34 Raquel and Vidas: Jewish merchants cheated by Ruy Diaz and Martin Antolinez, who offer them two chests filled with sand for pawn (*Poema del Cid*, I, vi–xi).

l. 36 menie: (ME.) 'meynee' ('retinue' or 'army').

l. 37 Valencia: Diaz captured and ruled Valencia (1094–9).

l. 38 Ignez da Castro: Inez de Castro (?1320–55), a Castilian noblewoman, secretly married to Pedro, heir to the throne of Portugal, and murdered by King Alfonso IV. After Alfonso's death Pedro had her body exhumed and placed on a throne by his side, exacting homage from the court to the dead queen. The story is told in Camoëns's *Os Lusiadas* (*The Portuguese*) and summarized by Pound in *The Spirit of Romance* (pp. 218–19). Pound returned to it in Canto XXX (ll. 26–35).

l. 41 Mantegna: Andrea Mantegna (1431–1506), Italian painter who executed frescoes for the Gonzaga family, under whose influence Mantua became a centre of civilization. In particular Mantegna painted the fresco *Gonzaga, His Heirs and His Concubines* in the Palazzo Ducale, Mantua, referred to by Pound in Canto XLV (l. 10).

l. 42 "Nec Spe Nec Metu": (Lat.) 'with neither hope nor fear', a motto in the rooms of Isabella d'Este in the Palazzo Ducale, Mantua.

from Canto IV

Canto IV first appeared in a private edition of 40 copies in October 1919, and then publicly in June 1920 in the *Dial* and *Poems 1918–21* (1921).

ll. 1–2: the sack of Troy. Pound's source is Virgil's *Aeneid*, Bk. II, perhaps in John Dryden's translation (ll. 417–20):

> The palace of Deiphobus ascends
> In smoaky flames, and catches on his Friends?
> Ucalegon burns next: the Seas are bright
> With splendour, not their own; and shine with *Trojan* light.

(Cf. Bradford Morrow, 'A Source for "Palace in smoky light. . ." ', *Paideuma*, III, no. 2, 245–6, who suggests also that

Pound's economy is a rebuke, via Dryden, of Virgil's 'long-windedness'.)

l. 3 ANAXIFORMINGES: (Gk.) 'Lords of the Lyre', from the opening of Pindar's *Olympian* II, 'Lords of the lyre, ye hymns, what god/ what hero, what man shall we honour?' – an example for Pound of Pindar's 'big rhetorical drum' (*SL*, 91). Cf. its use in *Hugh Selwyn Mauberley* III (ll. 26–8).

Aurunculeia: Vinia Aurunculea, the chaste bride of Manlius and the subject of Catullus' epithalamion (LXI). Cf. Canto V (21/17).

l. 4 Cadmus: the legendary founder of Thebes.

Golden Prows: cf. the description 'Cadmus, of the gilded prows' (Canto XXVII, 137/132). Its source is uncertain. Cadmus was a Phoenician who travelled (presumably by sea) from Tyre to Thebes (Ovid, *Metamorphoses*, Bk. III, l. 6/8), and Phoenician ships are described as loaded with gold in Virgil's *Aeneid*, Bk. I, l. 363 (John E. Hankins, 'Notes and Queries', *Paideuma*, II, no. 1, 142–3).

l. 10 Choros nympharum: (Lat.) chorus of nymphs, gathered perhaps in Dionysian festival.

l. 16 Ityn: Itys was the son of Procne, the wife of Tereus, king of Thrace. Tereus raped Philomela, Procne's sister, and cut out her tongue. In revenge Procne killed Itys and served his flesh to Tereus. The story is told in Ovid, *Metamorphoses*, Bk. VI (ll. 424–674/ 542–853) and is alluded to in T. S. Eliot's *The Waste Land* (ll. 99–103, 203–6).

l. 17 Et ter flebiliter: (Lat.) 'And thrice with tears'. Pound alludes to Horace's phrase 'Ityn flebiliter gemens' (*Odes* IV, xxii, 5). The phrase is recalled in Canto LXXVIII (508/477).

l. 19 swallows: according to Greek legend Philomela was changed into a swallow, Procne into a nightingale.

l. 21 Cabestan: Guillen da Cabestanh (1181–96), Provençal troubadour and lover of the lady Soremonda. He was killed by her husband Raymond of Castle Rossillon who had Cabestanh's heart cooked and served to Soremonda for her infidelity. Soremonda vowed to eat no more food and in her grief committed suicide.

l. 29 Rhodez: i.e. Rodez in west central France.
l. 32 'Tis. 'Tis. Ttis!: a conflation of 'It is' and 'Itys' and an onomatopoeic imitation of the swallow's cry (cf. Canto LXXXII, 560/525).

Canto IX

One of the 'Malatesta Cantos' (Cantos VIII–XI), first published in the *Criterion* (July 1923) as 'Cantos IX–XII of a Long Poem' and dealing with the martial exploits, political intrigue and patronage of the arts of Sigismondo Pandolfo Malatesta (1417–68), lord of Rimini and professional soldier. Malatesta is popularly presented as a cultured but barbarous opportunist, guilty of treachery and atrocious brutalities. Pound recognized an element of 'boisterousness and disorder' in him, and a need for it in these Cantos 'to contrast with his constructive work' (letter to John Quinn, 10 Aug. 1922, in Pearlman, Appendix A, 302–3). But Pound's view of Malatesta is not the generally accepted one. Cantos VIII–XI were, he said, 'openly volitionist, establishing, I think clearly, the effect of the factive personality, Sigismundo, an entire man' (*GK*, 194). Malatesta then is an example of Odyssean 'polumetis', or many-mindedness, whom Pound celebrates as integrating art and politics, and particularly for his construction, against the odds, of the Tempio Malatestiano in Rimini on which he employed a number of distinguished Renaissance artists including Matteo da Pasti, Agostino di Duccio, Piero della Francesca, Cristoforo Foschi and Matteo Nuti. Said Pound,

If you consider the Malatesta and Sigismundo in particular, a failure, he was at all events a failure worth all the successes of his age. He had in Rimini Pisanello, Pier della Francesca. Rimini still has 'the best Bellini in Italy'. If the Tempio is a jumble and junk shop, it nevertheless registers a concept. There is no other single man's effort equally registered.
(note to frontispiece, *GK*, and cf. also pp. 159–60)

The Malatesta Cantos are the first sustained example in the poem of an attempt to 'include history', and of Pound's reliance to this end on an external source, chiefly Charles Yriarte's *Un Condottiere au XVᵉ siècle* (Paris, 1882). The result, in its selected details, its raids in Canto IX on the documentary evidence of Malatesta's post-bag, and in its rugged prose qualities, questions both what constitutes historical method and 'original' poetry.

Very useful background and corroboration of Pound's views on the Tempio is supplied by Adrian Stokes's *Stones of Rimini* (1934), a work inspired by the Malatesta Cantos. Cf. also Eva Hesse, *Paideuma* (I, no. 2, 147–8), for Pound's sources; *The Analyst*, v, on Canto VIII; and the discussion in John Drummond's 'The Italian Background to the *Cantos*' (Russell, esp. 106–13).

ll. 1–16: the reference is to events in 1429–33 when Malatesta was involved in defending his inheritance.

ll. 4–5: repeated in Canto XI (54/50).

l. 10 Astorre Manfredi of Faenza: a member of the ruling family of Manfredi at Faenza, Romagna, north central Italy.

l. 14 Fano: a town of the Marches, east central Italy. Sigismondo became heir to Rimini and Fano in 1431.

l. 16 Emperor: Sigismund V (1368–1437), Holy Roman Emperor 1433–7. Malatesta and his brother Domenico (known as Malatesta Novello) were knighted by Sigismund at Rome in 1433.

l. 18 Basinio: Basinio de Basanil (1425–57), Italian poet under the patronage of Sigismondo.

ll. 18–21: a reference to the incident in 1456 when Basinio defeated Parcelo Pandone (the 'anti-Hellene' of line 21) in a literary debate in which Pandone argued that it was not necessary for an Italian poet to study the Greeks.

l. 23 Madame Genevra: daughter of Niccolò d'Este, wife of Sigismondo Malatesta. At her death in 1440, Pope Pius accused Sigismondo of poisoning her.

l. 24: Malatesta served the Venetians in the early 1440s in the struggle between Venice and Milan.

l. 26 Rocca: fortress built by Sigismondo at Rimini 1437–46.

l. 27 Monteluro: village north-east of Florence.

l. 29 old Sforza: Francesco Sforza (1401–66), ruler of Lombardy and regions in north Italy. After an uneasy alliance Sigismondo broke with Sforza in 1445 over the affair of Pesaro and Fossembrone which he had expected Sforza to help him secure. Cf. Canto VIII (36/32).

Pèsaro: port city and capital of Pesaro e Urbino province in east central Italy.

l. 30: (1445).

l. 31 Messire Alessandro Sforza: Alessandro Sforza (1409–73), brother of Francesco Sforza, became lord of Pesaro in 1444 through some reputedly underhand agreement with Galeazzo Malatesta whose granddaughter, Constanza Varna, Alessandro married.

l. 33 Illus. Sgr. Mr. Fedricho d'Orbino: Federigo da Montefeltro (1442–82), first Duke of Urbino, famous soldier of fortune, politician, patron of the arts, and Malatesta's great rival.

l. 34 Galeaz: Galeazzo Malatesta, lord of Pesaro, cousin to Sigismondo. Known as 'L'Inetto' ('the Unfit'), he was involved in 1444 in the deal by which Pesaro was sold to Alessandro Sforza.

l. 35 Messr Francesco: Francesco Sforza (cf. line 29 above).

l. 37 Alex . . . Fossembrone . . . Feddy: Alessandro Sforza (cf. line 31); Fossembrone, a town in the Marches of central Italy, was sold to Federigo da Montefeltro (cf. line 33) in the same deal by which Alessandro obtained Pesaro.

l. 39 bestialmente: (Ital.) 'in a beastly manner', from Gaspare Broglio's *Cronaca*; cf. line 102, and Canto VIII (36/32).

l. 40 per capitoli: (Ital.) 'by the chapters'.

l. 46 Ragona, Alphonse: Alfonso, king of Aragon (Ragona) in the north Iberian peninsula.

ll. 46–55: a reference to Sigismondo's breaking his contract with Alfonso (1448), in which he had agreed to fight Florence, and siding instead with the Florentines, who offered better terms.

l. 50 Valturio: Robert Valturio (d. 1489), Sigismondo's first secretary, and engineer of Rocca. He urged Malatesta to support Florence rather than Alfonso.

l. 51 (hæc traditio): (Lat.) 'this tradition', i.e. of Italian *condottiere*, serving those who paid best.

l. 52 old bladder: probably Pope Pius II; cf. Canto X (48–9/44–5).

"rem eorum saluavit": (Lat.) 'saved their state'.

l. 56 TEMPIO: the unfinished Tempio Malatestiano in Rimini, built between 1446 and 1455, and then sporadically until 1461, in honour of Isotta degli Alti, Sigismondo's third wife (cf. line 147).

l. 57 Polixena: Polissena Sforza, daughter of Francesco Sforza. Sigismondo married her in 1442 and on her death was accused of poisoning her.

l. 58 Venetians: Sigismondo besieged Crema in 1449 in the service of the Venetians against Milan. Pound shows him as more concerned with the Tempio.

l. 64 Wattle-wattle . . . Milan: in 1441 Francesco Sforza ('Wattle-wattle'; cf. l. 107n.) married Bianca Maria Visconti, daughter of Filippo Visconti, Duke of Milan; after the latter's death, in 1447, Francesco became Duke of Milan in 1451.

l. 65 Sidg: Sigismondo.

l. 66 Feddy: cf. line 33.

l. 67 Foscari: Francesco Foscari (?1372–1457), chief justice or Doge of Venice 1423–57.

Caro mio: (Ital.) 'my dear'; cf. Canto X (47/43).

l. 68 Francesco: cf. line 29.

l. 72 Classe: town near Ravenna from whose church Sigismondo rifled marble for the Tempio.

l. 73 Casus est talis: (Lat.) 'this is the case', i.e. against Sigismondo. Cf. line 76.

l. 77 Filippo: Filippo Maria Visconti (1392–1447), who as Duke of Milan warred with Venice and Florence.

abbazia: (Ital.) 'abbey'.

l. 78 Sant Apollinaire: the church of Sant' Apollinare, Classe, from which the marble was stolen.

Cardinal of Bologna: Filippo Calandrini.

l. 79 quadam nocte: (Lat.) 'one night'.

l. 80 Illmo D^o: illustrious duke.

l. 81 Arimnium: (Lat.) Rimini.

porphyry: purple stone.

serpentine: dull green marble with markings resembling those of a serpent's skin.

l. 84 Santa Maria in Trivio: a church in Trivio, Rimini, the former site of the Tempio.

l. 89 plaustra: (Ital.) 'wagons', 'carts'.

l. 90 Aloysius Purtheo: the abbot of Sant' Apollinare, Classe, who agreed on the payment of 200 ducats to Sigismondo's taking marble from the church.

l. 93 German-Burgundian female: a noblewoman, thought to have been assaulted and killed by Sigismondo while passing through Verona *en route* for Rome, 1450. Malatesta's guilt was not established, but this event, together with his half-hearted service, caused Venice to release him (cf. line 104).

l. 94 Poliorcetes: (Gk.) 'taker of cities', an epithet applied to Sigismondo by Pisanello.

l. 95 POLUMETIS: (Gk.) 'many-minded', applied to Odysseus in Homer's *Odyssey*.

l. 102 Broglio: Gaspare Broglio, a soldier in the service of Malatesta, and author of one of Pound's sources, the *Cronaca*, on Malatesta's life and campaigns in Rimini.

l. 103 m' l'a calata: (Ital.) 'he put one over on me'.

l. 105 Istria: a peninsula on the north-east coast of the Adriatic. Istrian stone was used for the façade and flanks of the Tempio (Stokes, *Stones of Rimini*, 177).

l. 106 the silk war: a war between Venice and Ragusa. Malatesta's father, Pandolfo, led the Venetians against Ragusa in 1420, but failed to capture it. Cf. Canto XVI (74/70).

l. 107 Wattle: Francesco Sforza, so named because of his fleshy, pendulous nose and wartiness.

l. 109 bombards: an early form of cannon.

Vada: a village in Livorno province, Tuscany.

l. 114 Siena: the city in Tuscany. In 1454, Malatesta was

253

appointed Captain-General of the Sienese troops in their war
with the Counts of Pitigliano.

l. 115: the Sienese suspected Malatesta of intriguing with the
enemy, and intercepted his letters. In fact, Malatesta did
receive one letter from Pitigliano, paraphrased in Canto X
(46/42).

l. 117 Pitigliano: Count Aldobrando Orsino, lord of Pitigliano;
he was besieged by Malatesta at Sorano in August and in the
winter of 1454.

l. 124: they found, that is to say, evidence, not of secret intelligence, but of domestic matters and Sigismondo's concern
with the Tempio.

ll. 125–30: this first extract of the letters from Malatesta's
post-bag is from the architect, Matteo Nuti. In his Rome
Radio broadcasts, Pound said, 'Now when I was doing my
job on Sigismundo Malatesta I came to the conclusion that
documents, personal letters and what not proved one thing.
A letter proved what the bloke who wrote it wanted the
receiver to believe on the day he wrote it. The rest of history
has to be derived from computation.' 'With Phantoms',
Certain Radio Speeches of Ezra Pound, ed. W. Levy, 1975.)

ll. 125–6: (Lat.) 'From Rimini the 20th of December/ "My
very excellent lord, magnificent and potent'.

l. 128 Alwidge: Luigi Alvise, carpenter on the Tempio (cf. line
136).

l. 132: (Lat.) 'Magnificent most excellent'; (Ital.) 'My lord'.

l. 134 Mr. Genare: Pietro di Genari, Malatesta's secretary and
author of the last letter in the series (ll. 202–33).

l. 136 Giovane: Giovanni, son of Luigi Alvise (l. 128), and
author of the second extract (ll. 132–8).

l. 137 Albert: Leon Battista Alberti (1404–72), designer of the
Tempio. Cf. the reference to 'Messire Battista' (l. 140).

l. 139 Sagramoro: Sacramoro Sacramori, secretary to Sigismondo.

l. 140 Illustre signor mio: (Ital.) 'My illustrious lord'.

l. 145 danars: the danar was an early Italian coin.

l. 147 Isotta: Isotta degli Atti (?1430–?1475), the mistress and subsequently third wife of Sigismondo, in whose honour he built the Tempio. Their sons were Sallustio and Valerien.

ll. 147–8 Sr. Galeazzo's/ "daughter: a girl, reputedly seduced by Sigismondo.

l. 152 Ixotta: Isotta (cf. l. 147n.).

ll. 152–3 Mi/ pare che avea decto hogni chossia: (Ital.) 'It seems to me that he has said everything', from the original 'a detto al mio parere ogni cossa' (Yriarte, *Un Condottier e au XVe siècle*, 159).

l. 156 Madame Lucrezia: daughter of Malatesta and Isotta degli Atti.

l. 159 21 Dec: in the year 1454.

D. de M.: (Lat.) Dominus de Malatesta.

l. 160: continues line 139 above.

l. 163 Messire Malatesta: Sallustio Malatesta (1448–70). Cf. note on line 147 and line 196.

l. 166 Georgio Rambottom: Giorgio Ranbutino, a stonemason who worked on the Tempio.

l. 174 LUNARDA DA PALLA: probably the tutor and secretary to Sallustio Malatesta.

l. 176: perhaps a continuation of line 161 above.

l. 177 small medal: Malatesta employed the medallists Pisanello and Matteo da Pasti.

l. 178: (Lat.) 'To the magnificent and potent'.

ll. 180–1: (Lat.) 'Malatesta of the Malatestas to his Magnificent Lord and Father'.

ll. 182–3: (Lat.) 'Most excellent, and Lord without Lord, Sigismondo son of Pandolfo/ Captain General Malatesta'.

l. 186 Gentilino da Gradara: an agent for Sigismondo.

l. 187 ronzino baiectino: (Ital.) 'a small bay nag'.

l. 196: Sallustio Malatesta.

ll. 200–1: a snatch from a letter by Servulo Trachulo, Sigismondo's court poet. The letter is mentioned in Canto X as 'Trachulo's damn'd epistle' (46/42).

ll. 202–3 Magnifice . . . permissa: (Lat.) 'To the magnificent and potent lord, my most excellent lord, a humble/ advice permitted'.

l. 204 Veronese marble: for the Tempio.

l. 205 Ferrara: the town in north Italy.

l. 222 aliofants: elephant motifs in the Tempio (cf. Stokes, *Stones of Rimini*, pl. 28). The elephant was Sigismondo's personal emblem; the rose, Isotta's.

l. 224 Messire Antonio degli Atti: the brother of Isotta.

l. 226 Ottavian: Ottaviano d'Antonio di Duccio (1418–?), Florentine sculptor and designer of decorations in the Tempio.

l. 230 Messire Agostino: Agostino di Duccio (?1418–81), Italian sculptor, thought to have executed the bas-reliefs in the Tempio.

Cesena: a town in Forli province, Emilia, Italy, held by the Malatestas 1385–1465.

l. 233 PETRUS GENARIIS: Pietro di Genari, Sigismondo's secretary.

ll. 237–42: (Ital.) ' "and he loved Isotta degli Atti to distraction"/ and "she was worthy of him"/ "constant in purpose/ "she was pleasing to the eyes of the prince/ "beautiful to look at"/ "she was liked by the people (and the honour of Italy)'. Derived from Yriarte, *Un Condottiere au XVe siècle* (p. 155). 'Italiaeque decus' was the epithet of Isotta: the inscription on the Matteo da Pasti medal (1446) and a concealed inscription on Isotta's tomb both read, 'Isote Ariminensi. Forma et Virtute Italie Decori'.

l. 243: Malatesta's arch-enemy, Aeneas Silvius Piccolomini, Pope Pius II, allowed in the midst of his excommunication of Malatesta (1460) that 'he built at Rimini a splendid church dedicated to St. Francis, though he filled it so full of pagan works of art that it seemed less a Christian sanctuary than a temple of heathen devil-worshippers' (*Analyst*, v, 14). Cf. Canto X (47–8/43–4).

l. 245 "Past ruin'd Latium": an echo of Walter Savage Landor's 'Past ruined Ilion Helen lives' in the poem 'To Ianthe'.

l. 249 San Vitale: a sixth-century church in Ravenna; its Roman sarcophagi may have been a model for those in the Tempio.

Canto XIII

The first of the 'Confucian Cantos', amalgamating material from the three canonical texts, the *Ta Hsio* (*The Great Digest*), the *Chung Yung* (*The Unwobbling Pivot*) and the *Lun-yü* (*The Analects*). Together with the text *Mencius*, these form the 'Four Books' of Confucianism. Pound's source was the translation by J. P. G. Pauthier, *Les Quatre Livres de philosophie morale et politique de la Chine* (1840). He had been handed a text of the *Chung Yung* with the Fenollosa papers in 1913, and in January 1915 began to read Confucius in earnest, probably in Pauthier's translation (Stock, *Life*, 220). Pound's own English translations of these texts appeared between 1928 and 1950: the *Ta Hsio* in two translations, in 1928 and 1947, *The Unwobbling Pivot* in 1947 and *The Analects* in 1950. These translations are collected in the volume *Confucius* (1969) and all references in the notes below are to this edition.

Canto XIII first appeared unnumbered and with lines 3–6 omitted as the first of 'Two Cantos' in the *Transatlantic Review* (January 1924). Pound considered it the 'announcement of backbone moral of the *Cantos*' (Angela Chih-Ying Jung, 'Ezra Pound and China', Ph.D. dissertation, University of Washington, 1955, 69).

l. 1 Kung: K'ung Fu Tzŭ, i.e. Confucius (551–479 B.C.), the philosopher and statesman whose thinking was a major influence on Pound.

ll. 5–30: largely a paraphrase of *The Analects*, Bk. 11, xxv, 1–8 (pp. 242–3). Cf. also the version included in the seventh of the 'Imaginary Letters' by Walter Villerant (*P and D*, 71–3).

l. 5 Khieu, Tchi: Jan Ch'iu, a disciple of Confucius (the comma is a misprint).

l. 6 Tian: Tien or Tsêng Hsi, a disciple of Confucius.

ll. 7–9: from *The Analects*, Bk. 9, ii, 2 (p. 228).

l. 27 Thseng-sie: Tsêng Hsi; cf. line 6.

ll. 31–7: from *The Analects*, Bk. 14, xlvi (p. 262).

l. 31 Yuan Jang: Yüan Jang.

ll. 38–42: from *The Analects*, Bk. 9, xxii (p. 232).

ll. 43–4: Pound's idiom betrays its French source. Pauthier has 'dès l'instant qu'il aura attiré près de lui tous les savans et les artistes, aussitôt ses richesses seront suffisamment mises en usage' (quoted in Kenner, *Pound Era*, 446).

ll. 45–51: indebted to 'Confucius' Text' 4 and to chapters VIII and IX of *The Great Digest* (pp. 29–31, 53–65). Pound placed special stress on the *Ta Hsio* which he twice translated. In answer to Eliot's 'indirect query as to "what Mr. Pound believes" ', Pound answered in 'Date Line' (1934), 'I believe the *Ta Hio*' (*LE*, 86). In 1928, he had written to René Taupin on the seeming usefulness of the *Ta Hsio*, 'pour civilizer l'Amérique' (*SL*, 217), and in 1937 suggested the first chapter (probably the only part of the classic 'Four Books' that can be assigned to Confucius' authorship) might function as a *mantram* for the Occident ('Immediate need of Confucius' in *SPr*, 89–94).

ll. 52–3 "order" ... *"brotherly deference"*: key principles reiterated through the 'Four Books'. Pound's application of the first is evident in his view of Mussolini as standing 'not with despots and the lovers of power but with the lovers of/ ORDER/ tò kalón' (*J/M*, 128).

l. 54: a chief recommendation of Confucianism *vis-à-vis* Christianity. Cf. *The Analects*, Bk. 11, xi (p. 239), and Pound's 'Imaginary Letters' (*P and D*, 71–2). 'The concentration or emphasis on eternity', wrote Pound, 'is not social', and opposed this with 'The sense of responsibility, the need for coordination of individuals expressed in Kung's teaching' (*GK*, 38).

ll. 56–8: probably derived from *The Unwobbling Pivot*, Part One, III and IV (p. 105). Cf. also *The Analects*, Bk. 11, xv (p. 240).

ll. 59–62: from *The Analects*, Bk. 13, xviii (p. 251).

ll. 63–6: a version of *The Analects*, Bk. 5, i (p. 209).

l. 63 Kong Tchang: Kung Yeh Chang, Confucius' son-in-law.

l. 65 Nan-Young: Nan Jung, a disciple of Confucius.

l. 67 Wang: Wu Wang, the title given to Fa, son of Wen Wang, opponent of Cheou-sin and author of the *I' Ching*. Wu Wang defeated the emperor Cheou-sin in Honan province, 1122 B.C., thereby ending the Shang (or Yin) dynasty, and ruled as first emperor of the Tcheou (or Chou) dynasty, 1122–1115 B.C. Cf. *The Classic Anthology*, poems 235–44 (pp. 148–50); *The Unwobbling Pivot*, Part Two, XVIII, 2 (p. 137); and Canto LIII (276/265–6).

ll. 69–72: from *The Analects*, Bk. 15, xxv (p. 267).

ll. 73–5: for Confucius' stress on the Odes, see *The Analects*, Bk. 16, xiii (pp. 272–3) and Bk. 17, ix, x, xi (pp. 275–6).

l. 75 the Odes: the *Shih Ching* or *Shy-King* (Book of Songs), composed of 305 poems, thought at one time to have been compiled by Confucius. Pound quotes Confucius as saying that 'their meaning can be gathered into one sentence: Have no twisty thoughts' (*Confucius*, 192). Pound translated the Odes under the title of *The Classic Anthology defined by Confucius* (1954).

ll. 76–8: not a direct quotation from Confucius, but an allusion to the apricot orchard, in Ch'iu-fu, Shantung, where Confucius was born and where it is believed he conducted his teaching (Angela Palandri, 'Homage to a Confucian Poet', *Paideuma*, III, no. 3, 301).

from **Canto XIV**

One of the 'hell Cantos' (XIV and XV). Pound opens the Canto with a quotation from Dante, 'Io venni in luogo d'ogni luce muto', 'I came to a place utterly without light' (*Inferno*, V, l. 28) and therefore at least at this point invites comparison with the structure of Dante's *Divine Comedy*. As he wrote to his father in 1927, 'You have had a hell in Canti XIV, XV; purgatorio in XVI etc' (*SL*, 210). Cantos XIV and XV were drafted in 1919 (Stock, *Life*, 286) and they were, as Pound wrote to Wyndham Lewis in 1924, 'a portrait of contemporary England, or at least Eng. as she wuz when I left her' (*SL*, 191), and to John Drummond later, 'specifically LONDON, the state of English mind in 1919 and 1920' (*SL*, 239). Pound had attempted such a portrait earlier in 'Mœurs Contemporaines' (1918), but wrote to James Joyce already in that year of the 'need of bottling London, some more ample modus than permitted in free-verse scherzos, and thumb-nail sketches of Marie Corelli, H. James etc. (in Mœurs Contemporaines)' (P/J, 149). Joyce, in fact, and his *Ulysses* in particular, which Pound was reading and helping to publish in these years, seems to have influenced the conception and imagery of Pound's hell, just as it guided him in his revisions of the earlier Cantos. In 1938 in *Guide to Kulchur* Pound was to recall,

> In 1912 or eleven I invoked whatever gods may exist, in the quatrain:
>
>> Sweet Christ from hell spew up some Rabelais,
>> To belch and. . . . and to define today
>> In fitting fashion, and her monument
>> Heap up to her in fadeless excrement.
>
> 'Ulysses' I take as my answer . . . . 'Ulysses' is the end, the summary, of a period, that period is branded by La Tour du Pin in his phrase 'age of usury'. . . . The sticky, molasses-covered filth of current print, all the fuggs, all the foetors, the whole boil of the European mind, had been lanced.
>
> (p. 96)

Pound saw Joyce's imagination, because analytic and satirical, as tending towards the excremental (while Pound himself tended towards the phallic) and commented particularly in his response to the Sirens episode of *Ulysses*, on Joyce's 'cloacal . . . obsession' (cf. P/J, 147, 158). Joyce's type of imagination corresponded directly, moreover, to the character given to hell in the scheme of things proposed elsewhere by Pound: 'Three channels, hell, purgatory, heaven, if one wants to follow yet another terminology: digestive excretion, incarnation, freedom in the imagination' ('Postscript to *The Natural Philosophy of Love* by Remy de Gourmont', 1922, reprinted in *P and D*, 212).

l. 68 liars: cf. *Hugh Selwyn Mauberley* IV, lines 13–19, 'walked eye-deep in hell . . . and liars in public places'.
l. 73 slum owners: cf. T. S. Eliot's 'Gerontion':

My house is a decayed house,
And the jew squats on the window sill, the owner,
Spawned in some estaminet of Antwerp,
Blistered in Brussels, patched and peeled in London.

(Collected Poems, 1958, 37)

l. 74 usurers: cf. *Hugh Selwyn Mauberley* IV, line 18, for Pound's first use of this word in his poetry, Canto XII (59/55), and especially Canto XLV (including Pound's definition of usury). Dante placed usurers as 'the Violent against Nature and the Art derived from Nature' in the seventh circle of hell (*Inferno*, XVII).

l. 75 pets-de-loup: (Fr.) 'wolf-farts', perhaps pedants.

l. 76 philology: Pound had suffered from philologists in the response particularly to 'The Seafarer' and *Homage to Sextus Propertius*.

l. 81 preachers: Pound was inveterately anti-Christian; of many statements, he wrote in 1916 to H. L. Mencken, 'Hell is a place completely paved with Billy Sunday and Ellis. . . . Religion is the root of all evil, or damn near all' (*SL*, 97–8).

l. 82 Invidia: (Ital.) 'envy'.

l. 83 corruptio: (Ital.) 'corruption'.

fœtor: 'foetor' and 'foetid' are common terms in the 'hell Cantos'; cf. *Hugh Selwyn Mauberley*, 'Yeux Glauques', line 5; ' "Siena Mi Fe' " ', line 1.

l. 86 without dignity, without tragedy: T. S. Eliot felt that Pound's hell was lacking in the necessary spiritual struggle associated with the idea of original sin:

> It is, in its way, an admirable Hell, 'without dignity, without tragedy'. At first sight the variety of types – for these are types, and not individuals – may be a little confusing; but I think it becomes a little more intelligible if we see at work three principles, the aesthetic, the humanitarian, the Protestant. And I find one considerable objection to a Hell of this sort: that a Hell altogether without dignity implies a Heaven without dignity also. If you do not distinguish between individual responsibility and circumstances

in Hell, between essential Evil and social accidents, then the Heaven (if any) implied will be equally trivial and accidental. Mr. Pound's Hell, for all its horrors, is a perfectly comfortable one for the modern mind to contemplate, and disturbing to no one's complacency: it is a Hell for the *other people*, the people we read about in the newspapers, not for oneself and one's friends.

> (*After Strange Gods: A Primer of Modern Heresy*, 1934, extract reprinted in *EP*, ed. Sullivan, 182)

Pound, for his part, replying to John Lackay Brown in 1937, wrote,

> that *section* of hell precisely has *not* any dignity. Neither had Dante's fahrting devils. Hell is not amusing. Not a joke. And when you get further along you find individuals, not abstracts. Even the XIV–XV has individuals in it, but *not* worth recording as such. In fact, Bill Bird rather entertained that I had forgotten which rotters were there. In his edtn. he tried to get the number of . . . . . . correct in each case. My "point" being that not even the first but only last letters of their names had resisted corruption.

> (*SL*, 293)

l. 87 Episcopus: (Lat.) 'Bishop'; cf. Canto XV (68/64).
ll. 88–9: Pound wrote to John Drummond,

> It is NOT expensive editions that discourage circulation. The sacks of pus which got control of Brit. pubctn. in or about 1912 or '14 and increased strangle hold on it till at least 1932 have done their utmost to keep anything worth reading out of print and out of ordinary distribution via commerce (booksellers). . . .

> There is no reason why young England shd. pardon the ineffable polluters and saboteurs. What they have done to stifle literature in Eng., tho not so important as the press-bosses' stifling of economic discussion, is all of piece.

> (*SL*, 239)

l. 89 obstructors of distribution: perhaps distribution generally, of 'goods, air, water, heat, coal (black or white), power, and even thought' (*SPr*, 183). 'Usurers', Pound wrote in *Guide to Kulchur*, 'do not desire circulation of knowledge' (p. 62). More specifically, he refers to economic distribution, 'Probably the only economic problem needing emergency solution in our time' (*ABC of Economics*, 1933, reprinted *SPr*, 204). Pound's proposed solution, based on a shortening of the working day and a fair distribution of paper certificates (equal to the work done) so as to close the gap between available cash and the money required to buy available goods, owes much to the theory of Social Credit as propounded originally by Major C. H. Douglas. Cf. Pound's reviews of Douglas's *Economic Democracy* (*SPr*, 177–82), the *ABC of Economics* and Canto XXXVIII (ll. 102–25nn.).

Confucius perhaps offered Pound added authority here. The *Ta Hsio* (*The Great Digest*), x, 19, for example, states,

And there is a chief way for the production of wealth, namely, that the producers be many and that the mere consumers be few; that the artisan mass be energetic and the consumers temperate, then the constantly circulating goods will be always a-plenty.

(*Confucius*, 83)

Canto XVII

Notable for the analogy Pound perceives between stone and water. His subject is primarily Venice, although this is only suggested at the close of the Canto. Cf. Adrian Stokes, *Stones of Rimini* (1934) and *Venice, an Aspect of Art* (1945), and the discussion in Donald Davie's *Poet as Sculptor* (1965), pp. 127–9.

l. 6 ZAGREUS: Dionysus, god of wine and fertility; cf. Canto II.
10: (Gk. ἰώ), an exclamation invoking the aid of a god.
l. 9 goddess of the fair knees: perhaps an evocation of Artemis

(Roman Diana); cf. Canto IV (18/14), and Ovid, *Metamorphoses*, Bk. III (ll. 155–72/178–224).

l. 17 palazzi: (Ital.) 'palaces'.

l. 20 Chrysophrase: i.e. chrysoprase, the ancient name for a golden-green precious stone, or an apple-green variety of chalcedony, a transparent or translucent sub-species of quartz.

l. 24 Nerea: probably an allusion to Thetis, wife of Peleus and daughter of Nereus, Homer's 'old man of the sea'. Peleus first saw and desired Thetis while she slept in her cave at Thessaly (Ovid, *Metamorphoses*, Bk. XI, ll. 229–65/261–302).

l. 37 salt-white: an epithet used by Adrian Stokes to describe Istrian marble in his *Stones of Rimini* (p. 19). Cf. Davie, op. cit., pp. 127–8.

l. 38 porphyry: a purple stone taking a high polish.

l. 41 malachite: a green stone.

l. 43 panthers: one of the beasts associated with Dionysus; cf. Canto II.

l. 46 choros nympharum: (Lat.) 'chorus of nymphs'.

l. 47 Hermes: son of Zeus and Maia, the messenger of the gods and himself patron of wealth and good fortune, of thieves and of travel.

Athene: the daughter of Zeus and Metis, a warlike beauty and the goddess of cities, especially Athens.

l. 51 sylva nympharum: (Lat.) 'wood of nymphs'.

l. 57 Memnons: probably Memnon the son of Tithonus and Eos (the goddess of dawn). His statue was reputedly near Thebes, in Egypt, and was thought to give off a musical sound when struck by the morning sun.

l. 62 One man: probably an imagined visitor to Venice who is heard reporting on the city in the lines that follow.

ll. 64–72: an association of the Istrian marble, from which Venice was built, with water was elaborated by Adrian Stokes: 'For this Istrian stone seems compact of salt's bright yet shaggy crystals. Air eats into it, the brightness remains. Amid the sea Venice is built from the essence of the sea.' (*Stones of Rimini*, 19.) Cf. lines 15–16 and 104–9. Later Stokes was to write, 'We have seen that Venice herself inspires a lively sense of poetry, of metamorphosis, of inner and outer' (*Venice: an Aspect of Art*, 55).

ll. 64–5: there is perhaps an echo here of the line with the 'magical quality of poetry' from Lope de Vega's *La Circe*, 'The white forest of the Grecian ships', by which Pound distinguishes Lope de Vega from Camoëns (*SR*, 221).

l. 71 ply over ply: cf. the use of this expression in Canto IV (19/15) and the line 'phase over phase' in Canto XCVII (709/678), both derived perhaps from Mallarmé's 'pli selon pli' in *Remémoration d'amis belges* (Brooke-Rose, 92).

l. 73 Borso: Borso d'Este (1413–71), son of Niccolo d'Este and lord of Ferrara. His attempt to keep the peace between Sigismondo Malatesta and Federigo d'Urbino is referred to in Canto X (47/43).

Carmagnola: Francesco Bussone da Carmagnola (1380–1431), who served under Filippo Visconti, Duke of Milan, but later led Florence and Venice against him. He was tried for treason by the Council of Ten at Venice, and executed.

i vitrei: (Ital.) 'glassmakers'.

l. 77 Dye-pots: Venetian painters, according to Stokes, were directly influenced by the glassmakers of Murano (*Colour and Form*, 1937, 111).

ll. 83–4: slight variations of this expression appear in Cantos XI (55/51) and XXI (102/98). Its source is either the opening of Pindar's *Olympian Ode* I ('Best blessing of all is water/ And gold like a fiery flame gleaming at night'), a quotation from the first line of which opens Canto LXXXIII (563/528), or Virgil's *Aeneid* (Bk. VI, l. 204), at the point where Aeneas plucks the golden bough ('and there, through the branches, shone the contrasting gleam of gold').

l. 85 Now supine in burrow: probably an allusion to Odysseus, beached on Scheria, or Ithaca (*Odyssey*, Bk. V, ll. 470–93; Bk. XIII, ll. 117–19).

l. 88 Zothar: probably Pound's invention.

l. 89 sistrum: an Egyptian metal rattle.

l. 91 Aletha: an invented goddess of the sea. Cf. Canto XCI (ll. 16–17n.).

l. 95 Koré: (Gk. Κόρη), Persephone, daughter of Demeter and queen of Hades, abducted by Hades from the vale of Enna.

l. 97 brother of Circe: Aeetes, the king of Colchis, from whom Jason retrieved the golden fleece; cf. *Odyssey*, Bk. X, l. 137.

l. 99 fulvid: i.e. fulvous, tawny.

l. 110 Borso: cf. line 73 and a reference to the same incident in Canto X (51/46).

l. 112 Sigismundo: Malatesta; cf. headnote to Canto IX. *Dalmatia*: the eastern shore of the Adriatic.

from Canto XX

Pound gave an account of this Canto to his father (*SL*, 210–11). *l. 152 lotophagoi*: (Gk.) 'lotus-eaters'; 'the main subject of the Canto', said Pound, suggesting also that it presented a 'general paradiso' after the 'hell in Canti XIV, XV; purgatorio in XVI etc.' (*SL*, 210). Odysseus visits the land of lotus-eaters in Bk. IX of the *Odyssey* (ll. 82–104). Three of his crew feed on the lotus and succumb to the lassitude and oblivion it induces, before Odysseus forces them back to the ship and departs in haste. Cf. the presentation of Mauberley in ' "The Age Demanded" ' and 'IV' from the sequence MAUBERLEY (1920). *ll. 155–7 With . . . Lotophagoi*: recalled in 'Addendum for C' (29/799).

ll. 155–6 spilla . . . ball: the stalk which supports the ball of the lotus plant, or an allusion to the ball of opium or hashish. Cf. the lines from the lusty Juventus in Canto XXIX, ' "Matter is the lightest of all things,/ "Chaff, rolled into balls, tossed, whirled in the aether' (148/143). Pound probably intends a sexual analogy in both cases.

l. 158 Voce-profondo: (Ital.) 'deep-voiced'.

ll. 159–60: cf. 'the heavy voices' which condemn themselves in Canto XXV, 'Nothing we made, we set nothing in order' (l. 108).

l. 161 clear bones: the remains of Odysseus' crew.

ll. 163–86: a jealous protest on behalf of Odysseus' crew, spoken, Pound suggests, by the opium-smokers, giving a 'resumé of Odyssey, or rather of the main parts of Ulysses' voyage up to death of all his crew' (*SL*, 210). Odysseus tells of his voyage in Bks. IX–XII of the *Odyssey*.

l. 164: Odysseus' ship and crew are destroyed by a thunderbolt and spun in a whirlpool after their sacrilegious killing of the cattle of Helios (the sun god) on Thrinacia (*Odyssey*, Bk. XII, ll. 403–19). In Dante's *Inferno*, Odysseus tells of his last voyage beyond the pillars of Hercules to the Mountain of the Earthly Paradise, where his ship is caught in a whirlpool and both he and his crew drowned (*Inferno*, XXVI, ll. 90–142).

l. 166 stolen meat: perhaps the sheep that Odysseus steals from Polyphemus, the Cyclops (*Odyssey*, Bk. IX, ll. 170–566), or the meat of Helios' cattle which Odysseus' crew slaughter in spite of his warning.

chained to the rowingbench: Odysseus ties the crew members who had tasted the lotus under the rowing bench (*Odyssey*, Bk. IX, l. 99). Perhaps the more general meaning is that his crew are constrained to sail where he bids them.

l. 168 goddess: either Circe (cf. line 177) or Calypso (cf. line 178).

l. 170 Elpenor: Odysseus' companion who falls to his death from the roof of Circe's palace. Cf. Canto I, lines 42, 50–3.

ll. 172–4: cf. Canto LXXIV, 'olivi/ that which gleams and then does not gleam/ as the leaf turns in the air' (466/438), an image of the paradise that 'exists only in fragments'. Pound's lines echo the account given by Allen Upward of the word 'glaukopis' associated with the goddess Athene:

> We may see the shutter of the lightning in that mask that overhangs Athene's brow and hear its click in the word glaukos. And the leafage of the olive whose writhen trunk bears, as it were, the lightning's brand, does not glare but glitters, the pale under face of the leaves alternating with the dark upper face, and so the olive is Athene's tree and is called glaukos.
>
> (*The New Word*, quoted by Pound in 'Allen Upward Serious', *SPr*, 377–8)

In the first of the ur-Cantos, there appeared the explicit reference, 'colored like the lake and olive leaves,/ Glaukopos' (*Poetry*, June 1917, 116). Cf. also Canto XXI, 'Pallas . . . Owl-eye amid pine boughs' (104/99).

l. 172 Spartha: the city-state of Sparta, famous for its military efficiency, and the home of Menelaus and Agamemnon, who led the Greek forces against Troy.

l. 175 bronze hall: the houses of Menelaus and Alcinous – to whom Odysseus tells his story – are decorated with bronze (*Odyssey*, Bk. IV, ll. 71–5; Bk. XIII, l. 4).

ingle: hearth, or chimney.

l. 176 waiting maids: Circe has four handmaidens who attend upon herself and Odysseus (*Odyssey*, Bk. X, ll. 348–70).

l. 177 Circe Titania: Circe, the sorceress who detained Odysseus on Aeaea for a year, was the descendant of Titans (cf. Ovid, *Metamorphoses*, Bk. XIII, l. 968/1130; XIV, l. 376/430). Odysseus sleeps with her after resisting the potion by which she has transformed his men into swine (*Odyssey*, Bk. X, ll. 135–574). Cf. also Canto I, note on line 7.

l. 178 Kalüpso: the goddess Calypso. When Odysseus' crew are destroyed he alone is saved and borne to Ogygia, the island home of Calypso, who detains him there as her husband for seven years.

l. 181 Ear-wax: on Circe's advice, Odysseus plugs his crew's ears with wax so that they will not hear the song of the Sirens (*Odyssey*, Bk. XII, ll. 173–7).

l. 182 Poison: probably the potion offered to members of the crew by Circe (*Odyssey*, Bk. X, ll. 233–41).

l. 184 neson amumona: (Gk.) 'noble island' (*Odyssey*, Bk. XII, l. 261), i.e. Thrinacia. Pound offered the annotation to his father, 'literally the narrow island: bull-field where Apollo's cattle were kept' (*SL*, 210). Cf. note on line 164.

their heads . . . foam: a paraphrase of the *Odyssey*, Bk. XII, line 418, in which after being thrown overboard Odysseus' crew bob on the sea, like sea crows.

l. 186 Apollo: i.e. Helios, the sun god.

l. 187 Ligur' aoide: (Gk.) 'clear sweet song', a reference to the enticing song of the Sirens (*Odyssey*, Bk. XII, l. 183). Pound annotates, 'keen or sharp singing (sirens), song with an edge on it' (*SL*, 210).

from Canto XXV

One of the so-called 'historical Venice Cantos' (XXIV–XXVI), presenting Venice in the passage from maturity to decline.

ll. 72–9: Pound's source for these details of building alterations was Giambattista Lorenzi, *Monumenti per Servire alla Storia de Palazzo Ducale de Venezia* (1868). The Palazzo Ducale, at the eastern end of the Piazza San Marco, was the official residence of the Doges, the elected heads of the Venetian Republic. It was built first in 814, reconstructed in the early fourteenth century and extended and altered in the fifteenth.

l. 75 vadit pars: (Lat.) 'a part goes'. The dungeons were removed because of their smell.

ll. 77–9: probably votes cast for and against rebuilding: 254 in favour, 23 against, 4 invalid or undecided.

l. 81: cf. Canto XXI (102/98).

l. 83 murazzi: (Ital.) 'walls'.

l. 87 Sulpicia: Roman poetess, whose six love poems to Cerinthus are included in Tibullus, III, 15 (*Oxford Book of Latin Verse*, 196–7). Pound quotes a line from her 'To Phoebus: A Prayer in Sickness' at lines 96, 103, and 115–16 below.

l. 89 cortex: bark; cf. the line 'white ivory under the bark' in Canto LXXXIII (565/530).

ll. 90–5: the important notion for Pound of a pre-existent 'forma', given expression, or drawn forth, in execution. Cf. his statement in the essay 'Medievalism',

> The god is inside the stone, *vacuos exercet aera morsus*. The force is arrested, but there is never any question about its latency, about the force being the essential, and the rest 'accidental' in the philosophic technical sense. The shape occurs.
>
> (*LE*, 152)

Cf. lines 133–5, 137–8, Canto LXXIV, 'stone knowing the form which the carver imparts it/ the stone knows the form' (457/430), and Canto XC, 'the stone taking form in the air' (641/608).

l. 96: (Lat.) 'Lay fear aside, Cerinthus', from Sulpicia; cf. note on line 87. The phrase is repeated in Canto XCIII (663/630).

l. 97: cf. Canto LXXVI, line 170.

l. 102 Zephyrus: the west wind.

l. 103: (Lat.) 'God does not harm lovers', from Sulpicia; cf. note on line 87.

l. 104: (Lat.) 'For me this day was holy'. Pound suggests that the union of Zephyrus and Sulpicia confers divinity; cf. Canto XXXVI, 'Sacrum, sacrum, inluminatio coitu' ('a sacred thing, a sacred thing, the knowledge of coition', 185/180).

l. 105: compare the 'voce-profondo' of the lotus-eaters and the complaint of the 'clear bones, far down' of Odysseus' crew (Canto XX, ll. 158, 161).

l. 107: (Lat.) 'too late, too late'.

l. 108: cf. 'I neither build nor reap' from the proletarian 'tovarisch' in Canto XXVII (137/132), and Canto LXXXI, line 166, 'But to have done instead of not doing' and line 173, 'Here error is all in the not done'. Compare also the emphasis on 'order' in Confucius (Canto XIII, l. 52).

l. 110: cf. Pound's reference to Remy de Gourmont 'when he says that most men think only husks and shells of the thoughts that have been already lived over by others', as showing his 'very just appreciation of the system of echoes, of the general vacuity of public opinion' (*LE*, 371–2).

ll. 115–16 Pone metum/ . . . laedit: (Lat.) Sulpicia's 'Lay fear aside/ Fear, nor does God harm'; cf. note on line 87.

l. 118 bolge: (Ital.) a circle of hell.

l. 120 Civis Romanus: (Lat.) 'Roman citizen'.

l. 122 blood rite: cf. the blood rite performed by Odysseus in Canto I, lines 19–24.

l. 123 Ferrara: the town in north Italy. Cf. Canto XXIV (119/114).

l. 125 Phaethusa: daughter of Helios, who tended his cattle and

270

sheep on Thrinacia (*Odyssey*, Bk. XII, l. 132). Pound imagines her in Hades; cf. Canto XXI (104/100).

l. 129 Phlegethon: the river of fire in Hades.

l. 130 pone metum: cf. lines 96, 115.

l. 133 forms and renewal: cf. Canto XX (96/92) and Canto XXI (104/100).

l. 135 Napishtim: Utnapishtim, the wise man in the Babylonian epic *Gilgamesh*, who directs Gilgamesh to a plant which will restore youth (Tablet XI).

l. 136 νοός: (Gk.) 'Nous', i.e. the mind, reason or intellect. Pound believed in a neo-Platonic relation between mind and god; cf. the dictum in *Religio or, The Child's Guide to Knowledge*, 'A god is an eternal state of mind' (*SPr*, 47). In *Guide to Kulchur* Pound talks of the Platonists who 'have caused man after man to be suddenly conscious of the reality of the *nous*, of mind, apart from any man's individual mind, of the sea crystalline and enduring, of the bright as it were molten glass that envelops us, full of light' (p. 44).

l. 137: cf. note on lines 90–5.

l. 138: cf. Pound's statement in the essay 'Medievalism':

> We appear to have lost the radiant world where one thought cuts through another with clean edge ... magnetisms that take form, that are seen, or that border the visible, the matter of Dante's *paradiso*, the glass under water, the form that seems a form seen in a mirror.
>
> (*LE*, 154)

l. 139: in the second Homeric Hymn to Aphrodite, the goddess tells her lover Anchises that she is the daughter of King Otreus of Phrygia. Pound quotes from this poem at the close of Canto I, and alludes to it again in Cantos XXIII (114/109) and LXXVI (l. 144).

from Canto XXX

ll. 1–18: Pound's lines invert the emphasis of Chaucer's 'Complaint unto Pity' (*Works*, ed. F. N. Robinson, 1957,

526–8), where pity is presented as a lost but indispensable virtue. Pound comments in *The Spirit of Romance* on Dante's *Inferno*, XX.

> When Dante weeps in pity for the sorcerers and diviners, Virgil shows classic stoicism:
> 'Art thou, too, like the other fools? Here liveth pity when it were well dead. Who is more impious than he who sorrows at divine judgment?'
> (pp. 134–5)

Cf. also Cantos LXXVI, lines 245–6; XCIII, lines 166–7; XCIV (668/635).

l. 2 Artemis: the sister of Apollo, a virgin huntress and goddess of wild life. She appears in Canto IV as the Roman goddess Diana, who transforms Actaeon into a stag (18/14).

l. 19 Paphos: a town on the south-west coast of Cyprus and a famous place of worship of Aphrodite, who was thought in one version of her legend to have landed there after emerging from the sea.

l. 21 Mars: the Roman god of war and the lover of Venus (the Greek Aphrodite). Pound is supposing Aphrodite, the goddess of sexuality, to have been chaste.

l. 22 doddering fool: probably Hephaestus, the Greek god of fire and of smiths, and the husband of Aphrodite, to whom in fact she was consistently unfaithful.

l. 25: cf. Canto LXXIV, line 655, 'Time is not, Time is the evil, beloved'.

l. 27 Pedro: Pedro I, son of Alfonso IV and king of Portugal 1357–67. He was secretly married to Inez de Castro.

l. 29 Ignez: Inez de Castro. Cf. Canto III, note on line 38.

from Canto XXXVI

The present selection consists entirely of Pound's second translation of the *Canzone d'Amore*, 'Donna mi priegha', by the Tuscan poet Guido Cavalcanti (1250–1300), the only poem incorporated *in toto* into the *Cantos*. Pound's earlier translation appeared in the *Dial* (June 1928), and in *Guido*

Cavalcanti Rime (1932), *Personae* (1949) and *Translations* (1953). As part of the essay 'Cavalcanti', it appeared also in *Make It New* (1934) and *Literary Essays* (1954). Both the essay, particularly the section titled 'Medievalism', and the earlier translation are indispensable aids to an understanding of the poem as it appears in Canto XXXVI. Of the first translation Pound said he had not attempted 'an English "equivalent" . . . at the utmost I have provided the reader, unfamiliar with old Italian, an instrument that may assist him in gauging *some* of the qualities of the original.' Even 'the atrocities' of his translation were, he hoped, 'for the most part intentional, and committed with the aim of driving the reader's perception further into the original than it would without them have penetrated' (*LE*, 172).

For a detailed discussion of both translations and of the significance of Cavalcanti for Pound, see George Dekker, *Sailing After Knowledge* (1963), pp. 111–25; Dekker concludes that the version in Canto XXXVI is 'something of a *tour de force* in rigorously controlled obscurity' (p. 125). Georg M. Gugelberger ('The Secularization of "Love" to a Poetic Metaphor: Cavalcanti, Center of Pound's Medievalism', *Paideuma*, II, no. 2, 159–73) argues that Pound was drawn to the 'Donna mi priegha' because he found here a conjuncture of the subjects of love, poetry and form.

The Italian text of Cavalcanti's poem, given by Pound in company with his earlier translation, is corrupt. A superior text is contained in Guido Favati, *Guido Cavalcanti: Le Rime* (Milano, 1957).

l. 2: a departure from the Italian, 'perch'i volglio dire' ('if I would tell'). It is suggested to Pound perhaps by the Malatestan motto 'Tempus loquendi, Tempus tacendi' ('A time to speak, a time to keep silent'), quoted earlier in Canto XXXI (157/153).
l. 3 affect: desire or passion. Pound follows Dino del Garbo (*LE*, 182) in using this word in both translations for Cavalcanti's 'accidente', a term implying the scholastic distinction

between substance or essence and accident, and carrying the sense basically in Cavalcanti's poem of love as an essence or *forma*, actualized in the 'accidente' of individual love. Pound wrote in the essay 'Cavalcanti', 'I am aware that I have distorted "*accidente*" into "*affect*" but I have done so in order not to lose the tone of my opening line by introducing an English word of *double entente*' (*LE*, 159). In the same essay he suggests Cavalcanti's

> definition of '*l'accidente*', i.e. the whole poem, is a scholastic definition in form, it is as clear and definite as the prose treatises of the period, it shows an equal acuteness of thought. It seems to me quite possible that the whole of it is a sort of metaphor on the generation of light.
>
> (ibid., 161)

Pound is thinking here of Cavalcanti's possible indebtedness to the treatise *De Luce* by the medieval philosopher of light, Bishop Grosseteste (1175–1253), and states earlier in the essay, 'the whole canzone is easier to understand if we suppose, or at least one finds, a considerable interest in the speculation, that he [Cavalcanti] had read Grosseteste on the Generation of Light' (ibid., 149).

Pound had used the term 'affect' earlier, in MAUBERLEY (1920) II, line 31.

l. 12 virtu: (Ital.) 'virtù' ('virtue' or 'potency'). Cf. Pound's comment in his introduction to his translations of Cavalcanti, where he defines '*La virtù*' as 'the potency, the efficient property of a substance or person' (*Tr*, 18), and also Canto LXXIV, note on line 138.

l. 16: Pound recalls Cavalcanti's Italian, 'In quella parte/ dove sta memoria' ('in that part where one remembers'), elsewhere in Cantos LXIII (370/353) and LXXVI (480/452 and line 160).

l. 18 diafan: Pound retains Cavalcanti's word. James E. Shaw offers the gloss on the original, 'The diaphanous is the medium of visibility: it *receives* its actual *form* from light, without which a diaphanous body is dark and only potentially diaphanous'

(*Guido Cavalcanti's Theory of Love*, 1949, 21). In the essay 'Cavalcanti', Pound quotes from Grosseteste's *De Luce* as it appeared in Baur's *Die philosophischen Werke des Robert Grosseteste* (Münster, 1912): 'p. 73, *aut trànsitus radii ad rem visam est rectus per medium diaphani unius generis . . . aut transitus . . . modi spiritualis, per quam ipsum est speculum . . . transitus . . . per . . . plura diaphana . . .*' (*LE*, 161). The phrase 'per plura diaphana' ('through more things diaphanous') recurs or is alluded to several times in later Cantos; amongst other references, cf. Canto LXXXIII, line 81; XCIII, line 148; and Canto C (749/722).

George Dekker's comment on this word is probably the most apposite, and applies to other scholarly terms in Pound's version: 'diaphan', he says, is 'a very odd word indeed' with 'no contemporary equivalent'. The point is that this oddity, 'its air of precision', should alert the reader to 'depths of meaning' in the original (op. cit., 123–4). Pound, in his notes to Cavalcanti, directs the reader to Dante's *Paradiso*, X, line 69 (*LE*, 184). Dante's lines 68–9 read, 'vedem tal volta, quando l'aere è pregno, sì che ritenga il fil che fa la zona'('Sometimes when vapour has so charged the air/ That it retains the thread that makes her zone'; Binyon, 114–15).

ll. 23–4: in his notes to Cavalcanti, Pound cites Spinoza's 'The intellectual love of a thing consists in the understanding of its perfections' (*LE*, 184). Cf. also Canto LXXVI, note on lines 157–60.

l. 34: Cavalcanti's 'E l antenzione/ per ragione/ vale' as given by Pound (*LE*, 165). Pound openly confessed his difficulties here: 'does "*intenzion*" mean intention (a matter of will)? does it mean intuition, intuitive perception, or does the line hold the same meaning as that in Yeats's Countess Cathleen, *intenzion* being intention, and *ragione* meaning not reason, but "being right"?' There is, he adds, 'a mare's nest in "*intenzione*"' (*LE*, 162, 178).

l. 59: cf. Canto XLIX, line 46, 'The fourth; the dimension of stillness'.

l. 70: Pound's note in 'Cavalcanti' refers the reader to Dante's *Paradiso*, VIII, ll. 112, 42 and X (*LE*, 190).

ll. 75–6: compare Pound's earlier version, 'In midst of darkness light light giveth forth' (*LE*, 157), and the phrase 'In the gloom the gold/ gathers the light about it', Canto XVII (ll. 83–4; cf. note).

Canto XXXVIII

A miscellaneous critique of the moneyed interests behind the prosecution of war, producing in Pound a tone which moves into areas of broad comedy.

Epigraph: (Ital.) from Dante's *Paradiso*, 'the woe which he on Seine,/ By making the false coinage, is to bring' (Binyon, 225).

l. 1 Metevsky: Sir Zenos Metevsky, Pound's name for Sir Basil Zaharoff (1849–1936), European munitions magnate who sold arms for Nordenfelt & Co. and Maxim & Vickers, and had interests in Schneider-Creusot, Krupp and Mitsui, international banks and newspapers. Zaharoff, called the 'Mystery Man of Europe', was knighted in 1918 for services to the Allies, and endowed chairs in French Literature at Oxford and in English Literature at the Sorbonne. In *Guide to Kulchur* Pound wrote, 'I doubt if Zaharoff knew much of what he was doing' (p. 302), and in the article 'Peace' how Zaharoff's life would be a 'fascinating document' in studying the causes of war, the first of which is listed as 'Manufacture and high pressure salesmanship of munitions, armaments etc.' (*SPr*, 192). Cf. also Cantos XVIII and XCIII (660/627).

America del Sud: (Sp.) South America.

l. 2 Pope: Achille Ambrogio Damiano Ratti (1857–1939), Pope Pius XI (1922–39), who between 1907 and 1914 had supervised students at the Ambrosian Library, Milan, amongst them Pound himself. It must have been here that Pound gained an impression of the future Pope's manners. Cf. Canto LXXX (536/502).

Mr. Joyce's: James Joyce, the novelist. Pound alludes probably to Joyce's education by Jesuits.

l. 4 Marconi: Marchese Guglielmo Marconi (1874–1937), the Italian physicist and inventor of the wireless. In one of his talks over Rome Radio Pound drew an analogy between money as distinct from credit, and lightning and the use of electricity:

> Then somebody found out they could do without metal counters.
>
> Just like Loomes found out you could paint an electric signal without using wire, found out electricity would travel through the air. Nothing practical came of it until Signore Marconi put it into a system. Credit had existed just like lightening existed.
>
> ('The Fallen Gent', Levy, op. cit.)

l. 5 Jimmy Walker: James John Walker (1881–1946), American politician and Mayor of New York 1925–32.

l. 9 Lucrezia: Lucrezia Borgia (1480–1519), daughter of Pope Alexander VI and sister of Cesare Borgia. At her third marriage she became in 1500 the wife of Alfonso d'Este, later third Duke of Ferrara. Though tainted with the crimes associated with the Borgias, and herself accused of incest, she died as a respected patroness of the arts. Cf. Canto XXX where she is referred to as 'Madame "YΛH" ('Madame Matter') (153/148).

l. 10 rabbit's foot: a good luck charm.

l. 12: possibly a reference to Lucrezia Borgia who died of her last delivery, although she had six rather than three children, and no reported abortion (*Paideuma*, 'The Televort' no. 3, 21 Mar. 1977, 3).

ll. 14–18: a direct quotation from Dexter Kimball's textbook *Industrial Economics* (1929), pp. 79–80, where the example is cited as evidence that repetitive work 'is not necessarily deadening to the intellect'.

l. 18 Dexter Kimball: (1865–1955), American economist; his *Industrial Economics* is recommended elsewhere by Pound (cf. *SPr*, 153, 319, 411).

l. 24 Akers: probably Vickers Ltd. or Maxim & Vickers, the British armament manufacturers, both of which employed Zaharoff (cf. l. 1n.). Pound corresponded with Vincent Vickers, one-time director of Vickers and of the Bank of England, and possessed his pamphlet, 'Finance in the Melting Pot' (Stock, *Life*, 436–7). Cf. Canto XVIII where Vickers is referred to as 'Humbers' (85/81).

l. 27 Mr. Whitney: Richard Whitney (1888–1974), banker, president of the New York Stock Exchange, and credited with attempting to halt the Wall Street panic of 1929. Later he was sent to prison for embezzlement. Pound wrote in the *ABC of Economics*,

> The whinings of a Whitney and the yowls of stock jobbers are no better than any other form of gangster's sobstuff. . . . no one ever yet claimed to have sold short, or rigged the stock market, save in the hope of picking other men's pockets.
>
> (*SPr*, 228)

l. 31 two Afghans . . . Geneva: Amanullah Khan (1892–1960), as emir of Afghanistan, made treaties with Russia and Great Britain at Geneva in 1921 to secure the import of munitions via India.

l. 36 Mr. D'Arcy: William Knox D'Arcy, American oilman who founded the Anglo-Persian Oil Company after obtaining the oil concession from the Shah of Persia in 1901. Lines 36–8 are all but repeated in Canto XI (205/197).

l. 39 Mr. Mellon: Andrew William Mellon (1855–1937), American financier, Secretary of the Treasury at the time of the Wall Street crash in 1929 and U.S. Ambassador to Great Britain 1932–3. Pound saw Mellon as an obstruction to economic justice: 'What has capital done', he asked, 'that I should hate Andy Mellon as a symbol or as a reality?' (*SPr*, 199), and in *Guide to Kulchur* railed against the complacency

> which can see without boiling, a circumjacence, that tolerates Mellon and Mellonism, the filth of american govt. through the reigns of Wilson, Harding, Coolidge and the supremely uncultivated, uneducated gross Hoover, the England that swelters through the same period and the France of that period, and every man who has held high

office in these countries without LOATHING the conces-
sions made to foetor and without lifting hand against them,
and against the ignorance wherein such mental squalor is
possible.

(pp. 155–6)

l. 40 Mr. Wilson: Thomas Woodrow Wilson (1856–1924),
President of the United States 1913–21. Pound saw Wilson's
Presidency as 'a period of almost continuous misfortune to the
organism of official life in America', and as a time in which
'All American and republican principles were lost' (*SPr*, 189,
213).

prostatitis: inflammation of the prostate gland. After the Treaty
of Versailles (1919), Wilson suffered from nervous and physical
strain, resulting in a thrombosis.

ll. 43–4 her Ladyship . . . Jenny . . . Minny Humbolt: unidentified.
Possibly fictitious persons. *The Cantos* (1975) has 'Agot Ipswich'
for 'Minny Humbolt'.

l. 45 that year: 1914, at the outbreak of World War I.

l. 47 louse in Berlin: perhaps Kaiser Wilhelm II (1859–1941),
Emperor of Germany 1888–1918. Cf. Canto XLVIII (250/
240).

l. 49 François Giuseppe: i.e. Franz Joseph, Emperor of Austria
(1830–1916), who declared war on 28 July 1914. Pound repeats
his opinion of the Emperor in Cantos XVI (75/71), XXXV
(177/172) and L (258/247).

l. 50 Miss Wi'let: possibly Violet Hunt (1866–1942), the writer
and mistress of Ford Madox Ford.

ll. 50–2: the statement from the 'soap and bones dealer' has
not been located.

l. 53 Mr. Gandhi: Mohandas Karamchand Gandhi (1869–
1948), known as Mahatma ('Great Soul'), the leader of the
Indian Nationalist Movement and an instigator of non-
violence as a means to social and political change.

l. 56 Monsieur Untel: (Fr.) 'Mr. So and So'.

the Jockey Club: a famous social club in Paris.

l. 58 Mitsui: the central bank of Japan and the name of a

Japanese holding company connected with Vickers (cf. line 177).

l. 59: derived from *The Diary of John Quincy Adams, 1794–1845* (1928), where Adams records his experiments with black walnut seedlings and a visit to the armoury in Springfield, Massachusetts (pp. 374–5, 551–2). Cf. Canto XXXIV, 'Black walnut, almond planted in spring . . . Gun barrels, black walnut' (173/169, 176/171).

ll. 60–2: Pound alludes to industrialization in Russia after the Bolshevik Revolution (1917), and to Lenin's and Mussolini's efficiency: 'Practical men like Lenin and Mussolini differ from inefficients . . . in that they have a sense of time' (*The Exile*, Autumn 1928, 3, quoted in Pearlman, 161).

l. 60 Muscou: Moscow.

ll. 61–2 Italian . . . time: Pound praised Mussolini for 'Having drained off the muck by Vada/ From the marshes, by Circeo, where no one else wd. have drained it./ Waited 2000 years' (Canto XLI, 210/202).

l. 62 Tiberius: Tiberius Julius Caesar Augustus, Roman emperor A.D. 14–37.

l. 63 Beebe: Charles William Beebe (1877–1962), American biologist, under-water explorer and author. Pound catches the excited tone of Beebe's prose in, for example, his *Beneath Tropical Seas* (1928).

l. 64 Rivera: Miguel Primo de Rivera (1870–1930), Spanish general who became Premier in 1921.

l. 65 Infante: probably the son of Alfonso XIII, the last king of Spain, deposed with the establishment of the Second Republic, 1931.

l. 68 Schlossmann: apparently a U.S. correspondent in Vienna at the time of Pound's visit there (Eva Hesse, 'Notes and Queries', *Paideuma*, v, no. 2, 345).

l. 69 Vienna: Stock reports that Pound was in Vienna in May 1928, and that amongst other survivors of the Austro-Hungarian Empire, he met there Count Albert von Mendsdorff-Pouilley-Dietrichstein (1861–1945), agent for the Carnegie Endowment for Peace. Together they drafted a letter to

the Executive Committee, later published as the article 'Peace'
(*SPr*, 192–3).

l. 70 Anschluss: (Ger.) a political merger, as between Austria
and Germany in 1938.

l. 73 white man: Leo Frobenius (1878–1938), pioneer German
archaeologist and anthropologist, author of the seven-volume
Erlebte Erdteile (1925–9), and a seminal influence on Pound.
(Cf. the references to Frobenius in *Selected Prose* and *Guide to
Kulchur*; Pound had wished to title the latter work 'Paideuma',
adopting Frobenius's own term, as Pound defines it, 'for the
tangle or complex of the inrooted ideas of any period', *GK*,
57–8).

ll. 73–5: the story is told in *Erlebte Erdteile*, v (pp. 49–53), of
Frobenius's arrival amongst Babunda tribesmen in Biembe,
and of how their initial hostility was dampened by a storm
they took to be of his making. Later they restored a knife to
Frobenius, identifying him by drumbeat, given in German as
'Der Weisse der in Biembe das Gewitter gemacht hat' ('The
white man who made the tempest in Biembe'). Pound's
incorrect 'Baluba' (l. 74), a region and tribe in the south-west
Belgian Congo, appears in Frobenius's preceding volume iv
(Kenner, *Pound Era*, 508).

l. 74: repeated Canto LIII, line 69; alluded to Canto LXXIV,
line 319, and Canto LXXVII (494/465).

l. 76: cf. Canto XXXV, 'We find the land overbrained'
(179/174), where Pound refers also to a 'jewish Hungarian
baron'. The 'hungarian nobleman' is otherwise unidentified.

l. 77 1923: Pound was living in Paris in this year.

Kosouth (Ku'shoot): Ferencz Lajos Akos Kossuth (1841–1914),
Hungarian noble, leader of the Party of Independence, and
son of Louis Kossuth (1802–94), a leader of the Hungarian
Revolution.

ll. 81–4: an imaginary conversation with Schlossmann (cf. ll.
68–71).

l. 85 the Tyrol: the Austrian province, acquired by Italy after
World War I by the Treaty of Versailles, 28 June 1919.

l. 89 Bruhl: Lucien Lévy-Bruhl (1857–1939), French anthropologist with a special interest in the mentality of primitive peoples. Pound wrote in 1935 that Lévy-Bruhl was 'just a professor. Frobenius *thinks*' (*SL*, 266), and later that Lévy-Bruhl had 'a number of excellent ideas about savages and primitive language, but he leaves no conviction that he understands savages' (*SPr*, 273).

ll. 89–92: a summary of Lévy-Bruhl's account of primitive languages, as it appears, for example, in *How Natives Think* (1925), pp. 145–74.

ll. 93–8: Pound is thinking no doubt of the events at the close of Shakespeare's play, where Romeo, believing Juliet dead, poisons himself, and Juliet waking from the effects of a potion, herself then commits suicide. Lévy-Bruhl in *How Natives Think* mentions the practice of premature burial amongst primitive tribes (pp. 309–10), and of widows committing suicide upon their husbands' graves (p. 332).

l. 99 Blodgett: probably Lorin Blodget, author of *The Textile Industries of Philadelphia* (1880).

l. 102 (Douglas): Major Clifford Hugh Douglas (1879–1952), the British economist; cf. Canto XIV (l. 89n.).

ll. 107–25: an exemplification of the so-called 'A plus B Theorem' at the centre of Douglas's thinking. The total of wages, profits and production costs is divided into two: 'A' payments to individuals (in wages or dividends), and 'B', payments for the cost of raw materials, bank charges and other overheads. The price of any commodity should be the sum of 'A' plus 'B', but since 'B' takes money out of circulation, the money made available as purchasing power can never catch prices. Cf. Douglas's *Economic Democracy* (1920), p. 120; Pound's *ABC of Economics* (*SPr*, 221–2); the expositions in Gorham Munson, *Aladdin's Lamp* (1945), p. 150; Earle Davis, *Vision Fugitive; Ezra Pound and Economics* (1968), pp. 23–4; and also Dennis Klinck, 'Pound, Social Credit, and the Critics' (*Paideuma*, v, no. 2, 228–40). Klinck demonstrates how Pound (and most of his commentators) have misunderstood Douglas's proposals, showing that while Douglas and Pound agreed that a nation's social credit belongs rightly to the people, Douglas did not suggest, as Pound did, that the control of this credit be transferred from banks to the State.

l. 115 per forza: (Ital.) 'perforce', 'of necessity'.

l. 129 Krupp: Alfred Krupp (1812–87), who converted the Krupp cast steel works at Essen in 1843 to the manufacture of munitions, producing his first cannon in 1847 (cf. line 132). Krupp's field guns helped Prussia to victory in the Franco-Prussian War (1870–1), and the Krupp works became the world's largest supplier of arms.

ll. 129–31 guns . . . side: the remarks attributed to Krupp are derived from an account in Richard Lewinsohn's *À la Conquête de la richesse* (Paris, 1928). (Cf. Hesse, 'Notes and Queries', *Paideuma*, v, no. 2, 347.)

ll. 132–3: Krupp cannon were shown at the Paris Exhibition in 1855, and Krupp sold 36 two years later to the Viceroy of Egypt. Fenner Brockway in *The Bloody Traffic* (1933), a book Pound consulted, suggests that Krupp had sold weapons to France and later to both Britain and Russia at the time of the Crimean War, 1854–6 (pp. 53, 55).

l. 134 Pietro il Grande: (Ital.) Peter the Great of Russia (1672–1725). The use of Italian suggests Pound's source is Corbaccio's *I mercanti de cannoni* (Milan, 1932), a text he recommends elsewhere (*J/M*, 61, 79). Cf. also lines 115, 143.

l. 135: Sir Basil Zaharoff was appointed Commander of the French Legion of Honour in July 1914, and in June 1930 promoted to Grand Officer.

l. 136 Napoleon Barbiche: Charles Louis Napoleon Bonaparte (1808–73), Emperor Napoleon III (1852–71), called 'Barbiche' because of his goatee beard.

l. 137 Creusot: the city of Le Creusot, Saône-et-Loire in east central France, was the home from 1836 of the Schneider iron and steel plant. Schneider dominated French weapons production in World War I.

Sadowa: a village near Koniggrätz and the site of the Prussian defeat of Austria, 3 July 1866.

ll. 140–1 "The Emperor . . . humanity": Pound's summary of a reply from Leboeuf, on behalf of Emperor Napoleon III, to whom Krupp sent a munitions catalogue in 1868 (cf. Brockway, op. cit., 56–7).

l. 141 Leboeuf: Edmond Leboeuf (1809–88), French general, Minister of War 1869–70, Marshal of France 1870, and a relative of the Schneiders. In 1868, Leboeuf was aide-de-camp to Napoleon III and commander of the military camp at Châlons.

l. 142 Schneider: Joseph-Eugène Schneider (1805–75), who established the Schneider works at Le Creusot with his brother Adolphe.

l. 143 operai: (Ital.) 'workers'.

l. 144: derived from Brockway, op. cit., 58.

l. 145 Bohlem und Halbach: the former Prussian diplomat, Gustave von Bohlen und Halbach (1870–1950), who assumed the name Krupp and the control of the Krupp works on his marriage to Bertha, eldest daughter of Alfred Krupp.

l. 147: Pound assumes that the French Schneiders were one in their greed with the German Krupps.

l. 148 Eugene . . . tractiles": one line in the Faber *Cantos* (1975). *Eugene, Adolf and Alfred*: Joseph Eugène Schneider, Adolphe Schneider and Alfred Pierrot Deseilligny (1828–75), son-in-law of Joseph-Eugène and co-manager of the Schneider plant with Henri, Joseph-Eugène's son.

ll. 149–51: Joseph-Eugène Schneider was elected deputy for Saône-et-Loire in 1845, and served as president of the legislative body under the Second Empire from 1867 to 1870.

ll. 160–1: both Schneider and Krupp established amenities for their workers.

l. 163 Herr Henri: Henri de Wendel, director of a French steel company which cooperated with the Schneider plant in 1880, and father of François de Wendel (l. 166), President of the Comité des Forges (l. 169). François de Wendel's grandson was also called Henri.

l. 164 Chantiers de la Gironde: the Gironde shipyards, part owned by Schneider.

Bank of the Paris Union: La Banque de l'Union Parisienne, an investment bank, founded in 1874, reorganized in 1904 and controlled by Zaharoff and the Schneiders.

l. 165: the Franco-Japanese Bank was closely connected with the Schneider interests.

l. 166 Robert Protot: probably Robert Pinot, Secrétaire Général du Comité des Forges in World War I, author of *Le Comité des Forges de France au service de la nation (Août 1914–Novembre 1918)*, published in 1919. This is the source perhaps of Pound's lines 168–9.

l. 169 the Comité des Forges: the French Steel Trust, which subsidized several French newspapers; cf. *Selected Letters*, p. 243.

l. 170 Hawkwood: Sir John de Hawkwood (d. 1394), an English mercenary who served the Black Prince in France and the Italian republics, before accepting a pension from Florence. In *The Spirit of Romance*, Pound records an exchange between Hawkwood and a monk: 'Passing Monk: "God give you peace, my lord." Capt. Hawkwood: "And God take away your means of getting a living" ' (p. 70).

ll. 171–3: French newspapers in which the Comité des Forges had a controlling voice.

l. 174 Polloks: unidentified.

ll. 179–80: (Fr.) 'to put his own concerns/ before those of the nation'.

Canto XLV

First published in February 1936 in the English monetary reform journal *Prosperity*.

Usura: (Lat., Ital.) 'usury'. This Canto and Canto LI, the first half of which closely follows XLV, are Pound's summary complaint in the poem against usury, after the evidence which has been accumulating since Canto XII. Usury occupies a central place in Pound's thinking and therefore in his view of history, and in the Cantos as a whole. Against its malpractice, and the associated rise of Protestantism, Pound sets the strength of the Catholic Church in the Middle Ages, and presents in this Canto examples of the architecture and painting of the period as the outward token of its non-usurious economics. Cf. also 'Addendum for C' (28/798).

In the Foreword, dated 4 July 1972, to *Selected Prose*, Pound notes,

> re USURY:
> I was out of focus, taking a symptom for a cause. The cause is AVARICE

ll. 5–6: from Villon's 'Au moutier vois, dont suis paroissienne,/ Paradis peint où sont harpes et luths', in 'Ballade pour Prier Notre Dame' (*Oeuvres*, ed. André Mary, Paris, 1951, 61). The phrase 'paradis peint' is recalled in Canto XCV (676/643). Pound saw Villon as 'the first voice of man broken by bad economics' and as representing 'the end of the mediaeval dream' (*ABC of R*, 104).

l. 6 harpes et luthes: (Lat., O.F.) 'harps and lutes'.

l. 10 Gonzaga: probably Francesco Gonzaga (d. 1444), lord of Mantua. Pound refers to the painting in fresco, *Gonzaga, His Heirs and His Concubines*, by Andrea Mantegna (1431–1506). Cf. Cantos III, note on line 41, and XXVI (128–33/123–7).

ll. 11–12: cf. the lines ' "These sell our pictures"! Oh well,/ They reach me not' in the poem 'In Durance' (*CSP*, 34), and the much later 'what art do you handle?/ "The best" And the moderns? "Oh, nothing modern/ we couldn't sell anything modern" ' (Canto LXXIV, 476/448).

ll. 17–18: in *Guide to Kulchur*, Pound suggested 'that finer and future critics of art will be able to tell from the quality of a painting the degree of tolerance or intolerance of usury extant in the age and milieu that produced it' (p. 27). The point is repeated in *Selected Letters* (p. 303) and in 'Carta da Visita' (1942), reprinted as 'A Visiting Card' in *Selected Prose* (p. 293).

l. 17: Pound explains this 'means the *line* in painting and design. Quattrocento painters still in morally clean era when usury and buggary were on a par' [i.e. both condemned by the Church] (*SL*, 303). For relevant statements by Pound before and after this insight was connected with usury, cf. *The Spirit of Romance* (p. 166), *Literary Essays* (pp. 150–1), *Guide to Kulchur*

286

(pp. 108–9) and *Selected Prose* (p. 235). Cf. also the reference in *Hugh Selwyn Mauberley* to 'usury age-old and age-thick' (IV, l. 18) and Cantos XLVI (245/234) and LXXIV (458/432).

l. 25 murrain: plague, pestilence. In *Guide to Kulchur* Pound describes usury as 'a murrain and a marasmus' (p. 109).

l. 27 Pietro Lombardo: (1435–1515), Italian architect and sculptor, who ornamented Dante's tomb at Ravenna and carved the mermaids at the church of Santa Maria dei Miracoli, Venice, which Pound mentions elsewhere in Cantos LXXIV (457/430), LXXVI (489/460) and LXXXIII (564/529). In the *ABC of Reading* he writes, 'A few bits of ornament applied by Pietro Lombardo in Santa Maria dei Miracoli (Venice) are worth far more than all the sculpture and "sculptural creations" produced in Italy between 1600 and 1950' (p. 151).

l. 29 Duccio: Agostino di Duccio (?1418–81), Italian sculptor who is thought to have done the bas-reliefs for Malatesta's Tempio; cf. Cantos IX, line 230, and XX (94/90).

l. 30 Pier della Francesca: (1420–92), Italian painter employed by Malatesta on the Tempio in 1451, for which he painted the fresco *Sigismondo Malatesta Before St. Sigismund*; cf. Canto VIII (32–3/28–9) and MAUBERLEY (1920) I, line 14.

Zuan Bellin': Giovanni Bellini (1430–1576), the leading painter of the Venetian school. Pound seems in this as in the previous line to be thinking of Sigismondo Malatesta's Tempio, built 'In a Europe not YET rotted by usury', and where Malatesta 'had a little of the best there in Rimini. He had perhaps Zuan Bellin's best bit of painting. He had all he cd. get of Pier della Francesca' (*GK*, 159). Bellini's painting in the Tempio is his *Pietà*.

l. 31 "La Calunnia": a painting by Sandro Botticelli in the Uffizi Gallery, Florence; cf. Canto LXXX, line 623.

l. 32 Angelico: Giovanni da Fiesole, Fra Angelico (1387–1455), Florentine painter.

Ambrogio Praedis: (?1455–?1506), Milanese portrait painter and miniaturist.

l. 33 Adamo me fecit: (Lat.) 'Adam made me', derived from the inscription on a column in the church of San Zeno, Verona,

'ADAMINUS/ DESCO/ GEORG/IO.ME/ FECI/T', first seen by Pound in the company of Edgar Williams, architect and brother of W. C. Williams, in 1911. Cf. *Hugh Selwyn Mauberley* v, note on line 7, and Canto LXXIV (476/448).

ll. 34–5: cf. the elaboration of these lines in Canto LI, 'Nor St. Trophime its cloisters;/ Nor St. Hilaire its proportion'. Pound refers to their 'clear lines and proportions' as examples of the 'Mediterranean sanity' in 'Medievalism' (*LE*, 154).

l. 34 St. Trophime: the church of St. Trophime at Arles, visited by Pound in May 1919.

l. 35 Saint Hilaire: the church of St. Hilaire at Poitiers, probably visited by Pound in 1919; cf. also Canto XC (639/605).

l. 39 weave gold in her pattern: Pound offers the information, 'in Rapallo Middle Ages, industry of weaving actual gold *thread* into cloth' (*SL*, 304).

l. 40 cramoisi: (Fr.) crimson cloth.

l. 41 Memling: Hans Memling (?1430–?1495), painter of early Flemish school; cf. Canto LXXVI (484/455).

l. 46 CONTRA NATURAM: (Lat.) 'against nature'. Reviewing John Buchan's *Oliver Cromwell*, Pound wrote, 'By great wisdom sodomy and usury were seen coupled together. If there comes ever a rebirth or resurrection of Christian Church, one and Catholic . . . it will come with a recognition and an abjuration of the great sin *contra naturam*, of the prime sin against natural abundance' (*SPr*, 235). Pound is at one here with Aristotle's condemnation of usury as 'of all forms the most contrary to nature' (*Politics*, I, 3, 23).

l. 47 Eleusis: the town in Attica where the Eleusinian mysteries to Demeter were celebrated. The mysteries were in origin agrarian rites of purification and fertility, culminating in visionary illumination for their initiates, and came later to be associated with the underworld and the after-life. Pound valued the Eleusinian celebration of the natural cycle as a counter-force to usury, which is 'contra naturam'. Commenting directly on this line to Carlo Izzo, he wrote:

"Eleusis" is *very* elliptical. It means that in place of the sacramental — — — — in the Mysteries, you 'ave the 4 and six-penny 'ore. As you see, the moral bearing is very high, and the degradation of the sacrament (which is the coition and *not* the going to a fatbuttocked priest or registry office) has been completely debased largely *by* Xtianity, or misunderstanding of that Ersatz religion.

(*SL*, 303)

Pound sharply distinguished between the cult of Eleusis and Christianity elsewhere, arguing also that the core of the Eleusinian mysteries persisted through the Middle Ages, in Provence and Italy ('Credo' and 'Terra Italica' in *SPr*, 53, 54–60), and was evident, for example, in the Order of Templars at Poitiers (Canto XC, 639/605). This tradition is discussed also by Jessie L. Weston in her *From Ritual to Romance* (1957).

l. 48: reminiscent of the story of Pedro I of Portugal, who had the body of Inez de Castro exhumed and set on a throne by his side; cf. Canto III, note on line 38, and Canto XXX, lines 26–35.

N. B. USURY: Pound's definition was reputedly composed in 1953 at the request of Hugh Kenner (Stock, *Life*, 563).

Medici bank: in Florence, established by Cosimo de Medici (1389–1464). It failed, says Pound later, 'from accepting too many deposits' (Canto XCIV, 666/633).

Canto XLVII

ll. 1, 3–9: a version of Circe's words to Odysseus (*Odyssey*, Bk. X, ll. 490–5), the Greek lines of which are given in Canto XXXIX (202/194). Odysseus follows Circe's instructions in the Nekuia passage of Bk. XI of the *Odyssey*, of which Canto I is a translation.

l. 1: a description of the blind Theban prophet Tiresias, who retains his powers in hell.

l. 5 Ceres: Pound's addition to Homer. Ceres was a Roman goddess, identified with the Greek Demeter, and likewise a goddess of corn and of agriculture.

Proserpine: the Roman equivalent of Greek Persephone, daughter of Demeter, and queen of Hades.

l. 12 drugged beasts: perhaps Odysseus' crew, transformed into swine by Circe's potion, or the drugged panthers, leopards and lions mentioned in Canto XXXIX (201/193).

ll. 12–13 phtheggometha/ thasson: a transliteration of the Greek given in line 14. The words are Polites' cry before Circe's palace, 'let us raise our voices without delay' (*Odyssey*, Bk. X, l. 228).

ll. 15–16: reiterated at lines 21–2, 92–3, 95, and in Cantos XC (641/607) and XCI (646/612). Cf. note on line 18.

l. 17 Neptunus: (Lat.) Neptune, the Roman god of the sea.

l. 18 Tamuz: Thamuz is the Syrian equivalent of Adonis, the lover of Aphrodite; he was killed by a boar while out hunting but revived in the form of a rose or anemone which Aphrodite caused to spring from his blood. As such, Adonis is symbolic of the course of vegetation and the object of many fertility rites, such as Pound presents here where the 'small lamps' (ll. 15, 25), 'the red flame going seaward' (l. 19), and the 'lights in the water' (l. 21), are symbolic of Adonis' loss of blood.

l. 20 gate: the estuary of a river, perhaps, or the stretch of water Odysseus must navigate between Scylla and Charybdis. Cf. note on line 56.

l. 23 Scilla: Scylla, a sea monster with six heads, three rows of teeth in each, and the bark of a dog, who devours six of Odysseus' crew (*Odyssey*, Bk. XII, ll. 80–100, 222–59). Cf. also line 73.

ll. 26–9: (Gk.) 'You Dione/ And the Fates [weep for] Adonis' from Bion's *Lament for Adonis*, line 94 (*The Greek Bucolic Poets*, Loeb edn., 1928, 392). Dione is not named directly in Bion's poem, and presumably it is Aphrodite as the lover of Adonis who is meant here. In Homer, Dione is the mother of Aphrodite (*Iliad*, Bk. V, ll. 370–417). Cf. also lines 100–1, 104–7.

ll. 32–3: an allusion perhaps to the so-called 'gardens of Adonis' belonging to Adonis' cult. As described by Sir James Frazer in *The Golden Bough*, they were baskets or pots filled with earth, in which wheat, barley, lettuces, fennel, and various kinds of flowers were sown. . . . Fostered by the sun's heat, the plants shot up rapidly, but having no root they withered as rapidly away, and . . . were carried out with the images of the dead Adonis, and flung with them into the sea or into springs.

(p. 396, quoted in Pearlman, 173)

Cf. also line 103.

ll. 34–47: compare the definition of woman in Canto XXIX, 'the female/ Is an element, the female/ Is a chaos/ An octopus/ A biological process' (149/144).

l. 41 naturans: (Lat.) 'in accordance with nature'. The moth, the bull and Odysseus obey natural instincts. Cf. the designation of usury as 'CONTRA NATURAM' (Canto XLV, l. 46).

l. 43 Molü: (Gk.) 'moly', the herb given to Odysseus by Hermes, by which he resists Circe's drugs and gains entry to her bed (*Odyssey*, Bk. X, ll. 302–35).

l. 46 her: the generalized woman of line 34, but perhaps in particular Circe, who has not the same concern for the stars as the departed seaman Odysseus.

ll. 48–55: Derived from Hesiod, *Works and Days*, lines 383–91 (*Homeric Hymns and Homerica*, Loeb edn., 1926, 448). Cf. also lines 96–9.

l. 49 Pleiades: a group of stars in the constellation Taurus, thought in Greek mythology to be the seven daughters of Atlas. They are easily identified and an important measurement of the seasonal cycle.

l. 56 gate: the gate of morning and night, or of life and death. The Roman god Janus, represented as the opener and fastener of all things, as looking inwards and outwards and backward and forward in time, is regularly associated with the door or gate (Lat. 'janua'). Cf. line 20, and the repeated phrase, 'And that all gates are holy' in Cantos XCIV (667/634) and C (744/716).

l. 63 small stars: the small white flowers of the olive, but recalling also line 49.

l. 65 martin: (also marten), a bird of the swallow family which builds a mud nest on the walls of houses.

l. 69 Tellus: the Roman goddess of the earth.

l. 74 cunnus: (Lat.) the female pudendum.

ll. 79–92: an experience of combined mystical illumination and sexual rapture, guaranteeing regeneration, and associated with the fertility rites to Adonis and probably also to Demeter (cf. line 5, and Canto XLV, note on line 47).

l. 79 Io: in Greek, an exclamation; in Italian, the first-person pronoun.

l. 87 Zephyrus . . . Apeliota: respectively the west and east wind.

l. 109: recalled in Canto XLIX (l. 47). Cf. also the later reference to Apollonius of Tyana as having 'made peace with the animals' (Canto XCIV, 668/635).

Canto XLIX

The 'Seven Lakes Canto'.

ll. 1–32: very largely derived from a manuscript book given to Pound by his parents, consisting of sixteen poems (eight Japanese, eight Chinese) with accompanying paintings, which describe eight famous scenes in the lake region of Hunan, China, where the rivers Hsiao and Hsiang converge to form numerous lakes. Daniel Pearlman gives translations of both sets of poems, reproduces photographs of four poems and four paintings from Pound's original book and collates the translated Chinese poems with lines 1–32 ('Appendix B', p. 304–11). Hugh Kenner has since published paraphrases of the eight Chinese poems, included in a letter by Pound intended for his father, but never sent ('More on the Seven Lakes Canto', *Paideuma*, II, no. 1, 43–6). These would appear to be Pound's immediate source for the present section. Angela Jung Palandri has been able to add the information that Pound was assisted in making these translations by a Miss Pao-sun Tseng who visited him in Rapallo sometime between 1 March and 17 May 1928 ('The "Seven Lakes Canto" Revisited', *Paideuma*, III, no. 1, 51–4).

l. 1 seven lakes: since Pound's source was a copy of the 'Eight Scenes of Hsiao-Hsiang' one would expect the number eight here. A possible explanation lies in the fact that though Pound worked from rough translations of the total of eight Chinese poems, the title of the fourth of these appears in lower-case type with 'TITLE' in upper case added in brackets by its side. Perhaps Pound overlooked this correction. More simply the reason may be that of the many lakes formed at Hunan, 'seven', as Palandri reports, 'are better known' (ibid., 54).

no man: the eleventh-century original 'Eight Scenes' is much copied and its poems virtually part of an anonymous tradition. In Pound's manuscript book, though the poems were probably composed by Japanese sinologists, all but one, written by 'Genryn', appear to be unsigned (Pearlman, 308; Palandri, 54). 'Noman' is also the name Odysseus gives himself in answer to the Cyclops, Polyphemus (*Odyssey*, Bk. IX, l. 336); cf. Canto LXXIV (453/426).

ll. 2–6: derived from the poem 'Rain', the first in the series of Pound's rough translations of the Chinese. (All other references to the order of the poems are to how they appear in the letter quoted by Kenner. Pearlman infers a different order for Pound's original manuscript and suggests, p. 305, that the scenes are 'always listed' in this order.) The following poem corresponds to Pearlman's poem VI, 'Night Rain in Sho-Sho':

> Rain, empty rain
> Place for soul to travel
> > (or room to travel)
> Frozen cloud, fire, rain damp twilight
> One lantern inside boat cover (i.e. sort of
> > shelter, not awning on small boat)
> Throws reflection on bamboo branch,
> > causes tears.

ll. 7–12: derived from the title and lines 1–3 and 5 of the second poem, 'Autumn Moon on Ton-Ting Lake' (poem V in Pearlman):

West side hills
Screen off evening clouds
Ten thousand ripples send mist over cinnamon flowers:

   . . . . .

Blows cold music over cottony bullrush.

ll. 13–14: derived from lines 1–2 of the sixth poem, 'Monastery Evening Bell' (poem VII in Pearlman):

Cloud shuts off the hill, hiding the temple
Bell audible only when wind moves toward one.

ll. 15–17: derived from the seventh poem, 'Autumn Tide, Returning Sails' (poem II in Pearlman):

Touching green sky at horizon, mists in suggestion of
 autumn
Sheet of silver reflecting all that one sees
Boats gradually fade, or are lost in turn of the hills,
Only evening sun, and its glory on the water remain.

ll. 18–19: derived from lines 1–2 of the eighth poem, 'Spring in Hill Valley' (poem III in Pearlman):

Small wine flag waves in the evening sun
Few clustered houses sending up smoke.

ll. 20–4: derived from the third poem, 'Snow on River' (poem IV in Pearlman):

Cloud light, world covered with milky jade
Small boat floats like a leaf
Tranquil water congeals it to stillness
In Sai Yin dwell people of leisure [this line crossed out]
The people of Sai Yin are unhurried.

ll. 25–7: from the title and lines 1–2 of the fourth poem, 'Wild Geese Stopping on Sand' (poem I in Pearlman):

Just outside window, light against clouds
Light clouds show in sky just beyond window ledge [this
  line crossed out]
A few lines of autumn geese on the marsh.

ll. 28–30, 32: from lines 1–3 of the fifth poem, 'Evening in
Small Fishing Village' (poem VIII in Pearlman):

Fisherman's light blinks
Dawn begins, with light to the south and north
Noise of children hawking their fish and crawfish.

l. 31: Pound's addition. Tsing is probably Kang Hi, fourth
emperor (1662–1723) of the Ch'ing dynasty.
l. 34 Geryon: the three-headed or three-bodied monster slain
by Hercules. In Dante, Geryon, the guardian of the eighth
circle of hell and a symbol of fraud, is represented as having
a man's head, a beast's trunk and a serpent's tail (*Inferno*,
XVII); cf. Canto LI, lines 62, 65, where Geryon is presented
as 'twin with usura'.
l. 35 TenShi: (Jap.) 'son of God', but a place-name seems
intended.
ll. 37–40: from a famous Chinese song, 'Ch'ing-yun ko',
accredited to the Emperor Shun (2255–2205 B.C.). A Japanese
version with English notes was amongst the Fenollosa papers
in Pound's possession, and is the source of the present lines in
romanized Japanese. Pound attempted a translation in 1958:

Gate, gate of gleaming,
  knotting, dispersing,
    flower of sun, flower of moon
  day's dawn after day's dawn new fire.

Both the Fenollosa version and Pound's translation are
included in Kenner's 'More on the Seven Lakes Canto' (op.
cit., 45–6).
l. 40 KAI: KEI in Fenollosa.
ll. 41–5: a translation of an ancient Chinese folksong 'Chi-
yang ko', dated from the time of Emperor Yao, Shun's

THE CANTOS

predecessor, and taken from a second version made by
Fenollosa:

Beating sod song
sun	go out	and work
sun	enter	and rest
dig	well	and drink
till	field	and eat
	might	
Emperor's	power	for me what is?

(Eva Hesse, 'More on the Seven Lakes Canto',
Paideuma, III, no. 1, 143)

l. 46 fourth . . . dimension: a reply perhaps to Einstein's notion
of the 'fourth dimension' in his theory of relativity. Pound found
it 'confusing in Einstein' (*Antheil and The Treatise on Harmony*,
1927, 56) and of 'no philosophic bearing' (*GK*, 34).
stillness: this recalls the Confucian doctrine of the *Chung Yung*
(*The Unwobbling Pivot*), 'What exists plumb in the middle is the
just process of the universe and that which never wavers or
wobbles is the calm principle operant in its mode of action'
(*Confucius*, 97). Cf. also Canto XXXVI, line 59, 'He himself
moveth not, drawing all to his stillness'.
l. 47: essentially repeats the last line of Canto XLVII.

Canto LI

The second usura Canto.
ll. 1–5: Pound's lines recall the idea of light in the medieval
light philosophers (particularly, as an influence on Pound,
Bishop Grosseteste and Scotus Erigena) as the first principle or
element in creation.
l. 6 mud: Napoleon's wry addition (after the experience of his
military campaigns) to the traditional four elements of water,
fire, air and earth. The line occurs earlier in Canto XXXIV
(169/166). The lack of punctuation between lines 6 and 7
makes Napoleon the speaker of the following complaint against

usury; Pound in this way honours the Emperor's resurrection of the Roman and canon laws against usury.

ll. 7–32: a condensed recapitulation of Canto XLV. See the notes to that Canto.

ll. 33–50: instructions for fly-fishing, derived from Charles Bowlker's *Art of Angling*, 1829 (pp. 119, 122). The passage is offered presumably as itself an example of precise definition (see the cheng⁴ming² ideogram at the close of the Canto), and as presenting a patient, skilled and non-usurious activity.

ll. 33, 50 Blue dun, Granham: names of types of fly used in trout fishing.

ll. 51–2: Pound wrote in *Polite Essays*, 'Forma to the great minds of at least one epoch meant something more than dead pattern or fixed opinion. "The light of the DOER, as it were a form cleaving to it" meant an ACTIVE pattern, a pattern that set things in motion' (p. 51).

ll. 53–4: (Lat.) 'Godlike in a way/ this intellect that has grasped', adapted from a passage by Albertus Magnus, quoted by Pound in 'Cavalcanti' (*LE*, 186).

l. 55 Grass . . . place: repeats an earlier line in Canto XLIII (228/219) and recalls its context of the Monte dei Paschi, Pound's example of an ideal bank whose security was founded on the Maremma pastures. The phrase is repeated later in Canto LXXIV (462/435).

Königsberg: the town in north-west Prussia.

l. 56: (Ger.) 'Between peoples [a way of living] will be achieved'.

l. 57: (Lat.) 'a way of life'. Apparently Pound believed Hitler to be the author of this statement. Eva Hesse has established that it is in fact a quotation from Rudolf Hess (Pearlman, 218n.).

l. 60 regents: bankers (ibid.).

l. 62 Geryone: cf. Canto XLIX, note on line 34. In Dante's *Inferno* Geryon appears at the seventh circle of hell, the abode of the usurers, and transports Dante and Virgil spinning down to the eighth circle (cf. line 65).

l. 69 League of Cambrai: an association of Italian states and European powers against Venice between December 1508 and

February 1510. Pound would seem to stress the temporary success of the League, and therefore of the forces of usury.

正名: cheng[4]ming[2], an important ideogram for Pound which appears several times in subsequent Cantos. In his translation of the *Ta Hsio* he renders it as 'precise verbal definitions'(*Confucius*, 31), and in Canto LXVI it is glossed as 'a true definition' (403/382). 'The art of not being exploited', Pound said also, 'begins with "Ch'ing Ming"!' (*GK*, 244).

from Canto LIII

The first of the 'Chinese History Cantos' (LIII–LXI), published in 1940 in *Cantos LII–LXXI*. As Pound's note to this series of Cantos makes clear (*Cantos*, 445/255), he here sets out the names and achievements in turn of the Great Emperors: the rulers of the first (Hia), second (Chang) and third (Tcheou) dynasties (2205–255 B.C.), and of Confucius (551–479 B.C.). His source for this Canto, as for the other Chinese History Cantos, was very largely Père Joseph-Anne-Marie de Moyriac de Mailla's twelve-volume *Histoire générale de la Chine, ou Annales de cet empire* (Paris, 1777–83). Pages reproduced from a facsimile of the de Mailla text (1969), together with an article by David Gordon on 'The Sources of Canto LIII' appeared in *Paideuma* (v, no. 1, 95–152), and the following notes are heavily indebted to this material. As Gordon points out, the period dealt with in the second half of the Canto forms the subject of the Confucian texts *The Spring and Autumn Annals* (a record of events in the state of Lou 722–481 B.C.) and *The Warring States* (dealing with the period 481–221 B.C.).

this period of struggle was a mirror of the meaning of all history for Confucius. . . .

These two eras of small feudal states battling and intriguing against each other provided an extremely fertile and influential matrix for those structural characteristics which would be dominant in China over the next two millennia. It is in this sense a period comparable to the

Italian Renaissance in regard to the formation of Western cultural patterns. The earlier mythic, prehistorical and quasi-historical periods in China serve as a parallel to the mythic and semi-mythic periods in Western culture.

(p. 152)

l. 1 Yeou: the legendary king of China Yu Tsao-chi taught his people to build bird-nest huts, and hence acquired his name meaning 'have nest family'.

l. 2 Seu Gin: the legendary king Sui Jen-chi who followed Yeou. His name means 'maker of fire and wood', the use of which he introduced. He also set up a stage from which to instruct his people, introduced the barter of fruit and animals, and invented an abacus for which knots were tied in string.

l. 4 Fou Hi: Fü Hsi, successor to Sen Gin and the first of the Five Emperors of the legendary period of China. He ruled 2953–2838 B.C., hence Pound's line 5. Amongst his several accomplishments – the regulation of marriage, instruction in hunting, fishing, animal-raising, the invention of a calendar and stringed musical instruments – Gordon finds no reference to the growing of barley (p. 124).

l. 6: Fü Hsi's grave is in modern Tchin-tcheou.

l. 8 Chin Nong: the Emperor Shên Nung (2838–2698 B.C.), successor to Fü Hsi, known as the 'Prince of Cereals' for his introduction of wheat, rice, millet, barley and peas (not chick peas). He set up markets to distribute goods across the Empire, studied pharmacology and introduced a plough that is still in use in China.

l. 11 Kio-feou-hien: Chüo-fou-hsien, in Shantung province.

l. 14 Souan Yen: Suan Yen, a favourite governor under Chin-Nong, who himself seized power and ruled as Emperor (2698–2597 B.C.) under the name of Hoang Ti, or 'Yellow Ruler' (cf. line 16). He tamed tigers for military use (the number 15 was perhaps suggested to Pound by the page number 15 of his source; Gordon, 125), derived the original 540 radicals of the Shuo-Wen dictionary from bird tracks, invented bricks, made money of precious stones, gold and copper, and made an organ of twelve bamboo lengths. Hoang Ti had four wives, one of whom, Si-ling-chi, began the silk industry.

l. 19 Syrinx: the nymph who, pursued by Pan, changed into a tuft of reeds from which he made his musical pipes.

l. 21: i.e. 2611 B.C.

l. 23 Kiao-Chan: Chiao-shan, in modern Chung-pu-hsien in Shensi province.

l. 24 Ti Ko: Ti Ku, the sixth legendary Emperor (2436–2366 B.C.), set voices to instrumental music for the edification and pleasure of the people.

l. 25 Tung Kieou: Tun-chiu, in Hopei province.

l. 26 a.c.: ante Christum, (Lat.) 'before Christ'.

l. 27 YAO: the son of Ti-Ko, and a model Emperor in Chinese history. He ruled 2356–2258 B.C. Pound's 'like the sun and rain' is drawn from de Mailla's 'éclairé que le soleil . . . aux nuages qui fertilisent' (Gordon, 125). Cf. also *The Analects*, Bk. 8, xix (*Confucius*, 227), and later references to Yao at lines 44, 192, 359.

ll. 28–9: a reference to Yao's wish to correlate the stars with the phases of the agricultural year (cf. de Mailla's '. . . quelle est l'étoile qui est au point du solstice d'été', Gordon, 125).

l. 30 YU: Yü, a descendant of Hoang Ti and founder of the Hsia dynasty, who ruled 2205–2197 B.C. Cf. *The Analects*, Bk. 8, xxi (*Confucius*, 228). Yü controlled the flood waters of the Huang River, and determined the relative productivity of the soil in the nine provinces, finding the area Lai-chou-fu in Shantung, noted for its production of wild silk, black and fertile. He established 'ammassi', accepted 'earth of five colours' as tributes in kind in Siu-ch'ou (Siu-tcheou) province, found pheasant plumes at Yü Shan (Yu-chan) mountain, Chiang-nan province, for use as standards; and at Ye Shan (Yu-chan) mountain in Kiangsu province, found the sycamore tree for use in making musical instruments. At Se-shui (Se-choui) River in Kiangsu Yü found 'ringing stones' for use as percussive instruments, and a herb, Tsing mao (Tsing-mo), for use in sacrifices. Cf. lines 46, 361.

l. 32 Ammassi: (Ital.) 'piles', 'stores' of grain; cf. Canto
(351/335), Canto LVI (317/303) and *Selected Prose* (p. 270).

l. 39 μῶλυ: (Gk.) the magical herb moly which Hermes gives
to Odysseus to protect him from the spell of Circe (*Odyssey*,
Bk. X, l. 305).

l. 40 Chun: Shun, Yao's chosen successor, whose rule (2255–
2205 B.C.) is considered exemplary. On taking office Shun
made a great sacrifice to Chang Ti (Shang Ti, roughly equivalent to the idea of God), the sun, moon, stars and four
seasons. He is referred to many times in subsequent Cantos.

ll. 42–3: (Fr.) 'that your verses express your intentions/ and
that the music conforms', derived from de Mailla's 'Que vos
vers expriment votre intention; et que la musique y soit
analogue . . .' (Gordon, 127). Shun emphasized the educative
function of music.

l. 44 YAO: the corresponding ideogram of his name means
'eminent'.

l. 45 CHUN: his ideogram means 'wise'.

l. 46 YU: his ideogram means 'insect' or 'reptile'.

l. 47 KAO-YAO: Shun's first minister, said to have introduced
laws against crime; cf. *The Analects*, Bk. 12, xxii, 6 (*Confucius*,
248). His ideogram means 'bless kiln'.

*   *   *

l. 59 Tching Tang: Ch'êng T'ang ruled 1766 1753 B.C. as
founder of the Shang dynasty (1766–1122 B.C.). In a period of
drought Tching opened a copper mine in Mt. Tchouang-
chan, from which he made and distributed money in the form
of discs with square holes. When the grain was exhausted, and
after seven years of sterility, Tching offered himself as a sacrifice on Mt. Seng-lin, producing a cloudburst which saved the
crops.

l. 69: (Ger.) 'who made the tempest in Baluba'. An allusion to
Leo Frobenius; cf. Canto XXXVIII, note on lines 73–5.

ll. 71–3: Tching wrote the phrase 'make it new' on his bathtub
to commemorate the end of the drought. It symbolizes the
regeneration issuing from his own acts and the foundation of

the Shang dynasty, and is a major principle in Cantos LI–LXI, as for Pound generally. The accompanying ideograms arc given in *The Great Digest*, with the gloss

AS THE SUN MAKES IT NEW
DAY BY DAY MAKE IT NEW
YET AGAIN MAKE IT NEW.

(Confucius, 36)

Cf. also *Guide to Kulchur*, p. 278.

l. 79 Hia: Hsia, the first dynasty (2205–1766 B.C.), followed by the Shang dynasty (1766–1121 B.C.).

l. 83 Chang Ti: cf. note on line 40.

l. 84 Tang: Tching Tang; cf. note on line 59.

* * *

l. 175 Kang: K'ang Wang, the third emperor (1078–1052 B.C.) of the Chou dynasty. He is generally considered to have been a weak emperor, dependent on Chao Kong, brother of Wu Wang (cf. line 179).

l. 177 Tcheou: the Chou dynasty (1122–255 B.C.). Confucius' support for this dynasty is expressed in *The Analects*, Bk. 3, xiv *(Confucius, 203)*; cf. also *Guide to Kulchur*, p. 19.

l. 178 Confutzius: K'ung Fu Tzǔ, Confucius (551–478 B.C.), the sage and statesman, born in Lou, part of modern Shantung province.

l. 179 Wen-wang: Wên Wang (1231–1135 B.C.) is the title of Ch'ang, duke of Chou, a celebrated opponent of the corrupt Emperor Cheou-Sin.

Wu-wang: Wu Wang (1169–1115 B.C.), Wên Wang's son, was the first king of the Chou dynasty. Cf. Canto XIII, note on line 67, and *The Analects*, Bk. 8, xx *(Confucius, 227)*.

l. 181: Cf. the reference to Borso d'Este, 'Peace! keep the peace, Borso', Canto XX (95/91).

l. 184 Chao-Kong: (Shao Kung), the duke of Shao (d. 1053), the brother of Wu Wang, and counsellor to Kang Wang, famous for his sense of justice (cf. *Cantos*, 279/268–9).

* * *

l. 350 Kungfutseu: Confucius, who was made minister in his home state of Lou in 497 B.C.

l. 351 T.C.Mao: Chao-tching-mao (Shao Ching-mao). On taking office Confucius had him arrested and executed for creating disorder in government.

ll. 356–7: objecting to Confucius' influence in Lou, the prince of Tsi, a feudal principality in Shantung and South Hopeh, sent singing girls to corrupt its prince. Confucius retired to the state of Ouei; cf. *The Analects*, Bk. 13, iv (*Confucius*, 280).

l. 358 Tching: (Ching), a feudal principality near modern Kaifeng, in Honan province, east central China.

ll. 359–63: a description of Confucius.

l. 360 Cao: Kao-Yao (cf. note on line 47).

Tsé Tchin: (Tsze Ch'an), the upright chief minister of the state of Chang.

l. 366 Tchin: (Chin), a feudal principality in Shanshi and Honan on the Yellow River in north-east China. Also at line 370.

l. 369 Yng P: Yng Pi, the illegitimate son of Ling-Kung, prince of Ouei. When Ling-Kung offered to make him his heir in 492 B.C., Yng Pi refused because of his birth.

l. 370 Tsai: a feudal principality in Honan province in east central China. The princes of Tchin and Tsai intercepted Confucius on his way to visit the prince of Tchou in 489 B.C., driving him into the desert. After days of privation, he was rescued by Tchou's troops.

l. 371 Tcheou: an error for Tchou (Chou), a principality in north-east China.

l. 372 Tsao: a principality in Shantung, lasting from 1122 to 501 B.C.

l. 373: Confucius retired in 493 B.C., aged sixty-eight, to edit the Odes; cf. *The Analects*, Bk. 9, xiv (*Confucius*, 231).

ll. 374–5: in 481 B.C., in the 39th year of King Ouang, Confucius protested to Ngai-hong, prince of Lou, against the assassination of Kien-kong, prince of Tsi. He was ignored. In the following year a comet appeared which extended from Star Yng to Star Sin (perhaps Antares in the constellation of Sin).

l. 375 King Ouang: Ching Wang, 25th Emperor (519–475 B.C.) of the Chou dynasty, during the life of Confucius.

* * *

l. 395 "Hillock": a nickname not for Confucius' father but for Confucius himself, who was called 'petite colline, Kiu' by his mother (Gordon, 146). Cf. *The Analects*, Bk. 7, xxiii and Bk. 18, vi (*Confucius*, 222, 280).

ll. 396–400: an episode concerning Confucius' father K'ung Shu-liang Ho (d. 548 B.C.), a military officer in the state of Lou. In a siege in 562 B.C., when his men were trapped behind a portcullis, he held it up so they could escape (cf. *Cantos*, 283/272).

from **Canto LXII**

The first of the 'Adams Cantos' (LXII–LXXI), derived in bulk from the ten-volume *Works of John Adams*, ed. Charles Francis Adams (Boston, 1850–6). John Adams (1735–1826) was the second President of the United States (1797–1801), and stands in the *Cantos* with the figures of Odysseus, Malatesta and Mussolini as 'an entire man', and on a par with fellow American statesmen John Quincy Adams and Martin Van Buren (cf. Cantos XXXIV, XXXVI) and especially Thomas Jefferson (cf. Cantos XXXI–XXXIII) as a founding father of the United States, a formative influence on early governmental policy and practice, and a necessary ingredient in a revival of American culture. As Pound presents Adams, at the close of this Canto, he is:

> pater patriae
> The man who at certain points
> made us
> at certain points
> saved us
> by fairness, honesty and straight moving

(Cantos, 367/350)

The sources of the 'Adams Cantos' are given in full in Frederick K. Sanders's *John Adams Speaking. Pound's Sources for the Adams Cantos* (Orono, Maine, 1975), to which the reader is referred, and from which the following citations are taken. (*Works of John Adams* is abbreviated to *WJA* followed by the volume number and page. Volume I on which Canto LXII is based is a biography of John Adams by Charles Francis Adams (1807–86), U.S. statesman, grandson of John Adams and son of John Quincy Adams.) Cf. also Pound's 'The Jefferson Adams Letters as a Shrine and a Monument' (*SPr*, 117–28).

ll. 1–5: Preface to *WJA*, I, vi–vii.
ll. 6–11: *WJA*, I, 3.
l. 10 Thomas Adams: one of the grantees of the charter of the Massachusetts Bay Colony (1629), and possibly a relative of Henry Adams, the founder of the Adams family in America.
l. 12: *WJA*, I, 4.
l. 13: Pound's comment.
ll. 14–17: *WJA*, I, 4–6.
ll. 17–19: *WJA*, I, 11.
l. 17 Henry: Henry Adams (d. 1646) was in 1640 granted 40 acres at Mount Wollaston, later called Merry Mount, and subsequently Braintree.
l. 18 Joseph Adams: (?1626–94), the youngest son of Henry Adams, who took over and developed the brewery established by him.
l. 20: *WJA*, I, 12, 643. John Adams's birth date is given as $\frac{19}{30}$ October, 1735, on the marble tablet at his tomb.
l. 21: *WJA*, I, 22. A description of Adams's condition as teacher of a grammar school in Worcester, 1755.
l. 22: *WJA*, I, 39.
ll. 23–6: *WJA*, I, 42.
l. 27: *WJA*, I, 80. The grounds on which Adams opposed the British Parliament's taxation of the colonies.
l. 28: *WJA*, I, 92.
Burke: Edmund Burke (1729–97), British statesman and famous

conservative thinker, author of a 'Speech on American Taxation' (1774) and a 'Speech on Conciliation with America' (1775, 1778).

Gibbon: Edward Gibbon (1737–94), British historian. Adams sees Burke and Gibbon as united in presenting public figures in British life in the most attractive terms, although 'figures' would also seem to carry the sense of 'figures of speech', with reference to these writers' studied prose styles.

ll. 29–32: *WJA*, I, 94.

l. 31 tcha: this and the accompanying ideogram mean 'tea'. Since tea was produced in India and shipped by Britain to America, Lord North saw fit to impose a tax on the colonies for its importation.

ll. 33–4: *WJA*, I, 95.

Lord North: (1732–92), British Prime Minister under George III (1770–82), who pursued a policy of British control of the American colonies, particularly in the imposition of the Stamp Act and the tax on tea.

ll. 35–40: *WJA*, I, 95–6. The reference is to the changing attitudes of the American colonists to British authority.

l. 37: Pound's comparison. Rapallo, in Liguria, north-west Italy, was Pound's home from 1924 to 1945.

ll. 41–4: *WJA*, I, 97.

l. 41: Adams records this disturbance as happening at nine o'clock at night. Its outcome was the so-called 'Boston Massacre', 5 March 1770.

Lard Narf: Lord North.

l. 42 Bastun: Boston. Pound's parody of the local pronunciation.

l. 43 Styschire: Pound's satirical addition.

ll. 44–9: *WJA*, I, 98.

l. 45: Adams has 'barber's boy'.

l. 46: Captain Thomas Preston and seven men of the guard came to the relief of the intimidated sentry.

l. 47 lower order: a mob of 40–50 of the townspeople.

l. 48 Charles Fwancis: C. F. Adams (cf. headnote) said, 'This was the first protest against the application of force to the settlement of a question of right.'

l. 49 Louses of Parleymoot: Pound's own witty deformation of 'Houses of Parliament'.

l. 50: *WJA*, 1, 99.

l. 51: Pound's question to C. F. Adams.

ll. 52–4: *WJA*, 1, 99.

l. 53 Cadmus: in Greek legend the founder of Thebes. After killing a dragon he planted its teeth, on Athene's instructions, and from these sprang up armed warriors, who set about fighting each other until only five remained. These five were the ancestors of the noble families of Thebes. Adams's text at this point runs, 'The drops of blood then shed in Boston were like the dragon's teeth of ancient fable. . . . the seeds, from which sprang up the multitudes who would recognize no arbitration but the deadly one of the battle-field.'

ll. 55–8: *WJA*, 1, 107–8.

l. 55 legal advisor: John Adams, from this time called upon by the colonists in his capacity as lawyer.

l. 58 Blaydon: Colonel Bladen, a member of the board of trade and plantations who saw in the opening words of legal documents (indicated by Pound in line 57) 'words of fear to the prerogative of the monarch of Great Britain'.

l. 59: *WJA*, 1, 109. The recommendation of a committee on which John Adams served.

l. 60: *WJA*, 1, 112. This and the following lines 61–81 refer to John Adams's defence in October 1770 of Captain Preston and the soldiery after the 'Boston Massacre'; cf. Canto LXIV (377/359), Canto LXXI (443/420).

ll. 61–9: *WJA*, 1, 113.

ll. 69–70 that is . . . manslaughter: Pound's elaboration.

l. 71: *WJA*, 1, 114.

ll. 72–5: Pound's elaboration.

ll. 76–7: *WJA*, 1, 113.

l. 78: (Lat.) 'mind without feeling', quoted from Algernon Sidney, *WJA*, 1, 114.

ll. 79–81: Pound's elaboration.

l. 82: the statement derives from Edmund Burke.

ll. 83–4 disputed . . . king: *WJA*, 1, 121–2. It was not Burke who disputed this practice but a reply of uncertain authorship to Governor Hutchinson's speech on obligatory allegiance to Britain.

ll. 84–90: *WJA*, 1, 126–8.

l. 88 "*The Spensers*": father and son, Hugh le Despenser, beheaded as traitors to Edward II, 1326.

l. 89 Coke: the English jurist, Sir Edward Coke (1552–1634), author of the four *Institutes*. This is the first of many subsequent references to Coke in the *Cantos*. In Canto CVII Pound calls him 'the clearest mind ever in England' (783/758). Cf. Canto CVII.

l. 91: *WJA*, 1, 129.

l. 92: *WJA*, 1, 132. Britain was seen to regard the colonies 'not as friends and brethren, but as strangers who might be made tributaries'.

ll. 93–4: *WJA*, 1, 138–9. It was Adams's wish to abide by the Constitution, and in this spirit that the legislature impeached Peter Oliver (1713–91), Chief Justice of the Massachusetts Colony and supporter of the British Crown.

ll. 95–6: it was Oliver's agreement to accept payments to the Massachusetts judiciary from the British Crown which prompted his impeachment. Pound's lines have no direct source in Adams.

l. 97: *WJA*, 1, 139; i.e. under Peter Oliver.

ll. 98–101: Pound's comment.

l. 99 Governor: Thomas Hutchinson (1711–80), loyalist Governor of Massachusetts 1771–4, who blocked the impeachment proceedings against Peter Oliver.

from Canto LXXIV

This and the following selections from Cantos LXXVI, LXXIX, LXXX, LXXXI and LXXXIII are from the sequence of *Pisan Cantos* composed by Pound between May and November 1945 while he was imprisoned on a charge of treason, following his broadcasts over Rome Radio, in the U.S. Army Detention Training Center (D.T.C.) near the village of Metato, north of Pisa. For about three weeks Pound was incarcerated in a high-security steel cage (the 'gorilla cage' of Canto LXXXIII, line 141) measuring six by six and a half feet with a concrete floor on which he slept before the issue of a military cot and pup tent. Thereafter he was in a tent in the medical section of the compound. With him he had the classic 'Four Books' of Confucius in one volume, translated by James Legge, and a Chinese dictionary, both brought from Rapallo, a copy of Morris Speare's anthology, *The Pocket Book of Verse*, 'found on the jo-house seat' (Canto LXXX, 547/513), and an Authorized Version of the Bible issued by the Army. As well as *The Pisan Cantos* Pound also wrote at this time, in the same notebooks but running in the opposite direction, his translations of *The Great Digest* and *The Unwobbling Pivot* of Confucius (published in March 1947).

In 1949, *The Pisan Cantos* was awarded the Library of Congress Bollingen Prize for Poetry.

l. 3 Manes: (?216–?276), a Persian sage, founder of the sect of Manicheans and crucified for his teaching.

l. 4 Ben and La Clara: Benito Mussolini (1883–1945), dictator of Italy 1922–45, and his mistress Claretta Petacci were executed and strung up by the heels in the Piazzale Loreto, Milan, 29 April 1945.

l. 7 DIGONOS: (Gk.) 'twice born', the epithet of Dionysus.

l. 9 Possum: Pound's name for T. S. Eliot. Pound here inverts the terms in the last line of Eliot's 'The Hollow Men', 'Not with a bang but a whimper' (*Collected Poems*, 90).

l. 11 Dioce: Deïoces (d. 656 B.C.), the first king of the Medes and founder of Ecbatana, the capital of Media Magna, in the sixth century. The Greek historian Herodotus describes the city in Bk. I of his History as surrounded by seven concentric walls, each one higher than the next, with their battlements painted in turn white, black, purple, blue, orange, and the last two coated in silver and gold.

l. 13 the process: the Confucian 'way' or 'Tao', expressing harmony between man and nature. Pound glosses the relevant

Chinese ideogram (道) 'the head conducting the feet, an orderly movement under lead of the intelligence' (*Confucius*, 22). Cf. also in Pound's *Confucius*, *Chung Yung* (*The Unwobbling Pivot*), Part One (pp. 99–115) and Part Three (p. 183). Also at lines 346–7 and Canto LXXXIII, line 96.

l. 14: From *The Unwobbling Pivot*, 1, 2 (*Confucius*, 101).

ll. 16–18: the source is Tsang's comment upon the death of Confucius, ' "Washed in the Keang and Han, bleached in the autumn sun's-slope, what whiteness can one add to that whiteness, what candour?" ' (quoted, *Confucius*, 194). Tsang's comment is reported again in Canto LXXX (529/495).

l. 16 Kiang and Han: The Yangtse and Han Rivers which meet at Hankow, China.

l. 18 candor: with the sense of both 'frankness' and 'brilliant whiteness'.

*   *   *

l. 120 smell of mint: cf. the later lines in this Canto, 'Le Paradis n'est pas artificiel/ but spezzato apparently/ it exists only in fragments unexpected excellent sausage,/ the smell of mint, for example' (465/438).

l. 122 a white ox: cf. Canto LXXVIII, 'and as for the solidity of the white oxen in all this/ perhaps only Dr Williams (Bill Carlos)/ will understand its importance' (515/483).

road: the Via Aurelia, running north to south past the D.T.C.

l. 123 tower: the tower of Pisa, visible from the D.T.C.

l. 125 guard roosts: Pound refers earlier in this Canto to 'the ideogram of the guard roosts' (454/428).

l. 126: cf. Canto LXXXIII, 'When the mind swings by a grass-blade/ an ant's forefoot shall save you' (ll. 143–4), and Canto CXVI (l. 34n.).

l. 128 Mt. Taishan: Chinese T'ai Shan, meaning 'exalted mountain'; a sacred mountain in west Shantung province, the birthplace of Confucius. It is mentioned several times in the *Pisan Cantos* and was Pound's name for a cone-shaped mountain in a range stretching north-east from Pisa (cf. the illustration in Kenner, *Pound Era*, 473).

l. 129 Carrara: the city in Tuscany, famous for its marble quarries.

l. 131 Kuanon: Chinese Kuan-yin (Japanese Kwannon), the Chinese goddess of mercy, worshipped for her infinite compassion and charity. Mentioned several times in the *Pisan Cantos*.

l. 132: the saints Linus, Pope ?67–76, Cletus (or Anacletus), Pope ?76–88 and Clement I, Pope ?88–?97.

l. 134 scarab: a beetle or beetle-shaped gem: Pound's metaphor therefore for the priest's appearance when robed and officiating.

ll. 137–9: cf. *The Unwobbling Pivot*, XXVI, 10:

> As silky light, King Wen's virtue
> Coming down with the sunlight,
> what purity!
>
> He looks in his heart
> And does.
>
> – Shi King, IV, 1, 2, 1.

Here the sense is: In this way was Wen perfect.

The *unmixed* functions [in time and in space] without bourne.

This unmixed is the tensile light, the
Immaculata. There is no end
to its action.

(*Confucius*, 187)

In *The Cantos* (Faber 1964 edn.) lines 137–9 are accompanied on the right by the ideogram 明 (Ming[2]) which Pound elsewhere glosses as 'The sun and moon, the total light process, the radiation, reception and reflection of light; hence, the intelligence. Bright, brightness, shining. Refer to Scotus Erigena, Grosseteste and the notes on light in my *Cavalcanti*' (*Confucius*, 20). *Cantos* (1975) substitute 顯 (hsien[3]), meaning 'manifest'.

l. 137 tensile: stretched, extended, sustaining tension. Cf. later in this Canto 'light tensile immaculata' (455/429).

l. 138 virtù: (Ital.) 'virtue', 'potency'. Cf. Canto XXXVI, line 12, and the *Ta Hsio* (*The Great Digest*), x, 7, where Pound translates, 'The *virtu*, i.e., this self-knowledge [looking straight into the heart and acting thence] is the root' (*Confucius*, 73).

l. 139 "*sunt lumina*": (Lat.) 'are lights', excerpted from the phrase 'omnia quae sunt lumina sunt' ('everything that exists is light') from the work *De Divisione Naturae* by the medieval theologian and philosopher of light Johannes Scotus Erigena. (Cf. Cantos XXXVI, 185/179, and LXXXIII, 563/528.) Pound's quotation is repeated later in this Canto (456, 457/429, 430).

l. 140 Shun: cf. note on lines 143–5.

ll. 143–5: the Chinese emperors Yao (2357–2259 B.C.), Shun (i.e. Chun), his chosen successor (2255–2205 B.C.), and Yu (or Yü) (2205–2197 B.C.), who succeeded Chun in place of his son, are esteemed as ideal emperors. Of many references in the 'Chinese History Cantos' cf. Canto LIII, notes on lines 27, 30, 40. Cf. also in this Canto (467, 469/440, 442).

l. 143 paraclete: advocate or intercessor, an epithet of the Holy Spirit. Cf. the earlier 'paraclete or the verbum perfectum: sinceritas' (453/427).

l. 145: Emperor Yü was noted for having controlled the flood waters of the Yellow River.

* * *

l. 163: (Lat.) 'A time to be silent, a time to speak'. The phrase 'Tempus loquendi, Tempus tacendi' (with the terms reversed) was the motto of Sigismondo Malatesta and was inscribed by him on the tomb of Isotta degli Atti in the Tempio. It appears in this form at the opening of Canto XXXI. The source is Ecclesiastes 3: 7.

l. 166 dixit: (Lat.) 'said'.

Lenin: Vladimir Ilich Ulyanov Lenin (1870–1924), the Soviet revolutionary leader. Pound seems to allude to the remarks by the English economist S. G. Hobson quoted by Lenin in his 'Imperialism, the Highest Stage of Capitalism' (1917) on the growth of the 'rentier' or 'usurer' state: 'The exportation of capital, one of the most essential economic bases of imperialism, still further isolates this *rentier* stratum from production, and sets the seal of parasitism on the whole country living on the exploitation of labour of several overseas countries and colonies' (quoted by Pound, 'What is money for?', *SPr*, 269).

l. 170 23rd year of the effort: i.e. of the Fascist regime established in 1922.

l. 171 Till: St. Louis Till, an American soldier executed at Pisa.

l. 172 Cholkis: perhaps Colchis, the land of the golden fleece, ruled by Aeetes.

ll. 174–6: repeated Cantos LXXVI (483/454–5), LXXVII (503/473).

l. 174 Snag: the nickname of a fellow prisoner at Pisa.

* * *

l. 218: this description occurs earlier in association with Odysseus (*Cantos*, 456, 457/430).

l. 219 hamadryas: (Lat.) 'hamadryad', a tree nymph.

l. 220 Vai soli: (Lat.) 'woe to the lonely', an expression in Jules Laforgue's poems 'Pierrots' (*L'Imitation de Notre-Dame La Lune*, 1886) and 'Dimanche' (*Derniers Vers*, 1890); cf. Pound's translation of the first of these poems (*CSP*, 264). The phrase derives from Ecclesiastes 4: 10.

l. 224 ʿΗΛΙΟΝ ΠΕΡΙ ʿΗΛΙΟΝ: (Gk.) 'the sun around the sun'.

l. 226 Lucina: 'the goddess who brings to light', sometimes associated with the Roman goddess Juno in her function as goddess of childbirth; 'tides' referring to the female menstrual cycle.

l. 227: cf. Canto LXXX, 'I have been hard as youth sixty years' (548/513).

l. 229 leopard: associated with Dionysus.

* * *

l. 265 color di luce: (Ital.) 'colour of light'.

ll. 267–78: cf. the lament for those lost in World War I in *Hugh Selwyn Mauberley* IV, V and Canto XVI (74–6/70–2), and the memory of the poet Joe Angold killed in World War II in Canto LXXXIV (572/537).

l. 267: from Pound's earlier translation of 'The Seafarer' (l. 95).

l. 268 companions: as well as the 'gone companions' of 'The Seafarer', Pound looks back to Tiresias' prophecy to Odysseus, that he shall ' "Lose all companions" ' (Canto I, l. 67).

l. 269 Fordie: Ford Madox Ford (Hueffer) (1873–1939), the English novelist, poet, critic and editor of *The English Review*. Ford was a personal friend of Pound's and consistently praised by him for his 'insistence upon clarity and precision' (*LE*, 377). The 'giants' are perhaps 'literary giants' assembled in Ford's *The March of Literature* (1939). Arthur Mizener, Ford's biographer, writes, 'The risk for Ford was always that he would indulge his fancy too far and turn his imagined giants into evidently imaginary ones or that his vanity would lead him to spoil his story with self-pity and self-congratulation' (*The Saddest Story*, 1971, 207).

l. 270 William: the poet William Butler Yeats (1865–1939), a friend and direct influence on Pound's early poetry. Cf. the comparison Pound makes between Ford and Yeats, Canto LXXXII (560/525) and the recollection of Yeats, Canto LXXXIII (569–70/533–4).

l. 271 Jim: the novelist James Joyce (1881–1941) whose novels, *A Portrait of the Artist as a Young Man* and *Ulysses*, Pound helped publish. The two met very rarely, first when Joyce visited Pound at Sirmione 8–10 June 1920. Pound's essays on Joyce are included in *Pound/Joyce*, ed. Forrest Read (1967).

l. 274 Plarr: Victor Gustav Plarr (1863–1929), poet, member of the Rhymers' Club and Librarian of the Royal College of Surgeons. He was amongst Pound's early acquaintances in London and appears as M. Verog in the ' "Siena Mi Fe' " ' section of *Hugh Selwyn Mauberley*. Pound referred to Plarr and 'another man' in 'The Wisdom of Poetry' (1912) as having 'developed the functions of a certain obscure sort of equation, for no cause save their own pleasure in the work. The applied science of their day had no use for the deductions, a few sheets of paper covered with arbitrary symbols – without which we should have no wireless telegraph' (*SPr*, 331–2).

l. 275 Jepson: Edgar Jepson (1863–1938), novelist. Iris Barry recalled that Pound, Edmund Dulac and Jepson were 'passionately fond of jade', and that Jepson, who was a collector, used to hand pieces of it round the table at the weekly gatherings held in the Tour Eiffel restaurant in Soho in 1917–18 ('The Ezra Pound Period', *Bookman*, October 1931, 167). Jepson apparently also exchanged a carved horse for a piece of Chinese jade Dorothy Pound had bought in 1914 with a wedding cheque, but grown tired of (Stock, *Life*, 193–4).

l. 276 Maurie: Maurice Hewlett (1861–1923). Amongst his historical novels were *The Life and Death of Richard Yea and Nay* (1900) and *The Queen's Quair* (1904). Cf. Canto LXXX where Pound records his stay with Hewlett at Salisbury, Christmas 1911 (ll. 741–9).

l. 277 Newbolt: Sir Henry John Newbolt (1862–1938), the English poet. Pound visited Newbolt with Hewlett, Christmas 1911. In 1939 in his obituary on Ford Madox Ford, he listed Newbolt as one of 'the arthritic milieu that held control of the respected British critical circles' (*SPr*, 432).

l. 280 Kokka: Urquell Kokka, cited by Pound as a source of information on high society in *Guide to Kulchur*, where he gives the item of etiquette repeated here. Urquell was, says Pound, 'an ex-diplomat, ex-imperial staff officer, reduced along with dukes k.t.l. to flats, restaurants and intercourse with untitled humanity' (p. 83). Cf. also the following lines in this Canto (460/433).

* * *

l. 317 Mr. Edwards: an inmate of the D.T.C., Pisa.

l. 319 Baluba: a tribe in the south-west Belgian Congo investigated by Leo Frobenius. Cf. Canto XXXVIII, note on lines 73–5.

ll. 319–20 "doan . . . table": the table was made, against regulations, out of an old packing case for Pound by a Negro prisoner at Pisa, named Benin. Cf. Cantos LXXIX (517/485), LXXXI (554/519).

THE CANTOS

l. 321 methenamine: hexamethylene tetramine. Pound alludes presumably to his own physical distress in the D.T.C., Pisa.

l. 328 nient' altro: (Ital.) 'nothing else'.

l. 331: the source is, as Pound indicates, Leviticus 19: 35. Cf. later in this Canto (467/440) and Canto LXXVI (482/454).

l. 335: the verse from Thessalonians is, 'And that ye study to be quiet, and to do your own business, and to work with your own hands, as we commanded you'.

l. 334 300 years culture: cf. Canto XCI, 'for 300 years,/ and now sunken' (ll. 9–10).

l. 339 constitution: The U.S. Constitution. In Canto LXXIX, Pound writes 'God bless the Constitution/ and *save* it' (518/486)

Dioce: cf. note on line 11.

ll. 341, 344–5: Pound alludes to the statue of Venus (Gk. Aphrodite) at the seaport of Terracina, in Latium, central Italy. 'Given the material means', he said, 'I would replace the statue of Venus on the cliffs of Terracina' (*SPr*, 53); cf. Cantos XVII, line 91; XXXIX (203/195); XCI, note on lines 16–17; CVI (779/754), and also the refrain 'aram vult nemus' ('the grove needs an altar') in this Canto (473/446).

l. 341 Zephyr: in Greek mythology, the west wind.

l. 343 Anchises: the lover of Aphrodite and father by her of Aeneas (founder of Rome); cf. Canto LXXVI, line 144.

ll. 346–7: cf. later in this Canto, 'By no means an orderly Dantescan rising/ but as the winds veer . . . as the winds veer in periplum' (471/443), and the reference to Zephyrus and Apeliota, line 831. For 'process' cf. note on line 13.

l. 348 Pleiades: a group of stars in the constellation Taurus and in Greek mythology, the seven daughters of Atlas. Their rising marked the beginning of summer and their setting the beginning of winter. Cf. Canto XLVII, 'When the Pleiades go down to their rest,/ Begin thy plowing', derived from Hesiod (ll. 48–9).

l. 349 Kuanon: cf. note on line 131.

this stone bringeth sleep: cf. earlier in this canto, ' "of sapphire, for this stone giveth sleep" ' (452/426), and Canto LXXVI,

316

'Her bed-posts are of sapphire/ for this stone giveth sleep' (ll. 235–6). Pound's source is perhaps partly in Dante's *Purgatorio*, I, ll. 13–18, 'The sweet color of oriental sapphire . . . to mine eyes restored delight, as soon as I issued forth from the dead air, which had afflicted eyes and heart' (*SR*, 137). More probably the allusion is to the bed studded with sapphires to preserve chastity listed among the items in the medieval Christian Utopia advertised as established in Abyssinia by the legendary Christian ruler, Prester John.

* * *

ll. 390–1: a double allusion to the city of Dioce perhaps (cf. l. 11n.) and to François Villon's line 'Paradis peint où sont harpes et luths' (*Oeuvres*, 61) incorporated into Canto XLV (ll. 5–6).

l. 393 magna NUX animae: (Lat.) 'the great' (Gk.) 'night' (Lat.) 'of the soul', an echo of St. John of the Cross's *Dark Night of the Soul*, though Pound's use of the Greek 'nux' would seem to distinguish his experience from this entirely Christian work. Cf. lines 431, 449–50.

Barabbas: the criminal released at the will of the crowd in Jerusalem when presented with the choice of his own or Jesus Christ's crucifixion.

* * *

l. 431 nox animae magna: (Lat.) 'the soul's great night'.

Taishan: Mt. T'ai Shan. Cf. note on line 128.

l. 432 the a.h.: the arse hole.

l. 434 morticians' daughters: cf. the mention of the funeral director's daughters whose 'conduct caused comment', Canto XXIX (147/142).

ll. 435–43: these precepts are all derived from the Confucian *Analects*, Bk. 1 (*Confucius*, 195).

ll. 435–9: cf. *The Analects*, Bk. 1, i.

ll. 440–1: cf. *The Analects*, Bk. 1, ii. An important Confucian principle. Cf. also Canto XIII, line 53.

l. 442: cf. *The Analects*, Bk. 1, iii.

l. 443: cf. *The Analects*, Bk. 1, v.

ll. 445–6: (Ital.) 'And in the corner, Cunizza/ and the other [woman]: "I am the moon." ' Reiterated Canto LXXVI (480–1/452–3).

l. 445 Cunizza: Cunizza da Romano, wife of Ricciardo da San Bonifazzio, noted for her ardour and passion, her affair with the Provençal poet Sordello between 1227 and 1229 and for freeing her slaves by a deed of manumission in 1265. (Cf. Cantos VI, 26–7/22–3; XXIX, 146–7/141–2.) Dante places Cunizza in the third heaven of Venus (*Paradiso*, IX).

l. 446 "Io son' la Luna": repeated in this Canto (471/443) and Canto LXXX (534/500).

l. 449: Νύξ *animae* (Gk.) 'night' (Lat.) 'of the soul'. Cf. note on line 393, line 431.

l. 450 San Juan: St. John of the Cross (Juan de Yepis y Alvarez) (1542–91), the Spanish mystic.

l. 451 ad posteros: (Lat.) 'for posterity'.

* * *

l. 655: cf. Canto XXX, 'Time is the evil. Evil (l. 25).

l. 656 ῥοδοδάκτυλος: (Gk.) 'rosy-fingered', the recurrent epithet in Homer for the dawn, but in Sappho used of the moon (Barnstone, 141; *Oxford Book of Greek Verse*, 145). The Sapphic fragment in which the word occurs formed the basis of Pound's ''Ιμέρρω' in *Lustra*, and of lines incorporated into Canto V (21/17–18). It is repeated in Canto LXXX, line 619.

ll. 657–60 as . . . profile: cf. the photograph of Olga Rudge in profile, silhouetted against a window and holding a violin, titled 'cameo and fiddle 1928' in Mary de Rachewiltz's *Discretions* (1971).

l. 659 le contre-jour: (Fr.) 'the false light'.

l. 660: Pound recalls the lines 'In profile . . ./ To forge Achaia' from MAUBERLEY (1920) I in *Hugh Selwyn Mauberley*. The allusion is to the Veronese painter and medallist Pisanello (Antonio Pesano) (?1379–1455), employed by Sigismondo Malatesta on the Tempio. Cf. also lines 755–6.

Achaia: the name of two regions in Greece, one to the north and the other along the southern shore of the Corinthian gulf. Later the name was given to the Roman province, established by Augustus, occupying most of Greece.

l. 662: (Ital.) 'Venus, (Lat.) Cythera "or Rhodes" '.

Cytherea: an island off the south coast of Laconia, where Aphrodite was said to have landed after her birth from the sea and therefore a title of the goddess herself. Rhodes is the most easterly of the islands in the Aegean and the site of the temple of Pallas Athene at Lindos.

l. 663: (Ital.) 'Ligurian wind, come'. Liguria is the region along the north-west coast of Italy from Tuscany to France.

l. 664 Mr. Beardsley: Aubrey Vincent Beardsley (1872–1898), the illustrator and author whose grotesques and depiction of inner corruption made him a representative figure of the decadent Nineties. The statement attributed to Beardsley is repeated in the immediately following lines and elaborated in Canto LXXX (ll. 611–17).

*   *   *

ll. 748–9: cf. the related 'now in the mind indestructible' (*Cantos*, 470/442), Cavalcanti's phrase 'dove sta memoria' in 'Donna mi priegha' (*Tr*, 134), and Cantos XXXVI, note on line 16; LXXVI, lines 157–60; LXXXI, line 134.

l. 750: (Ital.) 'in a prepared place' from Cavalcanti's 'Donna mi priegha' (*Tr*, 138).

l. 751 Arachne: in Greek mythology a girl who challenged the goddess Athene to a weaving contest. For her impertinence and for having depicted the loves of the gods in her web, she was changed into a spider.

mi porta fortuna: (Ital.) 'brings me good luck'. The line is repeated in Canto LXXVI (490/461).

l. 752 εἰκονες: (Gk.) 'pictures', 'images'.

l. 753 Trastevere: a district in Rome on the opposite shore of the Tiber to the main city.

ll. 755–6: cf. note on line 660.

*   *   *

ll. 824–6: Pound indicates a debt to the French poet Paul Verlaine (1844–96), probably to the close of his poem 'Clair de Lune' in *Fêtes Galantes* (1869), 'Et sangloter d'extase les jets d'eau,/ les grands jets d'eau sveltes parmi les marbres' ('And the fountains sob with ecstasy, the tall, slender fountains among the statues'). Cf. also 'The main thing is to illumine the root of the process, a fountain of clear water descending from heaven immutable' (*Confucius*, 99).

l. 824 crystal: amongst other references, cf. Canto LXXVI, line 147, and Canto XCI, note on line 26.

l. 826 diamond clearness: an echo of 'the radiant world where one thought cuts through another with clean edge' (*LE*, 154).

l. 827 Taishan: Mt. Taishan. Cf. note on line 128.

ll. 829–30: cf. the exit from hell in Cantos XV, XVI (70–73/ 66–69).

l. 831: respectively the west and east winds. Cf. line 341, note on lines 346–7.

l. 832 liquid: cf. Canto IV, 'Thus the light rains, thus pours, *e lo soleills plovil*/ The liquid and rushing crystal' (19/15).

l. 834 nec accidens est: (Lat.) 'it is not an attribute'.

l. 836 est agens: (Lat.) 'it is an agent'.

ll. 837–9: Pound's lines 837–8 echo Ben Jonson's 'Have you seen but a bright lily grow . . ./ Or swan's down ever?' from his 'Her Triumph' in *A Celebration of Charis: in Ten Lyric Pieces* (1624). Pound includes the poem in *Confucius to Cummings* (p. 173). Cf. also Cantos LXXXI, note on line 108, and CX, line 7.

The image of the rose pattern made in iron filings by the action of a magnet recurs in the essay 'Medievalism' (*LE*, 154) and in *Guide to Kulchur* where Pound writes,

> The *forma*, the immortal *concetto*, the concept, the dynamic form which is like the rose pattern driven into the dead iron filings by the magnet, not by material contact with the magnet itself, but separate from the magnet. Cut off by the layer of glass, the dust and filings rise and spring into order. Thus the *forma*, the concept rises from death.
>
> (p. 152)

Pound's rose also recalls here Dante's symbol of the divine and radiant snow-white rose along whose petals are ranked the saints and the blessed (*Paradiso*, XXX).

l. 840 Lethe: the river in Hades whose waters induce forgetfulness of this life and reincarnation. The line is repeated in Canto LXXVII (501/472). Pound is perhaps remembering Dante's passing over Lethe (*Purgatorio*, XXXI).

from Canto LXXVI

l. 136: (Ital.) 'the altar on the rostrum'.

l. 140 Mozart: Wolfgang Amadeus Mozart (1756–91), the German composer. Pound refers elsewhere to the Mozart festival at Salzburg (Cantos LXXVIII, 511/480; LXXIX, 516/484). Cf. also Canto CXV, line 7.

prise: (Fr.) 'a taking hold', 'purchase'.

ll. 141–3 Ponce . . . de Leon: Juan Ponce de Leon (?1460–1521), who discovered Florida on Easter Sunday 1513 in his search for the fountain of youth.

l. 143 alla fuente florida: (Ital.) 'to the' (Sp.) 'flowery fountain'.

l. 144 Anchises: cf. Canto LXXIV, note on line 343.

her: i.e. Aphrodite.

l. 146 Cythera potens: (Lat.) 'powerful Cythera', i.e. Aphrodite. Κύθηρα δεινά: (Gk.) 'dread (or fearful) Cythera'. Also at Canto LXXX, line 621, and cf. Canto LXXIX, line 271.

ll. 147 8: cf. the later 'but the crystal can be weighed in the hand' (l. 218).

l. 147 crystal: amongst other references cf. in the present Canto, line 152, Canto LXXIV, line 824, and Canto XCI, note on line 26.

l. 151 Κόρη, Δηλιά δεινά: (Gk.) Kore ('daughter', i.e. Persephone, daughter of Demeter), 'dread Delia' (i.e. Artemis, goddess of Delos); cf. Canto LXXIX, line 273.

et libidinis expers: (Lat.) 'to whom passion is unknown' (repeated Canto XCI, line 23). The reference is to Artemis—Diana in contrast to the passion of 'Cythera potens' (l. 146).

l. 156: (Gk.) 'to suffer much', from the *Odyssey*, Bk. I, line 4.

ll. 157–60: cf. Canto LXXIV, note on lines 748–9, and Canto LXXXI, line 134.

ll. 157–8: repeated Canto LXXVII (495/466).

l. 160: (Ital.) 'where one remembers', from Cavalcanti's 'Donna mi priegha' (*Tr*, 134); cf. Canto XXXVI, note on line 16.

l. 162 J. Adams: John Adams (1735–1826), second President of the United States (1797–1801), and the subject of Cantos LXII–LXXI. Adams's remark is given more fully in Canto LXXIV, 'every bank of discount is downright iniquity/ robbing the public for private individual's gain' (464/437), itself repeated from Canto LXXI (438/416). The source is a statement made by Adams to Benjamin Rush dated 28 August 1811 (*The Works of John Adams*, ed. Charles Francis Adams, 1850–56, vol. IX, 638).

l. 166 guard: at the D.T.C., Pisa.

l. 167 Sergeant XL: Sergeant Lauterback, Disciplinary Sergeant, D.T.C.

l. 170: cf. Canto XXV, line 97, 'lay there, the long soft grass'.

l. 175: (Lat.) 'and domesticated wild animals'.

l. 176 a destra: (Ital.) 'to the right'.

ll. 180–1: cf. lines 216–17.

l. 180 atasal: from the Mohammedan physician and philosopher Avicenna, meaning 'conjunction or contiguity with God' as distinct from the full hypostatic union. Also at line 217.

l. 181 nec personae: (Lat.) 'nor masks'.

l. 182 hypostasis: 'substance' (as opposed to attributes or 'accidents'), or 'person', but more especially 'the union of the human and divine'.

Dione: in Greek mythology probably an earth or sky goddess, sometimes represented as the consort of Zeus. In Homer she is the mother of Aphrodite (cf. Canto XLVII, note on lines 26–9).

l. 184 Helia: possibly 'Delia' is meant; cf. note on line 151.

l. 185 Κύπρις (Gk.) Cypris, i.e. Aphrodite, who was thought in one version of her legend to have landed from the sea at Paphos, Cyprus.

* * *

l. 203 Bracken: Brendan Bracken (1901–58), British publisher and politician, Minister of Information 1941–5.

l. 208 ego scriptor: (Lat.), 'I, the writer'.

* * *

l. 216 spiriti questi?: (Ital.) 'ghosts these?'

personae?: (Lat.) 'masks?'

l. 219 Thetis: in Greek mythology, a sea nymph, wife of Perseus and mother of Achilles.

l. 220 Maya: in Greek mythology, Maia, mother of Hermes.

'Ἀφροδίτη: (Gk.) Aphrodite.

l. 223 Zoagli: a town south of Rapallo on the Ligurian coast, north-west Italy.

l. 228 οἱ βάρβαροι: (Gk.) 'the barbarians', also at line 237.

l. 229 Sigismundo's Temple: the Tempio Malatestiano built in Rimini by Sigismondo Malatesta between 1446 and 1455. Amongst other references, cf. Canto IX, note on line 56.

l. 230 Divae Ixottae: (Ital.) 'divine Isotta', i.e. Isotta degli Atti (?1430–?1475), third wife of Sigismondo Malatesta, to whom he built the Tempio. Amongst other references, cf. Canto IX, lines 147, 237–42.

l. 234 La Cara: amo: (Ital.) 'the dear one'; (Lat.) 'I love'.

ll. 235–6: cf. Canto LXXIV, note on line 349.

l. 238 pervenche: (Fr.) 'periwinkle'.

l. 240: (Lat.) 'and the consequences'.

l. 241: (Fr.) 'Paradise is not artificial', a riposte to the French poet Charles Baudelaire's *Les Paradis artificiels*, a book on the hallucinatory effects of drugs. Also at line 248 and several times in the *Pisan Cantos*.

l. 242 States of mind: 'A god', said Pound, 'is an eternal state of mind' (*SPr*, 47)

l. 243 δακρύων: (Gk.) 'weeping'. Cf. later in this Canto (491/462).

l. 244 L. P.: 'Le Paradis'.

gli onesti: (Ital.) 'the honest ones'.

ll. 245–6 J'ai . . . assez: (Fr.) 'I had pity for others/ probably not enough', repeated Canto XCIII, lines 166–7. Cf. The 'Compleynt agaynst Pity' in Canto XXX, in Canto LXXX the lines 'Tard, très tard je t'ai connue, la Tristesse,/ I have been hard as youth sixty years' (548/513), and Canto XCIV, 'pity, yes, for the infected,/ but maintain antisepsis,/ let the light pour' (668/635).

l. 249: (Fr.) 'neither is hell'.

l. 250 Eurus: the east or south-east wind.

l. 251 la pastorella dei suini: (Ital.) 'the little shepherdess of the hogs'.

l. 252 benecomata dea: (Lat.) 'the fair-coiffed goddess'. The allusion here as at line 251 is probably to Circe, known for her fair hair, and who changed Odysseus' crew into swine (*Odyssey*, Bk. X).

*   *   *

ll. 335–6: cf. the close of Canto LXXVIII, 'there/ are/ no/ righteous/ wars' (515/483).

from **Canto LXXIX**

l. 165 *Old Ez*: Pound, of himself.

l. 166 Eos: the Greek goddess of dawn. Perhaps Pound intends 'Phosphor', the name of Venus as the morning star.

Hesperus: the evening star, i.e. Venus. Also at line 270. Hesperus and the dawn are linked in Sappho's 'Ode to Hesperus' ('Hesperos, you bring home all the bright dawn disperses,/ bring home the sheep,/ bring home the goat, bring the child home to its mother', Barnstone, 251; *Oxford Book of Greek Verse*, 146). Pound refers to this poem in passing in Canto V (21/17).

l. 167 Lynx: here and in the several references in the 'Lynx Song' which follows, an animal sacred to Dionysus.

Silenus: a satyr, and usually drunken companion to Dionysus.

Casey: perhaps the Corporal Casey at the D.T.C., Pisa, mentioned in Canto LXXIV (465/438).

l. 168 bassarids: Dionysian maenads. Also at lines 222, 238.

l. 172 Maelids: here and later in this Canto, fruit tree nymphs. Cf. 'The Spring' (l. 2n.).

l. 174 the cossack: cf. the earlier lines in this Canto, 'So they said to Lidya: no, your body-guard is not the/ town executioner/ the executioner is not here for the moment/ the fellow who rides beside your coachman/ is just a cossak who executes . . .' (520/488).

ll. 175–6 Salazar, Scott, Dawley . . . Polk, Tyler . . . Calhoun: inmates with Pound at the D.T.C., Pisa.

l. 176 half the presidents: Cf. Canto LXXIV 'and all the presidents/ Washington Adams Monroe Polk Tyler' (464/436). John Tyler and James Knox Polk were the tenth and eleventh Presidents of the United States.

l. 177 Calhoun: John Caldwell Calhoun (1782–1850), Vice-President of the United States 1825–32, a supporter of slavery and the Southern cause. Cf. Cantos XXXIV (172–5/168–170), XXXVII (187/181).

l. 183 Priapus: a Greek god of fertility, gardens and herds, said to be the son of Aphrodite and Dionysus. Also at line 260.

Ἴακχος: (Gk.) Iacchus, a mystic name for Dionysus under which he was celebrated, with Demeter and Persephone, in the Eleusinian mysteries.

Io!: (Gk.) an exclamation used in invoking the gods.

Κύθηρα: (Gk.) Cythera, i.e. the goddess of love, named 'Cythera' from her association with the island off the south coast of Laconia where she is said to have landed from the sea. Also at lines 224, 232, 271, 277.

l. 191 Sweetland: inmate at the D.T.C., Pisa.

l. 192 ἐλέησον   Kyrie eleison: (Gk. 'have mercy   Lord have mercy' (from the Orthodox liturgy and the Roman mass).

l. 198 Astafieva: Serafima Astafieva (1876–1934), a Russian dancer with the Maryinsky Theatre and Diaghilev company which visited London in 1911, and who later opened a ballet school in London. Pound introduced her to T. S. Eliot and she appears as 'Grishkin' in his poem 'Whispers of Immortality'; cf. Canto LXXVII, 'or Grishkin's photo refound years after/

with the feeling that Mr Eliot may have/ missed something, after all, in composing his vignette' (495/466), and earlier in this Canto (516/484).

conserved the tradition: perhaps indebted to Remy de Gourmont's 'Des femmes conservatrices des traditions milésiennes'; cf. *Hugh Selwyn Mauberley* XI (l. 1n.).

l. 199 Byzance: Byzantium, the ancient city on the Bosphorus (modern Istanbul).

l. 200 Manitou: Algonquin Indian name for the creative power in all things.

l. 201 phylloxera: 'phylloxera vastatrix' or vine-pest, destructive of the grape vine (associated with Dionysus).

l. 202 Ἴακχε . . . Χαῖρε: (Gk.) 'Iacchos, Iacchos, hail'; cf. note on line 183.

AOI: a common cry in the early French epic, *Le Chanson de Roland*.

l. 203: an allusion to the myth of Persephone who, carried off by Hades to the underworld, ate some pomegranate seeds (six, seven or eight seeds according to different versions) and had therefore to spend six months of the year in Hades and six on earth. Cf. the references to pomegranate at lines 212, 216–17, 228.

l. 205 Κόρη: (Gk.) Kore ('daughter'), i.e. Persephone, daughter of the goddess Demeter.

six seeds: the pomegranate seeds eaten by Persephone (cf. note on line 203).

l. 208 Demeter: Greek fertility goddess, especially of corn and agriculture.

l. 210 Pomona: Roman goddess of fruit trees.

l. 216 Melagrana: (Ital.) 'pomegranate'. Also at line 248.

l. 219 Heliads: In Greek mythology, daughters of Helios, the sun god, who were changed into poplar trees while mourning for their brother Phaethon, their tears hardening into amber. Also at line 252.

l. 223 crotale: (Ital.) 'rattlesnakes'; or perhaps Pound draws on the Gk. κρόταλον' ('a rattle'). Also at line 232.

l. 227 Red? white?: anticipates Pound's reference to the English rose in Canto LXXX, 'and every rose,/ Blood-red, blanch-white' (ll. 756–7). The rose is also sacred to Aphrodite.

l. 231 γλαυκῶπις: (Gk.) 'glaukopis' ('with grey-blue gleaming eyes'), an epithet of the goddess Pallas Athene, associated with the owl and olive (cf. Canto XX, note on lines 172–4).

l. 232 Kuthera: Cythera, i.e. Aphrodite; cf. note on line 183.

l. 237 ἰχώρ (Gk.) 'ichor', the juice (as distinct from blood) supposed to flow in the veins of the gods.

ll. 251–7: pausing at this passage in conversation with Hugh Kenner, Dorothy Pound said, 'That chorus was for me. . . . He said the lynx chorus was for me' ('D.P. Remembered', *Paideuma*, II, no. 3, 491).

l. 251 kalicanthus: prickly saltwort.

l. 260 Faunus: the Roman god of crops and herds identified with the Greek Pan.

l. 261 Graces: in Greek mythology generally three goddesses of vegetation who attend on a greater goddess.

'Ἀφροδίτην: (Gk.) Aphrodite; cf. note on line 183.

l. 265 "Ηλιος: (Gk.) Helios, the sun or sun god. Also at line 281.

l. 269 This goddess: Aphrodite, according to legend born of the foam (Gk. 'aphros').

l. 271: (Gk.) 'you are fearful, Cythera'. Cf. note on line 183 and Canto LXXVI (l. 146).

l. 273: (Gk.) 'Kore' ('daughter', i.e. Persephone) 'and Delia' (i.e. Artemis) 'and Maia' (the mother of Hermes). Cf. Canto LXXVI (ll. 151, 220n.).

l. 274: 'Trino as preludio' ('threefold [in Trinity] as prelude').

l. 275 Κύπρις Ἀφροδίτη: Cypris Aphrodite. Cf. Canto LXXVI (l. 185n.).

l. 277: (Gk.) Cythera. Cf. note on line 183.

ll. 278–80: (Lat.) 'the grove needs an altar'.

l. 281 Hermes: the Greek god of good fortune, the patron of thieves and merchants, and principally, the messenger of the gods.

Cimbica: Pound's invention. Forrest Read suggests 'stinginess'

('The Pattern of the *Pisan Cantos*', *Sewanee Review*, Summer 1957, 412).
Helios: the Greek sun god.

from **Canto LXXX**

l. 582 Nancy: possibly Nancy Cunard (1896–1965), American poet and editor of the *Negro Anthology* to which Pound contributed a note on Frobenius in 1934, and of *Authors Take Sides on the Spanish War* (1937), including Pound's reply under the category 'Neutral?'. A 'Nancy' is mentioned earlier in this Canto (528/495).
l. 583 vair: (Prov.) 'of varied colour, speckled, grey'.
cisclatons: (Prov.) a type of gown.
l. 584: cf. Canto XXIX, 'So Arnaut turned there/ Above him the wave pattern cut in the stone' (150/145), and also Canto CX (l. 2).
l. 585 Excideuil: a village in the modern Dordogne Departement, south-west France, visited by Pound and T. S. Eliot in mid-August 1919. Cf. 'Provincia Deserta' (CSP, 132).
l. 586 Mt. Segur: Montségur, the site of a fortress in the far south of France, near Perpignan, visited by Ezra and Dorothy Pound in the summer of 1919. Cf. Canto LXXIX (480/452) and the later reference in the present Canto where Pound supposes it to have been a solar temple 'sacred to Helios' (610/574).
city of Dioce: Ecbatana, founded by Deïoces, first king of the Medes. Cf. Canto LXXIV (l. 11n.).
l. 587: (Fr.) 'that every month we have a new moon'.
l. 588 Herbiet: Herbiet Christian, French translator of Pound's 'Mœurs Contemporains' (July 1921).
l. 590 Fritz: Fritz-René Vanderpyl (b. 1876), Dutch art critic who lived at 13 rue Gay-Lussac, Paris and whose apartment had a stone life mask on the balcony. Pound and he shared the view that the statue of Blanche de Castille in the nearby Luxembourg Gardens was like a 'Beer-bottle on the statue's pediment' (Canto VII, 29/25).

l. 592 Orage: Alfred Richard Orage (1875–1934), a supporter of Social Credit and editor of the *New Age* and *New English Weekly* to which Pound was a regular contributor. Cf. Pound's 'Obituary: A. R. Orage' and 'In the Wounds' (*SPr*, 407–21).

Fordie: Ford Madox Ford. Cf. Canto LXXIV (l. 269n.).

Crevel: René Crevel (1900–35), French author. Pound praised his novel *Les Pieds dans le plat* (*SL*, 249; *SPr*, 295) and wrote an article on him for the *Criterion* (January 1939).

l. 593: (Sp.) 'out of my solitude let them come', adapted from the line 'De mis soledades vengo' ('From my solitudes return I') from a poem by Lope de Vega quoted by Pound in *The Spirit of Romance* (p. 208).

l. 594 Rossetti: Dante Gabriel Rossetti (1828–82), Pre-Raphaelite poet and painter who found a remaindered copy of Edward FitzGerald's *Rubáiyát of Omar Khayyám*; cf. *Hugh Selwyn Mauberley*, 'Yeux Glauques' (l. 15).

l. 596 Cythera: Aphrodite, who took this title from the island where she was supposed to have landed after her birth from the sea.

in the moon's barge: also at line 620.

l. 600 Münch: Gerhardt Münch, a pianist who gave concerts at Rapallo and made the violin transcription of Clément Janequin's bird-song chorale which Pound gives as the substance of Canto LXXV (cf. *GK*, 151–3, 250–2).

Bach: Johann Sebastian Bach (1685–1750), the German composer.

l. 601 Spewcini: Giacomo Puccini (1858–1924), the Italian composer of whom Pound wrote, 'and to give hell its due, Puccini knows how to write for the bawlers. I mean he *knows* how. If that's what you like, be damned to you for liking it, but I take off my hat (along with your own beastly bowler) to the artifex' (*GK*, 155).

l. 605 man seht: (Ger.) 'man sieht' ('one sees').

ll. 609–10 Les hommes . . . étrange/ . . . de la beauté: (Fr.) 'Men have I don't know what strange fear/ . . . of beauty.' Pound makes this observation in *Guide to Kulchur* in relation to an incident when a British colonel shrank 'from a sheet of paper carrying my 8 Volitionist questions as if it had been an asp or a red-hot iron', adding to the French 'and that ain't the 'arf ov it dearie' (p. 250).

l. 610 Monsieur Whoosis: Pound's invention, after the manner of 'Mr. Whatsisname'.

l. 611: cf. Canto LXXIV (l. 664n.) Yeats is the poet William Butler Yeats (1865–1939). Aubrey Beardsley (1872–98), the author and illustrator, died of tuberculosis.

l. 613 Burne-Jones: Sir Edward Burne-Jones (1833–98), the painter and member of the Pre-Raphaelite Brotherhood, who was an influence on the early work of Aubrey Beardsley; cf. *Hugh Selwyn Mauberley*, 'Yeux Glauques'.

l. 618 'I am the torch . . . she saith': from the poem 'Modern Beauty' by Arthur Symons (1865–1945).

l. 619 ῥοδοδάκτυλος Ἠώς: (Gk.) 'rosy-fingered Eos' (goddess of dawn). Cf. Canto LXXIV (l. 656n.).

ll. 620–1: cf. Canto LXXXI (ll. 109–11) 'To draw up leaf from the root?/ Hast 'ou found   a cloud   so light/ As seemed neither mist nor shade?'

l. 621 Κύθηρα δεινά: (Gk.) 'dread (or fearful) Cythera'. Also at Canto LXXVI (l. 146).

a leaf borne in the current: cf. 'a leaf in the current', Canto LXXXI (555/519).

l. 622 eyes: cf. the reference to eyes in Canto LXXXI (l. 118n.).

ll. 623–6: the decline in artistic excellence. In the essay 'Cavalcanti' Pound wrote,

'Durch Rafael ist das Madonnenideal Fleisch geworden', says Herr Springer, with perhaps an unintentional rhyme. Certainly the metamorphosis into carnal tissue becomes frequent and general somewhere about 1527. The people are corpus, corpuscular, but not in the strict sense 'animate', it is no longer the body of air clothed in the body of fire: it no longer radiates, light no longer moves from the eye, there is a great deal of meat, shock absorbing, perhaps – at any rate absorbent. It has not even Greek marmoreal plastic to restrain it.

(*LE*, 153)

Cf. also 'with usura the line grows thick' (Canto XLV, l. 17).

Hugh Kenner offers the useful illustration for the present lines of representations of the head of Venus in paintings by Botticelli, Jacopo del Sellaio and Velásquez (*Pound Era*, 364).

l. 623 Sandro . . . Jacopo: Sandro Botticelli (1444–1510) and Jacopo del Sellaio (1422–93), Florentine painters.

l. 624 Velásquez: Diego Rodriguez de Silva y Velásquez (1599–1660), the Spanish painter.

l. 625 Rembrandt: Rembrandt Harmenszoon van Rijn (1606–69), the Dutch painter.

l. 626 Rubens . . . Jordaens: Peter Paul Rubens (1557–1640) and Jacob Jordaens (1593–1678), Flemish painters.

l. 627: Pound alludes to Chu Hsi's note to *Chung Yung* (*The Unwobbling Pivot*), 'The main thing is to illumine the root of the process, a fountain of clear water descending from heaven immutable. The components, the bones of things, the materials are implicit and prepared in us, abundant and inseparable from us' (*Confucius*, 99).

l. 629 Chu Hsi: the Confucian philosopher Chu Hsi (1130–1200), who arranged the Confucian texts into the classic 'Four Books' (the *Ta Hsio*, the *Chung Yung*, the *Analects* and *Mencius*).

* * *

l. 705: a variation on the opening lines of Robert Browning's 'Home Thoughts from Abroad', 'Oh to be in England/ Now that April's there' (*Poetical Works*, 1896, 431).

Winston: Winston Leonard Spencer Churchill (1874–1965), Conservative statesman and Prime Minister 1940–5. Churchill is decried elsewhere by Pound as a warmonger (Canto XLI, 213/204–5) and for returning Britain to the gold standard (Cantos LXXIV, 452/426; LXXVIII, 513/481).

l. 707: Pound believed in delivering the control of credit out of the hands of private banks to the government. The Bank of England was a prime example of a usurious bank, creating 'moneys . . . out of nothing' (Canto XLVI, 243/233). Cf. line 723.

l. 709 labour: the nation's work force, but also probably the British Labour Party, which came into power for a second term of office in 1945.

ll. 714–15, 718: Dorothy Pound recalled a visit she and Pound made to a medieval abbey in Yorkshire owned by a cousin, Charles Talbot, 'and once Ezra and I crawled over the roof to a turret to see a copy of the Magna Charta, kept there in a glass case' (recorded by Hugh Kenner 'D.P. Remembered', op. cit., 492). This copy (Pound's 'old charter') was an 'exemplification' of the original, probably that of 1225 issued in the reign of Henry III and presented to the British Museum in 1945 by Miss Mathilda Talbot (C. F. Terrell, '*Magna Carta*, Talbots, The Lady Anne, and Pound's Associative Technique in Canto 80', *Paideuma*, v, no. 1, 72). The 'tower' Pound mentions is therefore at Lacock Abbey on Salisbury Plain, Wiltshire, not Yorkshire.

l. 717 John's first one: The Magna Charta, signed under duress by John 'Lackland' (?1167–1216), king of England 1199–1216, at Runnymede in 1215. Cf. Canto CVII.

l. 723 Chesterton: Gilbert Keith Chesterton (1874–1936), the English writer. Pound disliked Chesterton's religion and his dictum that if a thing was worth doing it was worth doing badly. He twice avoided meeting him in London (Stock, *Life*, 250).

l. 729 Talbot: a hunting dog, said to be named after the ancient English family of Talbot to whom Dorothy Pound (*née* Shakespear) was related (cf. note on lines 714–15, 718). The Talbot crest and seal bears the emblem of a hound.

l. 730 pasterns: ankle.

l. 731 butt: a cask or barrel of wine or ale.

l. 733: from the refrain of a sixteenth-century drinking song, 'Jolly Good Ale and Old', attributed to William Stevenson.

ll. 736–7: cf. Canto LXXXI (l. 118), 'there came new subtlety of eyes into my tent.'

l. 739 boneen: perhaps a diminutive of 'bonny [ones]'.

l. 740 Claridges: the high class hotel in Brook Street, London.

l. 741 Maurie Hewlett: Maurice Hewlett (1861–1923), the

novelist at whose house, The Old Rectory, Broadchalke, Salisbury, Pound stayed at Christmas 1911 (Stock, *Life*, 108); cf. Canto LXXIV (l. 276). Hewlett wrote an historical novel, *The Queen's Quair* (1904) on Mary Queen of Scots (cf. line 753).

ll. 746–8: Pound echoes Shakespeare's 'Heigh ho! sing, heigh ho! unto the green holly' in *As You Like It* (II, vii, 180).

l. 750 the Lady Anne: Lady Anne Blunt (*née* Lady Anne Isabella King-Noel), wife of W. S. Blunt, mentioned in Canto LXXXI (l. 169).

l. 751 Le Portel: a French fishing village just south of Boulogne. (Another Portel, south of Narbonne in a region of interest to Pound, is famous for the discovery of Cro-Magnon cave paintings there in 1908.) The name was wrongly associated by Pound with a swim made by the poet Algernon Charles Swinburne from Étretat in Normandy. As recounted by Edmund Gosse, Swinburne got into difficulties but was rescued by a fishing smack and taken to Yport, regaling the captain and crew on the voyage with the doctrines of the *Republic* and the poems of Victor Hugo (*Portraits and Sketches*, 1912, 22–7). Cf. Cantos LXXXII (558/523) and C (744/716), where Le Portel is connected with Phaeacia and the rescue of Odysseus from the sea by Leucothea. Pound is also probably remembering in these lines Swinburne's trilogy, *Chastelard*, *Bothwell* and *Mary Stuart* (*Complete Works: Tragedies*, II, III, 1925, reprinted 1968).

l. 752 him: David Rizzio, Italian secretary to Mary Queen of Scots. Rizzio was murdered while at supper with Mary Stuart at Holyrood Castle, Edinburgh, 1566. Pound may have visited the castle in the summer of 1906 (Hutchins, 38).

l. 753 La Stuarda: (Ital.) 'the Stuart', i.e. Mary Stuart (1542–87), Queen of Scots 1561–68.

l. 754: (Prov.) 'Si tuit li dolh èlh plor èlh marrimen' ('If all the grief, and tears and wretchedness'), the opening line of Bertran de Born's 'Planh' on the death of 'the Young King', Henry Plantagenet, in 1183; cf. Pound's translation of this poem and Canto LXXXIV where it is recalled once more (572/537).

l. 755 leopards and broom plants: the heraldic devices respectively of Richard Coeur-de-Lion (1157–99), King of England 1189–99, and Henry II (1133–89), King of England 1154–89, father of Richard and Henry 'the Young King'.

l. 756: Pound adapts the line 'Iram indeed is gone with all his rose' from Edward FitzGerald's translation of the *Rubáiyát of Omar Khayyám*, 1859, 5 (cf. line 594). The following 'rose lyric' (ll. 756–67) follows the stanzaic form of the *Rubáiyát*.

l. 757 Blood-red, blanch-white: the red rose of York, the white rose of Lancaster. Cf. line 763 and Canto LXXIX (l. 227).

l. 759 Howard . . . Boleyn: Catherine Howard (?1521-42), fifth wife, and Anne Boleyn (?1507–36), second wife of King Henry VIII of England. Both were beheaded.

ll. 760–1 Nor . . . white: Pound echoes Tennyson's 'Now sleeps the crimson petal, now the white' in *The Princess* (VII, l. 161).

l. 763: an allusion to the Wars of the Roses (1455–61) between the Royal Houses of York and Lancaster.

l. 769 along . . . size: one line in Faber *Cantos* (1975).

l. 770 the Serpentine: the lake in Hyde Park, London.

ll. 771–2 the pond . . . the sunken garden: the Round Pond, made for Queen Anne in the shape of a hand-mirror, and the sunken garden in Kensington Gardens, London.

ll. 775, 778: cf. Canto LXXXI (ll. 151–2), 'Paquin pull down!/ The green casque has outdone your elegance'.

from Canto LXXXI

ll. 97–115: this section is accompanied in the Faber *Cantos* (1975) by the notation '*libretto*' in the left-hand margin. Pound's metre modulates over these lines from trochaic tetrameters through the anapaestic trimeters of Ben Jonson to the iambic pentameter of Chaucer (cf. Davie, *Pound*, 92–5).

ll. 99–100: an echo of the earlier 'as by Terracina rose from the sea Zephyr behind her' (Canto LXXIV, l. 341), suggesting therefore the birth of Venus Aphrodite who here speaks (or sings) in the first person.

l. 99 zephyr: in Greek mythology, the west wind.

l. 100 aureate: golden.

l. 101 Lawes: Henry Lawes (1596–1662), the Caroline musician and composer. In the *ABC of Reading*, Pound groups Lawes with Dowland, Young and Jenkins as marking 'the period of England's musicianship' (p. 151; cf. also pp. 154–6). Cf. also the reference to Lawes in *Hugh Selwyn Mauberley*, 'Envoi (1919)' (l. 2).

Jenkyns: John Jenkins (1597–1678), composer and musician to Charles I and II.

l. 102 Dolmetsch: Arnold Dolmetsch (1858–1940), French musician and early instrument-maker. Pound possessed a clavichord made by Dolmetsch and listed him among the faculty members of his proposed 'College of Arts' in 1914. In his *Pathways of Song* (1938), Dolmetsch published the musical setting by John Dowland of Ben Jonson's 'Have you seen but a bright lily grow' (cf. Canto LXXIV, note on lines 837–9 and lines 108, 113 below). Pound remembers Dolmetsch earlier in Canto LXXX (538/504). Cf. also the essays 'Arnold Dolmetsch' and 'Vers Libre and Arnold Dolmetsch' (*LE*, 431–40).

l. 103 viol: the musical instrument, having five, six or seven strings.

l. 104 grave . . . acute: marks in musical notation indicating respectively a slow and solemn movement and a sharp shrill tone.

l. 108 Hast 'ou: i.e. 'Hast thou'. Pound echoes the earlier 'Hast 'ou seen the rose in the steel dust' (Canto LXXIV, ll. 837–9), indebted to the idiom and metre of Ben Jonson.

ll. 109–11: cf. Canto LXXX, lines 620–1, 'with the veil of faint cloud before her/ Κύθηρα δεινά as a leaf borne in the current'.

l. 113 Waller: Edmund Waller (1606–87), poet. Waller was an example for Pound of poetry's proper relation to song, and his 'Go, lovely Rose' the source of Pound's 'Envoi (1919)' in *Hugh Selwyn Mauberley*.

Dowland: John Dowland (1563–1626), composer and lutanist.

ll. 114–15: from the poem 'Merciles Beaute', attributed to Geoffrey Chaucer (*Works*, 638).

l. 116 180 years: i.e. between Jenkins's death (1678) and the birth of Arnold Dolmetsch (1858). Pound had written in 1918 to Margaret Anderson, 'I desire to hear the music of a lost dynasty. . . . And I desire also to resurrect the art of the lyric, I mean words to be sung. . . . And with a few exceptions . . . there is scarcely anything since the time of Waller and Campion' (*SL*, 128).

l. 117: (Ital.) 'and listening to the light murmur'.

l. 118: cf. Canto LXXX (l. 736), 'Only shadows enter my tent'.

eyes: cf. lines 114, 122–4. The significance of eyes is many times apparent in Pound's poetry especially in connection with Pallas Athene, the protector of Odysseus. In one aspect it is summarized in the phrase 'eyes are the guides of love' in *Homage to Sextus Propertius* VII (l. 12). Here at a moment of (near) vision, the reference is primarily to Aphrodite, as goddess of love.

l. 119 hypostasis: a union of the human and divine. Also at Canto LXXVI (l. 182).

l. 121 carneval: (Ital.) 'carnevale' ('carnival'), when revellers go masked. Cf. line 133.

l. 124 diastasis: dilation (of the eyes); cf. Hugh Selwyn Mauberley who passes 'inconscient, full gaze,/ The wide-banded irides/ And botticellian sprays implied/ in their diastasis' (MAUBERLEY (1920) II, ll. 26–9).

l. 127 εἰδώς: (Gk.) 'knowing'.

ll. 129–33: Pound encapsulates the evolution of his verse line, passing from the iambic pentameter of line 129, to the imagist or hokku-like stress pattern and typography over the ten syllables of lines 130–2, to the distinctive personal measure, again over ten syllables, of line 133 (cf. Kenner, *Pound Era*, 491). The famous statement '(To break the pentameter, that was the first heave)' occurs earlier in this Canto (553/518).

ll. 130–2: cf. 'sea, sky, and pool/ alternate/ pool, sky, sea' (Canto LXXXIII, 570/535) and '– violet, sea green, and no name' (Canto CVI, 780/755). Pound, it seems, refers to three pairs of eyes and is perhaps thinking at one level of the 'Tre donne intorno alla mia mente' ('Three women on my mind') referred to in Canto LXXVIII (514/483). The three women were Dorothy Pound, Olga Rudge and Bride Scratton, whom Pound refers to as 'Thiy' in Canto LXXVIII (Stock, *Life*, 307). Mary de Rachewiltz reports that Olga Rudge's eyes were 'violet-blue' and Dorothy Pound's 'steel-blue' (*Discretions*, 117, 259).

l. 134: cf. Canto LXXIV (ll. 748–9n.), Canto LXXVI (ll. 157–60), the phrase 'Amo ergo sum' ('I love, therefore I am') in Canto LXXX (526/493), and earlier in this Canto 'What counts is the cultural level' (554/518).

l. 138: cf. Canto LXXX (l. 774), 'my London, your London' and Canto LXXXIII, 'The eyes, this time my world,/ But pass and look *from* mine' (570/535).

l. 140: an echo of Pound's ideas on artistic creation, particularly sculpture; cf. Canto XXV (ll. 90–5), 'as the sculptor sees the form in the air/ before he sets hand to mallet . . .'

l. 141 Elysium: in Greek mythology, the islands of the Blest, conferring eternal ease on heroes and patriots.

ll. 144–5: Pound borrows his reference and his rhetoric from the Authorized Version of the Bible, available at Pisa. Cf. Ecclesiastes 1 : 2, 'Vanity of vanities, saith the preacher, vanity of vanities; all is vanity', and Proverbs 6 : 6, 'Go to the ant, thou sluggard; consider her ways, and be wise.'

l. 144 ant: cf. Canto LXXXIII, lines 87 and 143–4, 'When the mind swings by a grass-blade/ an ant's forefoot shall save you.'

ll. 148–9: Pound's charge that man should learn his place in a natural order recalls Alexander Pope's versified 'Great Chain of Being', 'Far as Creation's ample range extends/ The scale of sensual, mental pow'rs ascends:/ Mark how it mounts, to Man's imperial race,/ From the green myriads in the peopled grass' (*An Essay on Man*, I, ll. 206–10).

ll. 151–2: cf. Canto LXXX (ll. 775, 778).

l. 151 Paquin: a Parisian couturier.

l. 152 casque: a helmet. Pound elsewhere borrows the phrase, 'en casque de crystal rose les baladines' ('in pink crystal helmets the mountebanks'), from Stuart Merrill's *Ballet*; cf. Cantos LXXVIII (512/480), LXXX (538/504).

l. 153: Pound adapts the line 'Reule wel thyself, that other folk canst rede' in Chaucer's 'Ballade of Good Counsel' (*Works*, 631). The advice follows also the Confucian teaching on 'self-discipline'.

ll. 166–7: Pound consistently held and practised the principle that 'ideas should go into action', or as it appears in *Confucius*, of 'looking straight into one's own heart and acting on the results' (pp. 27, 73). Compare Mauberley's 'Olympian *apathein*' (MAUBERLEY (1920), ' "The Age Demanded" ', l. 39), the scornful lassitude of the lotus-eaters in Canto XX, and the confessions, ' "Nothing we made, we set nothing in order' (Canto XXV, l. 108) and 'I neither build nor reap' (Canto XXVII, 137/132).

l. 169 Blunt: Wilfred Scawen Blunt (1840–1922), English poet and critic of imperialism, for whom Pound and others, including Yeats, Richard Aldington and Victor Plarr, gave an honorary dinner at his home on 18 January 1914. Pound contributed an address:

> Because you have gone your individual gait,
> Written fine verses, made mock of the world,
> Swung the grand style, not made a trade of art,
> Upheld Mazzini and detested institutions
>
> We who are little given to respect
> Respect you, . . .

(quoted in Norman, 137)

l. 170 from the air a live tradition: cf. Yeats's 'I made it out of a mouthful of air', cited by Pound in connection with 'the *forma*, the immortal *concetto*, the concept, the dynamic form which is like the rose pattern driven into the dead iron-filings by the magnet' (*GK*, 152).

from **Canto LXXXIII**

l. 64 Δρύας: (Gk.) 'dryad', a tree nymph. Also at lines 69, 79.

l. 75 Taishan-Chocorua: the sacred mountain T'ai Shan in China (cf. Canto LXXIV, note on line 128) and Mount Chocorua, in eastern New Hampshire, U.S.A.

l. 81 Plura diafana: (Lat.) 'more things diaphanous', from the medieval philosopher of light, Bishop Grosseteste (1175–1253). Cf. Canto XXXVI, note on line 18.

l. 82 Heliads: daughters of Helios; cf. Canto LXXIX, note on line 219.

l. 84 ὕδωρ: (Gk.) 'udor' ('water'); cf. ὕδωρ/ HUDOR et Pax' at the opening of this Canto (563/528) where the source is Pindar's *Olympian Ode* I.

l. 87 ants: cf. lines 143–4 and Canto LXXXI, line 144.

l. 91 rectitude: in *Confucius* Pound writes: 'the word rectify (*cheng*) can be illustrated as follows: if there be a knife of resentment in the heart or enduring rancor, the mind will not attain precision; under suspicion and fear it will not form sound judgment, nor will it, dazzled by love's delight' (p. 51).

l. 95 equity: cf. *Confucius*, 'The great learning . . . is rooted in coming to rest, being at ease in perfect equity' (pp. 27–9) and ' "EQUITY/ IS/ THE/ TREASURE/ OF/ STATES" ' (p. 91).

l. 96 process: the Confucian 'way'; cf. Canto LXXIV, note on line 13.

l. 103 Clower: perhaps Clowes, a member of the London printing firm, William Clowes & Sons Ltd., who printed Pound's *Gaudier-Brzeska* and *Lustra* in 1916, the latter in an abridged form after Clowes and the publisher Elkin Mathews had objected to certain of the original poems (Gallup, 37–41). Clowes is mentioned in Canto LXXXII (559/524).

*   *   *

l. 128 la vespa: (Ital.) 'the wasp'.

l. 129 Bracelonde: possibly Brocéliande, the forest mentioned in Arthurian legend.

Perugia: the capital of Perugia province and the Umbria region.

l. 130 Piazza: probably the Piazza Quattro Novembre in Perugia, which contains the Palazzo dei Priori, housing the National Gallery, the cathedral of San Lorenzo (1345–1430) and the Maggiore Fountain (1278).

l. 131 Bulagaio: a suburb of Perugia.

l. 133 Mr. Walls: an inmate at the D.T.C., Pisa, referred to also in Canto LXXXII (558/523).

l. 139 mint: cf. Canto LXXIV, note on line 120.

l. 140 Jones: lieutenant and Provost Officer, D.T.C., Pisa.

l. 141 gorilla cage: the maximum-security cage in which Pound was at first imprisoned at Pisa. Hugh Kenner writes,

> He was in a cage because he was very dangerous, as witness the heavy air-strip that was welded over his galvanised mesh with so many welds the acetylene torches blazed blue a full 36 hours . . . he alone was never led out for exercise. By day he walked in the cage, two paces, two paces, or slouched, or sat. By night a special reflector poured light on his cage alone, so he kept his head under the blanket. There were always two guards, with strict orders not to speak to him. Everyone, including the incorrigibles, had orders not to speak to him.
>
> (*Pound Era*, 461–2)

* * *

l. 225 Senator Edwards: Ninian Edwards (1775–1833), U.S. Senator from Illinois 1818–24.

l. 233: a snatch from the English folksong, 'The Keeper', which has the refrain, 'Hey down, ho down,/ Derry derry down/ Among the leaves so green O.'

from Canto XCI

This and the following selection from Canto XCIII are from *Section: Rock-Drill: 85–95 de los cantares*, first published in 1955. The title of this group of Cantos was suggested to Pound by Jacob Epstein's sculpture *Rock Drill*, a plaster figure of a man straddling a real pneumatic drill which Pound had seen in Epstein's studio in 1913. The sculpture was exhibited at the Goupil Gallery in 1915, but subsequently much changed to become the bronze torso, called *Rock Drill*, now housed in the Tate Gallery, London. Pound began the Rock-Drill Cantos in 1952, thirty-six years after seeing Epstein's first figure, and was probably reminded of it by Wyndham Lewis's review, titled 'The Rock Drill', of *The Letters of Ezra Pound* (1950) in the *New Statesman* (7 Apr. 1951). Lewis wrote there of Pound's dealings with Harriet Monroe, editor of *Poetry* (Chicago), 'His rock-drill action is impressive: he blasts away tirelessly, prodding and coaxing its mulish editress' (reprinted in *Perspectives*, ed. Stock, 198). Epstein's sculpture and the relevance of its Vorticist principles to the *Cantos* are discussed by Jacob Korg ('Jacob Epstein's Rock Drill and the *Cantos*', *Paideuma*, IV, nos. 2 and 3, 301–13).

Pound's main sources for the Rock-Drill Cantos were Séraphim Couvreur, *Chou King: Les Annales de la Chine* (1897, reprinted Paris, 1950; English trans. James Legge, *The Shoo King*, in *The Chinese Classics*, III, 1865, reprinted Hong Kong University Press, 1960); Thomas Hart Benton, *Thirty Years View: or A History of the Working of the American Government 1820–1850* (New York, 1854–6); and Philostratus, *The Life of Apollonius of Tyana* (trans. F. C. Conybeare, Loeb edn., 1919). The main source for references to King Khaty and the Egyptian material in Cantos XCI–XCV was three books by Boris de Rachewiltz, *Massime degli antichi Egiziani* (Milan, 1954), *Il Papiro Magico Vaticano* (Rome, 1954) and *Libro Egizio degli Inferi* (Rome, 1959).

ll. 1–4: Pound's square notes give at line 1 the rising/falling melody as of a chant, and a fusion at line 3 of the variant melodies for the fourth line of Bernart de Ventadorn's 'Quan vei la lauzeta mover' ('When I see the lark on the wing'). The line itself, 'per la doussor c'al cor li vai' ('through the sweetness that comes into his heart'), forms the basis of Pound's lines 2 and 4, Pound superimposing on it the first three words

341

of William of Aquitaine's Chanson 10, 'ab la dolchor del temps novel' ('with the joy of a new season'). In addition Pound changes the article from the feminine 'la' to the masculine 'lo' (perhaps because the related Italian word 'dolzore' is masculine), and the pronoun 'li' ('his') to 'mi' ('my'), thereby identifying with the lark. Pound's line reads therefore as 'with the joy that comes into my heart'. (For further details see the information supplied by James J. Wilhelm, 'Notes and Queries', *Paideuma*, II, no. 2, 333–5). Bernart de Ventadorn (1148–95) was a Provençal troubadour attached first to the court of Eblis III, Viscount of Ventadorn, and subsequently to the court of Eleanor of Aquitaine, to whom his poem on the lark was addressed. Duke William IX of Aquitaine, seventh Count of Poitou (1071–1127), was the earliest troubadour whose work has survived, and grandfather to Eleanor of Aquitaine. Cf. the discussion of both Bernart and William in *The Spirit of Romance* (pp. 39–42), including Pound's translation of 'Quant ieu vey la' lauzeta mover' (*sic*), and Cantos VI (26/22) and LXXIV (457/431).

ll. 5–6: cf. the later lines in this Canto, '& from fire to crystal/ via the body of light' (649/615).

ll. 7–8: there is perhaps an echo here and elsewhere in the Canto of Dante's *Paradiso*, III (ll. 10–15),

> As from transparent glasses polished clean,
> or water shining smooth up to its rim,
> Yet not so that the bottom is unseen,
> Our faces' lineaments return so dim
> That pearl upon white forehead not more slow
> Would on our pupils its pale image limn.

> (Binyon, 27)

A second echo is of Bernart de Ventadorn's 'Quan vei la lauzeta mover' in the lines Pound had in 1910 glossed as

> I had no power over myself nor have had ever, since it let me see in her eyes a mirror that much pleased me.
> O mirror, since I mirrored myself in thee, deep sighs have

slain me, for I have lost myself, as Narcissus lost himself in
the fount.

(*SR*, 42)

l. 9 Reina: (Sp.) 'queen', an ideal woman as is the 'donna' of
Provençal verse, composed here at least, so the context would
suggest, of Queen Elizabeth I ('Miss Tudor', line 29), the
goddess Diana, who appears later in the Canto and in whose
name Elizabeth was often celebrated in verse, Eleanor of
Aquitaine (cf. note on lines 1–4), Helen of Tyre (and of Troy)
and the Princess Ra-Set (line 37).
300 years: Pound's sense of cultural loss is akin to Eliot's notion
of a 'dissociation of sensibility', manifest, for example, in the
loss from the seventeenth century of the tradition of poetry as
song, and in the coarsening of art. (Cf. Cantos LXXIV, line
334; LXXX, lines 623–6).
l. 13: cf. Cantos XCII, 'Hilary looked at an oak leaf/ or holly,
or rowan' (654–5/622), and XCV, 'I suppose St. Hilary looked
at an oak-leaf' (679/647), and line 25 and note on line 51 below.
l. 14: (Lat.) 'who labours, prays'.
l. 15 Undine: suggested by the romance *Undine* (1811), many
times translated, by the German author Friedrich Heinrich
Carl de la Motte-Fouqué (1777–1843).
ll. 16–17: cf. Canto XXXIX, 'with the Goddess' eyes to sea-
ward/ By Circeo, by Terracina, with the stone eyes/ white
toward the sea' (203/195). And cf. also Cantos XVII (ll.
91–2), LXXIV (ll. 341, 344–5) and CVI (779/754).
l. 16 Circeo: Mt. Circeo, north of the gulf of Gaeta, western
Italy, once the island of Aeaea, the reputed home of Circe.
Pound alludes to the goddess Venus; cf. his statement 'Given
the material means I would replace the statue of Venus on the
cliffs of Terracina' (*SPr*, 53).
l. 18 Apollonius: Apollonius of Tyana in Cappadocia, a first-
century Pythagorean philosopher and wandering mystic who
is presented in Philostratus' *Life of Apollonius of Tyana* as a rival
to Christ. Cf. later references in this Canto (649, 650/616) and
especially Canto XCIV (668–70/635–7).

l. 20 Helen of Tyre: in a note, dated 1916, to the chapter 'Psychology and Troubadours' in *The Spirit of Romance*, Pound wrote

> Let me admit at once that a recent lecture by Mr. Mead on Simon Magus has opened my mind to a number of new possibilities. There would seem to be in the legend of Simon of Magus and Helen of Tyre a clearer prototype of "chivalric love" than in anything hereinafter discussed. I recognize that all this matter of mine may have to be reconstructed or at least re-oriented about that tradition.
>
> (p. 91)

G. R. S. Mead, the editor of the *Quest* (in which Pound's essay first appeared), was the author of *Simon Magus: An Essay* (1892) and *Apollonius of Tyana* (1901). In the first of these Mead quotes from the *Revelation* of Simon, as included in the *Philosophumena* of Hippolytus, a passage where Magus distinguishes between a 'Great Power, the Universal Mind ordering all things, male', and 'the Great Thought, female, producing all things' (p. 19). Helen of Troy is seen to represent this 'Thought', to have been responsible for the Trojan war and subsequently 'changed by the Angels and Lower Powers', as the story is told by Hippolytus, to have 'lived in a brothel in Tyre', from which Simon Magus delivered her (P. L. Surette, 'Helen of Tyre', *Paideuma*, II, no. 3, 419–21).

l. 21 Pithagoras: the Greek philosopher Pythagoras (?580–497 B.C.), who taught the doctrine of metempsychosis and developed a theory of musical intervals and of number. Pound seems to have valued Pythagoras particularly for the 'time of silence' attached to his teaching (*SPr*, 110), and Philostratus records that Apollonius, accepting the wisdom of this principle, imposed a five-year ritual silence on himself (*Life of Apollonius of Tyana*, Bk. I, xiv).

l. 22 Ocellus: Ocellus of Lucania, a Pythagorean philosopher; cf. Cantos XCIII (662/629), XCIV (675/642) and XCVIII (714/684).

l. 23 pilot-fish: small carangoid fish, thought to act as a guide to the shark.

et libidinis expers: (Lat.) 'to whom passion is unknown'. The phrase occurs also in Canto LXXVI (l. 151) in reference to Artemis/Diana.

Tyre: ancient Phoenician trading port.

l. 24 Justinian: Justinian I (483–565), Byzantine emperor 527–65, famed for his codification of Roman law, the *Corpus Juris Civilis*; he is mentioned several times in the later Cantos and in Pound's prose writings, where he is praised for helping to establish the hierarchy of values necessary to civilization (cf. *GK*, 40; *SPr*, 104, 120; and Canto XCVI (686, 689, 695/654, 658, 663–4).

Theodora: Justinian's wife, mentioned in Canto XCVI (686/654).

l. 26 CRYSTAL: as it occurs here and at lines 34, 41, 45 and 49, an image of paradisal clarity, Pound calling on the meanings of crystal as a structured mineral formed through the evaporation of water, as highly transparent cut-glass, and as a synonym for eyes (cf. notes on lines 5–8). The succession of fire: light: crystal in these lines suggests how crystal synthesizes the aspects of sun and moon and therefore perhaps corresponds to the Chinese ideogram 明, which Pound interprets as 'The sun and moon, the total light process, the radiation, reception and reflection of light; hence, the intelligence' (*Confucius*, 20). But cf. also the later lines 'Above prana, the light,/ past light, the crystal./ Above crystal, the jade!' (Canto XCIV, 667/634), and Pound's caution in his essay on Brancusi:

> the contemplation of form or of formal-beauty leading into the infinite must be dissociated from the dazzle of crystal; there is a sort of relation, but there is the more important divergence; with the crystal it is a hypnosis, or a contemplative fixation of thought, or an excitement of the 'subconscious' or unconscious (whatever the devil they may be), and with the ideal form in marble it is an approach to the

infinite *by form*, by precisely the highest possible degree of consciousness of formal perfection; as free of accident as any of the philosophical demands of a 'Paradiso' can make it.

(*LE*, 444)

l. 27: water, which reflects the pine, and evaporates.

l. 28: (Prov.) 'To think of her is my rest', from Arnaut Daniel's 'En breu brisaral temps braus' (*Tr*, 171).

l. 29 Miss Tudor: Queen Elizabeth I (1558–1603), who was of the Welsh house of Tudor.

l. 32 he: Sir Francis Drake (cf. note on line 47).

l. 36 compenetrans: (Lat.) 'penetrating'; cf. Canto C, 'as light into water compenetrans' (749/722).

l. 37 Princess Ra-Set: an invented synthesis of two Egyptian sun gods, Ra, the principle of good whose hieroglyph, the barge of dawn, appears later in this and subsequent Cantos, and Set, an evil deity of feminine attributes who slayed Osiris, the brother and husband of Isis.

l. 38: cf. Canto IV, 'The liquid and rushing crystal/ beneath the knees of the gods' (19/15).

ll. 42–3: from Dante's *Paradiso*, XXVI, lines 34–5. Binyon, lines 31–6, reads: 'Therefore to the Essence, whose prerogative/ is, that what good outside of it is known/ Is naught else but a light its own beams give,/ More than elsewhither *must in love be drawn/ The mind of him* whose vision can attain/ The verity the proof is founded on' (p. 305).

l. 45: cf. note on lines 7–8, and Pound's talk of a lost

radiant world where one thought cuts through another with clean edge, a world of moving energies '*mezzo oscuro rade*', '*risplende in sè perpetuale effecto*', magnetisms that take form, that are seen, or that border the visible, the matter of Dante's *paradiso*, the glass under water, the form that seems a form seen in a mirror.

(*LE*, 154)

l. 47 Drake: Sir Francis Drake (?1540–1603), famous sea voyager and admiral of the English fleet in the war with Spain.

l. 50 ichor, amor: the fluid (as distinct from blood) in the veins of the gods, (Sp.) 'love'.

l. 51 J. Heydon: John Heydon (1629–67), astrologer, Rosicrucian and author of the *Holy Guide* (1662), a work Pound had recommended in 1915 for its writings on the 'joys of pure form' (*G-B*, 127; cf. also 134), used in the abandoned Ur Canto III and then in the Rock-Drill Cantos. 'Secretary of Nature' is Heydon's self-applied epithet, implying his belief in a 'doctrine of signatures': the idea that natural phenomena contain discrete signs of their medicinal properties and of nature's harmonious grand design. Cf. Canto LXXXVII (609/573), Canto XCI (650/616), lines 13, 25 and the mention of 'the gt/healing' at lines 34–5 above.

from Canto XCIII

l. 146: (Lat.) excerpted from Ovid, *Fasti*, VI, 15, 'est deus in nobis, agitante calescimus illo' ('a god dwells within us; when he stirs we are enkindled') (Eva Hesse, 'Notes and Queries', *Paideuma*, III, no. 1, 136). The line is quoted in part later in Cantos XCVIII (l. 44) and CIV (765/739), and elsewhere in full in connection with Richard St. Victor (*SPr*, 74).

l. 148: (Lat.) 'Light [in its divine source] as a mist of light'. Pound alludes to Bishop Grosseteste's philosophy of light. Cf. Canto XXXVI, note on line 18.

ll. 149–50: 'Creatress,/ [Lat.] I beseech'.

l. 151: Ursula (Ital.) 'the blessed', probably St. Ursula, patroness of virgins.

l. 154: (Ital.) 'by the hours of delight'.

l. 156: cf. the mention of 'Ysaut, Ydone' in 'The Alchemist' (*CSP*, 87). Ysolt is the Isolde of the tale *Tristram and Isolde*. Cf. earlier in this Canto (657/624) and the poem 'Praise of Ysolt' (*CSP*, 29). The name 'Ydone' is perhaps suggested by the *Amadis and Ydoine* (cf. *The Spirit of Romance*, pp. 79–84).

l. 158: Piccarda dei Donati, sister of Corso and Forese Donati, was a nun of the order of St. Clare, forcibly abducted by Corso and married to Rossellino della Tosa. She is referred to in

Dante's *Purgatorio* (XXIV, l. 11), and tells her story to Dante in the *Paradiso* (III, ll. 34–125), where she is an example of inconstancy to vows made on earth, and represents the lowest order in the hierarchy of the Blessed. 'Picarda' is named in 'The Alchemist' (*CSP*, 87).

l. 160 wing'd head: the asp crown of the Egyptian goddess Uraeus.

l. 161 caduceus: Mercury's wand, which was entwined with two serpents. Pound seems to suggest an association with Uraeus, and perhaps also with Asclepius, the Greek god of medicine whose symbol was the snake.

l. 163 horns of Isis–Luna: Isis is an Egyptian fertility goddess, represented as crowned with a cow's horn. Pound appeals to her as goddess of the moon and as the liberator of the god Set, the murderer of Osiris. Cf. the conjunction of Isis with Kuanon, the Chinese goddess of mercy in Canto XC (640/606).

l. 165 panther: associated with Dionysus, but perhaps Pound means to suggest here also his Egyptian equivalent, Osiris.

ll. 166–7: (Fr.) 'I had pity for others./ Not enough! Not enough!' A similar confession appears earlier in Canto LXXVI (ll. 245–6n.). Cf. also Canto CXVI (l. 71).

l. 168 the child: perhaps Pound's daughter Mary de Rachewiltz, who visited St Peter's, Rome, with Pound in an incident recalled at the beginning of this Canto (656/623). Cf. Mary de Rachewiltz, *Discretions* (p. 115).

l. 169 basilica: a church in the shape of an oblong building with double colonnades and a semi-circular apse at one end; also a term for the seven churches in Rome, including St. Peter's, founded by Constantine.

l. 170: repeated in Canto XCV (677/644).

from Canto XCVIII

From *Thrones: 96–109 de los cantares*, published in December 1959. The title of this section is an allusion to the Seventh Heaven of Dante's *Paradiso*. Pound commented:

I was not following the three divisions of the *Divine Comedy* exactly. . . . But I have made the division between people dominated by emotion, people struggling upwards, and those who have some part of the divine vision. The thrones in Dante's *Paradiso* are for the spirits of the people who have been responsible for good government. The thrones in the Cantos are an attempt to move out from egoism and to establish some definition of an order possible or at any rate conceivable on earth. One is held up by the low percentage of reason which seems to operate in human affairs. *Thrones* concerns the states of mind of people responsible for something more than their personal conduct.

(*Writers at Work*, 52)

Pound is concerned in *Thrones* with Byzantine, Chinese and English legal systems; the 'governing *subject*' of these Cantos, as Hugh Kenner has pointed out, 'is law' (*Agenda*, VIII, nos. 3–4, 15). The main sources for these Cantos were Leo the Wise, *The Eparch's Book* (Pound's direct source was a version prepared by Jules Nicole with a modern Greek transcription, together with Latin and French translations in *Le Livre du Prefet*, Geneva, 1893; collected with an English translation by E. H. Freshfield in Variorium Reprints, London, 1970); Alexander del Mar, *History of Monetary Systems* (Chicago, 1896); *The Sacred Edict*, trans. F. W. Baller (Shangai, 1921); Joseph Rock, *The Ancient Na-khi Kingdom of Southwest China*, 2 vols. (Harvard–Yenching Institute Monograph Series, VIII–IX, 1947); Edward Coke, *The Second Part of the Institutes of the Laws of England* (1642, reprinted as *Coke on Magna Charta*, Square Dollar Series, Hawthorne, Calif., 1974). Canto XCVIII was first published on 1 September 1958.

l. 29 Anselm: St. Anselm (1033/4–1109), born in Piedmont, Prior of the Abbey of Caen, and later Archbishop of Canterbury; best known as the author of *Cur Deus Homo* ('Why did God become man?'), a treatise on the Atonement, designed to prove the necessity of the Incarnation. In Dante's *Paradiso*, as one of the Doctors of the Church, Anselm occupies the

349

ninth position in the outer ring of 'The Double Circle of
Souls' in the Heaven of the Sun (XII, l. 131). Pound here
asserts a divinity in man by way of Anselm's view that the
image of the Divine Trinity in which the breath ('spiritus') of
the Holy Spirit in the form of love passed between the memory
of the Father, or Highest Nature, and the intelligence of the
Son, or Word. Cf. Canto CV, dominated by Anselm, and
Pound's chief source, Anselm's *Monologium* (1077), esp. ch. 57
(contained in the *Patrologia Latina*, ed. J. P. Migne).

l. 31 Plotinus: (205–270), neo-Platonic philosopher who held
that the material world has no existence but as the emanation
of the soul, originating from the Divine Mind of God, or the
One. In Ritter and Preller's *Historia Philosophiae Graecae* (1898),
the statements appear, 'Plotinus does not allow that the
authentic, the separable Soul, is in the body: the body is in
the Soul. . . . The body is visible; the Soul is not. . . . The Soul
is in the body only as light is in the air' (appended to *Plotinus:
The Ethical Treatises*: trans. Stephen MacKenna, Medici
Society, 1926, 1, 153–4; quoted in Carroll F. Terrell, 'A
Commentary on Grosseteste with an English Version of De
Luce', *Paideuma*, II, no. 3, 451). The phrase 'the body is inside
the soul' occurs later in CXIII (18/788). Cf. also Canto XV
(70/66) where Plotinus rescues Pound from the hell of London.

l. 32 Gemisto: Georgius Gemistus Plethon (?1355–1450), neo-
Platonic philosopher, indebted particularly to Proclus in his
attempt to revive a polytheistic system which would be an
alternative to Christianity and 'make men of the greeks'
(Canto XXIII, 111/107). Gemistus was a representative of the
Eastern Church at the Council of Ferrara-Florence (1438–9),
as Pound mentions in *Guide to Kulchur* (p. 224) and Cantos VIII
(35/31) and XXVI (128–9/123–4). At his death in Mistra his
body was exhumed and transported to Rimini by Sigismondo
Malatesta, to be placed in a sarcophagus at the Tempio.
Pound suggests that Gemistus' view of Poseidon (Neptune) as
the primary source in Creation was an influence on the bas-
reliefs in the Tempio (Canto LXXXIII, 563/528).

hilaritas: (Lat.) 'hilarity', 'mirth', associated also with Scotus

Erigena from a description in an edition of *De divisione naturae* (1838), of his hilarity and wit before Charles the Bald, King of the Franks (Canto LXXXIII, 563/528). Pound draws attention to the term 'hilarity' in the expression 'l'ilarità del Tuo Volto' in an Italian prayer for fair weather, translated in *Guide to Kulchur* (p. 141).

l. 34: (Lat.) 'and in clouds', (Ital.) 'a likeness'. 'Simiglglianza' (mod. Ital. 'somiglianza') occurs in Cavalcanti's 'Donna mi priegha' (*LE*, 164).

l. 35: (Gk.) 'in the likeness' (Lat.) 'of gods'.

l. 36: an allusion perhaps to the philosopher Iamblichus' belief in fire as a manifestation of divinity (cf. Canto V, 21/17, and *Guide to Kulchur*, p. 223).

l. 37: an allusion probably to Gemistus' work known as *Nomoi* or the *Laws*, in which he revised classical mythology according to his neo-Platonic metaphysic, and to his advice to the Emperor Manuel II to build a wall across the Isthmus of Corinth to defend the Peloponnese against the Turks (cf. Canto XXIII, 111/107).

l. 38 Herakleitos: the Greek philosopher Heraclitus (fl. 500 B.C.) who held that all things are in constant flux and that their origin was fire. Heraclitus' dictum (πάντα ρεῖ, 'everything flows') is incorporated into *Hugh Selwyn Mauberley* III (ll. 9–10), and quoted in Cantos LXXX (547/512), LXXXIII (565/529) and CVII (787/762). Pound probably here refers to the thought in a fragment from Heraclitus, 'If we speak with understanding we must find our real strength in what is common to all just as a city is based on the law, and even much more strongly' (quoted in David Gordon, 'Pound's Use of the Sacred Edict in Canto 98', *Paideuma*, IV, no. 1, 122).

ll. 39–55: repeated with some variation in Canto CII (754/ 728).

l. 39 Leucothoe: the daughter of Orchamus, a descendant of Baal of Sumerian Babylon. Leucothoe resisted Apollo's advances, died and was buried, but drawn from the earth as an incense bush by the sun's rays. Her story is distinct from but evidently spliced by Pound with that of Leucothea.

l. 42 Commissioner of the Salt Works: Wang Iu p'uh, the Salt

Commissioner of Shenshi, who made a colloquial translation of the *Sacred Edict* of K'ang-Hsi. He is named on the next page (716/686) and later in this Canto (720/690) in association with Dante's *De Vulgari Eloquentia* ('The Common Tongue').

l. 44 est deus in nobis: (Lat.) from Ovid's *Fasti*, VI, 15, 'est Deus in nobis, agitante calescemus illo' ('a god dwells within us, when he stirs we are enkindled'). The second part of Ovid's phrase appears in Canto XCIII (l. 146 n.), and Pound quotes the full line elsewhere in connection with Richard St. Victor (*SPr*, 74).

l. 45 sea-gull: Pound's term for Leucothea, formerly Ino, daughter of Cadmus, driven mad by Hera and changed into a sea goddess. In the *Odyssey*, she appears as a bird to Odysseus and offers him her headdress or veil as a float, enabling him to reach Phaeacia (Bk V, ll. 333–462). Cf. the references in Cantos XCI (649/615, 650/616); XCV (678/645, 680/647) and earlier in this Canto (714/684). Pound supposes that Leucothea was still worshipped in Phaeacia after 500 years (cf. Cantos XCVI, 686/654, and CII, 754/728). For a suggested parallel between Pound and Odysseus at this point in his story, cf. Canto LXXX (547/513), 'when the raft broke and the waters went over me'.

l. 47: (Gk.) 'kredemnon' ('headdress'), offered to Odysseus by Leucothea, but with the sense also of 'battlements', as of a city. *Thrones* opens with this word (Canto XCVI, 683/651) and it is repeated in Canto C (744/716) in association with Swinburne and 'Le Portel' (cf. Canto LXXX, l. 751n.). Hugh Kenner supposes Pound's gloss on 'kredemnon' to be the 'bikini' referred to in Canto XCI (650/616). See his discussion 'Leucothea's Bikini: Mimetic Homage' in *Ezra Pound: Perspectives*, ed. Stock (pp. 25–40).

l. 48 Cadmus: the founder of Thebes, accredited with the invention of the Greek alphabet; cf. Canto XCI (649/615), 'KADMOU THUGATER', and XCV (677/644).

l. 49 sea foam: cf. Canto XCV (677/644), 'white foam, a sea-gull', associated with Grosseteste's 'per diafana' ('through mist').

ll. 50–3: Pound's assertion is that Yeats, Eliot and Wyndham Lewis were without a necessary grounding in economics. A. R. Orage (1873–1934), editor of the *New Age* and the *New English Weekly*, was, like Pound, a supporter of C. H. Douglas, and of Social Credit. Probably Pound is also punning on the 'ground' out of which Leucothoe, and the dragon's teeth planted by Cadmus, both rose. Cf. also Notes for Canto CXI, 'Orage held the basic was pity' (13/783), and Canto CXV (ll. 8–10n.).

l. 52: 'pu' ('none'), the ideogram for a bird in flight.

l. 54: (Ital.) 'equal to reason' from Cavalcanti's 'Donna mi priegha' translated by Pound as 'reason's peer and mate' (*LE*, 156, 165, and Canto XXXVI, l. 34).

l. 55 Demeter: the Greek goddess of grain, mother of Persephone and instigator of the Eleusinian fertility rites. Pound supposes a vestige of the rites to have survived in modern Venice; cf. Cantos CII (754/728) and CVI (777/752). For the significance of Eleusis see Canto XLV (l. 47n.).

from Canto CVII

The main source for this Canto, and a source for others in *Rock-Drill* and *Thrones*, especially Cantos CVIII and CIX, is the second of Sir Edward Coke's four *Institutes of the Laws of England* (1628–44). Coke (1552–1634) was Solicitor General and Attorney General, Speaker of the House of Commons and Chief Justice of England under Elizabeth I, but was removed from office and later imprisoned and charged with treason by King James I for his defence of Common Law, the rights of Parliament and the authority of Magna Charta. Though he was cleared and re-entered Parliament, where he was instrumental in shaping the 'Petition of Right', Coke was under suspicion and his writings suppressed until, eight years after his death, his commentary on Magna Charta was published by Parliament in 1642. This commentary, the *Second Institutes*, presents the evolution of Constitutional government in England from Henry III to Edward I, and in it Pound found the source for future legal and social justice. His estimation of Coke he found also ratified by the high praise accorded the *Institutes* by Thomas Jefferson and the framers of the U.S. Constitution.

References to 'Coke' in the following notes are to the 1974 reprint, *Coke on Magna Charta*. I am indebted also to the full discussion of Coke's appearance and significance in the *Cantos* in David Gordon's 'Edward Coke: The Azalea is Grown' (*Paideuma*, IV, nos. 2 and 3, 224–99). Cf. also the life of Coke, recommended by Pound, *The Lion and the Throne* (Boston, 1956) by Catherine Drinker Bowen.

l. 1 azalea: a shrubby plant, growing in sandy soil, with a profuse bloom.
ll. 2, 3 Selinunt' (Ital.; Gk. Selinous), *Akragas* (Gk.; mod. Ital. Agrigento): ancient towns on the southern coast of Sicily. Pound alludes in these lines probably to Frederick II (1194–1250), crowned king of Sicily 1198, king of Germany 1212 and Holy Roman Emperor 1220. In 1231 at Melfi Frederick issued new constitutions for the kingdom of Sicily, the first time the law of a European state had been codified since Justinian. In 1235 he married Isabella of England and in 1254, David Gordon records, the Sicilian crown was offered to Edmund, second son of Henry III (op. cit., 249). Frederick is referred to elsewhere at Cantos XCIV (674/641) and XCVII (712/682) and in *Guide to Kulchur* Pound commented that his attempt 'to enlighten Europe both culturally and economically was a MAJOR event' (p. 261).
ll. 4–6: in 'A Proeme' to the *Second Institutes*, Coke records that the Magna Charta should by Act of Parliament be distributed to all justices, all sheriffs and king's officers and cities, 'and that the same charters should be sent to all the cathedrall churches, and that they should be read and published in every county four times in the yeare in full county, *viz.* the next county day after the feast of S. Michael, and the next county day after Christmas, and the next county day after Easter, and the next county day after the feast of S. John.'
l. 7: the twentieth year of the reign of Henry III (1216–72),

the year in which Henry, free of evil counsel, confirmed *Magna Charta* and the *Charta de Foresta* (Coke, 'Proeme'). Coke's *Second Institutes* is based upon the Charter of Henry III, the 'old Charter' referred to in Canto LXXX (ll. 714–15, 718n.).

ll. 8–9: Coke writes at the end of 'A Proeme', of his own commentary on Magna Charta compared with others on matters of civil law, that:

> . . . our expositions or commentaries upon Magna Charta, and other statutes, are the resolutions of judges in courts of justice in judicial courses of proceeding, either related and reported in our books, or extant in judiciall records, or in both, and therefore being collected together, shall (as we conceive) produce certainty, the mother and nurse of repose and quietnesse. . . .

ll. 10–11: from Coke, Cap. II (10) (pp. 9–10), 'Certain it is that he that holdeth by castle-guard shall pay no escuage, for escuage must be rated according to the quantity of the knights fees', the point being that a knight was not required to perform military service and also pay tax. (Lat. 'scutum', i.e. 'shield'; O.F. 'escuage').

l. 13: (Lat.) 'Edward Coke, militiaman', the designation given Coke on the title-page of the *Second Institutes*.

l. 14: from Dante's *Paradiso*, Canto X (l. 136), 'essa e la luce etterna de Sigieri' ('"Tis Sigier's eternal light', Binyon, 119). Sigier is Sigier of Brabant, a thirteenth-century philosopher at the University of Paris where he was involved in a dispute with St. Thomas Aquinas over his teaching of the philosopher Averroës. Sigier left Paris but in 1277 was summoned before the Inspector-General of the Faith for France on a charge of heresy. Tradition has it that he was later executed for a political offence by order of the Court of Rome at Orvieto. In Dante St. Thomas and Sigier are reconciled and Sigier's integrity in teaching 'invidious truths' vindicated.

l. 15 this Eleanor: Eleanor of Provence (1223–91), daughter of Raymond Berengar IV, Count of Provence, wife of King Henry

355

III of England. Eleanor antagonized the English barons and when they seized power from Henry in 1264, she led the royalist exiles in France, organizing an unsuccessful invasion force. Eleanor returned to England with the defeat of the rebels by Edward, son of Henry, in 1265. Another Eleanor, Eleanor of Castile, wife of Edward, is referred to in Canto XCIV (674/641).

ll. 16–17: from Coke, Cap. v, on the upkeep of church property and the unlawfulness of it being let or sold by the Crown when vacated:

> The keeper, so long as he hath the custody of the land of such an heir, shall keep up the houses, parks, warrens, ponds, mills, and other things pertaining to the same land, with the issues of the said land; and he shall deliver to the heir, when he cometh to his full age, all his land stored with ploughs, and all other things, at the least as he received it.
>
> (p. 14)

l. 18: (Lat.) 'such custody shall not be sold' (Coke, ibid.).

l. 21: repeated towards the close of this Canto (787/762).

l. 23: (Ital.) as Pound indicates, from Dante's *Paradiso*, Canto X (l. 42), in the Fourth Heaven of the Sun. Lines 40–2 read, 'How must those spirits be in their nature bright/ Which in the Sun, where I had entered thus,/ Were visible not by colour but by light' (Binyon, 113).

l. 24 Custumier . . . de Normand': the Norman French law book, composed in the year '14 H 3', the fourteenth year of the reign of Henry III.

l. 25 de la foresta: the name of an ancient charter which together with Magna Charta earned the name of the 'greater charters of English Liberty' (Coke, 'Proeme'). David Gordon suggests that in these citations 'Pound registers the antiquity of the assize court', and, linking it with Coke's Cap. xII, 'the rustic beginnings of the jury system' (op. cit., 252).

l. 26 yellow-green: cf. 'Till the blue grass turn yellow/ and the yellow leaves float in air' (Canto XCIX, 724/694).

l. 27: from Coke, Cap. vIII (p. 18), a comment on the words

'Nos vero' in Magna Charta, the use of 'we' ensuring that regal power in a king is maintained in his successors.

l. 28: from O.F. 'eit ses auncient franchises' ('has its ancient liberties'), quoted in Coke, Cap. IX (p. 20); a reference to the ancient rights of London to levy aids and taxes, to elect a sheriff and other officers free from Crown appointment.

l. 29: (Lat.) 'not unjustly harass', an ancient writ in Common Law giving a tenant relief against the unjust demands of more than due rent (Coke, Cap. IX, p. 21).

l. 30: from the ancient rule of law, 'Sed rerum progressus ostendunt multa, quae initio praevideri non possunt' ('But the progress of things reveals much that could not have been foreseen at the beginning', Gordon, op. cit., 254), quoted by Coke (Cap. XII, p. 26) in a discussion of assizes, as an authority for an adjournment or transfer of the court on some difficult and unsettled matter to Westminster or Sergeant's Inn or any other place out of the justices' circuit.

l. 32 periplum: (Gk.) 'circumnavigation', used by Pound several times elsewhere to denote the sea voyages of Odysseus and Hanno. Here it applies to the justice travelling the counties to hold assizes.

l. 33 Kung: Confucius, who was made a minister of state in the principality of Lou in 497 B.C. at the age of fifty-four; cf. Canto LIII (l. 350n.).

l. 34: the ideogram 'root'.

l. 35: when King James attempted to arrogate the powers and privileges of Parliament, Coke responded,

> "The privileges of this House is the nurse and life of all our laws, the subject's best inheritance. If my sovereign will not allow me my inheritance, I must fly to *Magna Carta* and entreat explanation of his Majesty. *Magna Carta* is called The Charter of Liberty because it maketh free men. When the King says he cannot allow our liberties of right, this strikes at the root."
>
> (quoted in publisher's note, *Coke on Magna Charta*)

357

from **Canto CX**

From *Drafts and Fragments of Cantos CX–CXVII* (first published 1969). On this Canto see Donald Davie, 'Cypress Versus Rock-Slide: An Appreciation of Canto CX' (*Agenda*, VIII, nos. 3–4, 19–26).

l. 1 Thy quiet house: cf. the later line in this Canto, 'Galla's rest, and thy quiet house at Torcello' (10/780). Torcello is an island village in the Venice lagoon, and the site of the twelfth-century church of Santa Fosca. It is mentioned again in Canto CXVI (l. 67).

l. 2: reminiscent of the phrase, 'the wave pattern cut in the stone' describing Excideuil (Cantos XXIX, 150/145, and LXXX, l. 584); cf. also line 15 below.

crozier's curve: the curve of a bishop's crook.

l. 3 harl: or herl: 'the barb or fibre of the shaft of a feather, especially peacock or ostrich' (Davie, op. cit., 20).

l. 4 Verkehr: (Ger.) 'intercourse', 'friendly association'.

l. 6 caracole: in the shape of a spiral or helix.

ll. 7–11: Pound is referring, Hugh Kenner suggests, to Venice (*Pound Era*, 546).

l. 7: Pound's line recalls the earlier 'Hast 'ou seen the rose in the steel dust' of Canto LXXIV, lines 837–8, and the 'Hast 'ou fashioned so airy a mood' of Canto LXXXI (l. 108n.), modelled on Ben Jonson's construction 'Hast 'ou . . .' in 'Her Triumph' from *A Celebration of Charis*. Cf. also line 24 below.

l. 12 Toba Sojo: Abbot of Toba, also called Kakuyū (1053–1140), the 47th head priest of the Enryaku-ji, the headquarters of the Tendai sect of Buddhism, near Kyoto, Japan. Pound probably alludes to the narrative scrolls, 'Shigisan engi' ('History of Mt. Shigi') and 'Chōjū giga' ('Scrolls of Frolicking Animals'), traditionally attributed to Toba Sojo, the second using a new technique of free-line ink drawing against a white background.

l. 16: from the phrase 'E paion si al vento esser leggieri', describing the doomed lovers Francesca and Paolo da Rimini,

flailed by the dark wind of Dante's Inferno (*Inferno*, V, ll.
73–4), translated by Pound in *The Spirit of Romance* as (the
pair) 'that seemed so light upon the wind' (p. 130). Cf. also
the later line in this Canto, 'A wind of darkness hurls against
forest' (11/781).
l. 17: Peter Whigham offers the gloss, 'Har=fleetness of the
wind; Ilü=spirit of the hunt. The whole phrase is the name
of the Na-khi ceremony of propitiation, invocation and
exorcism of the demons of suicide', adding that the phrase is
'onomatopoeic of the wind's rush' ('Il suo Paradiso Terrestre',
Agenda, VIII, nos. 3–4, 32). Carroll F. Terrell translates the
phrase as 'wind sway perform' in 'The Na-Khi Documents I'
(*Paideuma*, III, no. 1, 105).

Pound's chief source in references to the landscape and culture of the Na-khi tribes in *Thrones* and *Drafts and Fragments* was
Joseph F. Rock's *The Ancient Na-khi Kingdom of Southwest China*
(1947). Pound writes, in the first mention of the Na-khi in
Canto CIV (764/738), 'Na-khi talk made out of wind noise'.
l. 19 fates: there were three Fates in classical mythology,
Clotho, Lachesis and Atropos. The Fates appeared sometimes
as the Three Muses and perhaps Pound derives the number
'nine' from the nine Muses, daughters of Mnemosyne. The
Fates were also credited with the invention of seven letters
(five vowels and two consonants) of the classical Greek alphabet, hence perhaps the number 'seven'.
l. 20 black tree: perhaps the black poplar tree, sacred to Hecate.
The line invokes at a distance the myths of Dryope, replaced
by a poplar tree by the Hamadryads, after being seduced by
Apollo, and of the two sisters of Phaethon, the Heliads,
metamorphosed into poplar trees after Phaethon had angered
Zeus. But the 'black tree' is more probably the cypress, the
symbol of mourning and resurrection, mentioned later in this
Canto (9/779) and sacred to Artemis (8/778), goddess of wild
life and childbirth, and as the virgin huntress associated
especially with the stag (l. 22).
l. 21: cf. the later 'The lake waves Canaletto'd/ under blue
paler than heaven' (8/778) and 'Over water bluer than

THE CANTOS

midnight' (9/779). Pound's descriptions recall earlier references to Sirmione in ' "Blandula, Tenulla, Vagula" ' (l. 10), 'The Flame' and 'The Study in Aesthetics' (*CSP*, 64, 105) and Canto V, 'Topaz I manage, and three sorts of blue' (21/17).

turquoise: the colour of juniper, mentioned later in this Canto, the prominent vegetation of the Na-khi landscape; cf. Canto CI, 'The hills here are blue-green with juniper' (752/725).

l. 24: cf. the later 'can'st 'ou see with the eyes of turquoise?' (8/778).

coral: cf. the reference to the nymph Ileuthyeria, transformed into coral, Canto II (ll. 121–9).

l. 25: cf. the later 'Laurel bark sheathing the fugitive' (9/779) and 'bare trees walk on the sky-line' (10/780). These lines recall the appearance early in Pound's poetry of the myth of men transformed into trees ('La Fraisne'), and especially of Daphne, transformed into a laurel when pursued by Apollo ('The Tree'). The 'oak' is listed with the 'purifications' of snow, rain, artemisia, dew and the juniper later in this Canto (8/778), where Pound is doubtless thinking largely of the oak forest of the Na-khi region (cf. Canto CI, 752/725, 'under Kuanon's eye there is oak-wood').

from Canto CXV

The lines given in *Selected Poems* are all that appear in published form of this Canto.

l. 3 Wyndham Lewis: (1884–1957), the chief instigator of Vorticism. Lewis was blinded by a tumour in 1951, and 'chose blindness' in refusing the risk of corrective surgery. While his sight was failing, however, he continued to paint, and after conceding to the readers of his art criticism in the *Listener* that he could 'no longer see a picture', he continued still to write; in keeping with his resolve 'to light a lamp of aggressive voltage in my mind to keep at bay the night' (quoted in Kenner, *Pound Era*, 549). Cf. the earlier 'Gaudier's word not blacked out/ nor old Hulme's, nor Wyndham's' (Canto LXXVIII, 510/479), and Canto LXXX (540–1/506–7).

l. 5 garofani: the garofano is a North American flower, its scientific name, 'dianthus', meaning 'flower of the gods' (Timothy Materer, 'A Reading of "From Canto CXV"', *Paideuma*, II, no. 2, 205).

l. 7: cf. Cantos CXIII (16/786), 'Yet to walk with Mozart, Agassiz and Linnaeus', and CV (771/746), '. . . Sulmona, Ovidio's,/ . . . Mozart obit aetat 35'.

Mozart: the composer; cf. Canto LXXVI (l. 140n.).

Linnaeus: Carolus Linnaeus, the latinised form of Carl von Linné (1707–78), the Swedish explorer and botanist. Linnaeus first introduced a principled classification of genera and species, bringing order and a model of terse description to the natural sciences.

Sulmona: the birthplace of Ovid (43 B.C.–A.D. 18) in the valley of the Apennines, east of Rome. Ovid was exiled from Sulmona to Tomi on the western shore of the Black Sea in A.D. 8 and remained there until his death. In Canto CIV, Pound writes 'Mirabeau had it worse, Ovid much worse in Pontus' (768/742).

ll. 8–10: Pound seems to have served as something of a liaison between Ford Madox Ford and Yeats in his early years in London, passing on what he learned from Ford in the afternoons to Yeats at his Monday evenings (Kenner, *Poetry of EP*, 307; Stock, *Life*, 173). There was also quite fierce antipathy between himself and some early acquaintances, for example Amy Lowell, and later some estrangement, but not hatred, in the 1930s and '40s and for different reasons, between Pound and close friends such as George Antheil, Louis Zukofsky, William Carlos Williams and Yeats and Eliot. But Pound's attitude towards these and others remained, and was, in the end especially, respectful and generous. In spite of the acrimony generated by Eliot's view of Pound in *After Strange Gods* (1934), for example, Pound confessed in his last years in the Tyrol, 'I should have listened to the Possum', and made Eliot's book compulsory reading (de Rachewiltz, *Discretions*, 306). Materer suggests that Pound is thinking in particular here of his failed attempt to re-launch Vorticism in the mid-1930s with a third issue of *Blast*, remembering Lewis's probable 'ten (invalid) reasons' against it, and Eliot's reluctance to print it (op. cit., 205–6). Cf. also Pound's castigation of Yeats, Eliot and Lewis for failing to share his belief in the fundamental importance of economics (Canto XCVIII, ll. 50–3).

ll. 15–16: a reply perhaps to Wyndham Lewis's *Time and Western Man* (1927), where Lewis viewed the *Cantos* as an example of the Bergsonian 'time-cult', a romantic sense of experience as a temporal flux and a process of becoming, as against an intellectual and classical sense of space and a condition of 'being'. Pound may well have thought that such summary judgement ignored his life's effort to synthesize such categories, admitting indeed that their effective relation had escaped him.

ll. 17–18: cf. Canto CXVI (ll. 61–2, 70) 'And as to why they go wrong,/ thinking of rightness/ . . . To confess wrong without losing rightness'.

l. 19 meiner Heimat: (Ger.) 'my homeland'. Cyril Connolly reports that Pound told him this 'roughly is Rapallo' ('A Short Commentary', *Agenda*, VIII, nos. 3–4, 46). The succeeding lines suggest, however, that Pound is recalling the living hell he diagnosed in London (cf. Canto VII, 30, 31/26, 27).

from Canto CXVI

l. 23 great ball of crystal: in a sense the poem itself. For the significance of crystal cf. Canto XCI (l. 26n.).

l. 25 acorn of light: Pound probably alludes to Dante's *Paradiso* (XXVIII, ll. 10–39) where Dante perceives reflected in Beatrice's eyes the point of pure light which is God, shining from the Empyrean through the Crystalline Heaven of the Primum Mobile. The phrase occurs earlier at Canto CVI (779/755). C. F. Terrell suggests the source of this image is Grosseteste's 'light shines in all directions so that a point of light will at once become a sphere of light of any size unless curbed by some opaque object' ('A Commentary on Grosseteste . . .', op. cit., 454).

l. 27: Pound adjudged in late interviews with Allen Ginsberg and with Daniel Cory that the *Cantos* were 'a mess . . . stupid and ignorant all the way through' and that he 'botched it . . . I picked out this and that thing that interested me, and then jumbled them into a bag. But that's not the way to make . . . a *work of art*' (*EP*, ed. Sullivan, 354, 375).

l. 29: cf. lines 55–6, 72 below. In his translation of Sophocles' *Women of Trachis* (1956), Pound emphasized Herakles' words 'SPLENDOUR, IT ALL COHERES', commenting, 'This is the key phrase, for which the play exists' (p. 66).

l. 30: Pound's daughter, Mary de Rachewiltz, reflecting on Pound's stay at Schloss Brunnenberg after his release from St. Elizabeth's, Washington, D.C., in 1958, writes, 'Yet something went wrong. The house no longer contained a family. We were turning into entities who should not have broken bread together' (*Discretions*, 305).

l. 32 blackness: cf. Canto LXXIV (l. 449), 'is it blacker? was it blacker? Νύξ animae?'.

l. 34: cf. Cantos LXXIV, 'A lizard upheld me' (l. 126; LXXXIII, 'When the mind swings by a grass-blade/ an ant's forefoot shall save you' (ll. 143–4); and CXVII et seq., 'Two mice and a moth my guides' (32/802).

squirrels and bluejays: visitors to Pound possibly at St. Elizabeth's, Washington, D.C., or at Pisa; cf. the many references to birds observed on the camp wires (Cantos LXXIX, 517/485, 518/486, 519/487; LXXXII, 560/525, 562/527). Cf. also the earlier references in Cantos XCIV (666/633) and CIV (767/741, 768/744) which suggest a classical association, most clearly with Cythera (Aphrodite). Pound therefore perhaps substitutes the blue jay for the doves and sparrows associated with the goddess, suggesting also (and querying) a parallel between himself as rescued by Aphrodite, and Odysseus rescued by Leucothea, the 'sea-gull' (cf. Canto XCVIII, note on line 45).

l. 35: not a quotation, as the context might suggest, from Jules Laforgue, but probably a rendering of the common saw 'Plus je vois des hommes, plus j'admire les chiens', variously attributed to Mme Roland, Ouida and Mme de Sévigné. Cf.

Pound's much earlier *Lustra* poems on this theme, 'Meditatio' and 'The Seeing Eye' (*CSP*, 111, 114).

l. 36: the daughter of King Minos of Crete. Ariadne gave Theseus the thread by which he negotiated the labyrinth and killed the Minotaur. Pound refers earlier to his own 'labyrinth of the souterrain' at Pisa (Canto LXXX, 548/513).

l. 37 Disney: Walt Disney (1901–66), film producer and pioneer of animated cartoon. Pound was impressed by what he called

> the serious side of Disney, the Confucian side. . . . It's in having taken an ethos, as he does in *Perri*, that squirrel film, where you have the values of courage and tenderness asserted in a way that everybody can understand. You have got an absolute genius there. You have got a greater correlation of nature than you have had since the time of Alexander the Great.

> (*Writers at Work*, 38)

the metaphysicals: the seventeenth-century poets John Donne, George Herbert, Richard Crashaw, Henry Vaughan and others, of whom Pound generally had a low estimation. In 'How to Read' (1928) he placed them in a class below the 'inventors', 'the masters' and 'the diluters', as 'men who do more or less good work in the more or less good style of a period' (*LE*, 23). Later he conceded that John Donne 'towers above the rest' and singled out Donne's 'The Ecstasy' as 'a clear statement, worthy to set beside Cavalcanti's "Donna mi Prega" ' (*ABC of R*, 140).

l. 38 Laforgue: Jules Laforgue (1860–87), the French poet, a demonstrable influence on Pound's early poetry, especially *Hugh Selwyn Mauberley*. Laforgue, wrote Pound, 'found or refound *logopoeia*' (*LE*, 33). Cf. also 'Irony, Laforgue and Some Satire' (ibid., 280–4).

l. 39 Spire: André Spire (1868–1966), French poet and Zionist. Pound wrote in 1918 that though not 'hard', Spire could be 'acid', that he and Arcos 'have delineated . . . and write "more or less as I do myself" ' (ibid., 288). Pound met

Spire in Paris, where he was introduced by him to the phonetician L'Abbé Rousselot in 1920 (cf. Cantos LXXVII, 502/472, and also LXXXI, 553/518).

in proposito: (Ital.) 'apropos'.

l. 42: Eva Hesse suggests Laforgue discovered these 'deeps' in the Berlin aquarium while Reader to the Empress Augusta (p. 29); they were 'the symbol of promised Nirvana', 'the silent deeps which know only eternity, for which Spring, Summer, Autumn and Winter do not exist' (*Moralité légendaire Salomé*, 1888).

l. 43 Linnaeus: cf. Canto CXV (l. 7n.).

l. 44: (Ital.) abbreviated from Dante's 'Ecco chi crescerà li nostri amori', *Paradiso*, V, line 105 ('Lo one, by whom our loves are magnified', Binyon, 57). Pound quotes from the line elsewhere at Cantos LXXXIX (625/590) and XCIII (664/631).

ll. 45, 47 terzo (Ital.) 'third', *Venere* (Ital.) Venus: an allusion to the Third Heaven of Venus in Dante's *Paradiso* (VIII–IX).

ll. 50–4: a reference probably to Dante's exit from hell, where clambering over the pelt of Satan, Dante and Virgil, as Pound recounts in *The Spirit of Romance*, 'enter the "cammino ascoso", the hidden road, and by this ascent issue forth to see again the stars' (p. 136). The 'take-off' (l. 52) is then the ascent of Mount Purgatory towards Paradise.

l. 51 some climbing: Pound incorporates perhaps a reference to Cacciaguida's prophecy that Dante would have to climb another man's staircase (*Paradiso*, XVII, l. 59), referred to also in Canto CXIII (20/790) and quoted in Pound's discussion of Dante (*SR*, 148).

l. 53 "see again": in the *Paradiso* (XXV–XXVI) Dante regains his sight after being blinded through looking into the brilliant depths of St. John to ascertain whether he was taken up to heaven in the body. When his sight is restored he sees Adam, the representative of redeemed humanity, the moral here being that Dante's temporary set-back, born of doubt and excessive curiosity, precedes a fuller vision.

l. 59 his hell: probably Mussolini's, who is said earlier in this Canto to be 'wrecked for an error' (25/795), but perhaps also

Dante's *Inferno*, a necessary prelude, Pound pointed out, to the 'more luminous' later movements; referring to Dante's early explanation (*Inferno*, I, l. 19) as translated by Pound, 'But to tell of the *good* which I found, I will speak also of the other things' (*SR*, 129).

l. 60 my paradiso: 'When you get out of the hell of money', Pound wrote in *Guide to Kulchur*, 'there remains the undiscussable Paradiso. And any reach into it is almost a barrier to literary success' (p. 292). Later he explained, in conversation with Donald Hall,

> It is difficult to write a paradiso when all the superficial indications are that you ought to write an apocalypse. It is obviously much easier to find inhabitants for an inferno or even a purgatorio. I am trying to collect the record of the top flights of the mind. . . .
>
> I am writing to resist the view that Europe and civilization are going to Hell. If I am being 'crucified for an idea' – that is, the coherent idea around which my muddles accumulated – it is probably the idea that European culture ought to survive, that the best qualities of it ought to survive along with whatever other cultures, in whatever universality.
>
> (*Writers at Work*, 51–2)

l. 63 palimpsest: a parchment or document which has been erased and written over; Pound's term also earlier for the record of Mussolini's wrecked career (25/795).

ll. 64–5: the first line of a sestina by Dante, 'To the short day and the great sweep of shadow' (*Vita Nuova and Canzoniere*, Temple Classics, 1948, 179). The line is quoted also earlier in Canto V (24/20).

l. 66 gold thread in the pattern: Pound noted to Carlo Izzo, 'In Rapallo, Middle Ages, industry of weaving actual gold thread into cloth'; cf. Canto XLV (l. 39) and the expression 'in the gloom the gold gathers' (Canto XVII, ll. 83–4n.).

l. 67: cf. Canto CX, note on line 1.

l. 68: (Ital.) 'in Golden Lane'.

l. 69: the Golfo Tigullio in the Ligurian Sea off Rapallo.